ALLEGRO

ALLEGRO

ROSLYN PATERSON

AuthorHouse™
1663 Liberty Drive
Bloomington, IN 47403
www.authorhouse.com
Phone: 1-800-839-8640

Published by AuthorHouse 8/10/12

ISBN: 978-1-4772-5525-4 (sc)
ISBN: 978-1-4772-5524-7 (dj)
ISBN: 978-1-4772-5523-0 (e)

Library of Congress Control Number: 2012913987

For love, truth,
and the butterflies who
know the difference.

TABLE OF CONTENTS

Chapter 1 It Had Begun, 2015

"I'm sorry, Miss, just a few more questions." Still, it was that voice.

Dreaming, Fiona recalled her struggle to remember that day in the hospital, right now, however, just not as vividly.

"Do you know where you are?" the voice said.

Her wedding and life with Kurt in Berlin had all been so real. What was it he had said? What is it with this voice and these questions; this man is a real pest. He won't leave me alone, Fiona thought, in her dream.

She remembered looking up searching for the man and his voice. Her eyes refused to focus, nor her brain for that matter. She wondered if they had heard what she just said. So she repeated it. But this time when she spoke, it was with a bit of sass and emphasis, the voice was not quite an irritation, but it was getting close. She so wanted them to stop asking her these silly questions. Not one to speak cheekily, maybe this time they'd let her alone. So they wouldn't ask her again, she thought.

She said, "I'm on a Mediterranean Cruise on the *Love Boat* with my husband Kurt Hochsaenger. We left port just yesterday and I woke up to what I thought was this morning. And you keep asking me these silly questions."

Those in her room gathered closer to her bed to listen to her comments. They included her parents, Maureen and Ian, her doctor, and Jake. They listened intently and with deep concern.

Fiona continued, "But when I woke up it was so dark, I decided that it was," she paused, "Well, it was still actually in the middle of the night. But the B-E-E-P was so loud; it was just like an alarm clock. I figured the last people in this cabin had unfortunately set the alarm clock for the middle of the night!

"Yes, Miss, it was quite loud."

She heard the voice again but still hadn't opened her eyes to see who it was that spoke to her, even now in her dream she wondered who it was. "Now kindly find my husband or send me someone who has some answers. All you seem to be doing is asking me stupid questions."

"I understand Miss, if you'd only open your eyes, and allow me to ask you one more question," the voice said again just like the last time. She remembered the doctor asking her these questions and that her answer was rather glib thinking if the doctor didn't know where he was they were both in a lot of trouble.

"Actually, Miss, could tell me, who is the President of the United States?" said the doctor.

She was hoping that he knew the answer to this mundane question. "Well that one is easy, George Bush." Fiona said with a nod of her head, "Yes, that's it. Why do you want to know about Mr. Bush, has something happened?" she said, questioning.

"I was hoping you would ask me that, Fiona. You see, I'm your doctor, you are in the hospital. Your Mother and Father have been sitting vigil in your room ever since you were brought in here two months ago." The voice paused, rather, the doctor paused.

"Hospital? Where am I?" Fiona said, as the alarm bells in her head were suddenly going off and were now showing on her face.

"You are in NYU Medical Center, ICU room number 1311," the doctor said.

Feeling more uncertain about her true surroundings, Fiona said, "No, I'm on the *Love Boat*. This is my honeymoon. You arranged it for me. Daddy, what have you done with Kurt?"

"Fiona, listen to me now," her Father said firmly. In her dream, she remembered her Father's tone. It was sweet and caring but yet it was still full of concern. "It is the year 2015, they told us that after your swimming workout at the YMCA you fell in the showers and hit your head pretty hard. They rushed you here and you've been in a coma ever since."

"A coma?" Fiona said even more alarmed at her health status revelation, then realized a bit more, though still her brain felt like the cobwebs were anchored in deep. "Doctor, am I alright?" She said in her dream.

Fiona's memory of her time in the hospital was fading in and out in her dream. She remembered hearing the "B-E-E-P" sound again, even now in her dream. That sound was a stranger in the dark, but she could hear it loud and clear. It wasn't the ship's horn, or from traffic outside. Finally, her more rational brain led her thinking, well, her dreaming. "B-E-E-P." There it was again, in her dream she finally remembered what it was, it was the nursing call button of a patient in the room next to Fiona's. Each time someone had come into or exited her room when the door was open, the too familiar "B-E-E-P" invaded the privacy of her hospital room and now the silence of her dreams.

She knew that if she was ever going to wake up to another alarm clock, she wouldn't have the alarm tone be set to beep; she would, instead, choose something else, something more soothing. Perhaps, she thought, the operas of Wagner on a sound machine, set to wake her up at the appointed hour. Perhaps the first opera he wrote, dedicated to a town he knew only too well, Füssen: Opus 1.

Chapter 2 First Impressions, 1988

Fiona and Jake met while they both worked as staff nurses at NYU Medical Center. He worked on a neurological unit where the wide variety of conditions included: epileptics, cranial surgery, rare orphan neurological conditions to the patients who recently suffered from a stroke or coma. He enjoyed the complexity of the cases with which he worked.

Cardiology had been Fiona's preference, working on a unit located just upstairs from Jake's. She took care of patients with arrhythmias, coronary bypass surgeries, heart and lung transplants, and the occasional rare cardiac disorder. Her subspecialty had come after a year or so and her specific interest was in abnormal heart rhythms.

One night when Fiona went to the hospital cafeteria for dinner break, she noticed a posting on the hospital internal community message board, "4th needed, golf outing Long Island-Saturday the 20th." Having played golf since she was about 12 years old, Fiona thought the idea of taking up golf again; a good idea. She hadn't played any golf since moving to New York. She responded to the notice by taking one of the tongued tabs with someone's phone number and made a mental note to call the number the next day.

When she called the number she wasn't surprised when a man answered, "Hello?"

"Hello, this is Fiona MacLaren from NYU, I'm responding to the posting about golf on Saturday?"

"Hi Fiona, this is Jake. I was sort of expecting a guy to call, but hey, we can be progressive men…" he said letting his voice trail off.

Sensing his apprehension, Fiona countered teasingly, "What, are you worried to play with a woman?"

"To be honest, a little."

"Well then we are even, it isn't every day I play golf with an entire group of men, but hey, I'm up for that challenge!" Fiona said, the smile on her face evident in her voice. "Do you play for money or beer?"

"Ah, what?" Jake said stumbling.

"You know bingo, bango, bongo, or match point or something?"

"You play, like that?" he said.

"It isn't a concept only for men," Fiona said flirtatiously.

"Then you are on, you don't want a handicap too do you?" he said.

Smiling broadly knowing she had finally been accepted to play, "Not if you don't."

"Touché, Fiona, touché. Where do you live Fiona? Sam is driving out to the course, perhaps we can all drive out together?"

"Oh gosh, I hadn't even thought of that!" Fiona stammered. "I live on East 78th Street."

"Ok, give me the exact address," he said and after she'd told him he said, "Got it, can you be in the lobby by 7:30am? Our tee time is for 10:28am and that should give us plenty of time to pick up everyone and drive out to the course. We usually play at 10:30 because we think it is perfect timing for lunch on the turn and time to clean up afterwards without rushing back to the city."

"Sounds perfect to me."

"Great," he said. "I'll call Sam and let him know. Nick is my neighbor so we only have a few stops and then head over to the course."

The remainder of the call was spent on finalizing the logistics, directions to her building, and if she needed to bring anything else. Thinking about the outing, Fiona smirked knowing she didn't mind being the only female, in fact, when she played golf, while she usually competed against just herself, playing against or with men only, always heightened her game. That was how she met Jake.

Jake informed his buddies that their 4th was woman named Fiona; she was another nurse from the hospital. He further explained that she was up for betting games on their round. He told them that one of her favorite games was bingo, bango, bongo.

Finally the day of the golf outing had arrived. Fiona wore her favorite red polo by Ralph Lauren and khaki middle length shorts. Her hushpuppy style golf shoes completed her look. She always wore a large brimmed straw hat, like Greg Norman-the shark. She wore her hair in a low ponytail underneath the hat. Tammy Jo, her New York golf pro, had shown her how to style her hair for women's golf hats, through the back of a cap or bonnet like Michelle McGann, ribbon and all.

Fiona was downstairs in the lobby of her building anxiously awaiting the men who were coming to pick her up. She spoke idly with her doorman, Neal, a retired police detective and pseudo-Father figure. When she first moved to New York and needed advice, she often stopped to ask his opinions. Today was no different.

As she walked into the lobby, Neal saw her carrying her gear and said, "Let me guess, going swimming at the YMCA?"

"Very funny, you are such a *card!*"

"Where are you playing today?"

"I'm joining three guys that needed a fourth. One of them is a nurse at the hospital who works on the unit downstairs from mine. They are picking me up. The course is out on Long Island, something public but they didn't tell me which one. At this point, they are all new and unfamiliar to me so it doesn't really matter. I am just looking forward to playing."

"Well, you look the part." He said looking out the window at traffic, "What time are they supposed to pick you up?"

"7:30. I'm a little early," Fiona reported.

"What kind of car? There is one parked up the street about 100 yards with some young men in it. They seem to be talking quite animatedly."

"Well, let's get this show on the road. If it is them, Jake knows what I look like, or at least he thought so from my description over the phone. If I'm outside on the sidewalk with you, waiting for them, perhaps if it is them, they'll drive up the rest of the way?"

"Good idea. Let me carry out your bag." Neal said walking back towards her bag and grabbing it. "What do you have in here, rocks?"

"No, I've still got my Father's old steel shafted clubs, heavy I know. It is why I ride when I play!"

"Darling when you get back to town, I'll have a list of the best women's club dealers for you. You must upgrade to titanium or help me when I'm laid up after my hernia surgery! OOF!"

"They aren't as bad as all that, you are a real tease Neal, you know that?"

Neal smiled knowing one of his favorite tenants was about to have a grand time on such a beautiful day.

Turning to look at oncoming traffic, Fiona saw the parked car merge back onto the street and stop in front of her building. As soon as the car lurched to a stop, Jake hopped out. Smiling as he did so, he assisted Fiona with her gear and she waved goodbye to Neal.

"Are you ready for a great day Fiona?" Jake asked eagerly.

"Ready, let's go!"

Inside the car, Sam turned to Nick who was sitting shotgun and said, "I love fresh meat."

Nick replied, "I think Jake does too."

On the outside, Fiona was busy settling into her seat and not particularly listening to the front seat conversation, Jake had heard his friends' comments and smiled while doing up his seatbelt. While on the inside, the butterflies were taking hold for both of them, keeping them alert and on their toes.

During their round of golf, Fiona and Jake shared a golf cart and Jake drove. Sam and Nick rode in the other cart. She had a feeling about him that she would hold throughout the golf match and try her best not to lose focus. Did she want to impress him? If she won, would that scare him away? He seemed to enjoy her company; he was often touching her knee as they drove through the course. He complimented her game even if that meant he was losing the bet.

"Where was this heading," Fiona thought, "Was this the making of a relationship?" A faint blush came to Fiona's cheek; she wondered about this man sitting next to her.

Chapter 3 Meeting the Parents, 1988

Fiona and Jake had been dating for over six months when they decided it was time to meet their respective parents. Fiona suggested they meet Jake's parents first, since they lived in southwestern Florida and that was a good place to escape the bitterness of a January winter in New York City.

Their flight to Florida was uneventful and surprisingly fast, probably because they both were so exhausted heading into the trip that they slept almost the entire flight. Their hands clasped in each other's grip while they slept made the flight attendants smile each time they passed them up with beverage or food service.

The announcement by the pilot that they were cleared for landing woke Jake, but Fiona still slept. It wasn't until the jostling of the landing that she woke up. "Wow, are we there?" she said.

"Yes darling. We just landed, welcome to Florida."

"Well that was fast, how time flies when you sleep on a plane!" Fiona said with a chortle.

After they collected their carryon bags and deplaned, Jake said, "Remember now, my parents always meet me at the gate. I can't wait for you to meet them!"

"I can't wait either!"

Sure enough, as they entered the gate area, standing there were Clifton and Bette Davies, just past the check-in desk of the gate. Their broad smiles beamed from their faces. Bette was the first to speak, opening her arms and enveloping her son in a huge bear hug.

"Oh Jake, it is so good to have you home." Turning to Fiona she said, "And this must be Fiona. It is so nice to meet you!"

"Hi Mom, Dad, yes, this is Fiona. Fiona, these are my parents Clifton and Bette Davies."

"By the end of the week Fiona, if you aren't calling us Mom and Dad something is wrong," said Clifton. "I am so glad to finally meet you."

They drove away from the airport trying to agree on where to take Fiona first, to their favorite place for lunch, to the ocean, or just what. So many choices awaited them. Jake decided he was hungrier for food than seawater and said, "Lunch first, ocean second."

The drive to lunch was picturesque but slow. They opted for the old highway instead of the new interstate. The restaurant was built on the beach tucked away amongst small and large resorts and island homes. Their lunch consisted of burgers and sandwiches at a picnic table outside on the veranda.

After lunch, the group took a walk along the beach. The devastation of recent hurricanes and storms was evident along the shoreline, as the beach was worn away in several places. Palm trees and fronds were scattered about. Fiona knew from her childhood that this was good timing for shelling and kept her walking path along the first few inches of surf. Every few minutes or so she found what looked to be a keeper shell but upon closer inspection, it was marred, flawed, or broken.

It was especially so for the multitude of sand dollars that she encountered, seconds after plucking them from the ocean, once what water was left in them drained away, the shells composition changed and they cracked in her open outstretched hand. She thought they'd have to figure out a way to keep at least one intact.

Jake caught up to her as she walked and reached for her hand. They walked silently, holding hands in the gentle surf, mesmerized by the incoming tide. Clifton and Bette watched the young couple and they shared the unspoken silent language of an older, more experienced married couple, keenly aware that this match at first appearances seemed quite good for their son.

Having walked enough for their post-lunch stroll, Jake's parents smiled as they turned into the walkway and headed back to the beachfront restaurant and their car in the parking lot. They'd wait for them in the shade of the veranda next to the car. Bette, a fair strawberry blonde, was feeling too much of the sun on her blushing face.

Almost an hour later, Jake and Fiona arrived at the car. They had walked all the way down to a lighthouse and found a secluded area to spend a little time away from prying eyes. Now parched and pink about the edges, they smiled as they approached his parents who were now resting eyes shut with the car doors wide open.

"Shhh," Jake began, "I think they're asleep. Let's go inside and get something to drink, and maybe they will sell us more drinks to go."

"Okay," Fiona whispered.

Inside the restaurant they ordered four sodas but while they were waiting, Jake and Fiona consumed two more drinks. "Remind me to hydrate when we come back to the beach tomorrow!" Fiona requested.

"Right. Down here it is so different. It catches you off guard with the humidity but the sun is what does it. How's my girl now?" he said, noting she had downed a soda in record time.

"Better, but I feel a bit gritty from the saltwater and the sand. I could really use a shower. How long before we get to your parent's house?"

"About an hour, you can rest in the car with another soda, and then grab a shower while I help Mom and Dad with dinner."

"Sounds like heaven," she said, stressed from the heat as she placed her opened hand above her head as further protection from the sun.

Just as suggested, Fiona fell asleep in the back seat holding Jake's hand, her head lolling to and fro with the gentle ups and downs of the Floridian roadway. The smile on Jake's face was a further sign to his parents that this was their son's future wife. While they weren't sure if he knew it, by the end of the week they'd make sure he knew how they felt about Fiona. It may have only been a few hours since they'd met her, but they were going to share with him what they were drawn to within Fiona in just their first impressions.

When the movement of the car finally came to a stop, Jake exited the car, careful to extricate his hand from a still slumbering Fiona. He went around the car and after opening her door, kissed her ever so softly to wake her up. She was slow on realizing where she was, then it dawned on her and she smiled and kissed Jake back.

"Fiona, we're here. Welcome to the crow's nest," Jake said, kissing her again, this time on her cheek, and helped her out of the car. Holding hands yet again, they walked into the modest two-story home. The plantings in the garden were a bit foreign to Fiona and certainly looked tropical. Bette had potted plants hanging from the eaves, impatiens mainly, but the colors were so vivid that Fiona stroked one of the plant's vibrant petals just to confirm it was real.

Inside, she immediately took to the orchids. Bette and Clifton had easily fallen for this house because of the design which included two sets of master suites: one upstairs and one down.

Bette said, “This way our guests feel right at home. Well, they are actually at home.” She informed Fiona that their room was on the second floor, a master suite away from any disturbances below.

“This type of home is different from those in the Midwest, or in Manhattan, it is so open and roomy.” Fiona remarked, “And, no basement, right?”

“Right,” Bette said, “Jake, why don’t you take your bags upstairs and get settled in, that will give me some time in the kitchen and I’m sure Clifton wants to take Fiona into his library.” Not waiting for his answer, Bette moved down the hallway apparently towards the kitchen.

“Sure Mom, I’ll see you soon darling,” Jake said as he began picking up their bags.

“Fiona, let me take you into my library, it’s just over here, why don’t you follow me.” Clifton added, “Meanwhile, what can I get you to drink,” he said.

“Your library has drinks?” said a somewhat confused Fiona.

“Well, mine does have a bar of sorts, and even a mini-fridge. I like to enjoy a nice cocktail while reading, don’t you?”

Fiona could hear the echoes of Bette’s work in the kitchen, and feeling a bit out of place but being flexible, she said, “What are you drinking?”

Soft humming sounds to Motown or similar songs were emanating from the kitchen. Clifton smiled, knowing Bette was checking on the appetizers and dinner; and with Jake upstairs, he said, “Well, ironically enough, I enjoy a good Manhattan or a martini. But I stocked up the bar in preparation of your arrival, so what’s your pleasure?”

“How about a rum and coke?” Fiona replied hesitantly.

“Gold or silver?” Clifton asked.

“Gold please,” Fiona replied.

“Very well, make yourself comfortable as I make our drinks.”

Looking around the library, Fiona was trying to take in the titles along the books’ spines. It seemed like an eclectic collection. Dickens, Keats, Chaucer, nautical charts, books on knots, tide movements, ocean-going yachting, even a few cookbooks-evidence of Bette’s contribution to the tomes.

“I see you’ve found my collection of cookbooks,” Clifton said, calling out from behind the bar.

"Your books," Fiona mustered, "The cookbooks are yours?" she said perplexed.

"Yes, you see I'm a bit of a renaissance man myself; I like to know a little about just about anything. Bette loves her romance novels packed in storage bags for the boat trips. They are smaller and lighter. Sometimes when we are having a cookout on the beach, I'll do the cooking and she reads to me from one of her raunchy stories. It doesn't seem all that bad in the end."

"Amazing, I'm sure."

Coming out from behind the bar, their drinks prepared and in hand, Clifton said, "So now, here we are," handing her a drink. "While they are away, Fiona, we can get better acquainted."

Just as Clifton began to take a seat, Jake walked in with another load of their bags. Smiling to Fiona, he said in warning, "Look out darling, the Spanish Inquisition has nothing on my Father!"

Kissing Jake on the cheek, Fiona replied, "Go settle our room, I'm ready for my barrage of questions, I can handle myself, I think," Fiona said, turning to follow Clifton as he took his seat.

An hour later, Bette waltzed into the library with a baked brie and apricot sauce, shrimp on ice with tangy cocktail sauce, and mini quiche. All of them were arranged on an acrylic platter, the inset of which was a legend of nautical flags and their definitions. "Here we are," she announced as she placed the tray table near the intense conversation between her husband and Fiona.

Looking over the array of options, Clifton replied, "Perfect timing, we were just concluding round one of the inquisition."

"Round one?" Fiona asked, "How many rounds are there?"

"Usually three," said Jake, entering the library as Fiona stated her question.

Looking up, Fiona smiled at Jake and welcomed him to the seat next to her on the tufted leather couch. As Jake sat down, his Father stood and headed to the bar. "Clearly, bartending is my second career choice," he said with a snort. "Jake, what can I get you? I'll just be a moment fixing another drink for Fiona and myself. And you dear?" Clifton said to his wife.

Jake replied, "I'll take a Heineken if you have it, if not, a Bud will be fine."

Reaching into the mini fridge, Clifton retrieved two Heinekens, knowing his wife loved a cold beer while cooking. She'd switch to wine; well, they all would, once dinner was served. Bringing the beers and refreshed drinks from the bar, as Clifton sat down, he passed out the drinks and then turned to his wife saying, "Round two, your turn dear."

"Well, not knowing exactly what you covered in round one, I'll limit my questions to why you are so attracted to our Jake," said Bette.

"Wow, you don't hold any punches, Jake sort of warned me about this." Fiona replied and began to describe all the things she had grown to love about Jake. Things she highlighted were his love of medicine and nursing, playing golf together, and that they had had similar experiences in schools growing up. It made it not so difficult to blend their lives together once they had decided to live together.

Hearing the buzzer from the stove, Bette excused herself from their conversations and returned to the kitchen to check on their dinner's progress. The day before their guests' arrival, Bette had gone down to the fish mongers and purchased four fillets of grouper and four of sea trout. She planned on baking them with a bevy of mixed vegetables and served family style with rice pilaf. The timer was set to give her another ten minutes of preparation time and to finish the vegetables; fresh waxed and green beans.

They ate dinner under the pergola just off the lanai, somewhat picnic style. The dinner was consumed in the darkness of the twinkling sky, the wine was consumed during non-stop conversation, and the apple pie à la mode dessert was served in complete darkness as clouds had slowly rolled in and blotted out the sky. Always prepared, Bette produced a few tea light candles and then the coffee.

The direction of their conversation changed when Bette announced, "Round three."

"What's round three?" Fiona asked, thinking to herself that she couldn't possibly answer any more questions, what else could they want to know?

"Well my dear, round three is when we tell you what we've learned about you and how we see you as a fitting match for our Jake." Clifton further explained their insights over the last few months with phone calls and letters from Jake about his growing relationship and deepening feelings he had for Fiona.

"I see," said Fiona, blushing. This family was very welcoming, a bit conniving, but completely hospitable and generous. Perhaps it was the trust she felt from them that settled her earlier fears about getting to know each other better. This was going to be an interesting weekend.

Two days later, at the airport, as the tears of goodbyes were shed, Clifton and Bette placed their son and the woman they knew would be their next daughter-in-law on a plane bound for Minnesota. They had had a wonderful time golfing, sailing, shelling, and eating over the weekend, and their time to meet this woman of Jake's was now concluded.

Fiona and Jake gave each of the elder couple a long hug, and Fiona promised to keep in touch. They waved back to the gate area all the way down the jet-way and into the plane. Standing by the wall of windows, Bette and Clifton waved as the plane taxied to the runway.

Exhausted but with hearts filled with newfound friends, Fiona fell fast asleep. In her dreams, she conjured up time spent on the "Ceilidh" (the kay-lee), Jake's parents' sailboat. She recalled Jake extolling its praises in detail: "A Pearson 323, 32' 3" long, a 10' 2" beam and a draft of 4.5'. She is a cream or almond color with black mast and sail covers. She has a red boot stripe and the red and black color scheme is used throughout by her 'decorator,' cushions, towels, sheets and comforters, and pillows."

She thought again, "Wow," but at the moment, Fiona was more concerned with the environment ahead of the bow instead of the designs in the cabin.

As the plane banked and turned, in her dreams, the sailboat rocked in response. She was just about to call to Jake to see the dolphins when she heard him calling her name.

"Fiona," Jake said, pushing her shoulder a little more firmly. "We're here. Dreaming again?"

"Guilty. This time I was on your parents' sailboat and I was just telling you about the dolphins swimming alongside us at the bow. I keep forgetting, Ceilidh means what?"

"I'm sure they were quite a sight. It means hospitality," Jake said.

"That's right, that's what we'll receive every time aboard her. I remember now, seems I can't keep that straight. Only things my parents named were the basement family room, "'Ye Inn of Ye Silver Knight' and their Japanese garden, 'Kamakura.'"

"Wow, I can't wait to see them."

"Well, I hope you enjoy meeting my parents, they have been talking non-stop about having us as their guests back home for some time."

"I can't wait to play some golf with Ian, and taste some of Maureen's culinary sensations. What will we do first?"

Almost in unison, Fiona and Jake said, "Golf."

Smiling at each other, they knew this was going to be a great few days, a few days back in Minnesota, and while her family home was in a less busy city than Manhattan, it was still home.

CHAPTER 4 GOLF PARTNERS, 1988

The rest, they tell their friends, was history. Over the next two years and after Jake moved into Fiona's apartment, they were able to gain a bit of seniority on each of their nursing units, and could coordinate their time off, so that in season, they could golf almost every week. Most of the time, they golfed at Jake's parents' club. Ever since Fiona met the female golf pro-Tammy Jo, her game seriously improved. Tammy Jo was instrumental in correcting Fiona's slice and added twenty or more yards to her drives. One season playing with Jake, Fiona had chipped in eight times, sometimes then winning the contest they had for that hole.

As their relationship developed, they'd go away for golf outings for long weekends or during their holidays off from work, especially if that holiday fell on a weekend. They would research resorts in the greater New York area for deals on golf for couples. They often avoided going out of town for the 4th of July.

Instead, they preferred to work that holiday, if possible, on the day shift. Their routine was to go out for a nice romantic dinner and then to take a walk, which often led them to Central Park and their favorite spot from which to watch the fireworks from the Hudson. Jake remembered to bring a blanket to rest on while they watched the fireworks. It was always more romantic to cuddle up on a nice piece of woolen tartan than to the prickly grass in their favorite viewing spot in the park.

For the upcoming July 4th holiday, since it fell midweek, the fireworks show was planned for Wednesday. So that they could have a mini vacation, they worked from Friday until Monday before the holiday. They took time off Tuesday through Thursday and traded to work the following weekend too, beginning on Friday evening. They planned a golf outing at his club, the Maplewood Golf Course, and dinner afterwards for Wednesday. "You remember we are playing with the Ferriers, right darling?" Jake said.

"Yes, I remember."

At home, while he was sorting out his clothing for the evening, he said, "Remember to pack everything you'll need, darling. We'll leave from the club."

"Ok, got it," Fiona shot back. "Where are we going for dinner?" Fiona asked, still thinking she could trip him up and he'd expose some clues to their dinner destination. No such luck.

She also overheard him reconfirming their tee time. Jake had made all the arrangements, something she always liked about him, his take charge attitude. That meant a few less things for her to think about which allowed her time to concentrate on other matters, things even thoughtful men like Jake sometimes forget.

"This is a surprise for my favorite golf partner. All you need to know is that your fuchsia dress and black pumps will look great with my off-white suit. The only thing I'll tell you is it takes a bit of time to get to dinner, and no, in case you are going to guess, it isn't at the Waldorf or L'Entrecôte!"

"Not one hint? Hmm," she thought out loud, "It takes a while to get to dinner, are we driving?"

"No more hints or clues. On this one, you will just have to trust me."

"Implicitly," she said smiling, and leaned over to give him a juicy kiss.

Thirty minutes later they were showering again, having detoured their packing for another romantic turn in their bed. He always liked that about her. She was unlike a lot of women he'd dated. She was equal to the task of initiating their romantic life just as much as he was. She could often be heard whispering quietly in his ear during their dances, "Oh, how I've missed you!"

Their golf that day was as typical as they expected playing with Dale and Etta Ferrier. Tammy Jo had paired them up last summer and they had all gotten along so well so quickly that they hardly played with any other couple.

Today, it seemed was ladies' choice and Etta proclaimed Jake as her golf partner.

Etta was always changing things up. Fiona smiled and moved her clubs to the cart next to Dale's bag. That's why Jake and Fiona enjoyed playing them so much. They always knew they'd have a great time.

Jake, though, had been in on this one. He'd secretly asked Etta to help him keep Fiona guessing about their dinner plans. This way, by having Fiona ride with Dale for 18-holes, perhaps her mind would remain on golf, and not be trying to figure out which restaurant they were going to, or about the rest of the plans for the remainder of their romantic evening together.

Jake reminded her that there should be no further interrogations or lines of questions, as Dale was off-duty! He worked as a Detective/Investigator for the Elizabeth Police Department. He handled cases that needed special attention or extra man hours in order to solve them. Basically, they left him alone to work out their cold cases.

Etta was about 10 years older than Fiona, and sported a handsome multi-carat diamond ring. She even had a golf glove specially made so the ring's prominent protrusion through her glove didn't rip the glove to shreds. It was along the same lines as other women who'd wear gloves with the finger tips exposed, especially if they had extra long fingernails.

To Fiona, she didn't understand how these women played golf with two inches sticking out the end of the fingers, much less wear any sort of glove. No, she preferred short manicured nails. Besides, at the hospital, long nails were forbidden, for they were just too good of a breeding ground for germs.

"Nice to see you again, Fiona," said Etta. "I'm looking forward to our game today."

"Nice to see you again too, Etta, Jake has been talking non-stop about this outing. When he told me who we were playing with, I was glad and so looking forward to it too," she said, smiling.

"I agree, Fiona, we were overdue," Dale said confirmatively.

"We'll be back momentarily, we want to freshen up before we tee off," Etta said.

As they golfed, whenever their shots were within speaking distance from each other, Etta talked about their young children, three so far. They were ages 8, 5, and 3. After the third child was born, the couple had decided to have Etta stay home with the children while Dale worked in town.

Dale and Etta met at a wedding, when he was best man and she was a bridesmaid. Before she was a stay at home Mother, Etta had worked as an Account Executive with AT & T. She knew once their children were old enough that she could jump back into her old career, she'd just need to buy some good track shoes for the running start she'd need to keep up with the newer, younger talent.

Their round of golf was almost perfect. Jake sunk a forty foot putt for birdie and Fiona drove a personal best on one of the par 5's. Then, she was able to show off her short game when she used an eight iron to chip in a curling bump and run that drained into the hole for eagle. In the end, Jake almost always won, including this round against Fiona.

Etta's game was comparable to Fiona's and the women often discussed hitting strategy, much to their men's approval. Jake was very fond of Fiona's golf prowess and was pleased to learn that Dale and Etta were staying in town for the holiday and had accepted their invitation to golf with them.

In the clubhouse, they shared a quick drink with each other and reviewed their outing. In the end, Dale won the match play with Jake, and Fiona won her match with Etta. It was just a friendly game and the stakes were drinks in the clubhouse. Dale and Etta explained that they were heading out to Long Island to view the fireworks from her sister's home in Smithtown so they didn't want to dawdle long over their drinks. Besides, Etta and Dale knew that Fiona and Jake were going out to dinner and they didn't want to keep them from getting ready for their date.

After drinks, Fiona and Jake said their goodbyes and retreated to their respective locker rooms to shower and dress for dinner. Fiona had been thinking of restaurants in the city that took a 'long time' to get to, and when she came up with more than ten, she decided to stop trying to figure out where and instead, concentrate on the here and now.

She got a bit of a scare when her flip flops slipped on the wet tiled floor of the locker room showers. She didn't want to fall and hurt herself before spending this incredible evening with Jake. She knew it would be the conclusion of a great day.

A good ten minutes before Fiona, Jake emerged from his locker room. He walked out of the club to the valet and gave his ticket to have the car ready and waiting when Fiona appeared. He knew she was well worth the wait. He only hoped the bulge in his jacket pocket and his plan for the evening were remaining camouflages.

He was dressed in a crisp off-white linen suit, by Perry Ellis. He wore a pink oxford cloth heavily starched shirt and Fiona's favorite tie, a thistle print in pastels. His brown leather penny loafers with tassels were buffed and shined. He even added a nautical theme to his wardrobe when he borrowed his Father's highly prized anchor cuff links.

He knew Fiona really liked his hair in style in one of two ways, either slicked back or in wavy curls, like tonight. She usually could determine his mood, whether playful or serious, depending on the hairstyle. But, that wasn't always the case. Either way, she was happy when he actually styled it and didn't leave things to chance. He was just pushing some stray curls off his forehead when the women's locker room door opened, stopping him cold.

It was like a scene from a movie. When the locker room door opened, a buildup of steam spewed out, ushering Fiona out amongst the vapor. She was a vision and her smile was an echo reflected upon his face. She was not wearing the fuchsia dress as he had suggested. Instead, she was wearing a dark black dress with a hemline just above the knee.

"Wow," was about all he could muster.

Her legs were covered with the sheerest of stockings, perhaps even the kind held up with garters, was the thought racing through his mind as he continued to watch her approach. Her legs were elongated with the jet black pumps upon her feet. No longer thinking pink, oh how he liked surprises.

"Thank you," she said seductively. "I take it you approve?"

He stammered, "Yes."

"Etta suggested it last night when we were talking on the phone. Remember when you were looking for us before the match?"

"Yes, you said you wanted to freshen up before we got started."

"Well, that wasn't all we did. Etta smuggled in this outfit for me; I hope you don't mind my not wearing the pink dress?" Fiona stated.

Still somewhat speechless, but slowly recovering, Jake said, "Yes, er, no, I don't mind. You look fantastic."

"Thanks. Are you ready to go?"

His senses returning, he thought to the small box in his breast pocket and smiled. "Yes, shall we?"

He escorted her to the car that the club valet had just retrieved. He paused at her neck before seating her and in a brief embrace; he kissed the side of her neck, just below the ear. He liked to kiss her there, knowing that was a location she applied her Oscar De La Renta parfum. He enjoyed this kiss knowing that when he rubbed against her, some of the scent was transferred onto his clothing.

He enjoyed her scent, enhanced in this way. That was one of the things that had drawn him to her. Even all sweaty from a round of golf, she smelled great. He remembered their golf outing the day before they consummated their relationship. She smelled good then too. He would have to remember that.

In opening the door, he assisted Fiona safely inside. Walking around to the front of the car, just as he passed in front, a feisty Fiona pressed slightly on the horn, making him jump. "Ready, my love?" he asked.

"Ready!"

"Then sit back and enjoy this ride, you remember it will take us a little while."

"I remember," she said, placing her hand palm up on the middle console waiting for him to place his into hers. "I'm all yours," she said.

That was what he was counting on. "Here we go," he said, placing his hand in hers, and left it there for the entire drive.

"This is actually fun not knowing where we are going. If I forget to tell you I had a good time, I'm telling you now!" Fiona exclaimed, then from her comfortable seat in the vehicle, sat back and blushed, thinking that Jake must have spent a lot of time putting this dinner together. She would sometimes pinch herself thinking how fortunate she was all those months ago to discover his note on the hospital bulletin board looking for a golf partner.

"Just relax and enjoy the ride darling," he repeated.

They made their way into Manhattan and followed the flow of traffic. Eventually, Jake pulled to the side of the road in front of a ticketing valet stand.

"What is this place?" Fiona asked, not recognizing the area.

"It is one of the best kept secrets at the hospital. Someone posted their menu on the break room bulletin board. But lately, all of us have been taking turns to come here with our wives or girlfriends ever since we heard about Charlene's experience eating here. She was the first person from work to actually look into this place."

"So have you eaten here before?" Fiona asked.

"No, I drove by on my way home from the hospital to check it out and stopped in to make our reservation. I don't know what to expect from the menu any more than you do. I just know when Charlene spoke of this place; she said both she and Isaac, her husband, had a really great time."

"It should be a great time then for us too!" Fiona said predicting their upcoming dinner experience.

The valet opened Jake's door and greeted him with his claim check. Jake then walked around to Fiona's door and in opening it, assisted her out of the sedan. They walked across the short sidewalk and continued to hold hands into the restaurant.

"Here we go," Jake said, giving her a soft peck on the cheek this time. He smiled knowing he had again given his nose a whiff of her enticing scent.

It was semi-dark inside, but very inviting. Inside the restaurant they were immediately greeted by a jovial hostess. "Good evening, my name is Cindi; I'll be your hostess for the evening. Welcome to O'Neary's, do you have a reservation?"

Jake answered swiftly, "Yes, eight o'clock."

"Name on the reservation," she asked sweetly.

"It is for Davies."

Looking down at her reservation book, the hostess said, "Very good, you're a little early, I'll just be a moment to confirm your server is ready. Perhaps you could wait in the bar?"

Jake and Fiona exchanged a quick look and they knew, "The bar will be fine," he said.

About five minutes later, the hostess reappeared from the darker recesses of the restaurant. She was smiling and when she realized that only Jake had seen her return, she gave him a wink. He winked back.

"Your table is ready. It is such a wonderful night, isn't it?" she said.

They said, "Yes it is."

"Well then, if you would simply follow me," said the hostess.

They followed her into the restaurant.

"Here we are," she said, pointing to a very secluded booth where the guests sit side by side. She pulled the table out from the space and assisted Fiona first to her seat and then Jake. Once they appeared comfortably seated, she smiled and said, "Your server tonight will be Federico. I certainly hope you enjoy your evening."

"Thank you," they said in unison.

Chapter 5 An Engaging Evening, 1990

Their table was covered with a crisp white linen table cloth, the flatware a traditional restaurant design, but the preset china place settings were anything but ordinary. The china design was that of handmade pottery direct from Ireland. The darker clay material was cast with a glaze in the rustic hues of heather and gorse. The combination of silver flatware with its simple lines, the drab greenery of the china made Fiona feel right at home. She would have to remember to thank Jake for thinking of their northern European ancestry when he looked for a place for their dinner date.

The waiter returned a few minutes later to take their drink order. Federico was a twenty-something young man with a medium build, dark wavy hair with brown eyes. He wore the traditional clean white shirt, black vest, black pants, and an apron tied about his waist. Fiona had always referred to wait staff dressed this way as penguins, which to Fiona, was an endearing term.

Tonight's focus for Fiona was to be a bit coquettish. It was her way of creating an overture. She knew that she really liked Jake and that spending time with him on or off the golf course was something she really looked forward to and planned her days around. She sat back in her chair squarely, elbows erroneously resting upon the table and her chin comfortably positioned in her hands. A pretty smile accented her flush face.

She leaned forward from the waist, for she didn't want to miss a word of their conversation. This wasn't likely to happen in the secluded booth but if the restaurant grew busy, the hustle and bustle would detract from her ability to hear. She didn't want that, not tonight.

"Would you like to order a drink from the bar? A glass of wine, a pint of Guinness perhaps," Federico asked.

"Yes, thank you. I believe the lady will have a glass of Merlot and I'll take a Guinness, please," Jake said, looking once at Fiona for confirmation of her drink order. He always enjoyed a beer or two before dinner and then a glass of wine with his meal. Fiona, the consummate wine sipper, often milked one glass the entire meal. Sometimes, she actually preferred soda over wine.

This restaurant, while more in the style of a pub, seemed to be confused with the milieu and choice of music. The soft lighting combined with the rustic brick walls proved to not be a good acoustically appealing location. The reverberations often confused the passive listener of the music piped in overhead. While Fiona reflected upon the menu, she was also listening intently to this music. It seemed somewhat familiar to her; she just couldn't put her finger on it.

"Do you recognize this music?" she asked.

"You mean the instrumental stuff they are playing now?" Jake replied.

"Yes, it sounds familiar to me but I'm not sure from where."

"I think this is a replaying of the background music from the fireworks. I think I read somewhere that it was the music of Richard Strauss, a German composer from the late 1800's. You remember we talked briefly about it in the cab on the way home from the fireworks. You said," he stopped. He looked into her eyes and saw them glistening and a slight blush upon her cheek. "What's the matter?" he asked gently.

"Oh, I just remember our conversation now. We spoke about the music and even though they chose Strauss, I had said how much it reminded me of Wagner and my time in Füssen. Do you remember?"

"Ah, Füssen. You are remembering your trip after college, before we met, right?"

"Yes, that is right. It was a remarkable trip and with wonderful company. I've shown you my photographs of Neuschwanstein with the group of us standing in front of the castle?"

"Yes, I do, it was a great shot. Do you miss Ellen now that she lives in Paris?"

"Ellen? Oh yes, very much. Please remind me to write a letter to her, I'm sure I'm overdue in my letters with her."

"Will do, what looks good on the menu?" he asked, noting his guilt in changing the subject. Ever since he had met Fiona, each time she recalled her trip, he would notice a change in her mood. Tonight, he thought, was for them and them alone. He didn't want the past to haunt them, haunt her, not tonight, not again.

"Hmm, I'm thinking about the chicken or maybe a steak. What looks good to you?"

"You do," he said bluntly, but with the most adoring composite look upon his face.

"Really…" she said seductively, knowing what he meant as soon as he said it. She slowly moved her leg to rest near his ankle and gave him a secret caress, joining their bodies at the bottom of their apex. Her flushed face was slightly more pronounced now but was no longer due to her memory, now she was in the present, she was here with her love. She was here with Jake.

"Yes my love, quite really." He said this very softly as he reached over and placed her hand in his. Her hand felt nice and warm there inside his hand. He had grown accustomed to holding her hand, so small in his much larger hand. He was more than a foot taller than Fiona, his hands as such, proportionately that much larger than hers. In the past, he was careful not to crush her hand. Tonight, he made sure to softly and gently caress it. He allowed his thumb to rub small concentric circles upon her palm.

His hands were warmer than hers and had a slight moistness to them. "It wasn't that warm in here, not for him," she thought.

Relaxing in their tender moment, she realized what his thumb was making upon her palm; it wasn't circles really, as she had first believed. No, it was the sign for infinity, the digit '8' upon its side. As she closed her eyes, in her mind, she conjured up the picture of her palm and a smear of his sweet sweat in the sign of infinity. The symbol '∞' was all she saw after a short time with her eyes closed.

Watching from the server's station, Federico waited to return to take their order even though their drinks were ready. He could sense that this was an important moment for his customers and he knew waiting was the best course of action. As he was thinking this, the hostess, Cindi, came to his post and said, "Is that the Davies party holding hands so sweetly?"

Federico replied, "Yes it is, why?"

"Well, Franklin, the manager on duty just gave me this note. It slipped his mind earlier in the staff meeting when we were all briefed about this booking."

"What does it say, here hand it over," he said impatiently.

"If you insist," she said in a teasing manner. She knew what the note said as she had done the same movement and words with Franklin only moments ago. "It asks for our assistance in his matrimonial proposal tonight."

"His what?"

"You know, he's going to ask her…" Cindi said but was cut off.

"Oh! The question is going to be popped! On my shift! I can't wait!"

"Now calm down, maybe I shouldn't have told you."

"I'll handle it; I'm not an understudy on Broadway for nothing! I'll be cool as a cucumber, just you watch."

"Shhh, you better," she said. They made sure to decrease the volume of their conversation as they looked out at the tables now filling in within the remaining areas of the restaurant.

Fiona was feeling very warm from the touch on her hand. Jake's fingers now drummed along with the music as the crescendo arrived. They sat in complete silence but volumes were exchanged in their non-verbal body movements. Anyone watching them could easily and readily see that as they watched with awe.

As the instrumental piece on the sound system faded as the piece concluded, Fiona slowly opened her eyes and leaned over to Jake to share a much needed, very moist kiss.

"If I forget to thank you and tell you I had a wonderful evening, I'll thank you now," she said, kissing him again.

He smiled knowing that this was her way of remembering, to prematurely thank someone, knowing in advance that indeed they would be having a wonderful evening. He simply said, "I will."

Seeing a momentary change in the atmosphere at the table, Federico took this as his cue to return to their table to take their dinner order. When in fact, this task was truly a farce concocted by Jake to fool Fiona into thinking their evening was normal, including the ordering of food off this restaurant's menu. It was, in fact, not entirely the case. Inside the envelope that Cindi showed to Federico were Jake's specific requests to order food from Chez Ebert, next to L'Entrecôte, it was Fiona's other favorite fine dining restaurant.

Federico recalled what he read in Jake's note: "Once we order dinner, please call this number, 212-555-2439 for Chez Ebert's kitchen to let them know they can begin to cook our food. Then in twenty minutes, call this messenger service, Scott's Bikers, at 212-555-2453, and they will bring our food over to you." Federico thought and agreed that at this time of night a bike service is actually faster than a cab. He continued with the note, "Please place the food on your china and serve us like it came from your kitchen. I have approved this with your manager. Thanks, Jake."

Federico knew that as soon as he would serve whatever food was pre-ordered, Jake's lady would know something was up. He also hoped that it wouldn't be fouled up with his facial expression and lingering, wanting to play the voyeur in this mini-drama. He knew that this night was giving him both ideas towards his own love life and the possibilities of making such tasteful arrangements with his own girlfriend. But he also knew it would make him that much better of an actor. In his upcoming leading role, he played Johnny Jennat, a young man killed by an accidental fall in front of a train.

Now in the character of Federico is Federico, the charming young waiter with a secret. As he approaches the stage, it is evident that he is now in his role 100%. As he walked up to Fiona and Jake's table, he thought to himself, I'm just Federico, their waiter. Nothing has changed. Nothing has changed.

"Hello again," he said awkwardly. "Are you ready to take your order?"

Looking confused, Fiona and Jake shared a look at each other and then back to Federico.

"I mean, are you ready for me to take your order? Have you decided?" he said, looking at Jake for some discreet indication that he hadn't already blown it.

"Ah, thank you Federico, yes we are. Darling, would you like to go first?" Jake said, smiling.

"Do you have béarnaise sauce?"

"I'm sure the chef will make something tasty for you," Federico stumbled out.

"I would like to have the sirloin since I don't see filet," she said.

"And for your starch, what kind of potato?"

"I'll have the twice baked please."

"Very well, the vegetables tonight are green beans. Would you like to refill your wine or change to another beverage perhaps?"

"Oh, I love green beans. Yes, I'd take a refill of my Merlot when you bring out the food."

"Very good, and for you sir?"

"Mmm, that sounds good. I think I'll change from the trout to the

steak like Fiona. Could you make that for two?" Jake said, smiling again.
"Certainly. A beverage for you?"

"Yes, I'll take the Merlot as well."

"Very good, sir. Two sirloins, twice baked, and green beans. I'll return with your dinner shortly," Federico said, bowing as he left the table, his dialogue and scene were now complete.

As Federico walked away, the music began again. It was the recent single of Luther Vandross's latest album, *Here and Now.* It struck Jake first and then Fiona that the purely instrumental music had suddenly changed to something from the top of the pop charts. Jake took this as a sign that the management was on his side. He smiled to Fiona and said, "Would you like to dance, darling?"

"What here and now?" Fiona giggled. "Yes, I'd be delighted."

The music was slow, their dance in time, and the lights seemed to fade as they made their way to an open area within the restaurant. When Luther sang, "I promise to love faithfully…" Jake pulled her in tightly to him. She rested her head upon his chest and he held her about her waist. Slowly, they took gentle steps, swaying skillfully from side to side, adding a small turn in the process. They were both aware of how much they were in love with each other, listening to the words, in their minds they echoed Luther's voice as he sang out about his most present love. They took turns adding emphasis to their frames and held each other until the song concluded. As Luther's voice faded at the end of the song, Fiona turned her face up to Jake's and they shared a long and wet kiss. The moisture in Fiona's eyes fell upon her face and mixed with their oral exchange adding to the saltiness of their lustful kissing.

Neither of them heard the next few songs, they were lost in their dancing embrace. When they did stop slow dancing, it was to share another passionate kiss. Not wanting to get lost in this embrace, while still holding hands, they eventually separated and returned to their table.

"That was lovely," she said first.

"I agree."

Federico and Cindi were watching them during their dance and kissing embrace. They knew it was almost time for the bike courier to arrive with their food. As they walked back into the kitchen from their hidden stance at the servers' station, they discovered the back door had just opened and the courier was unloading their special order.

"Let me help you with the plating," Cindi said.

The sous chef also helped making sure that the proper crockery was used for this special meal.

"Ready?" Cindi asked Federico.

"I've got the steaks and vegetables ready," said Federico.

"I'm ready with the béarnaise," Cindi said.

"Ok, then I'm ready. Here we go," he said.

"I'll casually walk to the front of the house, I have to see this!" Cindi exclaimed.

Walking carefully with their order on his tray, Federico arrived at their table just as they walked off the dance floor. "Here we go," he said.

"Perfect timing," Fiona said.

"Here darling, let me help you sit down," Jake said as he pulled out their table and helped her to her seat. In doing so, his body blocked the contents on the tray that Federico was carrying, thus delaying her surprise.

"Thank you," she replied to this gesture.

"Here we go," Federico said as he placed her still sizzling plate in front of Fiona.

"Mmm, just smell that beef," Fiona stated. When she actually looked more closely at the dish, she looked up at Federico with a questioning face. Federico and Jake did their best imitations of 'I don't know what happened,' when she said, "Hey, this isn't a sirloin, what is it?"

As Federico placed Jake's plate, he looked at him for guidance. Jake nodded, indicating something in male speak such as "I got this," without Fiona the wiser. To Fiona he said, "This is our order darling, doesn't it look wonderful?"

"Everything else is as I ordered it, the vegetables I mean, but this steak, is that Chateaubriand?" she asked. Federico was finished delivering their food and attempting to make a hasty retreat when Fiona said to him, "Now wait a minute, something is up."

"Enjoy," was all Federico could muster as he merely shrugged his shoulders, his work of bringing their order to their table, complete. He turned on his heel and made for the kitchen, taking a sharp right into the servers' station to watch the lovers and imagine their conversation.

Fiona was still bewildered but happily enjoying the surprise. They did remember a sauce and included a side of béarnaise, her favorite. Looking over at Jake, Fiona said, "Did you do all this?"

"Guilty." He smiled at her, reached across for her hand and kissed it again ever so sweetly.

"Oh, Jake..." was all Fiona could begin to say before she leaned over to kiss him once more.

"I love you so much," he added before his mouth was once again joined by hers. They didn't seem to mind that their exquisite and expensive steaks were cooling in the meantime.

"I love you too."

Eventually, their attention returned to their meal and they ate their meals tasting and sensing all the care and coordination that went into this feast. Never before had any food tasted as good, perhaps mood allowed their bodies to have heightened senses. It surely must be love and this time, it was real.

Nearing the end of the main course, the sound system returned to playing operatic music once again. They were accompanied on their date by the rich operas, music dramas, and symphonies of Wagner. As they listened to his compositions, they heard the allegro. It was during this lively tempo of robust notes that Jake signaled for dessert.

Federico returned from the kitchen to remove their dinner plates, the flush on his cheeks now evident. He has not recently been witness to such a production, with the music, the scene, and the actors. The couple was, in his mind, recreating a scene from some opera he thought he recognized. But to Fiona and Jake, this was their life. They too noticed the rarity of the moment as once again Fiona's eyes ran with warm moist tears of love.

Having removed the remnants of their first course, Federico returned with the scraper and pan to remove any excess crumbs. He wanted to assist Jake with the most pristine setting as possible, doing it man to man. His support showed in his movements which were candidly concealed in large sweeping gestures to capture the wayward food particles and prepare their table for their dessert.

Jake, from his position in their booth, could see the servers' station and was watching as Federico approached their table once more, this time with their dessert. Before Federico arrived at the table, Jake stood up and bent down on one knee next to Fiona. Ever the concern for others, Fiona was distracted by this sudden change in position. Fiona thought Jake had lost his silverware or perhaps his napkin. The rich tones of the brass and tympani now crashed into her concentration as the flutes and oboes invited her to pay attention to the music once more.

Fiona's eyes remain filled with unshed tears as she realized what the music had already foretold. She had hoped tonight would be their night when they would decide the rest of their lives together. That hadn't occurred to her until the music changed to another act in Parsifal-she had finally recalled the particularly lengthy piece that had been offered as helping to set the mood.

As Wagner's Parsifal changed acts to Act II, Jake reached up to cup Fiona's hands in his. He again noted the warmth and tenderness he found each time he held her hands. He sensed a sudden increase in her heartbeat and was smiling inside because of it. Outwardly, he appeared loving and serious.

Their collective heartbeats were racing at this important moment in their lives. Her hands were soft and supple, just as he remembered them. He loved the smell of her scented hand lotion for it was a mixture of lavender, vanilla, and rosemary and had been released anew with his direct contact.

In the muted lighting of the restaurant, their pupils were dilated. His eyes looked up and were deeply seeking hers. He saw his reflection in her eyes and smiled. He found that which he sought looking back at him in his chosen mate. He assumed she could see herself in his eyes, just as he saw himself in hers. Their eyes were mirrors, the instruments of measuring the love that was in their hearts. He saw her deep black orbs surrounded by the greenery that were her eyes. Her eyes remained moistened with tears of love, not sorrow.

He was down on his right knee, resting on the lushly carpeted restaurant's floor, his hands still grasping hers, ever so gingerly, taking it all in. He knew he could now begin.

"Fiona, my love," he said.

Instead of a verbally worded response, all Fiona was able to utter was a muffled and teary sigh of, "Uh huh?" Though there really wasn't any question in her mind, her voice reflected what was in her heart.

"Fiona, ever since our first date playing 18 holes of golf, I saw something in you. I saw what I had been searching for all these years. It was there in you, it was you, Fiona."

Again, Fiona was unable to verbally respond and instead merely nods her head causing the freshly released tears to spill their banks and run down her flushed cheeks. She didn't clear their remaining tracks, just pressed her body forward, listening. Listening to the man she loved.

"Fiona, it was you I have been looking for all my life. My perfect match, the golf partner who was patient with my short game and helped me discover more distance in my drives. I never thought it was possible to hit over 300 yards. After a few lessons with our pro Tammy Jo, you knew just where to start, to show me a better me and make me a better man through golf."

The music returned to a piece Fiona recalled from her tour of King Ludwig II's castle, Neuschwanstein, in Bavaria. It was the song of Füssen, the city she came to love. It was his first opus, Opus 1.

The restaurant patrons grew quiet as they were intently listening, or attempting to hear the words of love being professed before them. A moistened area on Fiona's dress denoted the flow of her unchecked tears. She didn't mind really, she hardly even noticed.

Looking down at Jake, propped there on the floor on one knee in front of her, she was hearing the most endearing, the most enchanting things. She knew this time it was real, that she wasn't dreaming, she wasn't making a wish in the fountain. Her heart raced and her mind tried to record every word she heard. She would want to recall this moment and his words forever. It was their own symphony they were composing. A symphony of love.

"Fiona, my love. It was you who taught me that which I was feeling and helped me learn that what I could not understand but saw between us everyday these last few years, that it was love. You showed me how to open my mind and listen with my heart to the music that I was playing there. You showed me how to believe what I was hearing, seeing, and feeling. It was you, Fiona who encouraged my work decisions and helped me make more out of what I had in my job, in my education, and in my future. I am returning to school in the fall, medical school, it was all because of you. It was you who allowed my unseeing eyes to focus. It was you who helped my ears to hear what my voice was saying when I spoke of you. And dearest Fiona, it was you who helped me understand that what we felt for each other was love."

Soft sobs were now emanating from Fiona's mouth, her shoulders were bouncing up and down as her breathing rate increased in response to the need for more air. She tried to take a deep breath, to settle herself but it helped only partially.

Jake continued, "Fiona, it was you. It was you that my mind, my body, and my soul have been searching for all these years. Fiona, it was you, when it finally occurred to me that when I looked at you, I saw everything I was yearning and searching for. Fiona, it was you that I see looking back at me now. The tears upon your face echo the rivers of joy in my body. When I knew, I finally understood what needed to be done. So Fiona, here we are, holding hands, sharing this moment with strangers, having a wonderful meal."

She took a deep breath knowing he was almost there, she knew it was him too.

"It was you, Fiona, who I finally knew, I knew you would become my wife. Oh Fiona, would you honor my request, here tonight, in front of these witnesses, in front of all these supportive strangers?"

She paused and looked around the room wondering why he had mentioned the occupants of the restaurant so significantly. While he had been speaking, during his operatic overture, gradually the former patrons of the restaurant had stepped out, and in their places now were seated her good friends, Gabriella, Ellen, and Jane. But, most of all, seated across the area where they had only so recently danced, were both sets of their parents; Fiona's parents, Ian and Maureen, and Jake's parents, Clifton and Bette.

The level of emotion in her diminutive body could no longer retain nor capture fully this moment. Her green eyes were now like waterfalls, as by now, the infrequent drop of a welled up tear had increased the flowage sharply in seeing her family and friends here to share in this moment. The music matched their sentimentality and produced a poetic tone of harmonic chords.

"Fiona, my love, will you marry me?" As he finally said the words, she felt an electrical charge spark in every pore of her being.

Her answer was immediately proclaimed and loud enough to be shared with those gathered thusly.

"Yes, I will. Oh, Jake, it was you my love, it was always you. Oh, yes I will."

Chapter 6 Requests and Permissions, 1990

Jake's parents, Clifton and Bette had flown in from their retirement community in southwestern Florida in order to attend the engagement dinner. Fiona hadn't been told that anyone was coming for this event. Even when she had last spoken with her own Mother a few days before their dinner, Maureen hadn't let on their plans. It had been all Jake's doing. He so wanted to profess his love for Fiona, what better way than to do so in front of family and friends.

Jake had always said, "You can't choose your family of origin, but you can choose your mate. You just pray that your choice blends well with your family to create a larger version of what you knew growing up. The better the blend, the better their marriage would be."

The month prior to this engagement feast, Jake had flown out to Minnesota. He had told Fiona that he was in upstate New York, claiming to be at an overnight conference on Brain Trauma in Albany. While in Minnesota, Jake spoke in depth with Ian and Maureen, Fiona's parents, about his intentions to marry their only daughter.

Over dinner in their spacious home that cool fall evening, the colors of the trees had already begun to change and the burr oaks and maples in their yard were ablaze in crimson, orange, and yellows. Taking their aperitifs on the veranda, Jake began to explain his plan and what his life would be like married to their daughter.

"Sir, if you will indulge me. I'd like to explain a few things." He had started with a head first dive into the deep end. For this important event, Jake had worn his best sport coat and dress pants. He felt a suit would be too formal and he would reserve the only one he had for their engagement dinner. Working as a nurse meant wearing uniforms, or scrubs, depending on the unit. He had foregone the outfitting of his wardrobe in lieu of outfitting his small apartment or banking his paychecks. He even wore a bit of cologne.

"I'm listening," said Ian. He was wearing one of his starched white shirts with a crisp collar and fold along the sleeve which was neatly tucked into his hard-pressed khakis and topsiders. He had removed his tie and changed to khakis from his normal business suit work attire upon hearing Jake's request for a meeting. He knew, or he thought he knew what the meeting's agenda would be, at least he thought he did. He really liked this young man and had seen how good he was for his daughter.

Maureen nodded from her perch. She sat across from Jake at the wicker table which was covered with ornamental glass and which glowed brightly with the reflection of the candles and the setting sun. The soft dwarfed bouquet of peonies, mixed with impatiens and snapdragons, from her garden reflected the glow. Even from across the table, Maureen could capture a sense of his cologne mixed with the flowers in front of her. The tanginess of his scent mixed well with the floral aromas wafting up from the table.

"As you know sir, Fiona and I met while we were working at the hospital. Initially, we were golf partners," he paused, and took a sip of his drink. "I was slow to catch on that I was always looking forward to my weekends or days off so that I could play golf with her. Eventually, though, I came around and realized it was Fiona I wanted, not the golf game."

"Yes, I can see that, based on her game. She is a fairly good player!" Maureen added.

"She gives me a run for my money, I knew it when she was 15 years old, and using an old persimmons driver she drove almost as far as I did," Ian shared.

"You are right about that. When she catches the sweet spot and drives it out straight down the middle, it could go almost 250 yards. It is almost like bringing a ringer when we play mixed doubles!"

"Yes, yes." Her Father said, "But, son is that really why you are here, to discuss Fiona's golf game?" In saying this, he looked away from his hoped future son-in-law and over to his wife of 35 years and smiled. He was remembering his own engagement and asking Maureen's Father, George, for his daughter's hand. Ian had asked George if they could meet at his office. George would recount that day as the day he thought this brainy kid wanted a job. Instead, he wanted his daughter!

Ian and Maureen took the train up to his parent's cottage by the lake and they dined in the fancy restaurant at place called Victoria Beach. Prior to meeting for dinner, Ian had deposited Maureen at the Inn where she stayed the weekend. Later, after their dinner concluded, while walking the beach near his cottage, he had stopped and proposed. For Maureen, like Fiona, being caught off guard had meant more in the moment than the actual act. The thought and planning had been inspiring.

"No, of course it isn't. Sir, I love your daughter."

"Yes, that I know," Ian said.

"You do?" Jake said awkwardly.

"Yes of course, it is written all over your face. Every time you look at her. I see it all the time, reminds me of how it was with Maureen and me." Ian said, reaching to hold his bride's hand.

Taking another sip of his drink, Jake continued. "Well sir, I am here to ask your permission for your daughter's hand in marriage. I know she loves me as much as I love her. I will respect her work, her life, her family, and most of all, how much she loves me. I love her so much…" he was lost in his own words. He took a moment to take in what he had been saying and was sure he had muddled it up. He was watching their faces for any reactions as to what he was saying. When puzzlement replaced austerity, he stopped dead in his tracks.

"Is something wrong?" he said.

"No my dear," Maureen said, "You just got a little lost in what you wanted to say, that's all. It is completely understandable. Ian did something to that effect with me too."
"I did?"

"Yes you did. And I've done it too. Remember my first love, the young man I told you about from junior high school?" Maureen inquired.

"Yes, are you speaking of the time you were walking and holding hands?" Ian asked.

"Yes, that is it. You see, Jake," she said, looking at him but at the same time having that far off look about one when you are looking into your minds' eye remembering the past. "He asked me to go 'with' him, meaning to go steady. I was so naïve, I simply said, 'go where?' like we were planning a date. He pulled at my hand and turned me to face him and he repeated, 'will you go with me?' That's when I realized he was asking me to go steady.

I wasn't that naïve with you though, was I dear?" she finished, looking at her husband.

"No, but I did fool you. You thought I was explaining where I was headed for my doctoral program and when I'd return to town. Instead, I asked you to marry me." Turning from his wife and back to Jake, he said, "You see son, it is important to plan this event and prepare yourself and your bride. This is the only time you will say those words, it is best to be as ready for the utterance as possible."

"What more can I say?" he asked.

"You have said enough. Jake, what we are trying to say is we are so pleased that you have fallen in love with our daughter. We will be so pleased to have you as our son-in-law and very glad to have you as a part of this family." Ian commanded an audience that was worthy of photographs. But, he let that moment remain in their memories and the cosmos, not on film.

"Yes, we do," added a teary-eyed Maureen.

"You mean it is all right with you?" Jake said, still a bit taken aback at how easy this task had been. In his mind, he had rehearsed over and over how this night would play out. He had never thought it was going to be as simple as it was. Being simple made it all the more the truth that she was the woman he had been searching for and he knew he was home. His heart beat harder in his chest and his breath caught.

"Are you all right son?" Ian said, noticing the hiccup in his posture.

"I will be," was all he could say. He placed his head in his hands and elbows upon his knees. She would be his and he would be hers. It was now only a matter of time. A flush came to his face as he recovered from the understanding of these implications to his life. "I have a request."

"Yes, you do?" said Maureen.

"Yes, will you two do me the honor of coming to the engagement? I want to show how much I love her and I want to ask her in front of our parents, other family, and our friends. When I have the plans in place, can you come out to New York to be with us?"
"Oh how marvelous," said Maureen. "We'd love to, wouldn't we Ian?"

"Sounds terrific. When is this taking place?"

"I am still working on the details but I'll let you know as soon as I can. Is three weeks' notice enough for you, for the airlines?"
"Don't worry about the airlines. We wouldn't miss this."

"Very well, I've asked my parents to join us too. It would be nice for all of you to meet. Perhaps you can stay in the same hotel and hide out together? But, please, please, do not breathe a word of this to Fiona. This is how I want to do this, and I want it to be our secret."

"007 it is," said Ian.

"Right, mum's the word."

Jake's flight home to New York the next day was a blur. He was thinking of where he could ask her and how all the details would fall into place. He knew he could count on his parents for assistance. When the plane landed, he called them and explained everything.

His Father answered the phone in the hall, "Hello son, how did it go in Minnesota?"

"Hi Dad, it went just like you said it would. They knew why I was there and didn't put on any airs. We sat down and discussed my plans. It was a really incredible evening."

As he was finishing this statement, his Mother walked down the hall saying, "I'm going to pick up the extension in the kitchen!"

To this, Clifton informed his son that his Mother was going to an extension.

"Oh good, I want Mom to hear all of this!"

"Hello Jake, how was it in Minnesota?" his Mother said as she picked up the kitchen line.

"Hi Mom! It was terrific. Fiona's parents were really nice to me and agree with my plans and they are willing to come if needed. Which brings me to my idea," Jake said.

"What idea is that?" his Mother asked.

"Well, I was thinking of having both sets of parents present when I asked Fiona to marry me. Can you and Dad fly to New York for such an event?"

"We wouldn't miss it dear," his Mother added. "When is it?"

"I'm thinking of a weekend this summer. When I know more I'll call. You probably want at least a two week notice for flight reservations. How is it in Florida?"

"We took the sailboat out for a ten day cruise around the Keys a week ago, still getting our land legs back," his Father said informatively.

"Well I'm sure you had a great sail. You know, someday, it would be just fantastic to show off the sailboat up here," Jake said suggestively.

"Good plan, son. Good plan."

"I'll be in touch when I know more. Goodnight then," Jake said.

"Goodnight son." His parents said in unison.

"Goodnight."

Jake clicked the receiver switch and called Fiona. He wanted to let her know he was back from his conference and set up their next date. He was pleased his parents had agreed to arrive with enough time prior to their special night to help him with all the details. They knew they were losing a son, but that was overshadowed by the gain of a daughter. Finally.

Chapter 7 Parties, Traditions, and Nuptials, 1990

"Can you believe it," Fiona said to her friends. "I'm so glad you could come and spend this time with me." Harriet, Gabriella, Ellen, and Jane smiled in response.

"Are you kidding Fiona? Your wedding wouldn't be missed; it is practically legendary!" said Ellen, teasingly.

"Legendary in that it is actually happening?" Fiona mused.

"Something like that," replied Ellen.

By this time, Harriet had married Wayne, a man she met while living in Orlando. Gabriella and Nate had now been married over 6 years and had two small children. Nate's dental practice was located in suburban northern New Jersey. Ellen and Pierre's wedding, 4 years ago, had been spectacular, held in the stunning Atlanta home of her parents. Jane was divorced and happy to be included. She was not the matronly type despite her additional 20 years in age.

"I've got tonight all arranged, Fiona. You just sit back and enjoy the ride!" added Gabriella, as their limousine pulled up to the curb in front of the apartment building. Neal, her favorite retired police detective turned doorman, was ready to hold the lobby door open for the boisterous group of women.

"Just as long as we have a ride and I'm not driving, I'm good to go!" Fiona exclaimed, with a double thumbs up. "Are you going to tell me about the first stop?"

"No, that one is a surprise. Trust me that we've listened to you for long enough to know what you would want for your bachelorette party experience. Before we go," Gabriella said, turning to Neal, "Do you have my bag?"

"Yes, it is just behind the desk here," he said, pointing to the floor area near his post. Walking out from behind his security station, Neal handed over a large paper shopping bag to Gabriella. "Here you go," he said. "Thank you, Neal." Then turning to the women, she said, "Now ladies, I'm going to need some help. I saw this once when I was out with some of my Long Island friends. Fiona, please close your eyes and work with me. Now keep your eyes closed, let me do this, and follow what we ask of you. You'll never regret it," Gabriella said, smiling broadly to the other women.

"I trust that you know me well enough to know I'm game for this but please don't make me look stupid!" Fiona replied, shutting her eyes and sitting down in a chair in the lobby waiting area just off from Neal's post.

Gabriella followed immediately behind her and placed the bag on the waiting area coffee table. "Ok ladies; please help me with these items! But contain your vocals to laughter and not words, or Fiona here will figure out her surprise!"

Inside the bag was a large plastic tiara that said 'Bride-to-Be' in hot pink sequins, an oversized tee shirt with the words "BACHELORETTE" written upon it, several hot pink feather boas, and party hats for the women. They turned Fiona to face Gabriella and struggled to get the oversized tee shirt on top of her outfit. Next she applied the tiara to Fiona's head, securing it with bobby pins.

The fall weather was perfect timing for this women's night out. Fiona didn't like the summer as it was often too warm for her, and winters in New York City can be downright messy, especially if there is a significant snowfall. No, Fiona had planned the timing of her wedding well in advance, and had seriously taken into account the season to hold the wedding that fit her plans. It was none other than fall.

Fiona was wearing a matching shirt and tea length skirt made of a cotton twill plaid she had sewn in college home economics class. Her espadrilles from Paris added to the Caribbean feel of her free flowing outfit. The faded plaid fabric was in soft pastels overset upon a vivid magenta. Most of Fiona's favorite outfits were in shades of pink or red.

Gabriella and Ellen both wore shirt dresses with crisp pleats and folds. Gabriella's look was more dressed up in white pumps and Ellen in a basic leather sandal. Jane wore her traditional slightly starched white dress shirt over a long jean skirt which she accented with very white tennis shoes. Her jewelry was in bulky white and silver on stretched thread. Her hair was freshly washed and bounced about her shoulders.

Waiting in the limo were the rest of the party. Harriet saw that Fiona was just about ready and she went out to the limo to get the rest of the waiting women out on the sidewalk. When the 'Fiona primping crew' finally exited the building, and Fiona made her way forward in the pack, she would discover her nursing colleagues or other friends: Stephanie, Muriel, Maggie, Georgie, Missy, and Wendy waiting for her there.

It took Fiona a few moments to realize the crowd on the sidewalk was waiting for her as they all began to shout her name, "FIONA!"

Smiling and blushing, Fiona surrendered to her friends who were now crowding around her. She was a bit overwhelmed. She bent at the knees and looked at Ellen and Jane for help.

"You aren't making a repeat of Salzburg now are you?" Ellen said boldly. She was recalling the time when they were in Europe, when Fiona, who had been feeling strange, fainted while in line to call home. In the end, she had been hospitalized and encouraged to have her ears checked for Ménière's disease once she came home. The doctor in Salzburg also thought it could just be the altitude but encouraged her to have it checked out nonetheless.

"No, I'm just so shocked. Look at all the people here. Are you all here for me?" she said, in a softly spoken, shocked sounding tone.

"Oh yes Fiona, when Gabriella and Ellen called, we made tracks to get here!" said Muriel who had flown in from Green Bay.

"That's right, we all made tracks to New York City and to witness, no, to partake in Fiona's 'Awesome Bachelorette Party!'" chimed in Georgie, who was one of the locals who didn't have to get on a plane to be there that night.

"How fantastic! Thank you all for coming. Georgie, I thought you said the other day you were working tonight?" Fiona asked.

"I was on the schedule just to fool you," she replied.

Fiona said, "Well it worked."

Eventually, Fiona learned that another co-worker, Emily, would not be coming because her Grandmother was very ill and she had traveled back to Michigan to be with her family and would be missing tonight's events, if not more.

Stephanie's train from Connecticut had arrived about an hour ago and she made it in time to be hiding in the limo. Neal would hold on to their schedule and Gabriella agreed to keep him updated as to their location so that those who missed them initially could meet up and join them later.

Wendy had just finished changing from work to party clothes and was walking outside to watch the goings on and Fiona's surprise. Maggie's boyfriend, Michael, and Missy's husband, Kitt, were meeting Jake's group for dinner. They couldn't get out of other work conflicts in time to participate in the golf outing.

Wendy, who had already changed from her work clothes, was just finishing up on Neal's telephone with her phone call with her husband, Hiro. She had just been told where the men were going and had accepted the challenge to explain to the women about the men's party, and when to do so. Hiro had explained the reservations at the Marriott. Wendy was also strongly encouraged to have the women appear at the Marriott by one o'clock in the morning.

As it turned out, the men had made arrangements for all of these couples to stay the night at the Marriott. They just hadn't informed their wives or girlfriends of it yet. Hiro was supposed to pass the news on to Wendy who would then explain it secretly to the other women.

"Wendy, why are you smiling and nodding?" asked Harriet.

It was then that Wendy began sharing the rest of the planning and told Harriet to tell a few of the women as she told the rest. Their network of friends had grown closer when Fiona and Jake's relationship grew more permanent. In varying groups, they had all shared dinner parties or dinner out together at Chef Rufalo's restaurant OHM. Its tagline was "it's electric" and was one of Fiona's favorites, next to L'Entrecôte.

Finally noting the time, Ellen walked over to Neal to ask him to get the women out the door. Neal offered to take their photo once he saw that Ellen had a 35mm camera over her shoulder. He had originally thought the skinny black strap belonged to her purse but when she turned to help with the tiara, he saw the lens of the camera connected to the long strap. As they posed, they pretended they were the models in a fashion shoot, similar to the time one of the men from an upstairs dorm room fashioned Fiona's hair and makeup for Ellen's photography class. Appropriately, all the women made over-the-top poses as Neal worked the lens and the group.

"Ok ladies. Let's work it!" Neal had said over and over. After exhausting an entire roll of film on the sidewalk of the building, Neal said, "Ok, I've got it."

"Thank you Neal," said Harriet.

"Thank you, I'm glad you took on that duty; that way I could be in these photos too!" Ellen shared her appreciation.

"My pleasure. Now, Fiona, remember, no drinking and driving!" Neal teased.

"Oh, we aren't driving," said Gabriella, who looked out the lobby window at the limousine driver who was still waiting for his fare.

"Wonderful," Neal retorted. "Then Fiona, I hope you have a wonderfully splendid evening!"

"Thank you Neal," Fiona said, and gave him a small peck on the cheek.

"Time to go! Ladies, start your engines! Time to go!" said Ellen, looking at her watch. She was concerned that they wouldn't fit in all that had been planned for this evening, and she wanted Fiona to enjoy every minute of it.

"Ok, ok," Fiona and Jane said in unison. "I'm ready!"

Now adorned with the princess tiara and the oversized tee-shirt, Fiona stood for one solo photograph-taken by Ellen.

In the limousine, Fiona asked pointed questions about her shirt. "Where are we going?" she said, looking down at her shirt and wondering why she needed to proclaim her status.

"Tonight we are celebrating your last night as a single woman!" shouted Gabriella.

Fiona said, "Yes, so where are we going?" She was wondering if they were keeping this night PG or X rated.

"Believe me, it isn't anything your Mother wouldn't approve of, in fact," Ellen said as they approached the limousine door, "She's coming too!"

"Or Jake's Mom!" added Gabriella.

As a surprise, Ellen and Gabriella had arranged for Fiona's Mother and Mother-in-law-to-be to join them for the 'early' portion of the evening. That included dinner, drinks, and dancing. The scheming friends had also asked that at some point in the evening that the 'Mothers' leave it to friends only. To which the Mothers readily agreed.

Looking inside the limo, Fiona saw her Mother and Jake's Mother already seated in the front end of the stretched car. "Ready?" Maureen said to her daughter.

"Oh I'm ready all right; I just didn't know you two were coming. Now I'm more than ready!"

Bette said, "I was so honored to be asked and included in this female ritual; back in my day we just had an overnight slumber party. This is way better!"

Looking now at her friends as they entered the limo, Fiona addressed them at once saying, "If I forget to tell you I had a great time tonight, consider yourselves informed!"

"You got it!"

"Let's go driver, first destination please," said Gabriella.

Over the course of the evening and after eating a fabulous meal, the women frequented several bars. At the last bar, the Mothers were excused and sent to their hotel in a taxi. With a wink from Ellen to Maureen, the Mothers knew Fiona was in good hands and going to have a great time.

In their taxi, Maureen asked Bette, "Do you have any idea what they were going to do?"

"Something X rated comes to mind. I hope the male dancers are handsome!"

"Male dancers," Maureen said, "Oh my! We didn't do that in my day."

"Mine either," Bette said.

"Well I hope they have fun!"

"Did you hear what the men were doing for my Jake?" Bette asked.

"Not entirely, Ian was a bit vague." "They all met earlier today for 18 holes of golf at Jake's club; Clifton and Ian, along with 7 of Jake's closest friends from college or work. I think Clifton said Nick, Jimmy, Pierre-Ellen's husband, Nate-Gabriella's husband, Wayne-Harriet's husband, Alfred, and Dale, were meeting up with Jake at the club. The men didn't share the rest of their plans other than saying they were staying in the Marriott and everything planned 'was coming to them.'"

"Yes, Ian did say something about golf and the Marriott, I'm sure he'll find it all quite interesting. I think for his bachelor party they played golf and went out for dinner. At least, that was all he ever told me." Maureen said, with a far off look in her eye.

"Don't worry, my Jake will keep it clean and fun."

"It was nice of Jake to include all of the husbands."

"Yes, it was. I'm sure they will have a great time."

Indeed, they all had a great time. After the women bar hopped a few places, they eventually crashed the men's party at the Marriott. The Moms had left the bar hopping to the younger generation of women and found their husbands back at the Waldorf for nightcaps.

It was about 4 o'clock in the morning when finally the last stragglers left Jake's suite. Nate took Gabriella to their room, a room she did not know that they had reserved. Similarly, Pierre took Ellen to their room, as did Wayne and Harriet. Fiona and Jake were finally alone. It was Thursday night, well, actually Thursday morning and the wedding was just a little over 24 hours away.

They had decided on a mid-afternoon ceremony with photographs before, during, and after the ceremony. Jennifer, their chosen photographer, had everything in hand and they knew and trusted all her ideas for posed and candid shots would be simply fantastic. Her artistic eye with the camera lens was still something left best unsaid; it was simply something to behold with the eye.

Fiona had decided to augment her auburn hair with a French roll up-do, graced with baby's breath, diamonds and a bit of lace. The diamonds and lace were set upon the bone of a hair comb Maureen had presented to her daughter to wear. It had been Grandmother Winnie's comb at her wedding, worn by Maureen in her wedding, and now was something old for Fiona in her wedding.

Her dress featured lace cutouts, a significant amount of beading and a very, very, full skirt. Fiona had always said she wanted to feel like Cinderella. Her dress reflected those wishes. It reminded her of the dress worn by a particular princess of people's hearts, worn almost a decade earlier. Her heels were ample but simple and supported her frame well. The last thing she wanted was to have sore feet and walk barefoot at her own wedding. While she knew plenty of hippies and their carefree attitudes, it just crossed with her own sense of style.

Jake, as she would later see, had chosen a full top coat, tails, and top hat. He had decided against the cane and gloves. He knew he was her Fred Astaire but in paying homage to his version of Fred, it would be sans accessories. His boutonnière included one tiny magenta rose, to match the multi-colored roses in the bridal bouquet.

The ceremony was typical in length, about half an hour. But to Fiona and Jake, it was both instantaneous and limitless. They had asked Neal to be their videographer while Jennifer captured their stills. They knew most of the day and night would be a blur but trusted in others to capture it for them. For they truly believed, the wedding ceremony was just that, a ceremony, something to invite family, friends, and other guests. The true honorarium of this day, they knew was not in what they did and who was there, no, it was really in how they lived and loved in their marriage. That was the true testament. That was real.

Maureen wore a Mother of the bride linen suit in her favorite color: red. Ian wore his kilt with full regalia. The MacLaren tartan was quite dashing when worn by especially well-dressed men. Similarly, Bette wore her favorite butter yellow sequined gown that she wore for their 25th anniversary gala a few years ago. Clifton wore his Davies tartan in his full regalia. Depending if they were in the respective MacLaren or Davies clans, or a member of the bridal party, guests of the wedding noted men in kilts everywhere.

The wedding was held at a Presbyterian church in northern New Jersey, one that Neal had turned the couple on to when they were searching for a suitable location in which to set the wedding. It was an older limestone structure which reminded both the bride and groom of buildings in Europe and of Fiona's college campus. Reverend Percival Fallow was in charge of the marriage ceremony. His name and derivations of it were not lost on Jake or Fiona. They affectionately called him Percy Fellow, a suitable name for a man who, while he married others to each other, had yet to marry himself. He was still in on the chasing of women at a young age of 32.

The reception was held at OHM and overseen by Chef Rufalo. Though a native of southwestern India and going by a first name westerners could pronounce without hesitation, Rufalo was the sort of chef one took stock of and from whom many a culinary lesson could be garnered. Similar to their engagement dinner, which Rufalo had prepared, the couple had decided on a Filet Mignon and a Roasted Turkey dinner. They knew most of their family and friends would take to chef Rufalo's beef, so in preparation of that fact, they planned ahead with 40 extra beef dishes.

The dinner and reception dance were held at the Plaza and featured the typical events of an American wedding, save a few Canadian nuances. Maureen cleared with Bette the issuing of a small piece of bridal cake to each guest, for it was customary to encourage guests to place this small morsel under their pillows the night after the wedding and wish for and dream of pleasant tidings for the newly married. Bette, upon hearing of this custom, was immediately in agreement and gladly assisted in the distribution of the tiny cakes so specially wrapped. Each bundle had been hand-tied with ribbon in both the MacLaren and Davies tartans. Ian had explained the history during the speeches.

For Ian and Fiona, the whirlwind of this evening slowed some as they danced their first dance. Now, his only daughter was a married woman.

Clifton soon joined with Maureen, Jake with Bette, then all three couples forming first a large circle of parents and the bridal couple and then a final circle of parents surrounding their married children. They walked slowly about the young couple as they again embraced for a long sought after kiss.

They concluded their dance by inviting their family, friends, and other guests out onto the dance floor. When the floor filled, Ian gave Jake an envelope, leaned over and said, "Open and read this later, my son." He led Jake from the dance floor and back to the head table for further instructions.

Once they were seated, Jake said, "Thanks, Dad."

"Now take your new bride and be off with her, get away while you still can. I know you have a flight to catch tonight. We will attend to your guests while you change for your flight. Maureen and Bette completed the packing of your bags and all that remains is your quick change. My chauffeur, Delaney, is waiting in the town car in the parking garage. Once you say your goodbyes to your guests, he will whisk you off to the airport where I've arranged a private jet to take you to Edinburgh. There, you will find another waiting car which will take you to your first destination and your reservation at St. Andrews. In your room, you will find the instructions for the rest of the arrangements your Mother and I have made. We hope you enjoy this time together as much as we did with our wives."

At this point in their conversation, Clifton had joined them and he too handed over an envelope for his son. "Bon Voyage son, have a very pleasant journey with your new bride."

Following the Fathers' lead, Jake took Fiona's hand and led her upstairs to their empty suite of rooms. Despite the closeness of timetables they faced, they hastily but lovingly consummated their marriage while still dressed in their wedding clothes. Their climaxes came quickly knowing their rush and they changed each others' clothes noting the physique of their partner with a slightly different tone. Now instead of witnessing and watching their lover change, now they were watching their partner, their chosen life mate, for now they were husband and wife.

They called for the bellman to carry their bags to the parking garage and into Delaney's care. Meanwhile, they took the guest elevator back to the grand ballroom and their remaining guests. They said their goodbyes quickly and stopped atop the grand stairway in order to toss the bouquet and garter. Jane caught the bouquet and Neal the garter. Many eyes watched as they shared a small kiss and a wink, perhaps something would come of it, after all they were the same age.

Flying first class is one thing, ample seating and space within the seat, but flying privately was something altogether different. It was the parental gift, the flight that launched this marriage. It was one these parents wanted to make sure was memorable and without glitches.

They landed in Edinburgh and the hired car was waiting for them. It took them north over the bridge of the Firth of Forth up to St. Andrews and the majestic golf hotel. The staff knew they were receiving a newly married American couple and were ready for them when they arrived. Jet lag notwithstanding, the couple managed a round of golf the same afternoon they arrived before they collapsed from pre and post wedding exhaustion.

After a few days in St. Andrews and remarkable golfing and sightseeing, they were off for the remainder of their honeymoon trip, which was really rather simple. A trip by rail and road was planned in order to tour their respective ancestral homelands of Scotland and Ireland. They spent a month driving about the lowlands and the highlands, looking for kin and clan remnants in Scotland. In Ireland, they found the old Davies castle in the north and felt the pure history in the old edifice. It was actually quite moving.

Many times while they were driving about these now all too familiar lands, Fiona would look over to Jake, simply smile and say, "I'm home."

"Here with you, I'm home too. I know it, I love you too my darling."

Leaning her head back against the small Volkswagen headrest, with the look of a siren, Fiona said, "I love you too."

Jake replied, "If I forget to tell you I had a great time…" his voice trailed off. With her eyes now closed and focusing on their future lives together, Fiona cut in saying, "I'm telling you now."

"I'm telling you now," was all he could say too.

Chapter 8 A Set Back, 2015

Her real life recollections were jumbled due to the brain injury and coma she suffered from the fall in the showers of the YMCA earlier that year. As directed by her physicians, the plan of her care, during her coma, was for family and friends to read their letters, postcards, and most importantly, her European trip diary from 1985.

She traveled Europe with Ellen and was later joined by Jane and because of the strong connection developed over those weeks in 1985; the women had remained in contact. Ellen and Jane took turns reading Fiona's trip diary along with their own diaries. They too had met Kurt, a young student traveling on holiday before beginning his studies at the University of Berlin. But in hearing of Fiona's comments when she first awoke from the coma, of her looking for Kurt, from on their honeymoon, had disturbed them both. They knew what was real and were now there to help their friend remember, even if that meant, by sending her encouraging letters once they'd returned to their respective homes.

Her distorted reality of events read to her from her trip diary clashed with her dreams, thus creating trauma-induced apparitions, the misguided apperceptions, and the true nature of the relationship, marriage, and life in Germany with Kurt. He was just a man they met in Füssen.

In room B 10, the doctor returned to continue his assessment of Fiona. Once she had her initial recovery from her coma and was indeed finally convinced that the year was 2015, she was moved to station 51, a standard room on the neurology unit and out of ICU. As she continued to recover more and more, Fiona was often depressed when thinking about the past and what had not happened during her trip to Europe.

To her, the reading of her diary had been so real. It was difficult for her to acknowledge what everyone was constantly telling her about things. These things in her mind, these things that hadn't happened as she thought they had. Likely, too, they were withholding more from her, waiting for a time when they thought she could handle reconciling her memories. Not just yet.

Free to have guests beyond immediate family, her guests piled in. Her parents were still there, as were Gabriella and Jake. He had been there all along-waiting. He knew what was real.

Alone in her room, no guests to make her focus, Fiona continued to pine for the memories of Kurt, whom she thought was her husband. When Ellen read from her own diary, it was clearer that Kurt was simply a man she met while traveling in Germany. Fiona remembered it was during her after college trip with Ellen and Jane. They met Kurt, a student, and Masato, a Japanese train engineer, on the train as it arrived in Füssen, in the region of Bavaria, Germany. Her memories continued to confuse Fiona. It was difficult for her to determine her reality from her memory, and what were the scrambled remnants of hallucinations that continued to affront her brain.

She learned from her parents that her doctor was down the hall and going to continue with his line of questions and they prepared her for the fright of the answers. The doctor walked in and after the pleasantries were concluded, he began again.

"You are rested now and ready to work again?" he asked, initially.

"Yes, I think so," said a still shocked Fiona.

"Very well, let's begin with a few more questions, all right?" he asked.

"Ok, ready," she said reluctantly. "I'll do my best."

She was beginning to think that this doctor had a German accent or was that just what she was expecting him to sound like. When the appropriate time arrived, she'd ask him about it. She was still looking about her hospital room for signs of her stateroom on the *Love Boat*, the Mediterranean Cruise she and Kurt had taken for their honeymoon. For now, she wanted to humor the doctor and his silly questions.

"That's right. Miss Fiona, it is all I ask. Now, can you tell me what year it is?" asked the doctor.

"Well, you were here when my Father explained things to me. That's when I said it was 1990. My memory isn't that bad, since he said that only a few hours ago, but I still remember what he said to me. He said the year was really 2015 and that I was in room 1311, in the ICU at NYU Medical Center. But I'm in a new room now," she added.

"Yes, that is also correct," the doctor replied flatly. "Just a few more questions, ok?"

"Ok," said Fiona.

"If it is the year 2015, where do you work?" he asked.

"At a hospital," Fiona said, doubtingly, with a vacant look.

"Can you be more specific," he pushed further.

"At this hospital?" Fiona said, questioningly.

"Ok, let's try a different question," the doctor said, after looking at her audience.

"Ok," replies Fiona.

"How old are you?" he asked.

"Well, that depends, what month and year is it?" Fiona said, jokingly.

"April," he replied. While he also indicated the year 2015, Fiona never heard that.

"Then I'm 27 years old," Fiona said, having counted out the decades on her fingers.

Looking about the room, the doctor shared a knowing glance with Fiona's parents, Jake, and Gabriella. Their faces said it all.

"And if I reminded you it was 2015?" the doctor asked.

"Then I'm not sure," Fiona replied.

Fiona reported her responses logically but without feeling or emotion. She was unaware of how she felt about this sudden change in time. Perhaps, that was more concerning to those watching this interview. They realized that Fiona was still looking for Kurt and her lack of emotions were her way of protecting herself from the unknown they were trying to explain to her.

It was Gabriella who deciphered Fiona's reluctances in her emotionless responses. In this realization, her eyes grew wet with unshed tears as she looked from Fiona to Jake and then to Fiona's parents. Gabriella recognized that her best friend, her classmate from nursing school, had not acknowledged her true husband, Jake, who was standing but five feet away from her. Looking up from Fiona's bedside, Gabriella caught Fiona's parents' gaze. Their shared realization was visible and they were shaken out of their seats. Now standing on either side of their only daughter, it was Maureen who picked up one of Fiona's hands and kissed it.

Jake looked on longingly and held himself together by a thread.

As far as Fiona was concerned, she thought she was merely Jake's patient, for when they first met, he had worked as a nurse on a neurological unit. To Fiona, after all, he was just someone she knew at the hospital. In her jumbled mind, they hadn't become golfing partners, lovers, or married yet.

Jake, feeling overwhelmed, left the room and Gabriella followed. In the hall, they discussed that now wasn't the time either to explain everything she was forgetting or had lost about her life since moving to New York City. They would explain their plan to Fiona's parents when they left her room for dinner.

Her parents now renewed their wish to help their daughter all they could. They again asked the doctor about when to begin to review her life, to help her remember. Previously, while Fiona was still in ICU, the doctor had told them then that it wasn't yet time to help; it was the time to hope. The doctor further suggested the plan he and Jake had decided. Waiting was the best for now.

They were told it was simply a time to wait and pray that Fiona came back to them, on her own as she wished. What she'd remember might be influenced if they continued to work with her on her stories, her recollections, and her real memories. That they could do readily, it just felt like they weren't doing enough. She'd been in a coma for the last two months, but as far as the current period, she was stuck in the past; an unreal past at that.

"Regaining the last twenty-five years will take some time," the doctor said, as ironic as it was.

Fiona hadn't questioned the missing time either, another sign of the depth of her injury. This gap, well, actually, it never even made a blip on her radar. As far as she was concerned, she was in the German countryside enjoying some Kir with Kurt, Ellen, and Jane. This nagging headache, though not diminishing much, was right now interfering with her ability to order another carafe of Kir for her to share with her friends.

She was unusually patient during this entire process, at least outwardly. This fact was gradually being taken in by family and friends. They had just reported it to the doctor when they were speaking outside her room just a few moments ago. But that was Fiona's way, they knew. She never displayed too much concern for her surroundings.

Since she wasn't in excruciating pain and she wasn't hooked up to life-saving machines, she would humor them with their stupid questions. She knew that much was a good sign, and didn't let her being 'in' the hospital as a patient bother her greatly. She'd been a patient before when she had her tonsils out, but then she was only five years old, and now she wasn't.

"All right now, Miss Fiona. Can you tell me how old you are?" asked the doctor, again.

"Well, let me think. If you said it was 1990, then I'd say I'm about 27?" Fiona surmised.

"Fiona, you are coming back to us! Are you remembering now?" asked her Mother.

"Well Mother, it wasn't too difficult to do the math," Fiona said, as a matter of fact.

"That's my girl, always logical and responsive to the scientific side of things," her Father said, beaming.

Gabriella interjected next, "Then how old are you in 2015?"

"Not as old as you, Gabriella." Fiona said, ducking the question, her headache growing.

The doctor spoke up next, "It is ok, Miss Fiona, if you do not know the answer. The math question was more simplified. We can ask you another question. Where are you?" He said, looking about her hospital room trying to coax her into looking for her own clues.

"Didn't you already tell me I'm NYU Medical Center?" Fiona retorted again.

"Yes I did, but what kind of place is this?" the doctor said, looking about the room again.

"Port Authority? Grand Central Station or Penn Station?" Fiona asked.

"What does Medical Center mean to you?" the doctor pressed her for an answer.

"I don't know. I'm tired, and my headache is getting worse. Father, do I have to answer all his silly questions?"

"No dear, you just rest now."

"Here you go," her Mother said, in a very nurturing way, as she eased her only daughter into her hospital bed and encouraged her to sleep.

Then in a panic, her Mother rushed out of the room, not wanting the sudden gush of tears to upset her daughter. As the door to her room opened, Fiona heard the B-E-E-P sound again. Instinctively, she rolled over in her bed and reached for the invisible alarm clock not positioned on her bedside table. "B-E-E-P" she heard it again, before her room door closed. It was as if, on automatic pilot, Fiona reached again for the non-existent alarm clock in her honeymoon cruise stateroom and for the second time, struck it to stop the beeping.

The doctor was growing concerned about Fiona's clarity of thought and her obvious hallucination. He said, "I think you best leave her to me for a few moments. I'll rejoin you in the family lounge shortly."

As the remaining guests turned to leave, silently they reached down and either attempted to hug or merely caress Fiona's shoulder and then they walked out of her room. Before she could rest, the doctor asked her to sit up and allow a small neurological exam. His findings were inconsistent. Most notably, her grip strength on the left was weaker than the right. Also, her arm reflexes were uneven in response. The doctor made note of these findings and walked out suggesting she sleep now but without uttering a word. He wanted his patient to rest and perhaps the apparent migraine she was currently experiencing would be over when he returned on his normal evening rounds.

She repositioned herself in the bed, doubling up the pillow and laying down. "Finally some peace and quiet," she thought.

Soon the hum of commotion that was the hospital's normal everyday sounds lulled her into a deep sleep. In her dream, she smelled the familiar salty sea air from her stateroom on the *Love Boat*. When she rolled over the next time, she indeed was forced to reconcile why she was alone in bed-again. She reached for Kurt in her dreams, and in her bed. He wasn't there, had he left her?

In the family lounge, the doctor began to recount his findings. "I'm concerned about her memory and her unequal reflexes. I may have to order another scan to see if we have missed something but I don't want to expose her unduly."

"She will recover, though, right, doctor," her Mother said, desperately pleading that her daughter would return to them.

"It will take a lot of work and rehabilitation. You say she has a strong mind and a strong spirit?"

Her parents, Gabriella, and Jake nodded in unison.

"Well, that will surely help her. You must reach out and support her. Now, as to what she isn't remembering, her real marriage and real life; this concerns me. Her coma has placed her mind back in 1990. To her, just like back then, she is still a young single woman. I think it would be best if we wait and see if interacting with Jake jogs her memory. I have written orders to use the utmost care, her psyche may depend upon it!"

"We will do as you say, thank you doctor," Ian said.

As the doctor walked to the nurse's station and clutched his next patient's chart, Ian turned his attention to Maureen and Gabriella. "Shall we go find ourselves some dinner? Gabriella, we'd be pleased if you would join us?"

"I'll stay behind and look over her chart," Jake mustered, still distracted that his wife didn't know him.

"I'd like that. Besides, we need to figure out how to handle Fiona's memory."

Back in Fiona's room, where she was still dreaming of Füssen and Mediterranean cruise ships, a jarring motion rocked her bed. It was like the large cruise ship hitting a mammoth wave and did in fact move her bed on the linoleum floor an inch or two. She would soon learn that sleeping in the hospital, as a patient, was reserved to the few overnight hours when all was quiet. The sudden change in movements of the peaceful waves from her dreamy ocean liner was now replaced with the bells, beeps, and lights of her hospital room. These noises consumed her mind.

No longer in a restful place in her dream, Fiona woke up. She was short tempered when she realized she was no longer alone in her private room; someone was standing just over to the side, by the window, watering her many plants and flowers. She used Fiona's water pitcher to do so. "Aren't I supposed to be drinking that?" Fiona asked.

"Oh, you are awake. That's good. I'm sorry, I just noticed these flowers needing water and I didn't want to waste the water in your pitcher when I had it refilled. Besides, you were talking in your sleep again. I thought perhaps if I made some noise in your room or maybe bumped your bed, as I passed by it, you'd wake up and your nightmare would cease. Was I right?" said the hospital worker who had yet to identify herself.

"Well, I can't really remember either way, that's why I'm here. I guess… was I bothering anyone?" Fiona asked, feeling a bit timid about her talking in her sleep, again.

"I don't think so, we are just getting ready to pass dinner trays, are you hungry? What can I get for you to drink?"

"What am I allowed to drink?"

"We have soda, milk, coffee, or tea," she said.

"Do you have Sprite?"

"Yes we do, I'll be right back with the soda. Oh, by the way who is Kurt? He isn't on the list of guests, family or friends on your care plan."

"Why do you ask?" Fiona questioned.

"That's who you were calling out to in your dream."

As the young woman walked out of her room, Fiona's face felt flushed. She'd been told more than once what she remembered about Kurt, their courtship, flying back and forth to Berlin while he attended university, their wedding, and working in Füssen. These very vivid memories were not memories at all, but were the very clear concoctions of a brain injured mind. Her fairytale was just that, a tale. Yet, she still yearned for the happy ending.

"Here we go," said the happy hospital worker.

"Thank you." Fiona began, "Are you my nurse?"

"No, but I will be a nurse some day. Right now I'm a volunteer. I'm a senior in high school, and I'll going to college next fall. I've already been accepted at CUNY. I'm so excited!"

"Did you know I'm a nurse?" Fiona asked. Fiona always knew she was a nurse, but her age and where she worked still eluded her.

"Yes, your nurse, uh, that's what Carolina told me."

"Who is Carolina?"

"That's the name of your nurse this shift. My name is Stacey," she said, finally introducing herself.

"Nice to meet you Stacey. My name is Fiona MacLaren Hochs…" Fiona stopped in mid-sentence, realizing that she was once again introducing herself as Kurt's wife. She made a mental note that she was going to have to watch that having been able to retain what her doctor, parents, and friends had said that she wasn't ever married to Kurt. "Maybe for now, I'm just Fiona," she said, thinking better of leaving her name at just Fiona and still not sure of her real name or just what she remembered.

"I'll be right back with your dinner tray," said Stacey.

In as long as it took Fiona to get out of bed, put on her hospital robe over her drafty patient gown, and sit in the patient armchair, Stacey had returned with her dinner tray.

"I'm hoping someone took care in ordering my dinner. I've a history of being a picky eater," Fiona admitted.

"Well, tonight it looks like someone did. You actually have food Jake brought up for you; I just swapped out the hospital food and placed the food he brought on your tray. I hope that was ok. He said you'd like what he brought for you," Stacey explained.

"Jake, you mean Jake Davies? From neuro?" Fiona asked.

"Yes, he has been watching out for you; he was with your family when you transferred down here. With the shift change happening almost at the same time as your transfer and since the doctor was here, he likely left before saying anything. He's outside now, can he come in?"

Stacey felt strange when she let Jake enter the room and not addressing him with his title in the process. Stacey knew that the doctor caring for Fiona was actually one of the physicians from Jake's practice. It was a challenge not to correct Fiona in her memory of Jake as still a nurse. All of this had been explained repeatedly to any hospital staff that would have direct contact with Fiona. According to her doctors and family's wishes, Fiona's personal life was that of 1990 even though it was now 2015.

Stacey attended the change of shift report and in sitting in on that important information sharing meeting, she learned what her role for the evening would be. They wanted to keep all stresses, excitable moments, and forgotten relations or relationships out of Fiona's purview until she recalled them on her own. Her doctor thought it best to at least humor her with her version of the present even though it was really her past.

This was a case he was going to write an article about and he didn't want Fiona's care to interfere with the natural course of events. Plus, he knew her mind would eventually sort itself out once she was constantly reminded of the year and other important factors of her prior life. All of this meant that Jake was to keep a low profile, maintaining the impression that he was still just her golf partner and would reveal more only when she remembered the present. Further, it meant no hospital staff could refer to him as "Doctor Davies."

To the hospital staff, following these orders felt a bit like playing a con game and they even developed signals to each other, like the flick of the nose from the movie *The Sting*. It was the general consensus that everyone who encountered Fiona wanted her to remember, but on her terms. They all easily and readily agreed with the doctor on this point. They didn't know what the shock of knowing about a real marriage or children would do to her.

"Yes please! Send him in." Fiona said, smiling and looking forward to seeing her golfing partner. She was pleasantly surprised to learn that he was here visiting her, but then again, if their positions had been switched, she'd be here for him too.

"Hey Fiona, how is it going tonight?" he said.

"Hi, Jake, how's neuro?"

Seeing her eye the food, Jake asked, “Do you like the food I got for you? It is from the diner down the street, I know it is way better than the Salisbury steak on the menu tonight!”

Looking back at her tray table and watching as Stacey left with the dish covers, Fiona found herself looking at one of her favorite meals: cheeseburger and fries. “Am I allowed to eat this?” she said puzzled.

“Sure, why not?” he said.

“No policy against it?” she said, still confused.

“No, I checked with the nurse, Carolina. She said it was just fine. It isn’t exactly prohibited food but eat it all up, as we don’t want to make the neighboring patients upset with the good smells wafting out of your room.”

“Come on in and sit with me Jake, won’t you?” Fiona said, then pointing with her boney white hand to the chair in the corner, the one reserved for guests. It was ironic, Fiona recalled, for the hospital’s guest chairs, that if this chair was anything like the ones on her unit a few floors up, they were the most uncomfortable chairs any of the nurses had ever sat in.

“Thank you,” he said.

What Fiona hadn’t seen was the to-go bag in his hand. He had another burger and fries for himself and a coke.

“Mmm, this is excellent. I hadn’t realized just how hungry I was. Thank you for bringing me such tasty food,” Fiona exclaimed.

“My pleasure, how are you feeling now? I talked with your parents just now in the hall. They told me you were still confused about your marriage and living arrangements. What are you remembering now?”

“I know Kurt was just a guy we met in Germany and that you all don’t really know where he is now, right?”

“Right, what else?”

“That my brain injured mind concocted this relationship with him?”

“Yes, anything else?” What he wasn’t saying was whether or not Fiona remembered him. They were more than golf partners when she fell and went into the resulting coma. Ever since that fateful day, she hadn’t remembered him as anything more than her golfing partner.

“That it isn’t really 1990 either?”

“Correct, it is much later than that. It is 2015, do you remember that?”

“Yes, that’s what my Father told me. So I can also tell you that I’ve been thinking. If I didn't marry Kurt in 1990, what have I done in all that time?" she said, innocently and with questioning eyes.

"The doctor suggested we not inform you about what you are forgetting but to work with you on remembering it on your own terms. That is why I'm here tonight, to see if we can jog out some memories."

"By the way my body feels, I could believe you that it is no longer 1990. I do feel a bit odd, maybe that isn't the right word, and maybe it is that I feel older in some ways and yet innocently younger in others due to all I cannot recall. Is that what you mean?"

"Yes, it is."

"Jake, why don't I remember anything else, there is more, isn't there? It feels so close and yet," she turned her face to look out the window and her thoughts drifted out beyond the smudged glass panes. "I feel like I'm missing something pretty important."

"Brains are interesting organs, they confuse even me and I've worked with them for a long time."

Feeling distraught but hiding it, Fiona allowed the welled-up tears to fall while she gazed out the window; she didn't want to let on to Jake that she too was worried about what she was forgetting. It was troubling her. It was like a word on the tip of her tongue, but the word, or words, just felt like they would never come.

Knowing how his wife sometimes initially kept her feelings to herself, Jake watched her face in the window's reflection and confirmed for himself that she knew something was missing. He would wait for her to realize it was him; he would wait for her-always.

Maybe with some sleep things would become clearer. Maybe she would remember him.

Chapter 9 Remembering London to Paris, 1985

Later, after awakening and turning away from the window of her hospital room, Fiona said to Jake, "This is what I remember, uh, of my trip. I first went to England to spend time with my cousin Gosnold and his wife Una and their three adult children. As I recall, it was the period of time when I left their home in London and was headed to Paris. For it would be in Paris that I would rendez-vous with my friend Ellen. I've told you about Ellen before, right?"

"Yes, you have been friends since college. You know, I don't think you ever told me about that part of the trip. I look forward to hearing it. Go ahead," Jake admitted.

"I know I've told you about my trip while we were golfing, but not this part?" Fiona asked, searchingly. She thought she'd recalled another feeling, something she was missing with Jake, but she couldn't quite connect the dots.

"That's right, while we've been golfing," Jake agreed, covering his faux pas about almost saying something that would ruin what steps and progress Fiona had already taken.

"Ok then, let me see," Fiona said. "It was after dinner one night…"

As announced prior to the dinner, Una and Gosnold would be ducking out early from their country home to take Fiona back to London. The three of them made their goodbyes, with Una and Gosnold concentrating more on Charlotte and Charlie. They'd see the cricket teammates soon enough. Charlotte and Charlie would be away for several years and they didn't know when they'd see Fiona again.

With their goodbyes concluded, Una made sure Fiona had all her belongings and had successfully packed everything. Now loaded with the carrier and her daypack, Fiona headed downstairs and out to the car. Gosnold hefted the bag into the boot and in a remarkably short period of time, they were on the road returning to their London flat.

Traffic into London was moderate and they returned in plenty of time for a good night's sleep before Fiona's big transition to traveling in Europe. In the car, they discussed how well they thought Fiona had acclimatized to England and to British travel methods, customs, foods, and slang. Fiona agreed that this section of her trip had gone very well, and had helped her identify with all the things she'd heard in her youth about her family, its history, and traditions. Fiona thanked her cousins for introducing her to most of what she had experienced, even the forehand shot to the nose.

She turned out the light in her guest room of the flat a few minutes after one o'clock in the morning, sleeping so soundly, that she almost slept through the soft sounds sputtering forth from her traveling alarm clock. After hearing the tones through her closed bedroom door, and realizing that Fiona hadn't yet turned off the alarm, Una knocked softly on the bedroom door, and then opened it before hearing permission. On the bed, Una found a softly snoring form of Fiona who almost looked like she was smiling through her dormant sounds.

Tapping her on the shoulder, Una woke Fiona who now heard the beeping alarm clock which now read 8:03AM. "Sorry, I was dreaming. The music in my dream was just like the alarm clock. Did it wake you?"

"No, I was already up. I wanted to send you on your way with another of your favorite British traditions, a cooked English breakfast. Get showered and when you are ready, so will be the breakfast."

"Thank you Una, how thoughtful of you."

"Not at all, it is my pleasure."

Thirty minutes later, Fiona entered the kitchen and was met with the wonderful aromas of cooked bacon, sausage, eggs and toast. The coffee was brewed and in a thermal pot on the table just in front of Gosnold. He was already enjoying his coffee with his morning copy of *The Times.*

"Good morning Fiona. I trust you slept well," Gosnold said, pointedly. He had already been informed of her over sleeping by Una.

"Yes, too well I'm afraid."

"Come sit, breakfast is ready now," Una said.

"Everything smells delicious."

Another thirty minutes later, breakfast was but a memory. Fiona appeared from her bedroom dressed in dark navy jeans and an aqua blue and hot pink striped polo shirt. The smile on her face was unmistakable. Una said her goodbye back at the apartment as Gosnold was helping Fiona carry the suitcase, carrier, and daypack down the five flights of stairs. Moments after hitting the final landing, Gosnold gave his bonnie cousin a final handshake, hug, and a kiss goodbye. They had shared an interesting and unique experience with this American branch of the family. He knew she'd thoroughly enjoy Europe; *he* always did.

Back in the apartment, Una went about cleaning up after breakfast, and preparing to strip Fiona's bed, wanting to take the laundry with her back out to the country house. Upon entering the bedroom, Una discovered that not only had Fiona stripped the bedding, but she'd left it neatly folded, and atop the pile on linens, was a small envelope and package.

Una opened and read Fiona's note:

"Dear Una and Gosnold,

Thank you for helping me adjust to and understand the English way of life and sharing your family with me. I appreciated all the support you showed to me while I was visiting with you. Spending my time in England with *__family__*, *made all the difference in my experience. Please enjoy this small token of my gratefulness.*

Love, your cousin,
Fiona."

Attached to the note was a small package, which Una opened after reading the card. As she ripped the wrapping paper, inside she discovered a small package of Minnesota wild rice. Una admired Fiona's time spent in her household. For at that moment, Una knew that Fiona's maturation and growth during her fortnight in her home had produced results beyond expectation. She was indeed proud of her husband's cousin, and the fact that Fiona had remembered the niceties and the art of the thank you note and gift. Muttering softly to herself, Una said, "Good show, Fiona, well done."

Fiona eased her way along the fairly crowded platform at Notting Hill Gate Station for her last egress. She was a bit pensive while waiting for the train. She thought back to the moment of personal connection with her Grandmother's past, reaching into her own future with the creation of her first kilt, and now, standing on this cement platform, she smiled at the face of the unknown that was awaiting her at the other end of the tracks. She was no longer concerned with what other people said or thought about her, she was one with the crowd and not alone in it.

Her train appeared after a few more moments, and then she was on her way. Ellen had confirmed their rendezvous during the dinner party last night. She was on her way back to Paris too, and had agreed to meet Fiona at Sophie's apartment the next day. At Victoria Station, Fiona exited the tube station and followed the 'To Trains' signs.

In consulting her *Cook's Timetables*, Fiona read that there was a train which went from Victoria Station to Dover, where she would then transfer to the Hovercraft terminal. She would cross the channel to France from Dover to Boulogne in the Hovercraft. Once in Boulogne, she'd take the French national railway, the Société Nationale des Chemins de fer Français (SNCF), train into Paris, Gare Du Nord Station.

Once Fiona arrived in Paris' Gare Du Nord, she'd have to follow the signs to the Métro trains, Paris' subway, and find the magenta colored line heading in the direction: Porte d'Orléans. She'd exit at the Odéon Station and then out on the street, she'd need to ask for directions to Sophie's street. During her phone call with Thierry before leaving Minnesota, Fiona had been given directions to Sophie's flat but when she most needed those directions, she couldn't find them. All she had were telephone numbers.

Fiona rationalized her dilemma by telling herself that if she needed a lot of help, she could always look for a policeman, or someone else who could help her in English. While Fiona's French speaking skills weren't bad, at times of stress, they weren't exactly reliable, either. Having thought through this far into her travel plans, Fiona almost forgot to exit the tube train at Victoria Station.

Soon the train to Dover arrived and just like her other solo train ride to and from Edinburgh, Fiona found a seat amongst other open seats with a table upon which she again played solitaire. With all her cargo piled next to her and about her feet, Fiona tried her best to concentrate on her card game. She missed numerous moves and a thirty-something looking man smiled as he watched her playing. After a few minutes, he said to her, "You missed several good moves already."

"I did?"

"Yes, you missed moving the jack of clubs onto the queen there," he said, pointing to the card in an empty column.

"So I did, thank you for pointing that out."

Eventually, these two got into a serious discussion about the rules for solitaire and the many, many ways to play it. The man introduced himself as Richard and he said he was spending a long weekend in Paris to take some photographs. Fiona figured his age to be close to thirty, with sandy brown hair and a mustache. His medium build suited his 6'2" frame. He was dressed in nice casual clothes with penny loafers.

It was a little hobby, he had said. After introducing herself in return, Fiona learned that they were heading in the same direction. That bit of information changed the demeanor of their conversation. A less formal discussion of cards gave way to a more serious conversation about how one would maneuver through the Dover train station, and how to board the Hovercraft.

"Did you buy your ticket yet," he asked.

"No I, well, to be honest, I bought my rail passes at home, so I think I don't need to buy any tickets," Fiona said, somewhat uncertainly.

"Well, you will definitely need to buy a Hovercraft ticket. It isn't the same as your rail passes. I haven't gotten mine yet, so when we get there, just follow me and I can help you get your ticket."

"Thank you very much. I didn't know that. I just assumed my rail pass worked on everything. I'm going to have to stop doing that," Fiona exclaimed.

"It's all right, happens all the time. I could tell you weren't a typical holiday or weekend traveler like me, so I thought I'd help you out by asking."

"Well it was a very good observation. You say you are going to take photographs? Is that all you are going to do?"

"Yes, I like to hop on the train and come here every change of season. I'm a little early for a Parisian fall, but I couldn't get away any other weekend for the next few months. Are you American?" he asked.

"Yes, I'm from Minnesota. We hop in the car and head to Green Bay or Chicago. You're hopping on a train and going to Paris just doesn't seem the same at all. How lucky you are to live so close to so many different cultures."

"I like it for that very reason. My fiancée and I are actually looking for places to get married. Marie has recently fallen in love with West Berlin, while I'm still partial to Paris. If I could convince her with just the right pictures, perhaps we'll have our wedding in Paris. I like West Berlin too, but, in my book, Paris triumphs over walls any day."

When the train pulled into the Dover station, Richard showed Fiona where to queue up to buy her channel crossing ticket. He stood off to the side to wait for her. Fiona couldn't believe her luck, finding someone who approached her to help her make her crossing and arrival into Paris uneventful.

Their luggage was taken from them to be stored below, similar to flying in more ways than Fiona first realized. While waiting in line to board the Hovercraft, Fiona wondered where in Paris Richard was going. Where was he going to stay? When she returned from purchasing the crossing ticket, Fiona asked him, "Where in Paris are you staying?"

"I'm going to Métro stop St. Michel, and you?" he asked.

"I'm supposed to go to Odéon Station and then look for Rue Charles-De-Gaulle. That's where my friend Sophie's apartment is located. I'm staying with her in Paris. Four years ago, I stayed with her parents in Triel-sur-Seine, a northwest suburb of Paris. That was when I was visiting France with my high school French class."

"No kidding," Richard said, in his obvious London accent. "I'm pretty sure your Métro stop is the next one right after St. Michel!"

"Now you have to be kidding me, really?" Fiona said; she couldn't believe it, what luck.

"Absolument, absolutely," he said, reassuringly in French and then in English. Finally the doors opened for the Hovercraft, and they were allowed to board. "Follow me, I know where the best seats are-up front!"

While waiting to board the Hovercraft, Fiona took a few minutes to observe the vessel for which she was waiting. The white background of the craft was accented with red and navy blue striping, following the ships form from stem to stern. The large fans on top of the craft were similarly painted in navy blue. By looking at the 'ship,' unless you covered from view the oversized fans and the soft coupling at the keel, one might think you were boarding a tug boat or ferry. In essence, the Hovercraft was a ferry, but Fiona found it odd that it actually looked like the ones she had taken in New York City or Seattle in her past.

Walking from the docks into the open bow was a bit unsettling. The bow of the craft was open like a large mouth bass awaiting the passengers to swim to their doom like bait fish. The passengers were instructed to board "The Princess Margaret" through her stem. Their luggage was secured below decks for the remainder of the journey. The passengers proceeded upstairs to the seats.

As they boarded from the docks, Fiona noted a sign indicating the weather conditions for the crossing. There were three options in the neon sign and the option 'moderate seas' was currently lit up. The other two were 'calm seas' and 'departure delays.' When they took to the seats that Richard selected for them, Fiona noted that they were only a few rows back from the bow of the ship. The glassed in windows at the front were positioned too high for Fiona to see out of, which was likely a design tactic. If she could have seen the seas she was to cross, through those windows, she might not have agreed to the crossing.

"What does 'moderate seas' mean?" she asked.

"It means we are in for a bumpy ride. I hope you like roller coasters," he replied.

"Sometimes, but as I'm looking there," Fiona said, pointing through the obstructed windows, "I can't really see where I'm going."

"Nor can the other 300 passengers, only the crew upstairs can see. That's what makes this kind of crossing so exciting!"

"Exciting?"

"Yes, you'll understand soon enough. Here's a waitress, do you want something to drink? I'm going to order a Whiskey Coke, what can I get for you?"

"I'd have a glass of Chardonnay, if they have it?" Fiona answered meekly.

"They don't serve any glass on here, only cans. Wait, you'll see," he said.

After receiving their drink orders, the waitress returned a few minutes later with their beverages. For Richard, it was a can of Coke and a small plastic bottle of Whiskey. He drank a few mouthfuls of soda before he poured the Whiskey into the can and handed the waitress the empty bottle. Then he looked at Fiona. She had a can of wine in her hands. The opening of the can was covered with a plastic strip like the tab on juice drinks. Richard assisted her in removing the plastic tab cover, and again handed that to the waitress.

"Cheers," he said animatedly. "If you can, try to drink as much of your drink before we leave port. You will have trouble drinking on moderate seas, and you can't take it with you in Boulogne."

"Ok, but I've never really been very good at chugging alcohol," Fiona admitted.

"That's ok, just get it started."

A few minutes later, the captain spoke over the loudspeaker saying, "All Aboard, departing in 5 minutes."

Now Fiona knew how long she had to try to consume her wine.

Looking at her watch, it was now a bit past noon. The Hovercraft didn't serve food, but Fiona figured the port in Boulogne probably had something. She'd look for a sandwich or something to tide her over when they reached the other side of the channel.

As announced, the Hovercraft departed Dover docks five minutes later. With 3 loud toots of an air horn, the craft began its retreat from port. What happened next, to Fiona was a bit of a blur. Richard was very calm in his seat, and happily watching Fiona's reaction to hovering. The moderate seas statement was now understood. This meant that the seas had significant swells on them, and in order to hover over them, the craft rose and fell much like a roller coaster combined with a flume.

Anyone who loves theme parks or their rides would have signed on to ride the Hovercraft back and forth all day long this Saturday in September 1985. For Fiona, one way was more than enough. Now she realized why there were windows up front and not just openings. When the craft was on the way down from a swell, it came crashing down into the wave and splashed grandly through it. It was like being on a massive boogie board and surfing along the shoreline's 1-2' swells. If anyone had been allowed to ride outside, they would have been drenched in seconds.

Fiona did manage fairly well to drink her can of wine, and balance the act of riding the Hovercraft's ups and downs without getting sick. She discovered that if she drank from the can while the craft was riding up a crest, she could finish her intake before the plunge to the bottom of the wave jarred the can away from her mouth. Richard was more of an expert and took pleasure in watching a novice figure out how to manage without spilling or vomiting.

In all, the hovering ride took 45 minutes to cross the channel, through the Straits of Dover, which are less than 25 miles wide at their narrowest point. They had to go across the channel at a bit of an angle to cover the distance to Boulogne. In the Boulogne Station, just as Fiona predicted, was a French café. Turning to Richard, Fiona said she wanted to grab something to eat on the train and would order something 'to go.'

"Great idea," he replied, "I'm hungry too. We can have a mini-picnic on the train, if you don't mind if I join you?"

"Not at all, I've enjoyed learning from you, the expert hovercraft beverage consumer."

"Ha, I just like to have a drink with my crossing, nothing wrong in that."

"Nothing at all, I'm sure it is better with calm seas, though," Fiona replied.

Standing in line at the café, Fiona saw a refrigerated section with prepared sandwiches and desserts. When it was her turn, Fiona ordered the cold Croque Monsieur. She knew it was the popular French version of a ham and cheese sandwich. She also ordered a coke and had to hand over more than half of her pre-ordered French francs.

She left home with 20₣, and her lunch cost 15.80₣. She recalled the exchange rate of US dollars to French francs (₣) was about 6 to 1. So doing the math in her head, Fiona concluded her sandwich was about $3.00. She now realized that when she left home, she really had very little in the way of French money, an oversight needing to be attended to whenever Fiona saw an "EXCHANGE" sign posted. She would also try to use her VISA credit card until she exchanged sufficient funds.

Fiona placed her sandwich in her daypack, and searched the station for a restroom. She finally found one on the other side of the terminal, on their way to the trains. She excused herself to use the facilities. After Richard watched her bags, Fiona watched his bags for his turn with the facilities. Then they headed to the train terminal and looked at the schedule of arrivals and departures. They saw that the next train to Paris was leaving from platform 7 and they followed the signs to platform 7.

In consulting her *Cook's Timetables*, Fiona learned that the trains here would be headed to Calais, Amiens, Lille, and Paris. The next train was leaving in about fifteen minutes. Their timing turned out to be lucky, so they had no significant layover in Boulogne. The high-speed train arrived on time, no surprise to Fiona, and departed about ten minutes after arrival. Climbing into the 2nd class car section, Fiona led the way to their seating options. This train had some individual compartments with opposing rows of seats, usually 3 across, or had open area seating, typical of an airplane.

In order to eat their lunch, Fiona searched for one of the compartments, and after walking passed a few occupied compartments, she finally discovered an open one. "Here we go," Fiona said, pulling her luggage carrier behind her and entering the compartment first, then bringing the bags over the threshold in one fell swoop. Richard followed behind like the true gentleman Fiona learned that he was, making sure that her carrier made it easily into their seating area.

After stowing her bag in the overhead compartment, Fiona watched as Richard removed his backpack and tossed it up into the same bin. Fiona sat so that she was facing in the direction the train traveled and Richard sat across from her. His view out the window was more or less the same as Fiona's, just watching where they'd been and not where they were headed. Neither of them were motion sickness sufferers so the train's movements from side to side and forward didn't affect them.

The day was getting long as Fiona realized she had about 3 more hours of train travel before her final destination within Paris. They unpacked their sandwiches, and in silence began to consume them swiftly. The scenery moved by in a green blur; Fiona realized that if you stare right at something along the train's path, but if you look ahead a bit, and let your eyes follow something, objects come into focus.

While Richard dozed off and on, Fiona made journal entries into her trip diary. In the pages of the tiny book, she recaptured all the places she had seen while in England. She wrote: London: Westminster Abbey and the Houses of Parliament, Big Ben, the Tower of London and London Bridge, Buckingham Palace and the Changing of the Guard, St. Paul's Cathedral, Trafalgar Square, Piccadilly Circus, Harrods and their famous fish display, Kensington Park, and Covent Garden. She rode on all available modes of public transportation: Double Decker Bus, London Taxicab, Bus, Train, and Tube.

For Edinburgh, Fiona commented on seeing: John Knox's House, Jenner's, walking along Princes Street, Holyrood Palace, Edinburgh Castle, Aunt Rhona and Julia Wing, and finally visiting Geoffrey Tailor's for her first kilt. Then for Oxford, Fiona listed Lincoln College, Oxford University, Radcliffe Camera, St Mary's Church and Tower, the River Cherwell, and All Souls College. Fiona asked in the diary, "What would be waiting in Paris and the rest of Europe?" She was too excited to imagine all the potential for fun that was still ahead. She hoped Ellen had a pleasant journey in the south of France and returned safely to Paris.

Fiona was brought back from her daydreaming by the overhead announcement, "Gare Du Nord," "Next station Paris North."

"Are we there?" Fiona said.

"Well, as far as the first train stop, yes. But now we must get out here. We need to change to the Métro and get on a subway train in the direction of Porte d'Orléans, remember?"

"Yes I do. I'll follow you," Fiona suggested.

When the train came to a complete stop, Fiona and Richard had gathered their belongings and cleaned up after their picnic and threw the trash in the bin on their way out. This station was very busy since it was a major hub of commuter trains, express trains from the countryside, and the Métro. Richard did well, making sure that Fiona kept him in sight, and that he didn't walk too fast to lose her.

They walked from the train platform into the multi-level station. The area was very well lit and the signs posted were direct. Fiona picked up a Métro map from the display and placed it in her daypack. They walked down several hallways of brick and mortar, some with graffiti, some just whitewashed. Eventually, they changed levels using an escalator. This was a challenge with the carrier but Fiona resolved to manage; she never saw an elevator here.

This is when she heard the familiar sound; it was the faint sound of an alto saxophone grew closer and closer, and finally they walked right past the player. His instrument case was open on the floor of the walkway, and inside it were various denominations of coins, even a US dollar bill. Fiona would try to remember to keep a few coins handy in her pockets. She liked to reward talent when she heard or saw it.

After about ten minutes of walking and taking escalators, they emerged on a platform with signs indicating that the terminus of the train was Porte d'Orléans. Fiona was relearning a critical lesson and reminded herself of when she had originally learned it. While taking the Métro during her trip to France with her high school French class, she'd one time missed her stop getting back to the hotel after some sightseeing. Since the children were allowed to roam the city sans chaperone, Fiona had been forced to navigate the Métro independently.

This was when Fiona originally learned that if you missed your stop, getting out at the next station might be the quickest and easiest solution, but finding the correct platform at the next station to be able to retrace the steps to trains heading in the other direction, wasn't. This was why on the English and Scottish trains, Fiona seemed consumed with checking and rechecking the *Cook's Timetables* and identifying the next stop. This way, Fiona confirmed she had boarded the correct train. This frustration with being on the correct train may feel like an obsession, Fiona rationalized, but if she learned one thing from childhood, she seriously detested being lost.

"Here we go," Richard said, as they finally reached the correct level in the station for the Métro and the direction they wanted.

"Yes I see it," Fiona said, as they entered the final turn to the platform. "No train here though, I guess we'll just have to wait."

"Shouldn't be long, at this time of day there is probably a train coming through here about every 5-6 minutes. See, hear that?" Richard said, as he heard the first rumblings of a train approaching.

"Yes, I do, good timing again. I hate waiting for something to arrive especially when I don't know the schedule!"

"Well, this is how I think about it. When I arrive at a station, if a train is already waiting by the platform, I should run to catch it. If I miss it, I know there will be another one coming along soon. If there isn't one already in the station, I still know that there will be one on its way. After a while, you get a sense of the timing of these trains. Some lines are faster and busier, while others are not. I'm sure as you go around Paris you'll discover this too."

"I think you are right about that," Fiona confirmed. Her analytical mind began thinking of charts and graphs of arrival and departure times, just for the fun of it.

They waited for the doors to open and for the other passengers to exit the train before they made their approach to the train. Fiona's carrier caused a wide wake and she didn't want to strike anyone in the close quarters. The seats of this train were plastic in a very ugly orange color. Sometimes seats were in opposing directions lengthwise, and then others were in singles or pairs, and were positioned at 90° angles. The humidity in the station was high, but the breeze from the approaching train had been soothing. Not having been outside since leaving for Notting Hill Gate Station, Fiona could only estimate the temperature by the degree of cloud cover.

They were able to claim seats at the front end of the train car in an area that had seats facing the direction of the train. Pulling her carrier in front of her, Fiona promptly sat down. She decided to sit out this last phase of the day's journey. She also knew, from her prior experience riding the Métro, she was now likely only 15-20 minutes away from Sophie's apartment. This realization quickened her pulse and added a bit of adrenaline to her already taxed system. The moisture on her face and neck grew proportionately to her happy anxiety to be finally arriving at her destination.

Richard reviewed his subway map and pointed to where they were on the map. Then he pointed out that from Gare Du Nord, they had 10 stops until Odéon. His stop was #9, St. Michel. He offered to help her find Sophie's apartment, but Fiona turned down his over-extending kind offer. She'd do the last part on her own.

"You've already been so kind to me, I'd like to repay you somehow.

Can I have your home address? I'd like to write to you, if that's all right with you?"

"Certainly, you are a different kind of American, Fiona; I'd enjoy being your pen pal."

"I think that is because I'm a first generation American. Perhaps you're seeing more of the Canadian and British traditions in my personality than American. Does that make sense?"

"Perfect sense. That was stop 6, Les Halles," he said.

"Getting closer, can you feel it?" Fiona said, making the movement with her arm like an old fashioned steam locomotive. "Coming down the track, woo, woo. Just like Casey Jones!"

"Casey Jones?" Richard asked.

"He was a children's train engineer on a local television show when I was growing up. I watched his show all the time," she said.

"Sounds interesting, we didn't have much television for children, just the BBC," he said solemnly.

"You missed out on a lot," she said, laughing.

"I am beginning to see that," he said, laughing with her.

"Next stop is St. Michel, my stop. I do wish you a pleasant journey. Make sure you go to Bavaria, there are some fabulous castles there."

"I will make a note of that in the *Cook's Timetables* book. We are putting dots next to destinations we want to see, that sounds like a good suggestion."

At the next station, Fiona said goodbye to Richard and thanked him for helping her find her way. She was on her own and she was in Paris, again. It seemed that the travel gods out there were watching over her and helping her along the way. Each time a different 'angel' would appear to help with this part or that. Fiona could only hope their help would last. In less than an hour, she would find out that her luck had run out. No more angels or Good Samaritans to see her along her way. That is, until she met Milton, the most unexpected assistant in a most unexpected place.

"Wow, it sounded like that Milton guy really came in handy for you," Jake said.

"Yes, he did," Fiona agreed.

Chapter 10 Still Remembering & Stranded in Paris, 1985

Fiona continued with her story by saying, the walk to Sophie's apartment wasn't difficult and easily found the building and entered it when she found the front door was conveniently unlocked. The doorway was one very large door with a smaller door for people; the larger door was big enough for a truck but it remained closed. Fiona passed through a small archway and then through a tunnel which opened out into a very quaint courtyard, which was surrounded by two stories of apartments. Each of the windows had ornate metalwork about them with curling ends. Further inside, Fiona saw a plump older woman sweeping the courtyard area with an old broom. The sweeping woman gave no recognition to Fiona whatsoever.

Fiona eventually found the stairs leading to the second story and followed the exterior walkway to Sophie's apartment #21. She knocked on the door, but no one answered. Realizing that Sophie was not at home, Fiona became flustered at her plight, walked back downstairs and approached the sweeping woman. She was so upset in her panic stricken frame of mind, that when she spoke in French to the older woman, her words were incomprehensible. Fiona thought to herself, "Where could Sophie be? She was expecting me? Now what should I do?"

Calming down, Fiona turned to the older woman and said, "Où est Sophie? Je suis une amie de Sophie." "Where is Sophie? I'm a friend of Sophie's." While Fiona was speaking, the older woman never stopped her sweeping.

The reply was so fast and furious in French that Fiona had no idea what was said by the sweeper.

Becoming anxious about Sophie's whereabouts, and thinking back, Fiona was certain she had made the proper arrangements to stay here. Before leaving London, Fiona had called to speak with Sophie's Father, Thierry, to reconfirm her accommodations with his daughter. Fiona then decided the next best thing to do was to find a pay telephone and call Sophie's phone. But, where was a phone, had she seen one on her way from the Métro station?

Leaving the panic producing person that was the sweeping woman behind, Fiona decided to retrace her steps which would take her back onto the street outside of Sophie's apartment building. She reversed her previous route to Sophie's front door by going back down the winding stairs, through the human sized door in the oversized doorway, and then Fiona was back out on the street. Looking both ways, Fiona decided to keep to the right, and if she walked long enough, she'd circumnavigate the neighborhood. While she was walking and passing other buildings, what Fiona noticed was the lack of other people about the street or sidewalk. Did she remember how to ask, "Where is a telephone?"

After walking about ten minutes, Fiona saw her answer: a post office. She remembered her high school French teacher explaining during their class trip to France, if they were ever lost, there would always be a telephone in a post office. She quickly crossed the street and read the posted placard in the window. The post office would be closing in about twenty minutes.

Next, Fiona peered inside through the shop's plate glass windows. Several people were lined up for service from the postal worker behind the counter. And then she saw them, three telephone cubicles of glass just past the people waiting in line along the far wall. She suppressed the urge to smile and smirked anyway.

Entering the post office was easy enough, and being noticed wasn't difficult. No one else in the office had a large suitcase on a carrier or a daypack. Fiona waited in line like everyone else. While she had enough money to make the call, she needed to exchange her franc bills for coins as the telephones were coin operated only.

With the proper change in hand, Fiona made her way into the first available telephone cubicle. She couldn't close the door behind her; it was too tight a fit with all her belongings, so she managed with the door slightly ajar. She dialed Sophie's phone number and then listened to the receiver. Long tones repetitively beeped, but no one came on the line. Fiona thought back to high school and tried to recall how many numbers in a Parisian phone number would she need to use when in Paris.

Her anxiety was growing as she then tried Ellen's number. Again, the long tones beeped away and no one answered. Next she tried to call Nicole and Thierry, Sophie's parents; surely they would be home on a Saturday at dinner time. Again Fiona heard the tones and again no one answered. Feeling dejected, Fiona said in the cubicle, "Now what am I going to do?"

With tears streaming down her face, Fiona felt extremely fragile. Her prior feelings of exhilaration at finally being on the European side of her trip had just about worn away. Her panic grew as she tried the numbers again. Each time, she attempted a number using less numbers. Like if she were calling Gabriella in New York, she'd drop a few numbers from the area code if she'd been calling her from say, Penn Station.

Using her suitcase as a makeshift chair, Fiona sat down and proceeded with her call. Again, the long tones and no answers as Fiona sobbed quietly. Alone in the metropolis that was Paris, with the equivalent of two dollars in francs in hand, Fiona didn't know what else she could do. What else was there?

She tried Ellen's number again, this time dropping the first 2 digits, and as the phone was dialing, Fiona dropped her pen. She reached down to grab it as it rolled almost out the open door to the cubicle. Absentmindedly, Fiona put down the receiver and chased after the pen, grabbing it before it made an escape to the post office floor. When she completely returned back into the telephone cubicle, as she picked up the receiver, she was thinking she'd continue to hear the long tones. To her surprise she heard instead, "Allo? Allo?" "Hello? Hello?"

Speaking into the receiver Fiona said, "Oui, allo. C'est Fiona, je veux parler avec Ellen? "Yes, hello. This is Fiona, I would like to speak with Ellen?"

The last remaining ounce of composure Fiona had regained from her astonishment that the phone was answered was completely obliterated when the other person spoke again. The rapid fire French was too fast and highly accented to be understood. Finally Fiona said, "S'il vous plait, parlez lentement," "Please speak slowly," but to no avail. Before she knew it the connection was lost. Fiona wondered if the party on the other end had hung up, if her credits had run out, or if there was some other explanation.

The reality of the matter was that Fiona was still alone; knowing what had really happened on that call was no longer of any consequence to her. The realization of these facts, coupled with the fact that Fiona was losing even more of what little French she had left, made her feel that when she needed help she had no one to ask to help her. These racing thoughts didn't help settle her growing panic. Not to mention the fact that she only had the equivalent of a few francs exchanged and it was growing late. She would need to find a place to stay the night, preferably before it got dark.

The only thing she had going for her, she realized at the moment, was that she still had several hours' daylight. It was evidently clear to Fiona, in times of significant stress, her ability to communicate, quite possibly in any language, was a lost cause. She had studied 5 years of French in high school and another year in college, all of which were seriously failing her now. Feeling almost completely dejected, with tears streaming down her face, Fiona heard the sound of metal wrapping on the glass door to the telephone cubicle.

Looking up from her dejected position on her suitcase, Fiona discovered the face of an older black man whose compassionate look was unmistakable. He was dressed in a suit and tie. He carried a briefcase in one hand and had some files in his other hand. His hair was cut short and his mustache looked freshly trimmed. He said in perfect English, "Do you need help, young lady?"

"Yes, I do," she said sobbing.

"I'm quite sure whatever it is we can figure it out, it can't be as bad as all these tears," he said, like a Father.

"Wait a minute," Fiona said, "How is it that you're speaking in English?"

"Well, I'm actually from Liberia; we speak English quite well there. My French isn't too bad, but they tell me I speak it with a British accent. My name is Milton, what seems to be upsetting you this fine evening?"

"I just arrived from England to stay with a friend. I found her apartment but she wasn't there. I think I figured out how to use the telephone to call her, but she didn't answer. I have only a few francs to my name, no place to stay tonight, and not much daylight left. I even called my girlfriend from college. She's supposed to have returned to Paris already. Someone answered, I think, but I can't find her either!"

"Ok, slow down, let's take this apart one thing at a time; let's do this by the numbers," he said, like an accountant or a banker. "What is the number to the girl in Paris, where you said you are to stay?"

"Her Father told me it was 45-78-16-23," Fiona replied.

"First, here," he said, handing Fiona a linen handkerchief, "Dry your eyes. Now, ok, let's dial it. I have a calling card, we can use that, then we don't have to worry about cash," he said. As he dialed the number, Fiona wiped her eyes and watched as Milton dialed Sophie's phone number.

The receiver was in Milton's hands but the connection was so loud that Fiona could hear the dialing. When Milton heard the long tones he said, "Ok, still waiting to be connected."

"Waiting to be connected? What does that mean?"

"It means the call is being connected but not all the way. Basically it means you wait."

"Wait? Oh my goodness. I don't think I ever stayed on the line long enough to connect these calls. Well, that is, until I dropped my pen."

"I saw you do that while I was waiting in line. Here we go, see," he said holding the receiver in her direction, "Now it is ringing." The long tones had now changed to a double ring, beep-beep, beep-beep, beep-beep, after several sets of double tones, Milton hung up.

"What's the matter?" Fiona asked.

"I don't think your friend is home, she never picked up the phone. What's the next number?"

"Ok, it is 45-77-04-01," she said.

"All right, let's see what happens," he said, as he dialed the number. The long tones were eventually replaced by the double beep tones and again no answer. "Do you have any other numbers?"

"No I don't, now what am I going to do. The post office is going to close very soon. I don't have any place to stay and I don't know how to find Sophie's apartment again. I barely found this post office let alone finding her apartment again. I don't know how long or how far I've walked since I left Sophie's apartment. I think I'm lost and ..." Fiona stopped talking and restarted sobbing. The tears flowed too easily. The stress of the long day of travel, coupled with trying to concentrate and speak in a foreign language, made her feel that everything she knew was rapidly unraveling.

"Well, if I can help you at all here tonight, I can help you find a hotel room. I'm sure I can make that happen for you. Will that help you? I live nearby and I know the neighborhood quite a bit. There are quite a few decent hotels near here. You couldn't have been walking that long or for that matter, around here, walked that far. Most of these streets run in circles, kind of like from *The Wizard of Oz* and following the yellow brick road," he said, trying to ease her tension filled tears.

"You will, there are?" Fiona said feeling a sense of optimism percolate up from the depths of her soul.

"Sure I will and I would say, based on what I know from you so far, you'd have done the same for me in America, right?"

"Yes, but how'd you know I was from America?"

"*That* suitcase and the accent were my first clues," he said with a smirk.

"That obvious?"

"I'm afraid so. Don't worry about it, we see people from all over. Honestly, I couldn't confirm you were an American until you talked. That was the clincher for me. Shall we see about you getting a hotel room now?"

"Yes, thank you." Fiona was indeed feeling much better. Her blotchy facial skin and red puffy eyes, however, remained.

Fiona followed Milton out of the post office where they took a left out on the street. A few blocks down, there was a small hotel. Milton said for Fiona to wait at the curb while he went inside to inquire about a room. He walked out too soon after he'd walked in, and as he exited the hotel, he was shaking his head. "They were all booked," he said.

"Ok, now where?"

"Let's keep going down this street, this is one of the busier streets in this arrondissement."

After rejections from the next five hotels, Fiona began to wonder if perhaps how the two of them looked might have had something to do with the sudden shortage of rooms. At the last hotel, the front door was open and Fiona could see Milton addressing the clerk at the desk. He even pointed at Fiona, waiting on the sidewalk. But, standing there with her suitcase, evidence of crying still fresh on her face, it was no wonder he was unable to find a room for her.

When Milton returned to the sidewalk Fiona shared her observation with him. "Do you think that is causing our troubles?"

"You know, it just might. If you look at us, I'm an older black man in a business suit. Despite my attire, you are still a young woman with a very obvious suitcase. That clerk there," he said, pointing into the hotel at the woman behind the desk, "She also spoke English, I heard her helping the people in front of me."

"Maybe if I go in and explain my predicament she'll find a room for me. It can't hurt to try, right?" Fiona said, "Especially if I try to speak in

French and then ask if she could help me in English. That worked for me quite well when I was here last time."

"That sounds like a good idea. I'll wait out here," Milton replied.

So, Fiona went inside and while she was waiting in line to be helped, she mustered up the courage to explain herself and her current situation. When it was her turn, she approached the clerk as tall as she possibly could. She wheeled her suitcase and positioned it in front of her just as though she were checking in. "Pardonnez-moi, pouvez-vous m'aider en Anglais s'il vous plait?" "Excuse me, could you help me in English please?" Fiona asked politely.

After looking at Fiona and hearing her request in French, the clerk said, "Sure, how can I help you Mademoiselle?"

Fiona then went through in rapid fire what had happened to her over the last few hours: her triumphant arrival in Paris, finding Sophie's apartment by herself, discovering Sophie was not at home, finding the post office and calling Sophie and Ellen, and either no one was home or their speech was too rapid for her to continue the call. She explained that she was traveling alone to meet her girlfriend from college, and that in a few days they'd be leaving to travel through Europe. Milton, she pointed to him standing on the sidewalk, just happened to offer his assistance to her at the post office when he heard her crying.

"This isn't what you think," Fiona said, "I just need a room. I can't reach my girlfriend or Sophie. It's dark out now and I have nowhere to go." Her tears were returning but perhaps this time they would actually be useful.

"I understand now, yes, you are correct, I did think something was questionable about you two. My mistake, I apologize, I see now that I picked up on something being a problem but came to the wrong conclusion. We really don't have any rooms," she said, picking up the telephone receiver, "But our sister hotel does. Let me place a call to them, just a moment."

The massive crushing tightness in Fiona's throat and chest just erupted like Old Faithful in Yellowstone Park. The clerk listened to Fiona's plight and appeared to be trying to help. When the clerk hung up the phone, she turned to look at Fiona. Her face changed from a blank look to a smile. "Yes, they have room and they are expecting you. Let me give you the address; you'll need to take a taxi. There is a stand just there," she said, as she pointed out the large paned window looking out on the street from the quaint hotel lobby. "You can wait there for the next available taxi. If there isn't one waiting when you leave, a taxi will come along shortly. The taxis know to drive by our hotel to see if we have waiting patrons. It works pretty well for us."

The clerk wrote down the address as Hôtel Capitol, 9 rue Viala and handed the card to Fiona. "Bonne chance," she said. "Good luck."

"Merci beaucoup," Fiona replied.

Outside, Fiona explained the new situation to Milton and told him she would be fine now. She had a reservation and the address for her hotel. And, just as the clerk predicted, there was a taxi waiting at their stand.

"I can't begin to thank you enough. You are so kind and I should know!" Fiona began all excited. "Can I take you and your wife out to dinner while I'm still in Paris? Would you accept?"

"That is awfully nice of you. Yes, I will accept, you are only too kind to offer. Besides, I'm so late for dinner now; she's going to want to meet you to corroborate my story!" He then opened his briefcase and removed one of his business cards. On the back, he wrote his home phone number. In the meantime, while Fiona was arranging the future dinner, the previously waiting taxi had been hired by another guest of the hotel.

"I usually get home about 7:00PM, but Jessica, my wife, is home most days. You can arrange it with her. Good luck," Milton said, as an unoccupied taxi pulled up and stopped at his hail.

"Thank you for your help. I really don't know what I would have done. I'll be in touch," Fiona said.

"Just be safe and have a good time. My adopted country isn't all that most make it out to be," he said, with a proud smile.

Fiona gave the suitcase and carrier to the driver, who placed her items in the trunk, and then helped her into the passenger side of the back seat. Fiona handed him the card with the hotel address given to her by the clerk. "I'd like to go here please," Fiona said in English, completely forgetting she was in Paris. A brief moment passed before she realized what she had just said. Then she said, "Ah, pardonnez-moi," "Oh, excuse me," to the driver. He smiled back, nodding his head in acknowledgement of her mistake.

The taxi ride was about ten minutes, including delays for red lights. The next thing Fiona realized was that she didn't have enough francs to pay for a taxi. Once at her destination, Fiona asked the driver to wait, and someone from the hotel, or Fiona, would be right out to pay him. He reluctantly looked on as Fiona disappeared into the slightly larger lobby of the Hôtel Capitol.

Fiona knew that hotels would exchange her traveler's checks, but by adding a hefty exchange rate in their favor. A small man from the front desk came out with a small piece of paper, a taxi voucher, Fiona assumed. Whatever the paper was, it wasn't French currency, but it was sufficient *payment* as the taxi left without argument.

"Bonjour, je m'appelle Fiona. J'ai besoin d'un chambre ce soir," "Hello, my name is Fiona. I need a room tonight."

"Oui, on m'as dit quelque chose de votre arrivée. Bienvenue!" "Yes, someone told me of your arrival. Welcome!"

After signing the registration card and giving the clerk her VISA® card, she was told the room charge was 380F. After swiping her credit card information on the ticket, the clerk handed Fiona a large key and gave her the instructions to find the elevator and her room on the third floor. Upstairs, Fiona opened her room door and discovered it was a corner room, with a queen sized bed, and a private bath and shower. This corner room's windows opened out to two sides of the building with great views of the street below. Fiona plopped down on the bed, placed both hands upon her face and resumed her open sobbing.

Resigned to her isolation for the evening, Fiona headed outdoors to find dinner. A local bistro down the street offered an excellent chicken dish and a half carafe of house wine for 145F. Fiona recovered from her housing ordeal over her dinner, where she paid no attention to the other diners and wasn't the least bit concerned about being seen eating alone. If she had been back at college, she would have felt differently about this type of situation. She was smiling to herself when she realized the progress she made with that part of her life. She would have to make a point of telling that to Ellen.

Using the telephone in her room, Fiona tried to call the Picoté's, but just like earlier, her calls continued to go unanswered, even when she stayed on the line long enough to be connected. She was beginning to think two things, first, she had the wrong numbers, and second, she was still dialing incorrectly. She tried Sophie's number before going to bed and got the same result.

The following morning was Sunday and Fiona allowed herself to sleep in until 9:30AM. After showering in the very pleasant and surprisingly private Parisian hotel room shower, Fiona dressed and tried to call Sophie again. To her shock and amazement, Sophie answered the phone on the third ring.

"Fiona, je suis désolée." "Fiona, I'm so sorry," Sophie began, empathetically.

Hearing the concern in Sophie's voice reminded Fiona of instances in childhood when she would be shopping with her Mother and had discovered herself lost. Hearing her Mother's voice, like hearing Sophie's at this moment, was like finding her Mother once again. She would feel great relief in just hearing her Mother's voice, even as an adult, for that voice had the power to make everything 'all better.' It was exactly what Mothers are known to do for their children, sometimes unaware of the ultimate end result of hearing their so familiar voices.

Sophie had been very concerned about not hearing from or seeing Fiona the night before. She knew that was when Fiona was due to arrive. Practicing her English, Sophie said, "It was such a beautiful day I went for a walk before work. I missed all your calls, Fiona! I'm so sorry." Then the questioning of Fiona's exact whereabouts ensued.

Fiona explained what happened and how the phones wouldn't work and how Milton had helped her ultimately find this room. "I'm at the Hôtel Capitol, on 9 rue Viala. Am I far away?" Fiona asked.

"Not too far, I can take the Métro over. I will leave in a few minutes. Have you had breakfast?"

"No," Fiona replied.

"Ok then, I'll be there in a few minutes. You can check out and wait for me in the lobby. We can pick up breakfast on the way back to my apartment. Oh, Fiona I'm so glad you are all right. I was really worried that something terrible had happened to you. I'll be over soon enough."

Fiona finished dressing and packing the remaining items into the suitcase. As Fiona queued up to check out, her gaze veered to the plate glass windows and the morning weather. It looked sunny and warm, a beautiful day ahead. She finished the checkout process before Sophie appeared, so she took a seat in the chairs in the small lobby.

The lobby door opened and in walked Sophie. She was dressed in a button down short sleeved shirt and jean cut-off shorts with sandals. Her face was a mixture of relief and joy, when she saw Fiona sitting in the lobby chairs waiting for her. "Hello Fiona!" she announced loudly. "I am so glad to find you."

"Sophie, it so nice to see you again. Thank you for coming to find me. I'm sorry about the phone," Fiona began.

"I know they are difficile," she said in her best Franglais, the art of mixing the French and English languages with words from each, all in one sentence.

On the way back to Sophie's apartment, they took the Métro and stopped at a bakery, in which they bought croissants and doughnuts. It was another beautifully sunny day, the temperature felt to be in the low 70's. A light breeze caught Fiona's curls, and accentuated their bouncing with each step. Sophie's long dark hair blew like a willow tree with long tendrils reaching to the sun.

Sophie was a year younger than Fiona. Her older sister Monique was barely a year older than Fiona. Like her sister, she had striking features and long flowing dark brown hair. Fiona had just graduated university, while Sophie was just a year behind and starting her final year in university. When Ian, Fiona's Father, had asked Thierry's permission for Fiona to stay with them during her high school French trip, Thierry instantly knew his daughters would love it. He had met Fiona a few times when he'd come to America for business meetings, and was over to the house for dinner. Fiona knew he was quite the character.

Sophie explained where she had been the day before and that when she got back she didn't know Fiona had been by. "I'm sorry, I didn't even think to leave a note, I was so flustered," Fiona said.

"I didn't either. I could have said 'gone for a walk and back in an hour.' Would you have stayed and waited for me then?" Sophie asked.

"I think that would have made a difference."

"I was thinking of taking you to an American nightclub that is very popular in Paris; it is a disco. We could go after dinner tonight. Oh, I forgot to tell you. After you called this morning, Ellen and Pierre called. They want to meet you for lunch. I told them I was going to go to the hotel and bring you back. I explained the hotel and all. They want to meet you by the Versailles Rive Gauche train station. I can help you find it, but let's eat first," she said.

"A disco sounds like fun, but I better see what plans Ellen has for us first. I'm sure they, Ellen and Pierre, want to do something today. Can I call you later to let you know? When do you work today?"

"I only work until one o'clock in the morning," she replied.

"Well, if we are still out at that time I'll call you," Fiona confirmed before leaving the apartment.

"C'est formidable!" "That's great!"

Fiona followed Sophie's directions to arrive at Versailles Rive Gauche train station to meet Ellen and Pierre at about three o'clock. She took the Métro from Odéon station to Montparnasse station where she changed to the train that went out to Versailles. Ellen explained that they would be driving to the station, and that Fiona should make her way out from the trains, and Ellen would be waiting just as she emerged from the trains.

Following Sophie's directions, in detail, Fiona trusted she was on the correct Métro train. Eventually, she heard the overhead announcement of the station she wanted. When the train came into the station, she stood up and as she approached the door, this time she was first in the line at the door and she became alarmed when it didn't open once the train came to a stop.

Fiona could hear other doors opening. She looked both right and left, and to her left she saw a person use the manual release to open the door. Turning the handle and pulling it to the side, the doors opened with a strained whoosh sound. Making another mental note of how to manage in the Métro, Fiona followed the signs to the exits. Ellen was waiting just as she had explained to Sophie. The reunion of these two women looked like they hadn't seen each other in years, much less only a few months. They almost made a scene.

"Fiona, it is so good to see you," Ellen burst out, reaching over to hug her friend. They greeted each other with formal French cheek swapping hello kisses.

"Hi Ellen! How was the *French Riviera*?"

"It was great as expected but you know we were camping. Really, we were camping!"

"I'll believe that when I see the proof in pictures. Where is Pierre?"

"He's out in the car waiting. Let's go!"

After greeting Pierre in similar fashion, they all climbed into Pierre's sister's car. Francine, Fiona later learned, was at home watching their younger brother Vincent. Pierre drove, while the women recounted their summers and the last few weeks. He drove them to a large shopping mall where they would have a late lunch. It was also a place, Fiona discovered, where she could get an excellent exchange rate. She chose to exchange $100US and received almost 650₣ in return.

Ellen was dressed in faded red Capri pants with a scoop necked grey cotton sweater and her new espadrilles. Her hair was in a chin length bob page-boy style. Her blonde hair appeared highlighted from weeks in the Riviera sun. Pierre was dressed in jeans, tee shirt and jean jacket. Fiona had chosen her jeans and a navy polo with tennis shoes.

Over lunch, Fiona explained Sophie's invitation to go out to the disco later that night. It would be a late night, but everyone seemed interested. They planned to call her later. After lunch, they went shopping. Here Fiona found a full skirt in a tan broadcloth material, and glassware with an iridescent sheen. In all, she purchased 6 water glasses and 6 high ball glasses, they were only 8₣ each. It was a bargain she couldn't turn down. Plus, if she had to, she could leave any extra objects or clothing in Sophie's apartment, and when they got back from their trip, Fiona could either pack them or ship them home.

As they were shopping, Fiona described her ordeal from yesterday afternoon, and meeting Milton. She explained that she wanted to repay him somehow, would Ellen know of a restaurant where they could meet him and his wife?

"Yes, I know a great place; it's called L'Entrecôte, they serve delicious steaks and fries in a family style, and it is really quite reasonable. How were you going to contact him?" she asked.

"He gave me his phone number."

"Well, tonight is as good as any night; I had thought we'd go out tonight with Pierre and Francine, but maybe we could have a family dinner with their family tomorrow, and then leave for the trip. Do you want to call Milton now?"

"Sure, I like your plan. Let's find a phone."

"Maybe after dinner we can go to the disco with Sophie?" Ellen suggested.

Always amenable to going out, Fiona replied, "Works for me."

Unaware that she had fallen asleep after sharing this part of her time in Paris, Fiona woke with a start to the loud warble of an overhead page. She looked about her hospital room, confused at the disappearance of Milton and her Jake no longer sitting in the guest chair. Instead, she saw the sleeping form of a woman, it was Ellen. There, laid open on Ellen's lap was Fiona's trip diary balancing on her stomach and displaying the heading, "Paris" at the top of the next page.

Chapter 11 Reality in Real Time, 2015

Hearing Fiona stir upon her creaky hospital mattress, Ellen opened her eyes. She paused before saying a meek and startled, "Hi."

Fiona replied a bit flustered, "Hi, what are you doing here, when did you get here?"

"I know it is confusing, Gabriella called me and I came over as soon as I could." Ellen said, and then she thought back to her instructions from Jake and Fiona's Father, Ian:

- Do not let on what year it is, let Fiona tell you first.
- Do not let on you know about Jake and Kurt, see what Fiona says first.
- Do tell her about your flight to New York, but let Fiona figure out from where.

Fiona repeated, "What are you doing here, why do you have my trip diary?"

"Well," Ellen started, "You fell asleep with a migraine over a week ago, I was told I should come and tonight was my turn to read to you from the diary." She didn't want to alarm Fiona with concern about a brief coma relapse and therefore, used the term 'asleep' to cover the truth.

Looking about her room purposefully, "Your turn, where is Kurt?" Fiona began, a bit more shaken at not knowing where her husband was-again. "Every time I wake up, he's not there!"

"What's the last thing you do remember?" Ellen asked.

"Arranging dinner with Milton, Sophie, and maybe the disco later, where is Pierre? Oh, I'm so confused!" Fiona exclaimed.

Using the training she had received about 10 days ago regarding the reorientation of Fiona, to be used each time she lives in the past in the present, Ellen turned to her dear friend and said firmly, "Fiona, look at me. How do I look? Do you see where we are? Focus now Fiona," her voice remained firm but held fast. Silently, the prayed that Fiona would come back to them, that she would remember, that she would remember Jake. He was still waiting for her to come back to him. Ellen admired that in Fiona's husband.

"You look different, you grew your hair long? When did you do that?" Fiona remarked.

"Yes I grew it out, what else do you see?" Ellen said, trying her best at not coaching her friend back from the past.

"Am I in the hospital in Salzburg, have I fainted again?" Fiona asked.

Concerned that her friend was now merging two time periods from their time in Europe, Ellen asked pointedly, "Does this hospital look like Salzburg to you?"

At that moment, her nurse Gretchen walked in and announced herself saying, "Hi, I'm Gretchen, I'll be your nurse for this shift. I need to do change of shift vitals and assessment." She performed a few tasks and listened to Fiona's heart and lungs, then to her abdomen. She took her temperature, pulse, and blood pressure, which at the moment was a bit elevated. "Before I go, do you need anything?" she said.

Ellen's face was trying to imply that the nurse needed to assess Fiona's neurological orientation. When Gretchen appeared to be leaving the room without asking, Ellen said, "Fiona, what were you just saying?"

Gretchen stopped at the room door to listen to the patient's response, having learned during change of shift report that this patient's orientation to time and place fluctuated especially after a migraine.

"What, about my headache?" Fiona asked.

"No, about Salzburg and Kurt," Ellen said, discouraged.

"Well, I was taken aback that you were here, since I haven't seen you in a while, I thought we were going out for dinner with Milton and Sophie, or maybe I thought I'd woken up from another migraine in Salzburg. Is that what you meant?" Fiona asked.

Nodding to the nurse, Ellen said, "Yes, that's it."

"Fiona, I know you and I haven't met and that this is the first time

I've been assigned to care for you. Do you know where we are?" Gretchen asked, as carefully as she could.

Reading the women's faces, Fiona concluded that she was wrong, again. "No, not really, maybe when Kurt comes back and he tells me, since you two clearly aren't telling me, maybe then I'll know something!" Fiona snapped, climbed out of bed and in walking to the bathroom, slammed the door behind her in a huff of displaced emotional energy.

"Maybe I'll go check with the charge nurse and place a call to her doctor," Gretchen said to Ellen.

"Good idea," Ellen replied.

"But before I do, Fiona, can you hear me?" Gretchen said to the bathroom door.

"Uh huh," was the muffled reply.

"I want to remind you that this is NYU and you are in the hospital following a coma and it is 2015. I'll go get your doctor; you just wait in there, ok?"

"Uh huh," was again the reply.

Out in the hall, Gretchen updated the charge nurse and together they called Dr. Logan.

In Fiona's room, Ellen sent a mass text to Gabriella, Ian, and Jake to return to the hospital ASAP for Fiona had stayed stuck in the past after the last migraine and Ellen, realizing she needed reinforcements, no longer knew how to approach Fiona.

Fiona, feeling scared, stayed in the bathroom, her safe place of retreat. The headache, which was pounding at the base of her neck, grew into another migraine, the retching and vision losses apparent to anyone on the other side of the door as she vomited and banged into things, her depth perception off again. So exhausted from retching, Fiona placed her head on her arm and fell asleep cornered upon the toilet, her mind returning to where she left off, meeting Milton for dinner with Sophie in Paris.

Chapter 12 Thanks to a New Friend, 1985

In her dream, she returned to Paris in 1985 from the confines of her hospital room bathroom in 2015. Ellen and her nurse were outside eagerly awaiting the return of her physician and unaware that Fiona was sleeping during her refuge in the ceramic tiled room.

The next morning, Fiona met up with Sophie and they went back to her apartment. Fiona hadn't realized how close it was. She turned to speak to Sophie and first explained about Milton and how he had been her angel on this leg of her journey. "I think Milton and I had been walking in circles."

Sophie led Fiona to her favorite neighborhood shopping area, the place where she conducted most of her daily marketing and other shopping. It was there that Ellen joined them by lunch time and they made their plans for the day. Fortunately, Fiona had Milton's phone number in her money belt with the receipt from the hotel. She hadn't moved either of them from their original place of safe keeping to the more long term storage place in the bulky maroon suitcase. The shopping mall they were in was large enough to contain a food court, and as well as many restaurants, and it also had a bank of public telephones lined up near the public restrooms.

Fiona reached into her money belt and from the coins section removed several francs to use to make the call. Then she realized that she wasn't in Minnesota and since she'd had some difficulty making French public telephones connect her calls, she turned to Ellen and said, "I think you better dial it, I can't ever seem to make these work," she said, while eyeing the receiver in her hand and handing it over to Ellen. "It's a long story," she said.

"Sure, what's the number?"

"It is 40-57-03-79," Fiona replied.

As Fiona called out the numbers, Ellen punched in the corresponding buttons on the key pad. "I think its ringing," she said. "Here, you take it," handing over the receiver.

As Fiona put the receiver to her ear, a woman's voice answered the call. Fiona requested to speak with Milton, and then realizing that it was Sunday, perhaps he wasn't home. "Un moment," the kind voice said. "One minute."

A few moments later, Milton came on the line. "Allo?" he said.

"Hello Milton, this is Fiona calling. Remember me from the post office yesterday?"

"Hello Fiona! Are you having more difficulties?"

"Oh no, I'm sitting here with Ellen right now, and Sophie came to the hotel this morning to pick me up. I'm calling to see if you and your wife could meet us for dinner tonight?"

"Dinner, tonight? Are you sure Fiona, that is really too much. I was just glad I could help you out. You seemed so sincerely shaken."

"I was and I want to thank you; this is what my parents always told me to do when thanking kind strangers. So can you make it?"

"Just a minute, let me just check with my wife, hold the line," he said. Then a few moments later after Fiona kept trying to overhear their muffled conversations, he came back on the line. "Are you sure this is what you want to do?"

"Yes, I'm positive."

"Ok, then we'd enjoy that, we accept. Where are we going?"

"Ellen and Pierre really like a restaurant called L'Entrecôte, do you know it?"

"Oh yes, that is not far from our apartment. What time tonight?"

"What about 8:30PM? Too soon or will that be ok? I realize we've called a bit late but I've only been out with Ellen a short time. You know, I tried to call her," Fiona said, and then broke out in cheerful laughter.

"Maybe you shouldn't be using the phones just now," Milton suggested.

"I know it. I had Ellen dial you now for this call!"

"Oh Fiona, what will we do with you?"

"Come to dinner and we'll see about that. See you in a few hours!"

"See you soon." He said as he hung up. Then he had some explaining to do with his wife. Apparently he hadn't told her all the story of why he was late getting home last night. Eventually, she stopped being mad when he explained how upset Fiona had been and how truly genuine was her dismay. She now realized that her husband had been some damsel in distress's knight and she didn't want to chink his armor.

The women reunited with Pierre who was scouting out computer gadgets and other electronic products in the local Parisian version of Radio Shack. They explained to him the updated dinner arrangements and suggested he call Francine to join them. That way, they could all drive together to the restaurant; Fiona could taxi back to Sophie's, and the rest could ride home with Francine. They were borrowing her car after all; they realized that they should really invite her to dinner too.

L'Entrecôte was located close to Sophie's apartment, and the drive to the restaurant was handled solely by Pierre. The two college chums were putting their heads together and figuring out the next portion of their journey and determining when they'd leave Paris. As Pierre was climbing the curb for a prime parking space, Fiona and Ellen had settled on leaving the next night. If they traveled at night on the night train and slept on the train, they'd kill the proverbial two birds with one stone: sleep and travel at the same time.

They exited the small car to Fiona's shock. She had never seen anyone purposefully park a car on the sidewalk. Pierre had explained that that was the only way to have parking here, no room on any streets, save the Champs Elysées. The street was slowly growing dark as the late summer sun was setting. The doorway to the restaurant was in shadows and softly lit from the neon lights. The smells upon the street were a mixture of mouthwatering to gagging, typical of Paris. No grassy areas to walk dogs, and some owners never cleaned up certain messes.

Inside the restaurant, the smells were of beef and fries. Fiona was searching for a posted menu and finally found it next to the checkout desk. The entire menu was devoted primarily to beef, all served family style and topped with their famous sauce. Fiona and Ellen were discussing the options listed on the menu when the hostess returned to assist them.

"Bon soir, combien?" she said.

"Oui, bon soir," Fiona began. "Nous sommes six, mais tout le monde n'est pas ici maintenant." "We are six people but not everyone is here yet."

As soon as Fiona fumbled in her French, the door opened behind them and in walked Milton and a woman Fiona assumed was his wife.

"Oui, c'est bon," the hostess stated. "Yes, very good."

"Non, maintenant, tout le monde est ici." "No, now we are all here."

"Suivez-moi," she said. "Follow me."

As they turned to follow the hostess, Milton said to Fiona, "This is Jessica, my wife."

"So nice to meet you Fiona. Milton has just explained everything to me. Have you quite recovered?"

"Oh yes, but I'm still staying away from the public telephones."

They turned and followed the hostess and were seated at a large round table with a vibrantly red linen cloth. In the middle of the table was a Lazy Susan, a turntable to help pass the family style dishes. They took their seats and ordered drinks when asked by the hostess.

Jessica was a shorter black woman with black hair that accented her face, especially her eyes and jaw line. She was wearing a long denim skirt with a red knit sweater and sandals. Her choice of accessories was gold chains, bangles, and a very handsome wedding ring set in platinum. She was carrying a Kenneth Cole briefcase and what looked like a Coach purse, the station bag, if Fiona recalled correctly.

Milton was dressed in suit which was an olive green that picked up the similar hue in his deep brown skin. His choice of necktie, Fiona thought, had been an excellent idea. He paired the olive green of his suit with a maroon paisley tie with flecks of greens, yellows, and brown. His brown dress shoes had a serious sheen and the tassels tapped as he walked. He, too, was carrying a briefcase, but his box style did not denote a brand.

Milton explained that he was an accountant for the Banque de France where he worked in the internal auditing department. He described it like a mouse living in a maze and numbers were his cheese. He lived in a cubicle in the basement of the bank, nothing fancy, but he enjoyed the work, which showed on his face as he smiled during his description of his daily duties.

Jessica, the group learned, was a child psychologist who worked with emotionally disturbed children in the French equivalent of foster care. She was part Mother, part social worker, part therapist, and part miracle worker, when she helped the most troubled youth change their behaviors and do well enough to be adopted. She too thoroughly enjoyed her work and said the challenge for her was dealing with a wish to take all the children home to live with them.

Over dinner Milton and Fiona recounted her ordeal again and again. Each time the story grew bigger and scarier. Jessica enjoyed hearing this tale and wondered, as a therapist, whether or not Fiona had truly recovered. It really wasn't her place to say either way; she just hoped the girl didn't have to deal with many more French telephones on her journey.

The food was something to write home about. The steaks were cooked and served to perfection with a special mustardy sauce. The accompanying platter of French fries would make Ray Kroc of McDonalds' fame upset. They originally placed orders for the equivalent of 4-5 servings and ended up eating enough to serve 8-9. Fiona commented that when they came back to Paris from their tour of Europe, she'd want to bring Ellen and Pierre back here to eat here again. Fiona, an amateur cook, was also trying to figure out the ingredients in the prize winning sauce.

When the waitress returned with the bill, Fiona instructed her to place the amount due on her VISA. "It would be my sincere pleasure," Fiona replied.

"Are you sure, Fiona, that is really unnecessary," Milton remarked.

"Avec plaisir," Fiona concluded.

Milton finally acquiesced and allowed the bill to be paid by his new friend. She was just trying to thank Milton for his graciousness and thoughtfulness, and in doing so, to include everyone else in on his treat. His helping a young person who was feeling so dejected in a strange yet familiar place had made a big impression. Fiona hoped that one day, his actions would be reflected in her own to be shared in the future with someone she could befriend or help out too.

Fiona took the next twenty or so minutes to say their goodbyes to Milton and Jessica. He understood now how much comfort Fiona felt from his actions. His wife was very proud of her husband.

The remainder of the group was still lingering at the table when Fiona remembered Sophie's suggestion of the disco. Her long day of travel the day before began to wear on Fiona, affecting her short term memory, or so she joked. She reminded the group about Sophie's suggestion of going to a nightclub, but they hadn't called her to confirm and figured Sophie was still at work.

Fiona remembered Sophie handing her a list of phone numbers, a 'just in case of emergency' sort of list for Fiona while she was in Paris. Fiona looked at her list of phone numbers and smiled, seeing the very number she had needed on the list. This time Sophie had thought ahead and had given Fiona her work number too. Feeling a bit energized by the preparedness of one particular French female friend, Fiona said to Ellen, "We need to call Sophie and let her know we want to go to the disco tonight."

"That's right. Let's find a phone and call her," Ellen said. "Actually you find the phone, Fiona, I'll call her."

"It was the perfect plan, as always, the perfect plan."

"I know, I'm so good at those," Ellen joked boastingly.

They used the phone in the restaurant to call Sophie at work. As long as they kept it brief, the manager had allowed them to use the phone. Sophie was excited to be going out and would be off work a little early. She suggested meeting at the disco on Rue De Rivoli. She could meet them in about half an hour.

"See you soon," Fiona said as she hung up the phone and thanked the manager.

Even Francine was excited about staying out. She hadn't been to a disco in a long time. It was especially exciting after a month of camping and not going out at night. She added that, since they had her car, she could drive the four of them to the disco and then take Ellen and Pierre home afterwards. Sophie and Fiona could find their own way home.

While they weren't out late by French standards, they certainly were for what Fiona and Ellen were accustomed to in Minnesota. The sun was beginning to lighten the eastern sky when they were walking out of the disco. The concept of bars or nightclubs staying open all night was rather foreign to the American women, but one with which they weren't completely unfamiliar. They had agreed to call each other the next day, well, as Ellen pointed out, in a few hours, and then they would decide on when they would leave for the rest of their trip.

Ellen called Fiona about 11:30AM and suggested meeting at Sophie's work for lunch and the planning of their trip. Pierre would help Ellen find the restaurant as long as Fiona thought she could find it too. "Oh, no, I'll have Sophie walk me there so I know how to find it. I'll have a dry run before you get there."

"That's a good idea, Fiona. Then you won't get lost and need Milton again!"

"Hey now, I was really and sincerely lost and couldn't get the blasted phone to work. Not funny Ellen," Fiona started, and then slowed as she heard her friend laughing at the other end of the line. "Ok, ok, I'll see you about three o'clock?"

"Yes, three o'clock," Ellen confirmed.

True to her word, Fiona asked Sophie to walk her to her restaurant and show her the way so that later, when they were meeting there, Fiona could make it there on her own. "No problem," Sophie had said.

"What shift do you work today?" Fiona asked.

"Mid-afternoon, so 1:00PM until 7:00PM," she replied.

So when Sophie went to work about one o'clock, Fiona tagged along, making sure she took note of landmarks, street names, and approximate distances so she could find it again. It turned out to be like walking to the corner store, down three streets, over one, and then another right.

Fiona took out her daypack and in it she placed the *Cook's Timetables*, a note pad, and the small map of Europe she'd brought with her from home. She realized that she didn't pack any maps or list of cities to go to, and that they hadn't really discussed where they would go next. Perhaps they'd go with the flow; just following the wind. Satisfied with her daypack's contents, Fiona looked about the apartment one last time for anything else she might need. She found a pen but that was all she felt she needed.

At quarter to three, Fiona left Sophie's apartment and made her way to the restaurant, L'Amanguier. She saw Sophie working tables when she walked into the foyer and with a nod, confirmed where Sophie suggested she sit. Ellen and Pierre hadn't arrived yet, so Fiona had the table to herself. A few minutes later, however, they appeared, with several books and maps in their hands.

"Wow, look at the two of you. Are you in college again?"

"No, just prepared to show you the maps and books we have as resources. I'm not really sure I want to carry all of this stuff with me, though. What do you think?" Ellen said, as she pulled out a chair at the table and sat down next to Pierre and across from Fiona.

"I don't think I'd want to either," Fiona replied.

Sophie walked over now that they were all there, took their drink orders, and gave them menus. Fiona placed her books and lists on the table next to her and took a look at what Ellen had brought along. Ellen did likewise.

"I like this book, the one with the timetables. I think this one is a keeper for sure," Ellen said. "We'll need one to plan the trains and destinations. Look at this," she said, pointing to the list of cities and the index to and from those cities from other places. "There is a night train, for example, tonight to Amsterdam. We could take that?" she suggested.

"How safe is that?" Fiona asked.

"I'm pretty sure you can lock yourself in your compartment," Pierre offered. "That's what my family does when we go out to Bordeaux on the last train out."

"How much is a compartment ticket?" Fiona asked.

"I'm not sure, but I suspect it will be a nominal charge in addition to your Eurail Passes," he replied.

"Can you handle my leaving tonight, sweetheart?" Ellen said to Pierre.

"Well, I better be, you aren't going to be gone long? Right? I mean, you have been with me and Francine for the last month. Maybe I'm ready to have some alone time," he said with a mischievous grin.

"If that was an attempt at humor, Pierre, you'd better work on it," Ellen began, "I'm ready to leave tonight. I think he is too. Just look at him, how are you going to manage without me?"

"Just like I did before," he said, quick as a whip.

"Touché," Fiona said, "I think he got you with that one Ellen. I'm ready to go tonight but I need a little time to figure out my luggage and all. I don't need to take *everything* I have with me," she said. "I know I don't."

Sophie came back just then with their sandwiches, a Croque Monsieur for Fiona, a baguette with strong smelling cheese and cold ham for Ellen, and a cheeseburger for Pierre. All sandwiches came with the most delicious fries. Before Sophie left their table, Fiona said to her, "It sounds like I might be leaving tonight. Can I leave some things in your apartment until I get back? You know, like those glasses and things I just bought?"

"Bien sûr, pas de problème," Sophie said. "Sure, it's no problem."

"Great, thank you," Fiona said to Sophie. "Pierre, do you want to see us off?"

"Where does the timetable book say the night train leaves from, which station?" Ellen said to Fiona, who was still holding the book.

"Let me look," Fiona said, studying the extremely busy page of information and statistics. "Here it is, it leaves from Paris Nord at 11:15PM. What is that?"

"That is Gare du Nord station," Pierre interjected.

"Oh, that's right. I remember that one. So, do you want to meet there, Ellen?"

"Sure. Pierre can help us buy the couchette tickets, you know, the sleeper compartments."

"How much time in advance do we need to get there to make sure we can get a sleeper compartment, a couchette?" Fiona asked.

"Good question, does the book say anything?" Pierre replied.

Before Fiona could answer, Ellen suggested, "Why don't we get there at least 30 minutes before the train is scheduled to leave. I have to believe that would be enough time. It is a Monday night, how many people would be going then? I'd think they would have gone last night."

"Yes, you are right. 30 minutes sounds good to me," Fiona said, looking at Ellen, and then regarding Sophie as she returned to their table. Thinking it a good idea to confirm their plans with another native, Fiona repeated their timing to Sophie.

"Yes, that would be good," she said in English.

"Ok then, where should I meet you?" Fiona asked Ellen.

"Pierre, sweetie, is there somewhere in the station to meet Fiona? Where do you suggest?" Ellen asked.

"I don't know about any other exact spot other than the ticket seller's window, what about there?" he said logically.

"Good idea, thank you Pierre. I think we should go now so I can take a shower, repack and return to the station in plenty of time." Fiona said, looking to Sophie for a bill.

Sophie saw them looking at her and returned to their table. She had been busy with her side work and preparing for the dinner crowd which would be coming in shortly. She brought them their bill, and smiled at them, knowing it looked as though they had a plan in place. "Here you go," she said, handing Pierre a bill for two, and then turning and giving one to Fiona.

"Are you sure this is right?" Pierre asked.

"Oui, Absolument. Mon superviseur a dit, demi prix pour tes amies Américanes," she said, "Yes, absolutely. My boss said half price to my American friends."

"Où est-il?" Pierre asked. "Where is he?"

"Là bas," she said, "Over there."

"Oui, merci." Pierre replied to Sophie and stood up at his chair and gave a bow to the manager, who bowed back in kind.

"Ok, then. Shall we go?" Fiona suggested.

"Yes, I'll see you at 10:45 tonight. Have a good evening and thank Sophie again for us," Ellen said.

They exchanged their traditional French cheek kisses, normally just two times, alternating sides, but these kisses are conducted three times between good friends. "Three times," Pierre had said, "was the sign of a good friend. Two times was just for anyone." Pierre and Ellen walked out ahead of Fiona and took the sidewalk to the left and found their parked car. Fiona turned right and walked finding her own way back to Sophie's apartment. Her first stop was the shower.

Chapter 13 Headaches & Hassles, 2016

Fiona and Jake would speak about her memory, rather the loss of memory and the replacement of those memories with delusional events. They spent a great deal of time working to retrieve her true memories. How fortunate for Fiona that Jake was now a neurologist. His keen understanding of the brain helped guide them through her longer than expected and bumpy recovery.

Unable to keep his professional distance, Jake asked Dr. Logan if he, Jake, could assume care of his wife post ICU. Jake wanted to be able to take off enough time from his medical practice to spend hands on time with his wife, to bring her memory and her, back to him. In the years to come, they would understand that her memory lapses and regressions often occurred during headaches, hassles with work, or the children, or when she was again up in altitude and once more experiencing the symptoms of dizziness and fainting that accompanied her European trip. Those Ménière's like symptoms, which had hospitalized her all those years ago, remained a pesky reminder of her time abroad.

Taking a few longer moments to dress this morning, Fiona recalled her hospitalization in Austria and the scare she gave her friends Ellen and Jane. Ellen, her dear friend from college, had been given the wrong directions to wait for Fiona and between the wait and Jane's anxiety, they finally realized they were in the morgue waiting room and not anywhere near Fiona's hospital room. Jane, an American school teacher they met in Amsterdam, had been particularly shaken when she and Ellen discovered they were down by the morgue.

This gloomy experience of waiting for news on their friend outside the morgue had eventually become a joke along their trip. Any time one of them needed more sleep, the others would simply reply, "I know a quiet waiting room where you can take a long nap!"

Smiling, Fiona looked away from the mirror and the brushing of her hair. She sat staring off into space when Jake walked in. He didn't speak upon entering her dressing area; instead, he made minor noises and even bumped the back of her dressing table's chair to see if she was daydreaming or perhaps having another of her immobilizing headaches or even if she was having a petit mal seizure.

He noted that her visage was of pleasant concentration but her actions were odd as she absently brushed at her hair, often missing the long tresses in the process. Watching her now, Jake realized that while her movements lacked purpose they were likely not the sign of a seizure so he just let her alone. In fact, he thought if she was reflecting on her European trip, which was often the case when she was daydreaming, he would assist her by playing some of her favorite Wagner music.

He retreated to their main bedroom salon and engaged their turntable with one of Wagner's longer pieces. Knowing it would conclude in about 45 minutes, Jake looked at his watch and paced himself for the next partial hour in order to return as the music finished. He left her there, stroking her hair with the far off gaze.

In Fiona's mind, she was standing on the train platform in West Berlin. All travelers into East Germany were forced to walk from the train station in West Berlin to East Berlin where they would undergo a checkpoint and customs interrogation. Fiona never liked this part of her journey home even though she had been through Checkpoint Charlie hundreds of times by now. The fact of going between freedom and communist territory, even though that was where she and Kurt lived, was still unsettling.

After their wedding in 1990, Fiona returned to East Berlin with Kurt while he was still a student at the University of East Berlin. They had discussed living in Füssen, where they met, and perhaps, working at Neuschwanstein, King Ludwig II's famous castle. While she was accustomed to traveling back and forth from Paris alone, each time she returned to Berlin she still was aware of the catch in her throat and the heaviness in her feet upon the train platform.

Their apartment was close to the campus and was regularly visited by Kurt's former roommate, Emanuel and his girlfriend Olivia. When Kurt returned from his race to Salzburg when Fiona had been hospitalized, the two men had gone back to Therese's office to thank her for assisting them in finding Fiona while she had taken ill in Salzburg. They asked Therese out for lunch and that was when the men learned of her daughter, a young woman about their age.

Overtime, Emanuel took a liking to Olivia and they began dating. Olivia was a beautiful young blonde woman with blue eyes and her heart skipped a beat each time she thought about Emanuel. She knew he was a foreign exchange student from Nice, France and was studying linguistics like Kurt, and together they often studied.

After Kurt found them a small starter apartment for married students, Emanuel was a frequent dinner guest and tonight, he brought Olivia with him. Kurt had stayed on at the university as a professor, while Emanuel continued towards his doctorate. He had been instrumental in their climactic reunion of 5 years ago, helpful in working with Kurt's assignments while he traveled to the states to see Fiona, and supportive of their need for privacy when she visited in East Berlin. She finally decided to move to East Germany before their wedding in order to get their home set up.

Fiona had been on the train because she was returning from a weekend in Paris, with Ellen and Pierre. During their meal, the conversation gravitated to Fiona and her stories about her trip to Paris. She also gave an update on Ellen and Pierre. This time, her news held an unfamiliar and slightly opportune echo; both Fiona and Ellen were pregnant. This would be Fiona's first and Ellen's second. Ellen's first child, a daughter, Amelie, was now three years old and didn't quite understand all the excitement over the last weekend that she was privy to.

Tonight, upon Fiona's return, Kurt had invited Emanuel and Olivia for dinner. Fiona always enjoyed her time with Ellen and when she returned, it was obvious the two women had been shopping, not only for clothes but for foodstuffs. Fiona returned this time with plenty of spices and new cooking ideas from Ellen. As was often their custom, Emanuel brought the finest baguettes he could find, Olivia covered dessert, and Fiona was in charge of their soup and warm courses. Kurt, who was not much of a cook, would usually make the cheese selections, and provide the wine, could, however, cook a salad. It was his only culinary skill and a standing cooking joke.

The walk from the train station into customs went as smoothly as it could. Fiona was still a bit skittish going through that place. Her mind recalled the time when the guards carried machine guns and might shoot a wayward East Berliner. As her thoughts drifted back to these images, her face screwed up and her brush got tangled in her long hair. She was now aware that she was back in 2016 remembering more than one event in the past. Yet, she was merging multiple events and doing so out of sequence.

She knew that the Berlin Wall came down in 1989, but in her memory, distorted by the coma, it was still present, as were the machine gun carrying guards. She wasn't confused about her feelings for the guards, or the efforts she'd typically put forth for their dinners with Emanuel and Olivia. Those images were clear, it is just that they occurred so often that they tended to blend together after all these years.

She recalled that tonight was the time when she explained that she was pregnant with their first child. She was reluctant to be pregnant in a foreign country and away from all things familiar, including her family-especially her Mother. They would need to discuss later where to give birth and now that they would be more than just a couple, what were they truly going to do with their lives.

The guards looked at her differently this time; she wondered if her growing belly and soon-to-be obvious pregnancy was now known by them too. The afternoon sun cast shadow combing her figure with her packages thus disguising her looks. In her mind, the shadow cast upon the cement platform was that of someone pushing a stroller.

The guard had been distracted with a passing vehicle's horn so that when he returned to look at Fiona, his face resumed the posture of power and mistrust. Her smirking face still reflected her view of the image seen in her shadow of her future motherly self. Realizing this, mismatch with his reaction did not result in a smile upon his face. When he looked at her directly, the smile disappeared. His intentions and attentions to her interrogation were not lost on Fiona.

He began, "Guten Tag, Frau, Dokumente bitte," "Good afternoon, Frau, papers please," looking at Fiona for her passport or other travel documents.

"Ja, hier sind Sie," "Yes, here you go," she replied, her obvious English accent apparent in her awkward German.

The guard was still trying to recover from the myriad of packages with which she was returning after her shopping in the west. Changing to English as he saw her struggle in his native German, "Where have you been, what are all these packages?" he asked.

"I've just returned from a weekend in Paris. We are having company for dinner tonight and I brought home some things from Paris for dinner." Fiona spoke calmly, acting 100%.

"Very well, Mother, where are the children?" he asked.

"No children," Fiona remarked, in her mind she added, "Not yet anyway."

While discussing her shopping in Paris, a group of school children approached with their teacher. They had been in the west for the day, attending a museum and were now returning and everyone could hear them.

"Proceed," he said to Fiona, distractedly.

Fortunately, Fiona and Kurt's flat was located just a few kilometers from the checkpoint and she made good time in her walk. She enjoyed walking again; it had been something she did frequently as a child but not as much as an adult. At her parents' home, everyone drove everywhere. In New York, it was mass transit, hired cars, or walking. Actually, in New York, she was spoiled by Jake's car ownership. In Germany, west or east, it was mostly walking. By now, she had grown accustomed to it. Packages and all.

As she entered their five story apartment building, she took in the various odors and smells of dinner preparations by other occupants. She was always guessing what they were cooking, mostly incorrectly. In the states, that never happened. She was just that unfamiliar with German food or cooking and the related spices.

As she approached the door to her apartment, she heard loud male voices in multiple languages, not in anger, but in serious debate. She put down her package wrapped in brown paper and rested her suitcase upon its trailer next to the door. In finding her keys, she slowly applied them to the lock and quietly entered.

Unheard and unnoticed, Fiona left her paper-wrapped package on the front hall table and took her suitcase with her to their bedroom. Inside the apartment, she heard not only Kurt's voice, but also Emanuel's and another female voice she did not recognize at first. If they were still discussing as loudly as now when she returned to the hall, she'd have to take a moment to listen more closely to determine what the conversation/argument was truly about.

She was able to unpack a few things and freshen up before Kurt caught sight of the package at the apartment door.

"Fiona, are you back darling?" he said questioningly.

From her retreat in their bedroom, she said quietly, "Yes. I am."

Walking and talking at the same time, Kurt spoke to her until he saw her when he stopped in his tracks, "I was just explaining to Emanuel…"

"Hello," she said, as he entered their small bedroom.

Kurt continued to approach her and with a passionate kiss on the mouth said, "Hello," as sexily as possible. He had missed her while she was gone. Even if it had only been three days.

"Wow, I was only gone a few days. To get kisses like that maybe I should be gone more often!"

"Maybe you should!"

Emanuel approached and showed Fiona his selection of baguettes for the evening's meal. "What is on the menu tonight?"

"You are in for a treat tonight, Emanuel. Ellen just showed me her recipe for roast duck with all the trimmings."

"Wow, it does sound like a great treat."

"Actually, we'll have that another time when I have more time for preparation."

"If time is what you need, based on what you describe, I'd wait for it!" Kurt added.

"Emanuel, can you stay long enough for me to prepare it?" Fiona asked.

"Sure we can, but do you have a duck on hand?" he asked pointedly.

"We?"

"Yes, Olivia came with me tonight."

"Hello Fiona," Olivia said walking into the hallway. "Can I help in some way? Duck sounds scrumptious."

"Do we have a duck?" Kurt asked.

"Ah, no I don't."

"Do you need me to go to the butcher and get a duck?" Kurt proposed.

"Yes, if that is what you want for dinner. I don't think we have any meat in the house. I'm sorry about all this," Fiona said.

"Or," Kurt said, "We could go out to dinner."

"Let's save dinner out for a celebration," Fiona said.

"Alright then," Kurt said, "Emanuel, shall we push on to the butchers?"

"Sounds like a plan to me."

Walking out to the hallway, grabbing his jacket, Kurt said, "We'll be back as soon as we can, duck or chicken in hand."

"Great, thank you darling."

While the men were away, the women began to talk while Fiona unpacked. About an hour later, the men returned with both a nice duck and a small chicken. Over the next few hours, they all worked on various portions of their meal. Kurt was responsible for the salad and setting the table. Emanuel broiled some smelly cheese on slices of bread and added some fresh basil. He cut them up into bite sized pieces and fed those whose hands were otherwise occupied with the dinner preparations. Olivia set about her famous chocolate mousse.

Emanuel brought out some wine, a nice Riesling and a full bodied Cabernet, and set the latter out to breathe. He had a. Looking at the table, he smiled. He had just detected something about the room, Fiona's demeanor, and the atmosphere. It was electrically charged, good news he hoped.

Emanuel and Olivia left after two o'clock in the morning with a very happy Olivia on his arm. His stomach was filled with a delicious combination of roast duck and roast chicken. Fiona had also prepared baked potatoes and green peas, still in the pod. His mind was a little foggy with all the wine and Scotch Kurt brought out after the wine was finished.

As they walked down the street, Olivia clutched his arm and brought his body closer to hers. When she sensed he was paying attention, she said, "I've got a secret."

"So do I," Emanuel said in return.

"Shall we announce what we know together?" she suggested.

"Yes, on the count of three: one, two, three!"

"Fiona's pregnant." Olivia blurted out.

"They are moving to Canada." Emanuel exclaimed.

Looking at each other, in disbelief, they truly mutually thought they knew the others' secret.

"Kurt has been accepted into the PhD program at the University of Alberta, in Edmonton, Canada," Emanuel said.

"Fiona's due in 7 months."

"They are going to be talking about these changes all night. Perhaps we should bring a robust breakfast or brunch for them tomorrow, eh, today," he said correcting himself.

"Good idea," she said holding his arm closer to her body. "If they move, I'm not going to have any western friends here."

Back at their apartment, as their door slammed shut, Fiona was slightly startled back to her brushing hair. Her face held an odd smile, one of sweetness but confusion as well. As she was returning from the past, she was even more confused as the Wagner piece on the turntable hit the allegro. Strangely, she smelled the duck wafting up from her own kitchen, a powerful scent memory. Even stranger still, she rubbed at her slightly pudgy belly and wondered what was real.

Chapter 14 A Brief Reorientation, 2015

While her room was empty and after Ellen had gone out to find reinforcements, Fiona carefully exited the bathroom and resumed her sleep upon the noisy hospital bed. She was still enjoying the taste of L'Entrecôte's fries and the sauce and could be heard smacking her lips. A faint smile was upon her still dreaming face.

"Fiona, wake up, its Jake!" Jake yelled from the doorway. He was hoping his sharp tones would jar her memory to their playful banter in their voices reserved for each other.

"What's the matter?" Fiona said, waking urgently.

"Fiona," Jake said, "Are you back?"

"Am I back from where?" Fiona replied, "Jake what's the matter, darling, you look like hell."

"Thanks a lot," he said, softly. Then, realizing her term of endearment, he said, "Say that again?"

"You look like hell?"

"No, the other part," he said.

"What's the matter?"

"No, the other other part," he said smiling knowing his Fiona was back and pulling his leg.

"Hello darling, what's going on?" Fiona said. "What are we doing here at NYU? Did something happen to me?"

"Yes, you could say it did," he said relieved. "What's the last thing you remember?"

"Swimming at the YMCA, how did I get here? Am I alright?"

"I think you are, I think you will be. Hang on, I've got some people that want to see you. They've been waiting such a long time too. They've been waiting with me."

Still tired, Fiona, losing the importance of the moment, yawned, and as Jake left the room, she fell asleep. Yet again.

Chapter 15 It had Begun-Again, 1985

Over the past few days, she was recounting her time in Paris to Jake. Now, she returned to Paris in her dreams. Her brief reprieve had ended.

Back at Sophie's apartment, Fiona had completed her shower and begun to lay out her things on the futon bed she used there. Sophie was due back in about an hour and Fiona wanted time to organize herself before the two women gabbed about their previous time together, and her trip now. Fiona also wanted Sophie's input on sights to see and any other important information she could gather from an experienced European traveler like Sophie.

As Fiona finished putting her selected items in her suitcase, she heard the apartment door open and close and the 'bon soir' 'good evening' yelled by Sophie, announcing her return. Fiona replied, "Je suis ici." "I'm in here."

"Bon soir Fiona, as tu finis avec tes baggages?" Sophie said, "Have you finished with your luggage?"

In French Fiona replied, "Oui, j'ai finis." "Yes, I'm finished."

"Bon, d'accord. Viens ici," she said, "Good, well then, come here."

"Ok."

"This is important, so I'll practice my English with you. I have heard stories of some dangerous people on the trains. If you take the night train, like tonight, always make sure the compartment door is locked, and that you sleep in the top couchette with your bags up there with you. Keep your money and passport with you at all times. Several friends of mine have been pick pocketed; I don't want that to happen to you."

"Yes, I know about that. Good idea on the couchette, as I probably would have slept on the bottom bunk. Can we really get a compartment all to ourselves?"

"I don't know exactly, but pray that you can and certainly ask the conductor. Make him a friend and you'll be fine. When do we need to leave to get you to Gare du Nord?"

"I don't have to be there until 10:45PM; it's only a little after 8 now; maybe we could sit and talk about your family, and anything else you would suggest we go see or places to go?" Fiona requested.

"Sure. Well, you remember helping Monique with her English when you were here four years ago? She was interviewing with Air France to be a flight attendant, you remember?"

"Yes I do. She had a lot of questions about pronouns, conjunctions, slang, and other grammar. It made me think that for a job interview that was a high expectation for a foreign language."

Sophie took a moment then to dig out some recent photos of her parents and Monique from last Christmas, and when Monique got her job with Air France. By the looks, Fiona thought, no one had changed all that much. She knew when she returned from their trip that she'd take the time to go out to see Sophie's parents and Monique. Perhaps Sophie would be off from work and could go out with her. The last time Fiona stayed with the Picoté's it was like living at home with parents that sounded a bit different but acted almost exactly the same. It was a wonderful experience.

"Yes, correct," Sophie said. "Well, she got the job and has been working for Air France now for three years or more. My Father is doing well and still working. My Mother is redecorating the house in Triel. So everyone is doing fine. As for me, I will finish university in another year or so. I'm studying art history, do you remember that?"

"I recall something like that was an interest of yours. Do you remember my olive green raincoat I brought with me in 1981? Remember when we were walking to the Métro by the Arc de Triomphe? Do you remember what the transvestite said to me?" Fiona said, reminiscing.

"Yes, he said, 'great coat.' I remember that coat, it was very chic."

"I still have it! I didn't bring it with me this time to save space. I have a little slicker instead."
"Oh, good idea. You will have rain at some point. You are going to Amsterdam tonight?"

"Yes," Fiona replied.

"Then where?"

"Well, that's what I'd like to ask you. Have you gone anywhere recently that you think is a really must see? Something you wouldn't want to miss?" Fiona asked.

Sophie thought for a moment, and then she said, "You are staying in Western Europe?"

"Yes, I don't think we want to go into a communist territory, why?"

"Oh, I was just concerned that you might want to go to Prague or Czechoslovakia, maybe even East Berlin. No, you don't want to go there, not this trip, maybe another time?"

"I think you are right. So in Western Europe, do you have any ideas?"

"Oh, yes. My high school class took a trip to Bavaria. It is so beautiful there and they were very good to classes, or groups of students traveling together with their teachers. We stayed in youth hostels, not hotels or with families like you did here 4 years ago."

"I know, that was nice staying with your family. I really got an idea of French provincial living. Have you seen any good movies lately?"

"Oh, the movies, they are slow in coming on tape in English. The last one I saw was Kramer vs. Kramer, and that one is old. It seems they take longer and longer to make them in French so I can understand them better. I know it is better in English, you remember watching Casablanca, c'était formidable," her language changed back to French suddenly startling both of them.

"Oui, c'est vrais, c'était formidable." "Yes, it is true, it was great."

"Other than Bavaria, I guess I'd go to Milan or Salzburg. I like those cities, lots of fashion and art for my studies. Where do you think you'll go?"

"We don't have a plan at all. I think it will be up to the wind and where the trains are going. We'll hop on and off as the mood suits us."

"Here, take this. I put together a small list of places to see. They are ones I'd want to go to, or ones I've seen, and want to see again. See, Bavaria is listed right there," she said, pointing to the name and the placement it took high up on the list.

"I'll mention to Ellen about your list and preferences on here. Thank you for making it for us."

"Do you need anything else, are you all packed?"

"Yes, I'm packed. I'm leaving a number of things here, you said it was ok, right?"

"Oh yes, just put them in the corner over there and I'll watch them for you. When are you coming back?"

"I should be back in about 3 weeks. My flight out is on the 30th. We will make sure to call you before we get into town. Can we meet you here?" Fiona asked.

"How about this, I don't want to repeat what happened when you arrived a few days ago. I'll begin to place an apartment key in my mailbox a few days before the 30th. Let me show you," Sophie explained.

Outside the apartment, there were some small boxes where the occupants received their mail. Sophie explained that she would let the matron of the building know that Fiona was coming back, and not to worry if she saw her. "Who is that?" Fiona asked.

"You've seen her, she's the woman who is always sweeping," said Sophie.

"I think that is a great idea. That way I can gain access to your place without you having to wait around for me. I'll do my best to call you when I'm coming back."

"Excellent."

"Do you think we should go now?" Fiona asked.

"I think so, we don't know how busy the Métro will be tonight; and I want to get you to Gare du Nord in plenty of time. Do you have everything?"

"Yes, I'm ready. Let's go."

Dressed in jeans, a red polo shirt and tennis shoes, Fiona put her daypack on her back and with her suitcase on the carrier, pulled it behind her. She had a bottle of Evian and the timetables book inside her backpack for easy retrieval. They walked from Sophie's apartment to the nearby Odéon Métro station and took the next train, indicating direction Porte de Clignancourt. Surprisingly, they only had to wait about 10 minutes, since at this hour of the evening; trains usually come at much longer intervals.

Once they arrived at Gare du Nord, Sophie expertly walked to the main terminal ticket window. As they rode up the last escalator, Fiona could see Ellen and Pierre already waiting just ahead of them. The American women exchanged waves. Just like Fiona hated the feeling of being lost, she also hated the feeling of not finding her destination and being late. Sophie had gauged their time well and they arrived at the ticket window at about half-past ten.

"Glad you made it," Ellen said.

"While I was paying attention, getting here at this time was really Sophie's doing. I was just along for the ride," Fiona joked.

"Well I'm glad she did. Let's get our tickets."

Pierre and Sophie watched from a nearby bench as the two American women approached the ticket window and requested their upgrades. They saw that Ellen was dressed in dark grey charcoal jeans with a black shirt and black sandals. Ellen would turn from time to time to smile at Pierre, her sweetie. The ticket purchasing process seemed to take only a few minutes before they both turned around and walked over with their tickets in hand. Ellen was showing signs of separation, just like any two-year-old being left in the nursery while the parents went to church.

"You'll be fine, ma chérie," Pierre said sweetly to Ellen.

"We'll be back before you know it," Fiona said.

"I know, I just don't like it when we are apart."

"Well, think of it this way," Pierre said, "I'm only a short plane ride or a long train ride away. If you have any problems, call my Father at work; he'll know how to contact me at school or work."

"Ok, I have that number in my backpack. Fiona, why don't you write it into your trip diary, just in case," Ellen suggested.

"I think you should get on the train," Sophie suggested. "You want your own compartment, non?"

"We already bought the entire compartment. We didn't want to have any surprises on our first train ride." Fiona said.

"Well, whose idea was that?" asked Sophie.

"Mine," Fiona said, "I didn't want us to worry. If one or both of us fell asleep, you know, we didn't want to wake up at the end of the line with no luggage, no passports, and worst of all, no money."

"Well, don't do that the whole time; it will be too expensive. Sometimes the trains will be full too," Sophie cautioned.

"Yes, we realized that. Just this time, it is the first trip out together; make it a good one was what we thought."

"Well, have a good time, I'm going to go back home now. See you in a few weeks," Sophie said, "Bon Voyage!"

Before Sophie could get away, Fiona made sure to explain a little something she left behind in the apartment. She didn't want Sophie to miss it. Fiona had the idea to leave another of her Minnesota gifts; this time she put it on Sophie's pillow. It was a 'Welcome to Minnesota' tee-shirt with the majestic scenes of the pines along the historic north shore of Lake Superior. Fiona exchanged a warm hug with Sophie and then she disappeared down the escalator, waving as each section of her body gradually disappeared until she was no longer in sight.

Fiona left her friends, the lovers, a moment alone to say goodbye. She even gave them more privacy during their farewell embrace as she was turned away, studying the big overhead schedule board. She saw their train was on time and leaving from platform 8. She even saw the 'To Trains' signs and which way to go to get to their platform. She waited until receiving the verbal 'I'm ready' from Ellen before she turned around.

"I'm ready, Fiona," Ellen repeated.

"So am I!" Fiona said. "Au revoir, Pierre, see you in a few weeks. I might even send you a postcard!" Fiona said, with a wink and a nod. They exchanged kisses and hugs.

"Go on, you need to board. I'll watch you leave from here," he said.

"Ok my love. Remember, mon cheri, je t'aime." Ellen said. "Remember, my love, I love you."

"Oui, moi aussi," he said in response, "Yes, me too."

The women waved from below the 'To Trains' sign and disappeared around a corner. Despite his internal jigsaw of emotions, Pierre was smiling as he watched the women leaving, for he could hear the mixture of their laughing and crying. He knew, as they did, their trip had begun.

Chapter 16 The Honeymoon Phase, 1991

The route they followed in Scotland, as suggested by Fiona's parents when they lived in England, took them to some of the most fascinating cities. Jake went on ahead into the Information Centre while Fiona wrote a few postcards home; one to each of their parents, one to Harriet, and one to Ellen. When Jake returned to the car, his hands were full of various bits of paper, one of which was a local map.

While Fiona was busy with pen and paper, postcards, Jake had been busy too. As they discussed prior to leaving home, and with the input of their respective parents, the couple had quickly learned that they didn't need to book a reservation in a large hotel in advance but a smaller inn or bed and breakfast actually suited them better.

Once they were accustomed to the information areas along their route, they quickly caught on to the nuances of traveling in Scotland. They also learned at one of the motorway's rest areas, which included charts and maps with various points of interest and other tourist information, that they could pre-book their next destination at one of these kiosks. They paid the Information Centre a portion of their lodging and paid the remainder to the innkeeper. This was the method they used when they didn't have a specific destination in hand when they set off one morning.

Their route took them up the A91 around the west side of "The Old Course" at St. Andrews and across the hillsides of southeastern Scotland. They made good time and were in Perth by tea time. Fiona wanted to try Scottish High Tea so they drove about looking for a teahouse or a grand enough hotel that would serve High Tea. After a quick survey of the smaller old part of city central, they finally got out and asked for a suggestion at the corner petrol station.

"Och, aye," said the cashier woman, "They serve a fine tea at Culdees. They are just up the road a wee bit, the whitewashed building with the shaved thatched roof. Not more than a few blocks, I should say, aye?"

"Thank you very much," Fiona replied.

"Did you understand that Jake?"

"Maybe, did you?" he said, unsure.

"I think she said there was a small place not far up this way," she said pointing up the street. "Shall we give it a go?"

As it turned out, the cashier had been correct and gave them perfect directions. They enjoyed a cup of Earl Grey, with some cakes and scones. For Maureen, Fiona added a bit of clotted cream on one of her cakes. In the days when her Mother lived here, clotted cream was like icing on the cake.

With their goal for today still Pitlochry, they didn't dilly dally long with their tea. In fact, they discussed how they could now manage driving in the dark and foregoing dinner until they found the bed and breakfast in Pitlochry. Everyone at the last Information Centre had raved about it and so they had made and paid for their reservation. They began calling it B & B for short soon after they made their reservation.

They took in a few more sights in Perth, including stopping to browse in the smaller shops they encountered. Maureen had explained to them that this was a wonderful way to find one-of-a-kind pieces and exceptionally good quality woolen sweaters. While driving, they held hands and only broke off this means of contact when they took a myriad of photographs of the countryside.

Pitlochry, as it turned out, was only about 45 minutes by car from Perth. They had delays up in the hills on account of wayward sheep milling about in the middle of the road. They had to stop numerous times to coax these timid beasts off their path and back into the hills. Fiona pointed out the sheep's ears to Jake. She had noted their upward direction when she had stayed with her cousin Gosnold and Una, at the beginning portion of her European adventure. Only it was solo during that time and without Ellen.

"See, I told you, here the ears of the sheep point upwards!" Fiona exclaimed.

"I am now a believer darling, I simply couldn't believe it before!"

"Speaking of ears..." Fiona said as she nuzzled in next to Jake's neck. "Are we there yet??"

"Not yet but soon or we'll have to pull off to the side of the road and 'park!'" Jake replied.

Smiling at her husband, Fiona was content with any option to attack his body once again. They hoped the B & B, now so dubbed, wasn't filled with other travelers so that their noisy love-making didn't disturb the other guests.

"Oh, I'm all for parking!" said Fiona exuberantly.

"You asked for it. Let's see if this Volkswagen can handle four wheel drive!" Jake said, pulling off the road and into the flock of sheep. He hoped they would be able to drive a distance on the grassy meadow and keep the sheep about them as camouflage. The further they drove up into the highlands, the fewer were the trees in which to use as cover. Their ongoing joke or invitation afterwards was a Volkswagen in sheep's clothing. Baaah! They said to each other with each crescendo as they composed and practiced their allegro.

Later than originally planned, they entered the city proper of Pitlochry and easily found their B & B. Taking their smaller bagged luggage inside with them, they signed in and registered with the front desk clerk named Tristan. Fiona let out a small gasp and giggled at reading his name tag. She recalled from her music appreciation class that Tristan was the male lead in one of Wagner's other operas. *Tristan und Isolde* was widely acclaimed and dubbed influential in the operatic cultures of the time. She wondered if he knew that, but decided now was not the time to ask.

Instead, they scurried up to their room, disrobed each other as quickly as possible and began again their composition of their own symphony.

Later when they had showered and dressed for dinner, they decided to go out for dinner and in lieu of a known restaurant, they figured Tristan would be up for a change in conversation and could give them a recommendation.

"Och, aye," began Tristan. "What kind of meal do ye fancy then?"

"We really hadn't decided, but probably something grilled at say a pub or traditional Scottish food?" suggested Jake.

"Och, aye, will ye be wanting to walk to it?" he asked.

"Yes, I think the night air will do us good," Fiona said, nudging Jake in the ribs. She was hinting at his verbal behavior about an hour ago. "Cool air to fill the lungs," she said, winking.

"Aye lassie, then I'd be sending ye to the Strathgarry Hotel and you'll find they have a handsome restaurant. Let me draw you a wee map," he said, reaching for paper and pen.

His map indicated they take a right out of the B & B and proceed south on West Moulin Road and when they came to the intersection of Atholl Road to take another right. The hotel would be just ahead on Atholl Road. He said in his note on the map that the hotel was made of limestone bricks and was flush with the sidewalk. If they got lost, he listed the B & B's phone number at the bottom of the map.

"Thank you Tristan," Fiona said, "If we aren't back by dawn, send out the search party!"

"Aye, aye, missus!" Tristan said, correcting himself having noted her fine wedding rings.

Turning to Fiona, Jake said, "Ready or not, here we come!"

Their walk to the Strathgarry took about twenty minutes and in their stroll, before the sunset, they took in all the sights and made notes of places they'd enjoy reviewing the next day or so. Being new in town, this walk helped them get a lay of the land and get a feel for the distances involved. Had they known the drive from Perth was so short, they would have booked into the hotel knowing that they would be staying 'in' most of the days here anyway.

The weather was cooperating with their walk. A soft breeze at their backs pushed them ever so slightly along Moulin Road. It was a bit to their sides once they turned onto Atholl and a slight mist developed as they entered the hotel. Fiona's naturally curly hair sprang into action with the slightly misty air. Jake's hair, a blend of thick dark brown growth, barely moved. They estimated the temperature about 65F but with the wind and mist, it felt more like mid 50's. Fiona was glad she thought to grab her slicker and umbrella. When in the United Kingdom, one rarely left home without it.

As they entered the hotel, they were immediately greeted by the front desk clerk, an older gentleman who looked a bit like Fiona's Father. His name tag said, "Heinie" and they both knew that there was a story behind it, had they had more time when they entered, they would have asked.

"Good evening folks, how may I assist you?" said Heinie in what was a surprisingly American accent, one rather familiar to Fiona.

"Good evening, could you show us to your restaurant, we'd like to have dinner?" Fiona said in her best Minnesotan accent.

A smirk developing on Heinie's face, "Sure thing, right this way." On the radio was a familiar song, "*Come back when you grow up, girl. You're still livin' in a paper-doll world…*" As the song continued, a faithful and large German Shepherd howled from behind the front desk. "Hush now, Killian, this is the good part!" Killian answered with a more muted howled none the less.

Heinie passed them off to the hostess saying, "Darling, these folks would be here for dinner, can you seat them?"

"Straight away," she said. "Follow me please." Her Texan or southern drawl was noticeable within the confines of the 'o's' in follow and the 'eee' sound in me. Her smile was bright and her attention keen.

"Thank you," Jake said as he took his seat.

"How about something to drink?" she said.

"I'm ready for a glass of wine, you want a beer honey?" Fiona said.

"Yes, I do."

"Very good, I'll be right back," she said.

Fiona looked at her name tag and saw it read Shania, a rather unusual name, thought Fiona. She'd have to ask her about it when she returned with their drinks.

"Did you see her name tag?"

"Yes I did, interesting names they have here!" Jake added.

Just then, Shania returned with their drinks. "Here you go folks," she said.

"Thank you," Fiona replied, "I'm wondering, may I ask you about your name? I haven't ever seen that name, can you tell me about it?"

"Why thank you," Shania retorted. "You folks are from the States, right?"

"Yes, I guess that wasn't too hard to figure out, huh?"

"Accent and dress, usually they give you away."

"Yes, they do. I'm actually from north Texas, my husband Heinie and I are covering the fall quarter for his friends who own this hotel. They met back when Heinie was in the Navy and was stationed in Edinburgh. He flew P3's, you know, antisubmarine warfare planes."

"Well, that isn't exactly what I was expecting you to say!" began Fiona. "So is Shania a southern name? I'm still puzzled by it."

"Oh, yes, in my town in Texas, you know, in Dallas, I think Shania is more like Sue, Jane, or even Beth. Quite common there," she concluded.

"Honey, let's keep what they are doing in mind for our future. If we ever want to live somewhere far away, say in a Scottish highlands hotel, perhaps the owners could be finagled in to taking some much needed time off in exchange. You know, house swap!" Fiona said with a tempting thought upon her face.

"It has been so much fun for us. Normally, we live in Dallas, but I'm from Rhode Island originally. I have my own interior design firm that is being covered by my interns. So what can I recommend to you from the menu?"

"Do you have anything of Scottish flair?" Fiona asked.

"Oh yes, just look, uh, here," she said, pointing to the "Scottish Favourites" section of the menu.

"Oh, look darling, they have 'Haggis'!" announced Jake. "I might just be game to try it!"

"I think I'll have the Mince n' Tatties," Fiona said.

"Very good, and for a starter?" asked Shania. "Our soup du jour is cream of wild mushroom."

"Oh, I like that, I'll take a cup of that please," Fiona said.

"Me too," answered Jake.

"Very good, I'll be back in a bit with your soups."

They sat back and began a recounting of the day, including a review of their dancing both while parking and in their room in town. They were making plans for their dance tonight and thought perhaps it might be interesting to find a secluded place in town on their way back, if not for a full dance, maybe just a taste.

Their dancing discussion was interrupted by Shania's return with their soups and a basket of warm bread and whipped honey butter. "I hope you enjoy, this is a fantastic recipe, unfortunately I'm sworn to secrecy," she ended, with a wink.

"It all smells terrific." Jake said, passing the bread basket and butter to his new bride. "Here darling, try some bread."

"Thank you," Fiona replied. Helping herself to the bread and butter, the first bite included a bit of butter melting and almost falling off the bread. Licking the butter and taking a bite, Fiona turned her gaze to Jake and seductively chewed her morsel.

Jake felt a stirring in his jeans and smiled. "Soon enough, soon enough," he said, taking his own bite, tempting her in the process.

Shania was watching their flirtatious display and walked over to the sound system and began to play some traditional Scottish Bagpipe Band songs. Among them, was "Amazing Grace."

When the sounds registered with Fiona, and she recognized the piece, her eyes began to tear. "Honey, have I ever told you that my Grandmother Winnie's favorite song was 'Amazing Grace?'"

"No, I don't think you have, it is an awesome song and even more so with the bagpipes."

"It feels like she is here with us, can you sense it?"

"Yes, darling, I think she is saying hello to us and she approves of our match. Perhaps through this song, she is wishing us well in our marriage?"

"Oh, I hope so," said Fiona, as she wiped a small tear from her eye. It was difficult being so emotional in more ways than one.

Distracted by the music and the memories, Fiona pulled at her pink sweater set. Jake removed his cardigan and placed it on her shoulders. He let his fingers linger just beside her breasts as he placed it properly. He hoped she would still be in the mood to dance the dance he had in mind later, on their walk back to the hotel.

Coming to her senses, Fiona responded to the gesture with her foot beneath the table when her foot sought out his ankle. Acknowledging she was still in the mood and that he felt her presence there, he simply nodded and smiled. It was real what they felt for each other. It was real.

They ate in relative silence, listening to the songs on the sound system, lost in their lustful thoughts. Like any couple, they wanted to make their honeymoon as special as possible. Sneaking about for a quickie seemed to be the special tonight.

When they left the hotel, they thanked Heinie and Shania for their hospitality and due to the lateness of the hour, assisted them in closing up. Fiona and Shania exchanged addresses and phone numbers and Shania agreed that when they finally retired, they had a trip planned to New York and would look them up. In the meantime, Heinie gave Jake a stash of the hotel stationery, saying, "Let's keep in touch."

On the front desk next to the register were the expected tourist listings of interest. It was here that Fiona found a map of Pitlochry and helped herself to it. While Jake was still talking with Heinie, and Shania had returned to clean up her mess in the kitchen, Fiona studied the map for a nice walk and perhaps to scout out a secluded area for their dance tonight. Actually, it was no longer tonight, it was now morning. About one o'clock in the morning, Fiona worried that the B & B would lock their doors and they couldn't get into their room. As a backup, she searched her daypack and discovered a second set of car keys. It wouldn't be the first time they actually 'slept' in their car, and it certainly wouldn't be the last.

She saw on the map that Atholl Road bordered what looked like a river, but upon further review, she discovered that it was actually a lake, Loch Faskally, to be exact. She traced Atholl Road to the east and found a small, dead end street that ended by the loch. The dead end street was Tummel Crescent, so surely there would be a park or a public resting place located at the end of that street. They would have to go on an adventure and find out. If they were interrogated by the police, they'd simply state they were lost and trying to find their way back to the B & B.

With her plan set up, Fiona waited for Jake's conversation to end and they said their final goodbyes. Holding Jake's hand and leaning into him for warmth, Fiona donned her slicker too. She showed him the map and said, "I have a plan. Follow me," she said, seductively.

"Looking like that, I'll follow you anywhere!" Jake replied.

"Good, you are going to enjoy this."

They walked for about half an hour until they were finally at the circled end of Tummel Crescent. As she had hoped, there was indeed a park here, now long deserted. They discovered muted street lighting, natural shrubbery and gorse, and a small park. Within the park, they discovered a tire swing hanging from one of the larger deciduous trees. Near the benches was a large marker; before heading to the swing, they went up to the marker to read it.

The marker was actually quite a find, historically speaking. It denoted the re-commencement of the Pitlochry Highland Games. "Apparently, they were held in town back in the last century," Fiona said, reading out loud. "It says there were contests of strength and other sports and that included the women's highland dancing."

"Dancing?" Jake asked.

"Highland dancing, not dancing," Fiona corrected him. "You know, when I was a little girl, I learned proper Highland Dancing, was in contests with my troupe and everything. We had these great little costumes with short skirts with lots of tartans. I wore ballet slippers too…" she said, gazing off into her memories.

"I'll show you highland dancing," Jake said, intruding her reflective thoughts. At this point, they had walked over to the tree swing and Jake sat down first, naked and aroused.

"I like the way you think, Mr. Davies," Fiona said, obligingly disrobing and mounting her dance partner.

"Me too, Mrs. Davies, me too," Jake said, propelling the swing pulling at both Fiona's body and the rope above them.

Their bodies did not last long in the coolness of the morning air and the swing sounded precariously like it would snap if they continued much longer. Instead, they made a nest with their removed clothing and finished their dance horizontally. Their dance that night was by memory and without much artificial light. While there was a bit of a moon out that night, the moonbeams that would have normally confronted them at home in New York, here in the Scottish Highlands; they were obscured by the mist that grew from the river only a few feet from their nest.

Their dance complete, their bodies spent, they fell asleep afterwards warmed by the coiling of each other's body. They had long ago learned to shut out all noises of living in a large city, the honking cars sounding like swans, the backfiring of delivery trucks the croak of tree frogs, and the dull hum of cars upon the concrete weren't any match for the solitude and silence they heard upon the grassy terrace at the end of Tummel Crescent.

Unlike their urban fortress with its thick draperies, and central heating and air, it was the combination of the brisk morning air and first light that finally stirred Fiona. Realizing that they were no longer cloaked in the cover of darkness and weren't in a secluded dead end, they were in fact in someone's yard, having stepped away from the park in their attempts at nesting. Nudging Jake, he woke up with his typical morning dance routine but shied away from it seeing that they weren't as secluded come the light of day.

They dressed quickly and walked more briskly than their normal New Yorker pace but at less than a jog. Checking his watch, Jake discovered it was just before six o'clock in the morning. They'd danced and slept in the park; well what they thought was a park and was instead the lavish lawn of the large dwelling at the end of the crescent. Thinking back, he smiled at the thought that they had danced all night long. Soon they knew, townsfolk and tourists alike would be exiting their abodes and heading towards the commencements and duties for the day. Unlike those people, Jake and Fiona sought the comforts of their room and a hot bath for two.

Along their return to the B & B, they found a bakery which had already opened. Inside, the smells of pastry and other baked goodies were all encompassing. Their movements throughout the night had burned off more calories than sleeping alone would do. They were famished. They quickly purchased four 'pain chocolat,' two bagels with cream cheese, four strawberry tarts, and hot coffee with cream and sugar. They packed it to go and devoured it once back in their room, while listening to the tub fill with enticingly hot water.

They drank their coffees au naturale in their bath for two. Once caffeinated again, they danced the dance of swans upon and within their porcelain lake. Drained from their dancing and low on sustenance other than themselves, they retired to their bed, where this time, they slept.

Chapter 17 More Hospital Activity, 2015

After finishing their dinner in the hospital cafeteria, Fiona's parents and Gabriella returned to Fiona's room on station 51. Maureen was at the door first and in knocking softly, she opened the door to find Jake and Fiona discussing their last golf outing. A week had passed since her last clear moment, but again she was looking for Kurt and only considered Jake as her golf partner, nothing more.

"Can we come in?" she asked.

"Yes, please come in. Jake and I were talking shop, golf shop that is!" Fiona joked.

"When Fiona feels up to it, and her doctor approves, we've discussed going back out to the golf course and seeing how her coma affected her game.."

"Is she really ready for physical activity?" Ian asked cautiously.

"I'm not sure," Jake began, "I wasn't in the room when the doctor was examining her. I'd expect they would want to make discharge plans to get her on her way home."

Her parents, nodding to Jake that they realized this line of questioning surpassed Jake's nursing skills and was closing in on crossing the line into Jake's medical expertise, they stopped pressing for this kind information in front of Fiona. They would wait until they were no longer in Fiona's room to ask him further questions. Ian shot a sideways glance at Maureen and raised his eyebrows knowing and owning his faux pas. Maureen crossed the room to her husband and gave him a small hug reassuring him that the elephants in the room, Fiona and Jake's relationship and his medical training, had not been divulged, well at least not to Fiona. She seemed none the wiser.

"When I'm ready and approved for the activity, I'm up for it," Fiona admitted. "Do you suppose they have a treadmill? Perhaps before I get discharged I can start walking and pretending I'm on a great journey and can track my progress."

"Sounds like a good idea, I could help you set up a spreadsheet to track your progress," Jake added.

"If you are up for a walk now," Gabriella said, "I'd take you out for a once around the block!"

"I don't know what my activity level is, maybe you should check? I mean, I'm up and around in the room, but I haven't been outside the room yet."

"Let me ask, I'll be right back," Gabriella added.

As they waited for Gabriella to return, the discussion in the room was focused on getting Fiona physically active as soon as possible. Jake took a back seat in these discussions whenever he was in Fiona's line of sight. If not, he would encourage either of her parents along their line of discussion. They again did not address the elephant and Fiona's memory. Tonight's topic was about her ability to begin her physical rehabilitation, not mental.

While they were discussing her future physical rehabilitation, the extremely intuitive Fiona felt there was more that wasn't said then was said. She wondered if her family had been withholding some bad news or other calamity, while she was comatose. She would continue to monitor this situation with her parents especially. They would be the easiest to read. Gabriella and Jake, she knew, were medically trained nurses, and they'd be able to duck a pointed question. She decided to focus on her parents for now.

After only a brief wait, Gabriella returned with her orders for activity. "I confirmed with your nurse that you are free to take short assisted walks, as long as you feel up to it. She encouraged me to take you for a walk tonight, you ready?"

"Oh that is good news," said Maureen.

"Yes it is, isn't it dear," Ian said to Fiona.

"I'm ready," Fiona said, "Jake, you want to come along?"

"I'd love to," he said. He was glad to have been asked. Perhaps, he thought, Fiona was remembering their relationship, but was fearful of letting on what she had recalled.

"Well dear, I think we'll call it a night and see you out into the hall as we head back to the Waldorf," Maureen said, looking at Ian for reassurance.

"Yes, Mother is right; we really should be on our way. We'll see you in the morning honey," Ian agreed.

"Ok then, good night," Fiona said as she held onto Jake and Gabriella for her first walk.

Her IV had been discontinued earlier in the day with the return of her appetite and sufficient oral fluid intake. So when she was walking this time, Fiona didn't have anything to assist her so she reaffirmed her hold on Gabriella's and Jake's arms. If she tired quickly, she would ask for more of Jake's help. They walked down the hall and off the unit towards the direction of the visitor elevators and then around to the staff elevators and the back hallway to the women's locker room. In this area of the hospital, there were double hallways, one for the public and one for patients and staff. That way, when not at their best, patients and public didn't have to interact unless by choice, or by accident.

"I never imagined that I'd be the patient walking around here. Not with you at my side," Fiona said to them both.

"I'll bet it feels a bit strange," said Gabriella, looking over Fiona's shoulder at Jake who was listening intently.

"You are doing very well, Fiona. Thank you for including me," Jake said.

"I have to admit I had an ulterior motive," Fiona began, smiling.

To this announcement, both Gabriella and Jake blushed and gasped.

"You did?" he said.

"Yes, I did. Well, I figured you are a strong man, so if I needed help, I'd overwhelm poor Gabriella pretty fast. Plus, I figured what better time to have the nurses gather than with walking the patient." Fiona said.

"It appears her logic has returned?" Gabriella replied.

"So it does," said Jake.

Fiona felt comfortable walking with her two friends. It felt a bit like old times. Maybe next time she'd ask only one of them to go with her so she could ask either one of them about it. "Probably," she thought, "Gabriella first."

"You seem to be holding your own pretty well," said Gabriella.

"Faking it, actually, I'd be ok with taking a short cut through station 41 and heading back to my room. Ok?"

"Whatever you say, we'll follow you and support you, you know that!"

This came from Jake and not Gabriella; who was distracted with the other RN's walking patients and the narrowing of the hallway due to their presence.

As another patient and an RN drew closer, the other RN recognized Fiona and Jake, and she also recognized Gabriella. She was looking back and forth from one nurse to the other. She smiled at them and almost greeted Jake with his title but she saw the caution on Gabriella's face and the shake of her head.

Fiona was watching the other patient and wanting to avoid a collision in the narrow space. She realized that in this moment, she was perhaps in better physical condition than the other patient so she moved to the side of the hall next to the wall out of his way.

"Thank you," was all that the other nurse said.

"No problem," said Fiona.

"Here, let me help you," Gabriella said to the other nurse when her patient started to waver. "Jake, can you take Fiona back to her room?"

"Sure," he said.

"Gabriella, what's going on?" said the other nurse, Linda.

"Didn't your unit get the update on Fiona?"

"What update? I've been on maternity leave for the last 3 months."

"Oh my, then you don't know!" Over the next ten minutes Gabriella explained how Fiona had fallen in the showers at the YMCA hitting her head quite hard on the tile floor and has just come out of a two month long coma. "The worst part is she doesn't remember her relationship with Jake!"

"Dr. Davies? Oh gosh! I'm glad I looked at you before I greeted him. I almost called him 'doc' like we always do," she said.

"It is ok, I don't think Fiona noticed."

"Is there anything I can do?"

"Well, we've spoken with her doctor, Dr. Logan."

"Oh good choice, I like Dr. Logan." "Well, as you know, he's the doctor from Jake's practice assigned to Fiona's case. He thinks it best to take things slow and perhaps the cobwebs of Fiona's memory will fill in on their own."

"Jake must have a lot of faith in Robbie Logan. He's pretty special in my book!" Linda said, blushing. Many a nurse had crushes on the dapper doctor.

"Yes, he does."

"Well, thank you for helping me with Mr. Stolkers," she said looking over at her patient as they eased him into the patient recliner in his room.

"Glad to help and to fill you in. Someday soon you'll have to come to Fiona's room with photos of your baby!" she said, as she left the room and headed over to Fiona's room.

As Gabriella walked back to station 51, she saw that Jake and Fiona had not gotten as far ahead of her as she thought. She saw them in intense conversation on the window seat opposite the staff elevators. Without being seen, she reversed turn and kept an eye out from around the corner of the hallway. She hoped Fiona was asking Jake about their relationship, "I hope she has remembered. Remembered him," she said softly.

Taking the public hallway back to station 51 instead of the patient hallway, where she watched Jake and Fiona's conversation, Gabriella sat in Fiona's room and looked at all the cards, letters, flowers, and other mementos hung with care. There were a lot of people concerned about Fiona's recovery, little did she know, and sadly, less had she remembered. This time the moistness in the tears belonged to Gabriella. She sat there quietly in Fiona's room and said a few prayers.

While she was lost in her prayers for Fiona's recovery, Gabriella's cell phone rang catching her off guard. In looking at the displayed number, she saw it was from her husband Nate.

Sniffing before answering, Gabriella said "Hi honey, no she hasn't yet, not right now. She's out walking with Jake. When I left them, they were sitting by the bay window talking quietly. Yes, I know. Me too. No not yet. Yes, I did, what did you eat? Ok, good, I'm going to leave when Fiona returns to her room. That will give them more time alone together tonight. Do you want me to call when I'm leaving? What?"

At the other end of the call, Nate said, "It's storming wildly out here. Tornado warnings were in all the northern New Jersey counties. Can you stay in town, perhaps at Fiona's apartment? You could park her car and wait out the storm in the city. Our power was out just now,"

"Ok then, I agree. I'll get a set of keys from Jake. I'll talk to you in the morning then?"

Waiting to hear his response, Gabriella took a deep wispy breath, the act of which was louder than she had hoped.

Her sigh was easily transmitted over the cell and her husband said, "Do you need me to come in baby?"

"No, Jake's here, I need to be strong for him. I'm all right, we can talk about things when I get home, whenever that is…" she said, her voice trailing off.

"Storm or not, I'll come if you really need me. She is improving, isn't she?"

"Yes, it is just so sad to watch her with Jake. The way she looks at him, it is like they are dating anew all over again. I watched their courtship the first time and while this one is almost the same, it just isn't the same, you know?" Gabriella said wistfully.

"Yes, I know it is hard on everyone. Imagine what Fiona is feeling."

"I am, that's why I'm sad tonight. With her coming out of the coma I thought everything was going to work out just fine," she said.

"It still can," he said.

Pausing before she replied, Gabriella composed herself. "I love you," she said slowly.

"Ditto," quoting his newest favorite movie line.

Gabriella smiled knowing her husband and she remembered each other, she wished that for her friend too. She knew for them it was real. "I'll see you soon, I love you sweetheart. Goodnight."

She closed the flip side of her phone and replaced it back into her pocket. She was strangely reminded of a time when cell phones were forbidden in hospitals. She wished she personally knew or was related to the computer guru who figured out the network and megahertz to allow the use of the cell phone technology in hospitals so that it didn't interfere with their telemetry. She imagined he or she was rather wealthy with that discovery.

Still lost in these random thoughts, Jake and Fiona returned to Fiona's room. They were all smiles but not necessarily romantically inspired. Gabriella figured Fiona was happy to be able to sit again; the walk was more work that she anticipated.

"Welcome back," Gabriella began, "How goes it?"

"Well enough," Fiona said, slightly out of breath.

"Well enough my ass," Jake claimed, "You did great! First walk around the corridor and with only one stop. That's practically a non-stop flight!"

"Very funny, Jake," Fiona said. "Maybe by tomorrow I'll add a non-stop flight, care to get more frequent flyer miles?"

"Oh the member's rewards!"

"Well, on that note," Gabriella began, "I was just talking to Nate. He said there are storms all along the northern Jersey shore and he suggested I stay in the city."

"So you are heading out then?" Jake said.

"Yes, want to see me out?" Gabriella suggested. "That will give Fiona a chance to rest a bit before you two talk away until the next shift change, like during your walk."

"Sure, I'll be right back d, ah, Fiona," Jake said, almost slipping and saying darling.

"I'll be here, they don't seem to want me to leave," Fiona replied, distracted with the television remote control. This was the first time she showed interest in watching TV, Jake made note of it. Something he'd ask her about when he got back.

"Thanks, Jake. I'll see you tomorrow," Gabriella said as she walked over to her friend and enveloped her in a large hug.

"I'll hold you to it!" Fiona said.

"Well if you don't let go of me now, you will be!"

"Very funny. Go be a storm chaser," Fiona suggested.

"Bye," she said.

In the hall, Jake asked Gabriella if there really was a storm. "Storms huh?"

"Actually, there are and Nate wanted me to stay here in the city. Is your apartment available?" she asked.

"Sure, I'll likely camp out in her room or go to the doctor's lounge. Here's a key," he said, handing over a small key ring with an assortment of keys. "The apartment door key has the teal cover on it. I always got it confused with my gym locker so we put a color code on my keys."

"Hey, maybe that will work with her," Gabriella said.

"It's a thought, I'll see if I can weave it into our conversation."

"What were you two talking about so intently during her walk?"

"Fiona is embarrassed at all the attention. She wanted to thank me for spending so much time with her and not apparently at work. She thinks I've traded or given away my 'nursing' shifts so that I can be here with her. I had trouble acting like it was easy to dismiss her and not to worry about me, but she kept after me, wondering if I worked enough shifts since she fell. Her logistical detective brain is working overtime. I can see it in how she is looking at me, she is just placing evidence from different cases into the wrong place. At some point, things will line up for her and I need to be there when that happens. Until then," he said, stopping to look at his audience.

"Well, if you need me to run interference tomorrow or any other day, just let me know. Maybe she is remembering more than we think and is afraid to check into things that don't make sense. Maybe she is afraid to ask that rhetorically 'dumb' question."

"Right."

"What about asking her to participate in a mock neuro status exam on points of memory, play truth or false, with all her evidence, the pieces of her memory that she has recovered?"

"Good idea, make a game or puzzle out of it. She likes puzzles."

"Yes, she does."

"I think that's what I'll suggest when I go back in. She'll likely wonder why her parents ducked out and why you are leaving now too. Wondering why it is that she is always alone with me. I don't know how much longer I can hold back how terrible I've felt watching my wife feel so lost. It is tearing me up inside," Jake confessed.

"I realize how tough this is for you, hopefully it will only be for a little longer," Gabriella said optimistically.

"I just hope we've decided the best course for her care. I feel guilty for not telling her the truth but I'm afraid that the truth, as easy as it is, may be harder for her to comprehend than placating her with her memories of Kurt, Jane, and Ellen."

"Think on it a bit before you go back in. Something will tell you what is best to do, you have good intuition and instincts Jake, use them," Gabriella said in her best nurturing tone.

"Maybe tomorrow morning, while she is bathing and eating, I can run over to the bio-medical library and ask the librarian to send me links to journal articles in this area," he said.

"Good idea, forward them to me. Nate and I'll help you look them over," she offered.

"Thank you. I'm glad you were here with us tonight. I feel we are close to breaking through…" Jake said, his voice and gaze trailing off down the corridor.

Watching her good friend and colleague struggle at a time like this wasn't easy for Gabriella. It isn't for anyone. What she wanted to do was hug him and tell him everything was going to be just fine. But, she couldn't, she didn't believe that completely yet herself, how could she say something like that to Jake? If not for the storm, she would have encouraged Nate to come into town to help her sort out how to best approach this situation, to guide and support her, and their friends.

After a few moments had passed, each of them realized that they had been silent for a brief time and the awkwardness of the posturing grew. "Well, I have to go," Gabriella said, turning to walk away.

"Wait," Jake said. "Thank you, Gabriella, thank you for being here and listening to what I didn't say."

Her non-verbal response, tears and a hug, said it all. She walked away trying to disguise the sobbing that had grown from those first few tears. She hadn't lost control of her emotions since Fiona's injury, everything was sinking in and now she knew it was time for her to grieve for the memory her friend had lost. She knew she hadn't lost her friend, but important parts of her and who she was to her, were still lost in the jumble that was Fiona's mind. She was still waiting for those pieces to fall back into place. So was Jake, he was there, and he was still waiting.

Chapter 18 Memories of Medical School, 1995

When Jake returned to Fiona's room after seeing Gabriella off, he found Fiona already asleep in her hospital bed. Not wanting to disturb her, and still wanting to stay in her room with her, he climbed in and settled himself into the more than uncomfortable recliner the hospital offered as a so-called guest chair.

As he was falling asleep, his mind wandered off to the time when they agreed he should return to school and fill out his medical school applications. Since their marriage four years earlier, he had been working full time as a nurse and over the last two years, studying part time for the MCAT's. He wanted to do as well as possible so that he would place with schools of his choice and not the other way around. Ultimately, they had discussed his attending medical school at one of the many schools in or near New York City.

Since deference was given to NYU Medical Center employees and undergraduates, it only seemed logical and financially responsible for Jake to attend NYU Medical School. With his higher than average MCAT score, undergraduate GPA, current career, and employment, Jake would be a shoe-in to NYU MS. And so he was.

He began medical school in the fall of 1995, and it would be weeks at a time between their dates of any substance. While they did see each other at breakfast, that was often the limit of their daily communication. If Fiona woke up early after working second shift, they'd have breakfast together. Better yet, now that they were living predominantly on only her income, she would often stay overnight at the hospital to work a double shift. On those mornings, Jake met her at the employee cafeteria for her dinner and his breakfast. They'd exchange a kiss after eating and she'd head back to their apartment to sleep and he'd head off to a long day of school.

As the years progressed, his ability to meet for meals depended on the rotations of his clinical experiences, classes, and on call shifts for new admissions. They would have to take his schedule apart and break it down into mini blocks of time in order to see each other as planned. If they didn't, it could easily be a month between scheduled 'dates.'

Fiona didn't mind and never complained. He was fulfilling a life dream, and for these few years, she could navigate as his first mate and be as supportive as was necessary for his sanity. Well, really for her sanity as well. To keep them both happy, they kept each other happy. They got into the habit of leaving each other notes from their respective day or night, and what part of that time had they thought of their spouse. Fiona always enjoyed reading these little notes of thoughtfulness and love, keeping them in a lavender folio for posterity.

It gradually became clear that his program was set up into blocks of achievements, whether during laboratory where he learned a skill; to studying for a test; to learning specific assessments for common diseases; from the classroom which involved a significant amount of reading; to finally clinical time on the wards where the medical students put all they learned together into practice. Throughout his program, there were four hell weeks, when something significant was scheduled or due from each segment of his program all in the same week. As a celebration, they pre-scheduled dates together for the day after each hell week.

She knew he'd want to regroup after the strain of all the coursework, and she wanted him to give undivided attention to his studies. They had determined this plan worked the best. They did, of course, have impromptu dates and times alone, but they couldn't plan around those during hell weeks. An example of an impromptu date was when Jake's assigned patient was on Fiona's unit. They spent most of her shift caring for the same patient and in a verbal seduction that assisted their next dance.

At the end of that shift, their bodies were so in tune with each other, they dashed off to the on call lounge to fulfill this passion. Only, once they got there, the door was locked and the 'occupied' sign was listed. Having spent the entire evening together, and Jake having completed his assessment, diagnosis, and treatment plan, when they discovered their rendezvous point wasn't available, they instead headed home.

Jake had the next morning off from classes and unless something significant occurred with his patient, he could be away for a few hours. They spent their time wisely, their foreplay had been conducted while working Fiona's shift. Their collective juices were flowing over and they took each other on the apartment floor as soon as they closed the door. They didn't even remove all of their clothes for this dance. It was a well needed hard and fast dance, one that they repeated the rest of the morning more comfortably from their bed.

After several rounds of pleasure, Fiona said, "Follow me," and she seductively wiggled from their bed into the bathroom where she immediately climbed into the shower.

He joined her there as the steam began to hide their view.

"You look so adorable when your body is lathered up with soap," Fiona said, helping apply the suds, her strong hands determined with their movements.

"Mmm," Jake softly moaned. "I think you like the application more than the production it makes," he said, looking at his own firmness. He enjoyed the way she played with him in the shower, knowing it would be his turn to play with her body in an oily backrub once they finished in the shower.

As the hours passed with each shared orgasm, their thirsts for each other's body was coupled with their true thirst. They were close to consuming all of the coffee, tea, juice, and soda in their kitchen when Fiona noted the time. They had one last body quench in the shower, as they shared the last dance dripping wet in the steamed confines of their bathtub shower.

They emerged from their apartment in time for a late lunch. They were pleased with themselves but still hungry for more. Patients and patience, they agreed, was how they would make it through the next 18 months. It was almost the finish line of Jake's medical school program when they were faced with another time consuming issue. It would be perhaps the biggest decision they would face as a young couple. Would they, could they, handle his acceptance into a fellowship program, with as few personal hours as in medical school? They knew if they proceeded this way, their lovemaking routines would have to become more succinct and measured.

Over lunch at a neighborhood café, they confirmed his future and concurred that her career would remain unchanged, at least for now. She was moving up in the nursing seniority on her unit, but they would figure out something for her down the road, and they had plenty of time to do so.

When their order arrived, following her first bite into her burger, a stray spray of ketchup lingered on the corner of her mouth. Jake leaned over from his chair. Fiona smiled, thinking he was coming in for another kiss. Instead, it was a lick, and then a kiss as he removed the traces of the redness that had run afoul upon her face.

"Mmm, thank you," Fiona said, "do we have time to go home?" She was hinting at a repeat of their morning's activities.

"Sorry, love, afraid not. I can be away a little but not all day. Maybe tonight when you get home, I'll be home and be ready and waiting for you," he said licking his lips with her scent and the ketchup mixed together.

"I'll finish up as fast as I can and taxi home for an offer like that!"

"Check please!" he called.

He fondly remembered their late morning and afternoon romps whenever he had a half day off. They were both surprised that in the process she had never gotten pregnant either. In the back of their minds, though, they both thought it was for the best, it would be difficult to care for a growing family while their careers were still in bloom.

"C-R-A-S-H!"

Jake heard the noise from his chair waking him up and bringing him back to the present. He took a moment to adjust to his surroundings and then recalled the nightmare that was now his life. Where was Fiona? Turning to the direction of the noise, yet in the darkness of her room, he couldn't quite detect where it came from. Had he fallen asleep? Had he been dreaming of their early life, so wanting to relive the past in view of Fiona's current mental state? Either way, he was now attending to the noises coming from the bathroom.

"What was that?" he mumbled. Then looking at Fiona's bed, his eyes had adjusted well enough to the darkness and he realized she was no longer sleeping and must have gotten out of bed. "I hope that noise wasn't Fiona falling!" he said.

"C-R-A-S-H!" a bit louder this time.

Again the noise came from the bathroom a few feet from Fiona's bed. Walking towards the bathroom door, at the end of her bed, Jake was surprised by Karin, the night nurse Fiona referred to as granny due to her plump frame and short bent stature.

"What was that?" she said, walking into the room and bumping into Jake in the process. "Oh, Dr. Davies, I didn't know you were in here, you gave me a start," she said with a hand to her chest.

They moved together into the area in front of the slightly ajar bathroom door and he watched for the interior contents of the bathroom as Karin reached for and opened the bathroom door.

"Oh, no!" Jake exclaimed. "FIONA!"

Lying on the floor of the bathroom, amongst a messy pile of dry and wet towels, lay Fiona, slumped atop the pile, eyes shut and unmoving. On the floor, next to her was a water pitcher, the remaining contents of which had been sprayed about the tiled floor, the jug leaking the remaining contents in time with the water running from the tap.

What they didn't yet know was in her late night stupor and sleepless state, Fiona awoke thirsty, and in finding her water jug empty, got out of bed. On her way to the bathroom sink, she put on the flimsy hospital slippers which she thought were more like socks than formal shoes, and she walked weakly into the bathroom and turned on the faucet. She reached out her hand to check the temperature when she dropped the water pitcher onto the floor. She had been trying to bring it up to the tap and had misjudged the height of the countertop, slamming the jug into the side of the countertop and in her surprise, let the jug fall to the floor. Her left hand was wet with water.

The first crash was her startled reaction to the clumsiness of hitting the jug on this surface. But the second, louder crash was Fiona herself, when she fell upon hearing the nurse say, "Dr. Davies."

She landed in a ball, coiled up right where she fell upon the tiled area just inside the bathroom and next to the toilet. Looking from Fiona's slumped frame up to Karin, Jake said, "I think she was thirsty, it looks like she managed to turn on the water but how and why she fell is a mystery."

"Wow, is she all right? Does she have a pulse?" Karin said urgently.

"Yes, she's fine, I think she's fainted. She has a history of fainting when she's excited, tired, hot, or all of the above. It is hot in here," Jake said, turning to the open bathroom door and the air conditioning vent back by his guest chair. "Let me get some air in here and see if she wakes on her own."

"Are you sure, don't we need to call a code?" Karin said, a bit out of sorts.

"No, she's fine. Look, her facial color is normal, her body is a bit warmer than normal, and her pulse is 85," he said, removing his hand from her wrist. "No, I think all she needs now is some air, and water-apparently."

He sat down next to his wife's curled up still unmoving frame and cradled her body onto his lap. And there he sat, waiting. Waiting for her to come back to him. Again.

Chapter 19 Scottish Highlands, 1991

It was well after three o'clock in the afternoon when they woke, their tub dance and buffet ending in the late morning. Jake was the first to stir, and feeling a bit stiff from their current repertoire, decided to repeat a few stanzas before beginning their day. But first, he regarded his new bride, she lay there upon her side facing away from him, her long hair flowing down her back and resting in a coil behind her. He loved her hair and the smell of it either dirty or right out of the shower; for it was these auburn tresses that had first caught his attention about the nurse ahead of him in the employee cafeteria line. He remembered thinking that day that she had the most beautiful hair, he'd like to get to know her, better, much better.

He pulled the covers off his legs and lowered them to just below Fiona's shapely bottom. He enjoyed waking her from behind when they woke up spooning. As he nestled himself between her legs, he could sense she was already waiting for him. Their dance that morning was slow and sweet and when they were finished they once again curled up into each others' arms and slept.

They knew that this may be one the few times during their honeymoon for them to sleep in and be together. They hadn't planned on staying in one place longer than 3-4 days, unlike other people who take cruises, go to the Caribbean or some other exotic locale the entire honeymoon. No, they had planned to see as much of Scotland as they could, while the weather held, and time permitted. They would pack up and leave in the morning; it had been agreed when they walked home from Tummel Crescent.

This time when one of them woke, it was Fiona, her stomach giving her away with its loud growling. She noted that Jake didn't move when she sat up in bed, so she quietly made her way to the bathroom to complete her rather tardy toilette. She emerged from the bathroom in a cloud of steam with a smile upon her face.

Sitting on edge of their bed was Jake, still naked but behind a room service trolley with a brunch for two fashioned upon it. "Coffee, tea, or me?" he said smiling.

"Hello darling, I thought that was my line?"

"Well," he snickered, "Can I borrow it this day?"

"Sure," she said softly, walking towards him.

"And lass, what is ye'r answer then?" he said in his best Scottish accent, still thickly Americanized.

"All three," she said. "But I'll start with tea."

"Very well, then, I'll have some coffee with my tart."

"We have tarts?" she mused.

"Fiona, darling, the most fanciful tart, eh, sweet I know!"

"Given our location, I'll tolerate and allow you 'tart' but not when we get home, deal?"

"Deal. Now come kiss your husband good day!"

He took her once more, briefly and smeared in strawberry jam. After showering again, they decided their sightseeing for the day would have to be cut short, or allow for darkness. They spoke with the front desk for a restaurant recommendation and made a reservation for nine o'clock. They decided in the end, that a walk about town, window shopping and snooping suited them the best given the hour.

They walked north on West Moulin Road and through the shopping areas, cut across some smaller alleys, when Jake saw the Pitlochry Golf Course. They turned left at the golf course and walked by more houses before they finally arrived at the Pine Trees Hotel. This charming little inn was as its name foretold, was nestled amongst some aromatic pines. Their walk took them the long way arriving about a quarter hour late for their reservation. However, this being mid-week and after nine o'clock, they could see only the patrons of the place were drinking in the bar.

As they entered, they also noted the gardener's touch about the front steps with all the wildflower hanging baskets and potted perennials dotting the front stoop. It was a pretty scene, especially in the fading evening sun. Jake positioned Fiona back outside for a photo. Seeing them creating and framing a shot, the hostess offered to take the photo for them so they would both be in the picture.

Once they were seated and had ordered drinks, they looked about their surroundings, and now noticed for the first time a few other dining patrons. The table by the window featured what looked like an elderly grey haired and diminutive Asian woman with her adult children, and grandchildren. From their vantage point, it appeared to be a birthday celebration. They couldn't quite hear how old she was but were happy for them just the same. Caring for the elderly in their duties at the hospital, any birthday was always one worth celebrating.

Fiona decided she was actually hungrier than she thought when they first walked in. She had thought of splitting an entrée with Jake but when she saw Parma Ham, and Celeriac Remoulade starter, she changed her mind. "Did you see the starters?"

"Yes, I know which one I'm getting; you love that thin ham don't you?"

"Yes, I love it, ever since Ellen and I ate it during our time in Germany. She was the one who encouraged me to try it. What are you getting for your main course?"

"I was thinking of the lamb, and you?"

"Well, while I see they have prime rib or fillets of beef, I actually think with the ham, I'd have the risotto with wild mushrooms and parmesan. That is, if you care to share a bit of your lamb with your sweetie?"

"Sounds good to me, I think I'll have a field green salad and cheese platter to start, that should be nice and light for the lamb. Which I'm quite willing to share," he smiled.

"What are you going to drink?"

"Wine?"

"Yes, I think I'll have some wine," she agreed. "Which one?"

She handed him the wine list which had been conveniently tucked inside her menu. She loved drinking wine but hadn't become as learned as Jake had when it came to actually choosing a brand from a list. "I think I'll have a Shiraz, they list several from Australia, sound good to you darling?"

"I'm sure it will be fabulous," she said agreeably.

Their waiter arrived a short time later, took down their order, and soon returned with their starters. They also agreed on a bottle of wine, which he brought up to them next. He poured a sample into a glass, and Jake tasted it and agreed it was more than suitable. The waiter left after pouring them half a glass each.

They ate slowly, savoring all the flavors and rich textures of the food from this region of Scotland. As Fiona had predicted, they also needed to order another bottle of wine. Since they were walking back to the B & B, they imbibed a bit more. Also, if they decided they drank too much, the innkeeper could call them a taxi. A small town such as Pitlochry surely still operated at least one taxi a night.

After their very delicious meal, they walked home, not too drunk to get lost and not too drunk to find their destination safely. Despite the long day, they danced once more before finally fading off into dreamland, satisfied, mind, body, and soul. Her dreams that night took her back to Edinburgh, retracing her family's ancestry in that historic city on the cliffs. Perhaps she would enjoy tea with crumpets?

Chapter 20 Remembering Tea and Crumpets, 1985

"Hello?" Jake said, answering their phone at their home in Elizabeth.

"Jake, Ian MacLaren calling," Ian said.

"Hi Dad, how are you?"

"Fine Jake, just fine. As you know, we've been home for the last week and we will be back in New York day after tomorrow. We wanted to check with you on the status of Fiona's care. Has Dr. Logan continued with his request for Fiona to continue her memory work from the past and is she still recounting her time in Europe?"

"Yes Dad, that's still the plan," Jake replied.

"Ok, we'll call you once we are settled at the Waldorf Astoria," Ian said, then muffling the phone with his hand. He spoke to Maureen. "Let's take him out for dinner, sushi again?"

"Oh, yes, that would be delightful," Maureen confirmed, smiling broadly.

"Jake?"

"Yes, dad?" Jake said, waiting on the line during the somewhat muffled silence.

"Are you on call on Friday night? How about we go to Maureen's favorite Sushi Bar?" Ian asked.

Checking his digital pocket calendar schedule, "No, I'm free. That would be nice Dad."

"Great, we will call you after we visit with Fiona."

"Alright Dad, sounds good to me. Have a safe trip. I know Fiona will be glad to see you. I know you've only been gone a week, but I'm hoping you will see the improvement that Gabriella and I are seeing. I hope we can get through that brain of hers and bring her back to the present."

"Me too son, me too."

They ended the call and were both a bit shaken. The waiting and the not knowing how Fiona's post-coma recovery would unfold were beginning to take a toll.

As planned, the flight was uneventful and once settled into their usual suite at the Waldorf; their hired car drove them over to NYU Medical Center. Fiona's parents were exchanging their unspoken language in the limo and as they walked through the hospital lobby, Maureen reached for Ian's hand.

Hand in hand they took the ride in the elevator to her floor and walked the short distance to her room. They entered after a quick knock.

"Come in," Fiona's voice replied from behind the closed door.

"Hello dear," said Maureen and repeated by Ian.

"Hi!" Fiona said, smiling and pleased at her new guests.

"We're back for a few days dear, what's new?" Ian asked.

"Well, I'm allowed out of my room for walks now. I can go either further out on the unit or even the around grounds for walks about three times a day. I'm even getting a bit stronger."

"I'm so glad to hear it," said Maureen, her eyes slightly moist. "How about a walk now?"

"Sounds good to me, let me bring my hot tea." Fiona said, looking at the large portable container of tea that her nurse had recently brought to her.

"Just tea?" Maureen asked, "No crumpets?"

"Tea and crumpets, that's what I had with Aunt Rhona, remember?" Fiona said. "Let's go outside and I'll show you the memorial garden."

Her parents followed as she lead them through the hospital and out onto the grounds to a small oasis of greenery amongst the gray cement that was the large city of Manhattan.

During his next visit, Fiona recounted her walk and talk with her parents, that they'd visited the memorial garden and had reminisced about Fiona's 'aunt' Rhona. Fiona was smiling at her recollection when Jake knocked on her patient room door.

"Come in," Fiona replied.

"Hi, Fiona, how are you feeling today?" Jake asked. "Are you up for another walk?"

"Hi Jake, I'm getting stronger every day. A walk sounds lovely," Fiona replied.

Fiona followed Jake's lead off her unit, through the hospital, and out to her favorite garden bench. Once seated Jake asked, "Shall we have another story today?"

"Sure, have I ever told you about the time I went to see my 'aunt' Rhona?" Fiona asked Jake.

Fiona started once they were situated on the cement bench, "These benches remind me of a taxi stand in Edinburgh and Winnie's best friend."

"Is that where Rhona lived?" Jake asked, not recalling the particular friendships of his mother-in-law's mother.

"Yes, that's where I met that great taxi driver…" Fiona said. "Let me tell you…"

Fiona began with the conversation with the taxi driver as she gave the driver the address to 'aunt' Rhona's apartment building and she sat back to take in the sights.

The weather was still mild and windy, making Fiona glad of her further plans for indoor activities. Sightseeing in a horizontal rain and trying to take quality photographs were seriously elusive on challenging weather days like these. She knew she would share with Ellen her thoughts about keeping backup plans in the case of inclement weather. An early fall in Europe was typically dry and the tourist traffic was lighter, and these were the two driving forces behind their choice of travel dates.

"Here you are, lassie," said the taxi driver, bringing Fiona back to the present.

"Thank you," Fiona replied, and handed him sufficient money to cover the meter and a modest tip.

She slipped out of the taxi and began looking at the street. It took her a few minutes to find the correct address; she discovered a private gate amongst all the row houses. "This was the address," Fiona said to herself, looking at her trip diary and the information her Mother had given her prior to leaving Minnesota. She approached the private gate and found a buzzer. Depressing the buzzer, she heard a quick click next to her as the gate popped open.

A voice on the intercom said, "Please come in, child," and Fiona hope that the voice belonged to Rhona.

Once inside, Fiona found the private gate was the entry point to a small cottage sized home nestled between multistoried buildings with multiple flats and larger apartments. The patchwork limestone walk had a mixture of stones and grasses that led to the front door. It was lined with simple flowers, perhaps perennials, Fiona thought, so it would be less maintenance for an older woman.

On the front stoop, however, was an arrangement of various sized terracotta pots, which held on one side marigolds and petunias, and a thickly foliaged green plant Fiona didn't recognize. On the other side there were pots of mums and snapdragons, daisies and violets, and above her head, Fiona saw some hanging baskets with petunias. The aroma in peak season must have been very pleasant, she thought. The bees were probably in Nirvana with all the tempting pistils to choose from in this small space.

Fiona walked inside the archway leading to the front door and before she could press the doorbell, the door opened and a small elderly woman was staring up at her from the open doorway. "Fiona?" she said.

"Yes, that's me. Are you Rhona?" Fiona asked gingerly.

"I certainly am, deary. Please come right in and warm yourself by the fire."

Fiona wasn't exactly freezing from the inclement weather, but warming her hands would be comforting just now and if that meant doing so by a fire, all the better. "Thank you."

"Come sit down in the parlor, I'll just put the kettle on."

Following Rhona from the hall, Fiona walked into the parlor and noticed two brocade covered armchairs aimed in front of a small peat fireplace. A few bricks of peat were already snapping and popping on the hearth cradle. The emanating scent was very distinctive.

"There now, isn't that better?" Rhona asked, as she returned from the kitchen and sat down opposite Fiona. "Tea will be ready momentarily."

"Actually, I didn't realize how nice this could feel; I really didn't think I was that cold. It does feel nice and cozy."

"I can't get over it," Rhona said, looking at Fiona and marveling at her sitting in her chair, in her wee house. "You are Winnie's granddaughter all right, just look at you. Wait a minute; I have some <u>verrry</u> old photographs taken before Winnie left on the ship. Let me get them, I pulled them out when I heard you were coming. They are just in the other room."

Fiona was getting more and more accustomed to the Scottish brogue and could understand more easily this elderly woman. Though, sometimes she had to repeat the words in her head to make sure she had fully understood what was said. She had hoped she would have been able to decipher the accent sooner than this.

"Here we are, now, take a look at these," Rhona said proudly. "I was about 13 or perhaps 14 in these. Winnie was a year or so younger. We were such good friends, I was sorry to hear she was moving so far away. See, look at this one, the resemblance is just remarkable."

"I know what you mean. One time when I was visiting Grandmother in Manitoba, she showed me her bobbed ponytail. She had preserved it intact in a shoebox. We took it out and held the long strands next to my own hair and it was an exact match. I do think though that I got my lack of height from Rachel, my Father's Mother."

"I'm sorry these are so faded, and only in black and white, that was all we had in those days. But I remember her beautiful long thick auburn hair, she wore it longer than you do and I think yours is curlier. Oh my dear, you have brought back so many wonderful childhood memories."

The conversation was now interrupted by the kettle's whistle from the kitchen. "Oh that will be the tea?" Fiona asked, "Can I help you with it?"

"Aren't you a sweet girl, I'd be delighted."

Fiona stood now and assisted her elderly friend to her feet and together they walked into the kitchen, primed the tea pot with a bit of hot water to heat up the porcelain, set out two tea cups and saucers, and then filled the pot after draining out the original hot water. Aunt Rhona suggested she carry the tray of goodies if Fiona would bring out the tea and they would pour in the parlor.

Rhona explained that the cracker looking cakes were groat cakes, the others a buttery scone with blackberries, and last, the very rich yellow pound cake. She had chosen English Tea Time for the tea and served both their tea with a splash of milk. Of the carbohydrate rich treats, Fiona could not select a favorite, they were all equally delicious.

They spent the rest of the afternoon and early evening reminiscing about life in Edinburgh at the turn of the century and what Rhona's life had been like, especially after Fiona's Grandmother had emigrated to Canada from her native Scotland. Fiona learned that the elderly women had stayed in contact by post and in person with visits about every 1-2 decades, mostly with 'Winnie' returning to Scotland.

As the afternoon sky drew dim, Fiona realized it was likely closing in on the time for her to depart. She asked permission to use the telephone to call for a taxi. She didn't want to take her chances, in this more remote section of Edinburgh, and the likelihood of not finding a taxi once she was out on the street. The timing she thought was good as she had noticed that Aunt Rhona had some difficulty keeping up with the conversation. Fiona thought that she was likely quite tired after spending an afternoon with a 22-year-old. As a parting thought, Fiona requested they pose for a few photographs; these ones would be in color. Fiona promised to send a copy to Aunt Rhona and to her Grandmother.

The goodbyes were bittersweet knowing that this frail bitty was closer to her end in years than she had wished. Fiona collected her entire postal code and promised to write when she returned home. As a parting gift, Fiona left a small package of Minnesota wild rice on the kitchen counter, something Aunt Rhona could discover after Fiona had left. Beside the rice was a little note explaining how much Fiona had enjoyed their chat and would share a fond hug with her Grandmother when she next saw her.

As predicted, the taxi's horn produced a short blast in a trio of tones indicating its arrival. Having already said her goodbyes, Fiona proceeded to the curb where the taxi was waiting. With her camera out in hand, Fiona requested one more photo from Aunt Rhona. Fiona posed the wee Scottish lady on her petite front stoop, amongst the colorful floral canopy she had so masterfully created. Waving from the taxi, Fiona watched the little woman as she faded and shrank into the backdrop with each roll of the taxi's tires.

Fiona took a few moments in the back of the taxi to make footnotes of her visit with her Grandmother's dear old friend, and hoped that the personal reconnection with her visit was as satisfying to Aunt Rhona as it was to her. Back at the youth hostel, the Austrian women weren't in the room. Fiona had spent the last few days touring castles and cathedrals with these two travelers.

Fiona took this time to write the postcards she had purchased at Jenner's. The five lucky recipients of these postcards were: her parents, Harriet, Grandmother Winnie, one to Muriel, and lastly, one to her Grandfather MacLaren.

As she was licking the stamps on the completed postcards, she heard voices in the hallway. These voices were gradually growing louder and louder until they entered her room. As Fiona expected, Farahilde and Annaliese, the Austrian women, were back from their sightseeing. They sounded a bit like they'd also spent some time in a pub, as their voices were much louder than the occasion called for.

"Glad to see you back Fiona. We found the most fantastic pub," said Annaliese.

"Really, I couldn't tell you'd been to a pub," Fiona said, playfully.

"Did you eat dinner yet?" Annaliese asked.

"No, I was thinking of eating the miscellaneous items I got at the grocery store since I didn't see you up here."

"Well, we've been waiting to go to dinner with *you*. The pub also has a kitchen, are you ready to go?"

"Sure, sounds like fun," Fiona replied.

"That's a good girl; we'll help you exchange that serious look for something else, anything but serious. And oh boy, are you in for a great feast for the eyes, just wait until you check out the bartender, Keith. We told him we'd be back with you. He loves Americans, so he's all excited to meet you!"

"Ok, let me just change out of these clothes into something more appropriate for a pub. Look at these sweaters I got today. I think I'll put on the green cardigan set with jeans."

"Oh, very cute sweaters, where did you find them?" said Annaliese.

"In the department store, Jenner's, it is across from the Balmoral Hotel on Princes St. I even found a huge steal on china and ordered some to be shipped home." Fiona said, as she disrobed and changed from her polo shirt into the warmer sweater set.

Annaliese was wearing a red pullover sweater with soft brown corduroys and a pretty silk scarf at the neck. Farahilde was dressed in a long sleeved oxford shirt with an argyle sweater vest in pastels and pinks. Fiona's green cardigan reflected the dress code the other women were sporting.

They made their way down to the street via the oversized freight elevator and walked along the vacant sidewalk to the pub. Fiona explained that her plans for the next day were to visit a library and do some research on her family tree. Meaning, she could be out late, and not be concerned with the consequences of a late night the next day.

The pub, as it were, was more a combination of a local's eatery that served alcohol. It was filled with people who were either on their way home from work or had decided to eat out like these three women. The atmosphere was highly charged and quite apparent within moments of entry. In one corner, people were singing to the juke box, while in another, there seemed to be a serious game of darts, with side bets and other wagers on each toss of the pointed miniature missiles.

Keith was still behind the bar and waved at the women as they made their way back to the bar stools they had left a short while ago. "Here she is, Keith. Isn't she a charmer?" said Farahilde.

"Aye, a very bonny lass indeed. What's your pleasure, lassie?" he asked congenially.

"I'd like a rum and coke please, and could we get some menus, as we'd like to have some dinner?" Fiona answered.

"Very good," he said, and reaching from below the bar, he produced three pub menus and handed them to the women. "Another pint of Guinness for you two?" he assumed.

"Yes, please," said Farahilde, while Annaliese nodded.

"I see what you mean. This is a nice place. You have popular American songs on the juke box, isn't that a Stevie Wonder song on right now?" Fiona questioned her ability to identify popular music. She was more of a listener than an aficionado.

"I think so, I like it," said Annaliese. "What are you going to order for dinner? Earlier we saw some great looking fish and chips, and the burgers looked really good too."

"I think I might have a grilled chicken sandwich; it looks like it comes with fries. I don't want to eat burgers every night," she said, with an emphasis on 'every night.' "What are you going to order?"

"I like fish and chips here better than at home, so I think that's what I'll have," said Annaliese. "Farahilde, what looks good to you?"

"Sounds like a good idea to me. I liked the looks of them too."

As the women looked up at Keith, practically in unison, he knew they were ready to order. Turning to Farahilde first, he said, "What can I order for you, lassie?" he said listening to her order and confirming it. "And for you?" he asked Annaliese, "And for the American lassie, what can I get for you? I'm sorry to say Keith is not on the menu," he said with a teasing smile.

So far this trip, that was the most forward of any of the men Fiona had met. She thought perhaps it was also the only man even remotely close to her age that she met either. She just smiled and said, "Chicken."

Her answer and timing were not lost on her new friends or on Keith. The laughter that erupted from that portion of the bar caused the locals to take notice. Keith looked up from the bar and explained he'd have to fill them in on the joke later.

After everyone's stomachs had recovered from laughing, they were filled with their dinners. Annaliese said she would have to share that joke with her friends at home. It was just the most perfect line to use in a foreign bar. She couldn't believe she had been a witness to it. "Well done, Fiona, well done," she repeated over and over, most of the rest of the night.

While they didn't close the pub like some of the locals might do on a regular basis, they were out much later than any of them had been in quite a while. When they were walking back to the hostel, it occurred to Fiona, would they be able to get back inside coming back this late? She looked at her watch and saw that it was almost 3:00AM. Then she remembered what Garrett had said when they checked in, "...and the front doors after hours." Then to the women she said, "Our room keys will let us in after hours, did you bring yours?" Fiona asked, slightly panicked that she had forgotten it. In the rush to change clothes and head out for dinner, Fiona recalled in her mind's eye, her key was left squarely on her bunk bed, no use to her now.

"I didn't, did you Farahilde?"

After a concerned look faded from her face, and a delay of pantomiming the search for said key, Farahilde said, "Yes I did, aren't you glad you stayed out late with me, now?"

She was slobbering her words but not slurring; there was a difference. Fiona knew the next day her new friend might not feel up to breakfast, but hopefully she could sleep off all the extra pints Keith had served her.

Upstairs again via the large lift, the women got ready for bed, and Fiona whispered to Annaliese whether Farahilde would need any help. "Oh no, she's got this routine down. She'll be fine. Goodnight," she whispered back.

"Goodnight," Fiona replied in her hushed voice. She was asleep moments after hitting the pillow. Her dreams this night involved an amazing assortment of china in large boxes loaded into a lift that opened onto a floral garden terrace with a peak-a-boo gate which had a buzzer that bleated like a fog horn.

Chapter 21 Still in Scotland Finding Family, 1985

"I can see why you were fond of those girls," Jake said at last, still sitting on the cement bench they found out on the hospital grounds during their walk.

"Yes, they made good traveling companions. You know, I think it was the next day that I went out to see where my Grandmother Winnie had lived. Did I ever tell you about that?"

"I don't think so," Jake said, settling in again on the grass, the cement benches had long since lost their allure.

"Ok, well, I started my day a bit earlier than usual," Fiona began.

It was now about 8:25AM, and as was her norm, Fiona woke up a few minutes before the alarm would chime. She left her watch on her bunk bed while she was in the shower room and she set her little travel alarm clock for 8:30AM. "I think today is Tuesday," Fiona muttered, softly, as she got up to shower and dress.

The weather report from Monday's *USA Today* had said Tuesday would be a repeat of Monday's cooler wet windy weather. She planned to get a head start on the day without her Austrian friends who said at the pub last night, after they nursed their hangovers, they would likely be going to the National Portrait Gallery and other such museums in Edinburgh.

Last night, Fiona had explained to them that her Grandmother was born in Edinburgh and she was going to go and look for her house. They knew that was likely why she hadn't had as much to drink as they did at the pub with Keith the bartender. They'd also been supportive of Fiona's decision to forego attending the viewing of old unknown peoples in lieu of searching for her own family. They knew they didn't need to spend all their time together; Fiona was an independent young woman.

Dressed in jeans and a long-sleeved shirt, Fiona headed downstairs for breakfast. The line was short at this hour, and also because the hostel didn't have as many occupants as it did just a week ago. Fiona felt fortunate that she'd spent those days in the English countryside instead of fighting the throngs of tourists up here. The food here was offered cafeteria style but without any hot food offering. Perhaps Fiona had been spoiled by Una with the cooked English breakfasts. Fiona would make a mental note regarding the hostels' food offerings, likely lighter fare than expected. One should carry a snack or access food whenever it was observed. To Fiona, that meant she could nibble her way across Europe, one snack at a time.

Settling for corn flakes, milk, toast, and coffee-the hot chocolate dispensing machine was on the blink, or so the sign indicated-and orange juice. When Fiona headed to the seating area after finishing through the cafeteria line, she missed her footing, tripped, and fell with corn flakes, toast, and all the liquids going flying through the air. Fiona landed with the tray in her hands but nothing else. Fortunately, her solo food fight remained a solo event, as her breakfast did not strike any would-be food fighting opponent. Instead, it was strewn all about the floor, save for a few corn flakes now in Fiona's curly locks.

Back at college, whenever anyone stumbled or dropped food or china like this, there would have been applause from the other diners. It was strange not to hear that now, as she most assuredly would take first place in the 'lacking grace this morning' category of breakfast time awards. Fiona moved quietly to help the hostel kitchen staff clean up her mess, and then she was allowed back through the line. At the end of it, though, was one of the kitchen workers who said, "I'll carry your tray for you, lassie," to which Fiona gratefully acquiesced.

At last successfully seated, Fiona began to eat her second first helping of breakfast in quiet solitude. She was still wondering how many pairs of eyes were watching her, and what they were thinking about her. Nothing could be helped, trips happen.

After finishing with breakfast in such exquisite fashion, Fiona dropped by the front desk to ask about the location of a good library for her research. The desk clerk suggested, "Oh lassie, I'd go to the National Library of Edinburgh, that's where I'd go." The way this clerk pronounced 'go' sounded more like goo than go which made Fiona smile.

The clerk also wrote down the address and drew out a wee map. The library was not far from the castle on George IV Bridge. Fiona thought she had seen this building when walking through town earlier, but wasn't sure. Sometimes old buildings begin to look the same, the viewer's challenge was to remember which building was in which city and what the occupants were.

"Should I take a taxi there?" Fiona asked, wondering if the library was within walking distance or not.

"If you walked to the castle, it is just about 6 blocks south, but almost all uphill. I can ring a taxi for you if you like. You could always walk back, no?"

"Yes, excellent point. Could you please call a taxi service for me?" Fiona requested. "Do you have any taxis you recommend?" "Yes we do, we recommend Drew's Taxi to our guests. When would you like him to arrive dear?"

"How about in 15 minutes? I should be ready by then. Do you have any paper I could have, you know, something to write a note on? Yes, that size would be great, thank you," Fiona said to the clerk, leaving him to his work. While she wrote the note, the clerk called for her taxi.

Back in the oversized bunk room, Fiona gathered up her suitcase and daypack. She would store the suitcase in the large lockers just like she did the previous day, and take the daypack with her. She also had the trip diary and her money belt. On the piece of paper from the front desk, Fiona had composed a note to the Austrian women indicating she'd be out most of the day and would be back in time for dinner. This was her last night in Edinburgh before heading to York and Oxford on her way back to London.

On her way downstairs, Fiona stored her suitcase and retained the key from the storage locker in her money belt. As she exited the hostel, she saw a car, the now familiar black vehicles that were used predominantly for United Kingdom taxis.

Fiona said to the driver, "Hi, I'd like to go to the National Library of Edinburgh, inside they said it was in the direction of the castle. I'm sure you know where it is."

"Oh aye, lassie. What do you want to go there for, have you forgotten to bring something to read?"

"Oh, no I have plenty to read, I'm researching tartans and family lines. I have Scottish ancestors on all sides and wanted to see if we could add to our information about family while I was here."

"Well then, I'd expect that would be the right place to go. Shall we?"

"Yes thank you."

Along the drive, Fiona was able to take in the castle high up on its perch. The weather today was improving with each hour. The wind had tapered off and the temperatures were climbing as the clouds faded. "No more horizontal rain," Fiona thought.

Moments later, the taxi pulled into the loading zone in front of the library. It was an impressively mammoth structure. The limestone edifice was showing its durable construction and was typical of larger buildings of the time. Inside, Fiona asked for the reference section. She was told that the entire library was essentially a reference library. No books were available to lend. "If you go upstairs, Miss, someone behind the circular desk can help you," said a clerk.

"Thank you very much," Fiona replied.

Upstairs was like going into the stacks at the library at Fiona's college, minus all the stacks. The grand open spaces replaced a good portion of the stacks of bookshelves Fiona had expected in the 'upstairs.' Eventually Fiona walked into the second floor far enough to see a circular desk, and as she expected, there was an older woman behind it, but, not dowdy looking as she would have supposed. Fiona approached the desk and waited for the librarian to look up from her work.

"May I help you, lass? I'm the head librarian and historian," she said.

"Yes, I'm interested in conducting some family ancestry work and tartan research. I'm not really sure where to start." Fiona began and then noticed her nameplate said, 'Mrs. Maira MacFarlane, Head Librarian/ Historian.' "Are you Mrs. MacFarlane?" Fiona asked.

"Yes, I am, but you can call me Maira. You are in the right place for all of that. You'll want to go into our secured reference section. You'll need a reader's ticket to enter that area. You'll need to provide evidence of your identification in order to enter."

Looking a bit flustered at this heightened level of security, Fiona said, "What kind of identification do you require?"

"Are you American?"

"Yes I am."

"Do you have a driver's license or a passport with you?"

"Yes, I have my passport with me. May I ask again why you need that? I was cautioned not to let anyone have access to my passport."

"Anyone entering the reading room must provide to the librarian, me, proof of their identity and that seems to be your only proof available to you."

"Alright, I understand. This is all new to me, I just wanted to be sure," Fiona said feeling small.

"Don't fret, it happens all the time. What are you looking for? Perhaps I can point out some good volumes for you in the reading room."

"Well, some of my lineage is really well documented, and we have names going back to the 1600's. Other lines are less informed and I'd like to look at those. Like my Grandfather McCallum, I don't have a lot of information about him or his lineage. Also, I'd like to get a kilt made, and I want to look at all my options. Is there an official book on tartans?"

"Well, that is a lot of work. How long are you staying in Edinburgh?"

"I'm leaving tomorrow. Why?"

"Well my dear, we have some people that have been doing what you are looking to do for the past year or longer. Sometimes, depending on the available information, it takes a lot longer. Maybe I could help you refine your research into a couple of key areas, would that be helpful?"

"I didn't realize this could take so long. Yes, what do you suggest that would accomplish some of what I want to do?"

"Maybe you could concentrate on answering a few things. Perhaps it would be good to determine the specific clan memberships and their tartans? Next time, when you have more time, you can do the full lineage work. It is a very slow process and a lot of reading, I'm afraid to say."

"Ok, that sounds like a good plan. I didn't realize I had bitten off more than I could chew. What about a book that explains the clans, septs, and related families? After I'm finished with that, I'll come find you for the tartan information. Would that be all right?" Fiona suggested.

"Now you have a good plan."

"Then here's my passport and let the research begin," Fiona said.

"Very good dear, let me just issue you a reading room reader's ticket. I'll need to get that back from you in order to return your passport. So it will be a very important document, don't lose it."

"Wow, you sound just like my Mother!"

"She's a good woman. Here you go," said Maira, who had finally warmed up.

"Thank you."

"Follow me," Maira said, and she led Fiona into the single story rows of bookshelves. "I think these books in this section will be the most useful.

There is scratch paper by the card catalog chest of drawers should you want to take more notes than the paper you have with you. Now is there anything else?"

"What about enough time to perform the research properly," Fiona said, with a slight laugh.

"That's all up to you deary," she said, with a knowing smile. "Good luck, now."

Over the next few hours, Fiona scoured over a host of oversized dusty reference books and felt like she was attempting to find the proverbial needle. She took notes of all the grandparents' names and what names she knew of their respective parents. Next, Fiona determined if each of the names was a clan or not. She also learned that a clan was made up of septs and other families that lived on clan lands. From this information, Fiona next wanted to see what the tartans looked like. Not seeing any volumes in the area on tartans, Fiona went back to the librarian for direction.

"Oh yes, those are kept in a different area," she said. "Follow me, please." Leading Fiona across the open area to a different set of stacks, the librarian retrieved a specific book this time. It was a very dusty old volume. Handing it to Fiona, she said, "This is the best we have."

"It looks quite official," Fiona commented.

"It's the best. Have you decided which tartan to use in the kilt?" Maira asked.

"No, I wanted to see what they looked like," she said, leafing through the book she was handed. Fiona discovered photographs of tartans throughout the text. "Oh, look at this one," Fiona said. "This one is McIntosh. Just look how vibrant that is."

"Oh yes, that one is a favorite amongst clothing designers too," she added, "how many scarves like this have you seen in America?"

"I've seen them plenty of times," continuing to leaf through the ancient volume, "Here it is, MacLaren, oh! How nice is this one?" Fiona said immediately, knowing that this was the tartan she would use to have her kilt designed in. "I think I'll pick this one," she said to the librarian.

"May I make a suggestion?"

"Sure, please do."

"When you go to the tailor, ask them to show you all the tartans of the clan, there are several versions you know."

"Yes, that much I knew."

"It may be that you would like a different one and seeing the tartan in the hand and with yards of fabric, you may change your mind," Maira said wisely.

"That is very good advice, thank you for sharing that with me. Do you have a kilt?"

"Yes, I do. I'm a MacFarlane," Maira said beaming. As she said her clan name, she rolled her R's even more pronouncedly.

"Where do you suggest I have mine made?"

"I always like Geoffrey's," said Maira. She then snatched a note pad from the desk and wrote down the address and in making a wee map, Maira showed Fiona how to get there. Then she handed the piece of paper to Fiona.

"Thank you so much," she said.

"You will be going to an historic portion of Edinburgh, you will, you'll see." Maira was rolling her R's again as she spoke. She so loved it when the tourists turned out to be kinfolk. "It is right next to John Knox's house!"

"Oh thank you. I'm sure they will do a good job. I'll head over there right away," Fiona said excitedly.

"There you go. Now, do you have your reader's ticket? Before you leave, I need to exchange that for your passport. You wouldn't want to leave here without that!"

"Yes I do, here it is," Fiona said exchanging the small piece of paper for her navy passport. "Thank you for all your help. I realize now that I should really have planned on having more time here. I'll have to do that on my next trip!"

"I hope I can help you when you come back. You are so enthusiastic, it warms me heart. You came all this way to look for family who left a long time ago."

"Well, not all of them have left, just the line I come from. Before I came up here I was staying with family, all descendents from cousins who lived here at the turn of the last century." Fiona paused, "I mean the early 1900's. It has been a wonderful experience getting to know these cousins. They live so far away and yet how we live our lives seems so similar, so familiar. They noticed it too. I've had an odd sense of belonging ever since I landed. It feels like this land is calling to me. Does that sound crazy?"

"No, not at all, it really feels like home."

"Exactly, it feels like home." Fiona left the library thanking the no longer dowdy librarian, realizing that must have been an act to stave off tourists. Once she learned Fiona was serious in her research, she really warmed up. With her map in hand, Fiona hit the pavement surrounding the library, turned south on George IV Bridge and east on High Street following the signs to John Knox's house and then saw the Geoffrey sign in the shop window.

When she entered the tailor shop, a chime rang out from the top of the door, alerting those within of her entrance. Shortly after walking inside, a man dressed in a crisp white dress shirt, black tie and pants, and wearing a work apron, approached her, "Hello. My name is George, how may I help you Miss?" he said.

"Yes, I would like to see some tartans and be fitted for a kilt. It will be my first one, I'm just a little excited about it," Fiona said, not having to be repeated, and showing her obvious excitement.

"Very good lass, what tartans may I fetch for your viewing?"

"For the MacLaren Clan please," Fiona said clearly.

"Very good, I'll pull some bolts and be right back. Please take a seat; I'll just be a moment," George stated.

"Thank you," Fiona replied, sitting down on the smaller sofa. The shop was laid out in a square frame with bolts after bolts of fabric lining the outside of the square, and the viewing areas, like the one in which Fiona was sitting, were on the corners. The one Fiona was using, however, seemed to be the master viewing area, for it was much larger than the rest and was afforded a small sitting area with the sofa and three arm chairs set around a low coffee table.

Before Fiona could concern herself with the magazines displayed on the coffee table, the man had returned with several different bolts of fabric. In all, the man had pulled 16 swatches from the bolts. "Does any one of these meet your fancy?" he asked.

"Yes, I like these two. Hmm, can you hold it up like it is a kilt, maybe then I'll be able to make up my mind?"

"Certainly miss, is that any better?" he said, holding the fabric and draping it from his waist and swooshing it a bit.

"Yes, much better, how about the one on the right? You said that one is MacLaren hunting design, right?" Fiona clarified.

"Yes, Miss that is correct. Please step over to the mirrors and up on the step so I can measure you. Have you thought about the buckles? What style you wanted?"

"Styles?"

"Yes, the leather buckles that hold the tartan's shape. We have several style models to choose from, just behind you over there," George said, as he pointed just beyond where Fiona was now standing on the mirrored fitting podium.

"What is the one used most often, the most popular?" Fiona asked.

"The one on the left miss, most people find that one works the best, easily fastens as well," he shared.

"Very well, can I get fitted for this now?" Fiona requested, keeping her fingers crossed but out of his sight.

"Certainly, just let me get the on duty ladies tailor to observe my work. I usually work on the men's kilts only. I'll see if Patrick is back from tea, and then we'll be back with a pad and tape," said George, and he was off like a flash to the workroom to retrieve his tape measure and pad to make notes.

George returned with Patrick who watched George fit Fiona for her kilt. Patrick made a few suggestions here and there, especially approving of her choice of buckles. He was very interested in Fiona stating, "I don't think we've had a bonnie American lass in here to be fitted for a kilt in what," he paused, "Well over a year, have we, George?" Patrick commented.

After Fiona was measured, and all the buckles chosen for the making of her kilt, she made one last important request. "Can you ship this to me in America? I won't be back here to pick it up when it is finished. I'm returning to England tomorrow."

"Oh, very good, Miss, that is not a problem at all. We frequently ship to America. I believe that means I don't charge you any tax, just the shipping charges. How would you like to pay?"

"Do you accept VISA?"

"Oh yes, lassie, all over town we do," George confirmed with a smirk.

At this point in the transaction, Fiona wanted to make sure these kilt makers understood the significance of her purchase today. "You have been so kind and helpful to me. You know, this is my first kilt," she said.
"My name is Fiona MacLaren; it's so very nice to meet you, Patrick, and thank you, George, for helping a wee American-Scottish lass order her first kilt," Fiona said, with her best Scottish brogue.

"I thought it might have been. It is always my pleasure to be of service."

"You both know your jobs quite well and do them very nicely. Thank you, again." Fiona said, as she walked out of the shop, thinking, "I'm the proud new owner of a Scottish kilt," and then she thought, "Well, the receipt for a kilt, anyway."

After concluding her business with the tailor, Fiona made her way back to the corner of High Street and Princes Street. She began to search the oncoming traffic for an unoccupied taxi. Her wait wasn't too long.

Her first stop was to look for the childhood home of her Grandmother Winnie. She told the driver to take her to Plewlands Terrace and just drive along. The family thought her Grandmother's house had been built in the mid 1890's and they knew it likely hadn't survived modernization that had befallen many an early budding metropolis. When asked, Winnie merely shrugged her shoulders, stating that addresses back then were mainly peoples' names and neighborhoods, not exact house numbers and postal codes. Maureen, Fiona's Mother, had cautioned her that the house had likely been replaced with something newer and better, and that the house numbering may have changed.

The driver drove slowly down the street, turning onto Plewlands Terrace from Morningside Drive and was instructed to go all the way to the end, which turned out to be Craighouse Terrace. His respectful driving methods added to Fiona's reverence. She was thinking, in the early 1900's, did they use a car, was there any pavement like today? The masons had created some majestic stone buildings about three stories high, and today, some homes looked old enough to be Winnie's, but there was no way to know for certain. She wondered how many of the buildings she saw now were the originals, perhaps even Winnie's, as the driver slowly passed by each dwelling.

Slowly, as the taxi made its way along this precious avenue, Fiona imagined her Grandmother, not more than 11 years old, receiving the news about the move to Canada. The ship's crossing to North America occurred when Winnie was 12 years old. Her family took passage on a ship one week after the inaugural sailing of the Titanic, having the good fortune to book just one week later. If that one variable had changed, Fiona thought, the outcome of her riding in this taxi might have been completely obliterated.

"Can you stop here a moment?" Fiona asked.

"Sure lassie, take your time." The driver hadn't seen any fare react so emotionally to a street in a long time. He wondered why this place had such a special meaning.

What kinds of childhood memories or belongings, or toys, did Winnie take with her and what was she forced to leave behind? Looking down the street one last time, Fiona wondered had Winnie played in the street with the other children? She took her time walking the sidewalk, sitting on the grass, running her fingers through the blades.

Looking at her fingers in the grass and speaking to the mossy spikes,

"Were you here then, did my Grandmother do this with you?" Fiona could feel the energy from this neighborhood, it was gentle and inviting.

Regarding this modern street, Fiona thought if she had lived here, she would have missed living here too. Perhaps that was why her Grandmother didn't speak of it much. Her Grandmother's heart ailed by rheumatic fever was perhaps more simply a broken heart. Perhaps she had merely survived and never allowed or had the chance to mend her broken heart after moving away from this majestic place. Leaving this beautiful and enchanting city in that mystical, distant land, would give anyone pause, even a curious but proper pre-adolescent girl like Winnie.

As a permanent way to commemorate her visit, Fiona quickly clicked off an entire roll of film. Now back in the taxi, Fiona decided that it must have been a nice place to live, and an even more difficult one to give up. How does one decide something like that? "Ok, I've seen enough," Fiona said with her eyes quite noticeably moist.

"I can feel it too," the driver said. "Someone lived here?" he asked.

"Yes, my Grandmother, but only until she was 12 years old, then they moved to Canada." She informed the driver then why they were just driving by, and not actually stopping at an address.

"I'm ready to leave now. But can you drive through the street slowly one more time? Then can you take me to the youth hostel on Eglinton please," she instructed the driver.

"Yes, lassie. You know, not many people get to see where they come from, that is a precious gift, aye?"

"Aye, it is." Fiona concurred.

"I know it may not mean much, take it for the intention behind it. If I may say something?" the driver asked with slight apprehension.

"Sure," Fiona agreed.

"You did something today that will affect you the rest of your life. Remember today, it is special, a gift from the past to your future. Aye?"

"Aye, thank you for saying so," Fiona said, wiping more tears from her eyes.

While trying to relax in the back of the taxi, Fiona wondered where to go for dinner that evening and whether or not the Austrian women got her message. She thought perhaps a taxi driver would know of good places and asked him. "Excuse me. I'm looking for a modestly priced pub or restaurant for dinner within walking distance of the hostel for me and my new friends. Do you have any suggestions?"

"Well as I'm sure you know by now, the area around the hostel is fairly residential. My friends and I like a pizzeria not far from Haymarket Station, you might be able to walk to it though. There is another restaurant, it is fairly good too, and Keith, the bartender is quite friendly."

"We went to Keith's pub last night. I'm not sure my friends can handle another night like last night. They were still sleeping when I left this morning."

"That sounds like Keith's place all right. Why don't you check with your friends, I'd be glad to drive you if you need a lift, here's my card," he said. "My name is Drew, I'd be glad to drive you."

"Thank you, Drew. I will talk it over with them and see what they want. They may already have figured it out." As Fiona exited the cab and paid the fare, a few raindrops landed with a smack on her head. "You know," she said through the cabbie's open window, "If it keeps raining, we'll want a ride after all."

"Very good, lass, perhaps I'll see ye again."

Inside the youth hostel not much had changed. The lobby was no longer a marathon of patrons, or full of students or young adults running about. This hostel was actually very peaceful, and Fiona hoped that with her newly found ability to get good quality sleep on a bunk bed in a room filled with countless other women, she'd do just fine all across Europe. She thought, besides, if she could get to the point just before exhaustion each day, she'd have no issues with sleep.

Taking the massive freight elevator to her floor, Fiona walked over to her storage locker and unlocked her suitcase and then walked into their room and placed the suitcase on her bunk. On her pillow was a note from the Austrian women. It said, "We will be back about 6:00PM and want to go out for dinner again with you. No pubs, Farahilde." Looking at her watch, Fiona knew they'd be back any time now as it was just about 6 o'clock now.

While Fiona waited for the Austrian women to return to the youth hostel, she decided to write a few quick postcards. She had stopped in a little shop that was near the hostel and purchased several cards with photographs of Edinburgh Castle, a map of Scotland, and one scenic card of the Scottish Highlands that was focusing on the thistles that grew amongst the heather. She wrote one card to her parents:

"Dear Mother & Father,

Hello from Scotland! Today I went to see Grandmother Winnie's house. I bought a kilt which will be shipped home, watch for it. I'm having a great time, meeting Ellen in a few days.

Love, Fiona"

Then she wrote out similar messages on the remaining cards; sending the map of Scotland to Harriet, and the thistle in the heather card to Gabriella.

Fiona understood completely the 'no pubs' comment and wondered what time Farahilde climbed out of bed today. She didn't have to wait long to find out as the women showed up as expected. And as in the past, Fiona heard their approach before she saw them. Once in the room, they were pleased to see that Fiona had returned from her day of research. They seemed to be buzzing about something, but changed the subject when they walked by the bunks.

"So did you find any long lost relatives?" asked Annaliese.

"Well I wasn't exactly looking for anyone in particular, more a line of people. I found out more about my Grandfather McCallum's family and where they came from. We already knew a good deal about my Father's side. What did you two do today?" asked Fiona. Fiona thought it best to keep her more personal discoveries today to herself, a gift to herself.

"We went touring in general, we only took in a few sights, but they were really good, you should see them."

"Where did you go, what did you see?"

"We went to St. Mary's Cathedral, Scottish National Museum of Modern Art, and then we had a picnic at a little park we came across while walking between places. We saw some restaurants we thought of going to for dinner tonight."

"Really, what are they?"

"The taxi driver we had earlier today told us about a pizzeria not far from Haymarket Station; we can even walk there if we want, but it is raining. He gave me his business card to call him for a ride if we wanted a ride to dinner," said Annaliese.

"You know, I asked a taxi driver for recommendations today, too. He said a pizzeria by the station to me too! You don't think it was the same driver?"

"What was your driver's name? Where did you put his card?" asked Annaliese to Farahilde as she walked over to the window to check for rain.

"I have it right here in my pocket. His name is Andrew MacDonald," Farahilde said.

"Did he say his name was 'Drew'? Fiona asked.

"Yes, he did. Is it the same one?"

"Let me see the card," Fiona requested.

Farahilde handed the driver's card to Fiona, who in looking at it immediately recognized it as the one from her own ride just a few moments ago. Nodding, Fiona said, "That's him. And that's really funny that he recommended the same place to basically the same group. Annaliese, is it still raining?"

"Yes, I'm afraid it is. Should we call Drew?" she asked.

"Let's call him. We can always walk home if it stops raining." Fiona said looking at her new friends, and in concurring with their dinner plans: pizza.

They gathered their essentials and slickers and traipsed back to the substantial elevator to the lobby where there was a free public telephone. The front desk clerk had finally informed them of this little convenience. Drew answered on the 2nd ring, saying, "I'll be right back to collect ye."

Downstairs, the women were out on the sidewalk when Drew's black taxi pulled up. When he saw the giggling gaggle of girls at the curb, his facial expression explained a lot. In unison the women said, "Pizza, Drew!"

"Don't tell me these are your friends," he said to Fiona.

"Aye."

"Well, I met them earlier today and they mentioned they had a new American friend who was off on family research today, but that they needed a place for dinner. Then you come into my cab, and ask me for a place for dinner. As I was pulling away from the hostel, I put it all together. I was waiting down the block and just circled round to collect ye. Are ye ready for pizza, ladies?"

"Aye," they said.

After dinner, the rain had stopped and they walked back to the hostel, following the directions Drew had given them when he dropped them off. They sat in the lobby to talk for a few minutes before heading upstairs. They knew that Fiona was leaving tomorrow and wanted to share a few more memories of their time in Edinburgh before parting company. Fiona's train was at 7:00AM and she would be skipping breakfast in the morning. Plus, she didn't want to have the women get up early to say their goodbyes in the morning.

"One of the customs or traditions I've implemented for myself is something I'd like to ask you to participate in too. If you agree, that is."

Fiona said looking from Annaliese to Farahilde. They hadn't had as much to drink tonight, giving their systems a bit of a rest.

"Sure, what is it?" Annaliese said first.

"Aye, what is it?" Farahilde said mocking Drew's accent.

"I'd like to become pen pals. Could I have your home addresses? I want to write to you after I get home. Who knows, I might even send you a card when I get a chance in the next few weeks. Would that be all right?" Fiona said, searching their faces for a glimmer of an indication of their agreement to this plan.

"I think that would be a wonderful idea, what about you Hilde?" said Annaliese.

"Excellent plan, I'd really enjoy that."

"Here's some paper," Fiona said, handing them some scratch paper she kept in her money belt.

"I've been meaning to ask you about that, motion. You aren't keeping things in your, uh, drawers, are you?" asked Farahilde.

"Oh no, I am wearing a money belt under my pants but OVER my underwear," Fiona said. "See look," Fiona said, and pulled her jeans a bit away from her body producing a view of said money belt which was conveniently covering her underwear. "I know it looks like I'm doing something else, but I thought it worked out better this way. If I were to wear the belt over my clothes, I'm just asking to be robbed. But here, hidden beneath, no one will bother me. They won't know I have any money or a money belt." She explained, thinking she'd covered the topic rather logically, but by hearing the laughter from her new friends, perhaps she'd missed the mark.

"Well, you certainly aren't going to catch me going in there for any money," said Annaliese with a mocking look.

"Here you go, keep that safe and sound in your money belt," Farahilde suggested.

"Yes, here's mine too, keep them safe. Now what about your address?"

"Sure thing, let me get some more paper!"

"Oh no, I'll ask the front desk clerk for something fresh," Farahilde said loudly.

Their laughter followed her all the way to the front desk where the clerk was waiting with a handful of scrap paper. Smiling, she handed it to Farahilde saying, "Freshly pressed today, lassie."

"Thank you!"

"You live in Salzburg?" Fiona asked.

"Yes we do."

"I'm fairly sure Ellen and I discussed going to Salzburg. We want to see *The Sound of Music* tour, among other things. When are you going home?" Fiona asked, contemplatively.

"I think we are going to Ireland after the rest of Scotland, likely not until November. That's after you return home, isn't it?"

"I'm afraid so. Well, perhaps next trip?" Fiona said.

"Yes, next trip for either of us. Sounds like fun to me," said Annaliese.

"I just wanted to say how much I enjoyed getting to know both of you and spending the last few days together. It was important to me that I come up here, and now I have, and I shared these poignant experiences with new friends."

"We've enjoyed spending time with you and getting to know you too. I think," Annaliese said, looking at Farahilde for confirmation, "We are going to miss you. I'll think of Scotland as the place to buy china and sweaters, and to do family research, kilts and all."

"Aye," Fiona said, "Kilts and all."

Chapter 22 Nurses Always Find Their Own, 2015

After walking in the hall with Jake, Fiona felt drawn to him, more than the normal nurse to nurse affinity. There has long been a feeling amongst nurses, Fiona also felt, that whenever out in public, and especially when not working in the capacity of a nurse, that nurses always find their own. It was the pleasant recognition when speaking in queue at the grocery store and striking up a conversation only to hear key words that indicated nurse training.

But walking with Jake felt more than that affinity and most certainly didn't feel like competition and the other unfortunate fact most nurses wish remained myth: nurses eat their own. Supposedly keen in supporting each other, it is a well known fact that in some cases, units, or departments, instead of striving for unity, some nurses strive for superiority. It is during these occasions of striving, that older nurses put down younger ones in some extraordinary fashion. Strikes are not unheard of results.

No, this feeling with Jake was more on the belonging side, but there was something more to it. It reminded Fiona of the days spent with Harriet when they were taking the nursing exam on two fine July days. When nurses find their own, it could be good or bad. Fiona, ever the optimist, always hoped it was for good.

Her glances out the window of her hospital room were left uninterrupted while the staff of the neuro unit was busy dealing with a new admission. No one noticed Fiona's gaze or for how long she had been looking, watching out the window, searching for that affinity, was it for Jake? Had she begun to remember him?

Chapter 23 Nursing Board Exam— Day One, 1985

Jake arrived at the hospital with mail from home. It was a letter from Harriet, in which he read that she was asking about their nursing board exam and the few months they shared together after college and before Harriet moved to Florida.

In Fiona's room, Jake finds Fiona resting quietly and before leaving to go check in at his practice, he leaves the open letter on her patient bedside table in hopes that she would read it when she woke up. He whispered, "I've left you a letter from Harriet, darling," and leaves the room.

While sleeping, Fiona smiled when she heard Jake's voice. But in her dream, Fiona agreed to meet Harriet at the entrance to the auditorium where they would be taking the exam. It was attached to the hockey stadium and seemed like an odd place to be sitting for their national exam, but they looked at it this way, where else are you going to put hundreds, if not, thousands of examinees than in a building like this? There had been rumors told in one of their nursing classes that people faint, vomit, or go into labor during these exams. They knew they were prepared for just about anything: side shows, tests, or weather.

Finally, the morning of the exam arrived. Fiona set her alarm for an early hour so that she had plenty of time to wake up properly, get ready, drive downtown, park, and get in line to enter the exam. The feeling in her digestive system wasn't a typical symptom they had studied: butterflies.

Fiona knew she was as ready as she could be with the preparation plan she had completed. Harriet had a similar plan and together they approached the test with the peace of mind of passing with the philosophy of significant optimism. They knew they had just graduated from one of the top nursing programs in the country, and would be qualified and ready for what was on the exam. They had been warned about trick questions with a lot of distracting fluff. They prepared for fluff extraction and learned how to not only dissect the human body, but also lengthy and fluff-contaminated test questions.

Harriet had a longer drive into downtown than Fiona did, and she was waiting at the entrance to the auditorium adjacent to the parking garage when Fiona walked out of the structure. Instantly, their mutual levels of stress were reduced when they saw a comrade in arms. Whether they were going to be seated near each other or not, just knowing that the other was somewhere in the room was a serious relief for them both.

Waving as she walked up the sidewalk, Fiona said, "Ready?"

"Good morning, yes, I'm ready." Harriet replied.

"Ok then, let's go!"

"Oh, we're off to see the wizard," Harriet said, smiling and laughing as they walked side by side, not into the lion's den, but it felt close enough.

"I'm ready to tame this exam!"

The pair walked across the skyway and entered the sea of would be hopeful other nurses-to-be already waiting in lines. They could see signs posted breaking up the lines into the registration numbers they received in response to their request to sit for the exam. They heard the overhead announcements indicating the examinees were to line up in the appropriate line by registration number. The lines were broken up in groups by number.

"I'm over here," Harriet said, pointing to the line where her registration number, 1310 would be accessible. "Meet you on the other side of these registration desks!"

"Ok, my line is over here," Fiona said pointing to the sign posted for 275. "See you in a few!"

As it turned out, they were fortunate in their arrival timing. The lines weren't that long when they queued up but were out onto the concourse and up into the skyway when they finished. There was a faint but lingering smell that permeated the atrium of this building. It was an odd mixture of smells- both good and bad, burnt popcorn, old hot dogs, and beer. This scent wafted up to their awaiting noses only to be pushed back out with a deep exhale. Fiona wondered if there had been a circus in town last night, an odd thought at this moment.

Turning to look behind her, Harriet said, "Just look at those lines now. Wow, we timed this just right!"

"I'm glad we decided to get here early," Fiona replied.

"Where is your assigned seat? I'm in section D, seat 1310," Harriet indicated looking at her admission pass.

"I'm in section C, seat 275," Fiona answered.

"Well, maybe they are near each other, maybe not. Either way, we should select a rendezvous point for meeting each other after we complete each round of the test. What do you think?" Harriet suggested and began looking around for an obvious spot to meet.

"What about down there at the end of that hallway by the sign indicating the stairs? Would that work?" Fiona suggested.

"Sure, I see it, yes that should work fine. When either of us is finished, whichever one of us is finished first can wait for the other one on the steps. That works for me. Boy," she paused, and in looking at the growing line and number of other examinees and added, "how many people do you think are taking the test today?" she asked.

"I don't know, looks like a lot more than we thought though, huh," Fiona replied.

Their conversation was overheard by another examinee waiting to go into her assigned seating, and she said, "I'm sorry; I overheard you commenting on how many people would be taking the exam. My professors at the university said there could be over a thousand here today. She told us that the summer exam has more people at it since most of us graduate in spring rather than in the fall."

"Well that makes sense. I'll bet that the February exam is practically empty if you compared it to this one," Fiona said as she turned to include the woman in their conversation.

"Where are your assigned seats?" said the other unidentified student.

"I'm in section 1310 and Fiona is in 275," Harriet answered. "Where are you assigned?"

"I'm in 694." She said, and then offered, "I'm Margaret, by the way, you look familiar to me, but I can't seem to put my finger on it, can you?"

Fiona replied to this question, "Didn't I meet you at the exam prep class at the hospital? I think you sat behind me in that auditorium? Aren't you from New Zealand?"

"Why yes, correct on both accounts. You have a good memory for faces and places."

Harriet spoke up now hearing that Margaret was from New Zealand, "How long have you lived in Minnesota?"

"I've been here over 10 years. My husband and I finally agreed that now was the time for me to go to school since he had already finished medical school and was working now. So I just finished, but I'd say I'm a good 15 years older than you," she said.

"It is never too late to start something like nursing," Fiona replied. "It is so good to see you again!"

They also learned that Margaret graduated in the last class from her nursing school as the school was closing at the end of the month, at the end of the hospital's fiscal year. Her program was a hospital-based diploma program. Long gone were the programs where the students worked as student nurses with on-the-job training. Back then, they were considered the doctor's handmaiden. But with the influx of men into nursing, the lowering and obliterating of the glass ceiling for women in the workforce, and with women's liberation, the modern nurse's education and role was vastly different than in years past. No more maidens, now teammates and colleagues.

The women spent the next 15-20 minutes comparing their nursing programs, their clinical stories-both good and interesting, how they prepared for this exam, and where they were going to apply to work. It turned out that Harriet had finally settled on a hospital program in Orlando but would be delaying her departure for some time. Margaret was looking to work locally at a large metropolitan hospital in the inner city. She preferred a medical-surgical type unit. Fiona hadn't decided yet because in about 6 weeks she'd be in England.

After another 20 minute period or so, the doors finally opened and the examinees were allowed to enter the testing facility, aka, the auditorium. They were herded in like a flock of sheep, simply following the person in front of them. Above their heads they could see the posted hanging signs directing them to the quadrants and the assigned seating layout. As it turned out, their numbers were actually the number to their exact seat, not a section. After Fiona found her assigned seat, while still standing, she looked across the crowded floor searching for Harriet. When she found her, they shared an acknowledgement that they had both found their seats. They nodded at each other and gave each other thumbs up for good luck.

After sitting down, she got a good sense of the expanse of space taken over by the examiners of this 2 day examination. She looked at row after row of long tables with attaching seats and remembered back to elementary school and the long center-folding tables that were wheeled out of temporary daily storage and set up for their lunches. Looking around herself again, she thought, these look to be almost the same kind of tables. Why not bring in separate tables and chairs? Perhaps chairs make noises when one sits or leaves. Still it was a strange sight and something she would forever wonder about: the choices of seating options made on her behalf.

Thankfully, the smells from the atrium had not spread to within the heart of the testing area. The tables seemed freshly cleaned; a hint of *Pinesol* wafted up from them. She didn't even think to look for gum underneath as she didn't need any further distractions.

Fiona began to situate herself and her supplies. She was allowed two pieces of Kleenex in a plastic bag, several No. 2 pencils, and an extra eraser. No calculators, pens, paper, or extra tissues. When Fiona looked up to take in her immediate seating area, a few seats away was Margaret. She too was just finishing her situating of her supplies and looked up, catching Fiona's gaze. It was such a striking coincidence; one Fiona figured she would remember for a long time.

The exam began on time and by all accounts with a full session of examinees; no spare or empty seats visible. At the conclusion of the first day's examination, Harriet was waiting for Fiona at their rendezvous point. The drain of the day was quite apparent on their faces and their mood. While they were glad the first day was finished, they knew they would be back in the morning for round two. "I'm starving. Want to stop for some dinner before going home?" Harriet asked.

"I was hoping you would say something like that. I hate exams; I was expecting to get a lot of my test anxiety today but I think I was lucky and didn't. Can you guess why?"

"Let me think, because a pesky proctor stopped by you all the time?" Harriet mused.

Fiona said, "How'd you know that?"

Harriet replied, "I had one too!"

"You too? Wow, wasn't that terrible? I complained after finishing that first section."

"I hope perhaps tomorrow will be better." Harriet suggested they check out a local restaurant she knew that was only a few blocks away and was just as easy to get to walking as driving.

"That sounds like a good choice, are you ready now?" Fiona asked.

"I've been ready to eat since prior to that last section. Move it MacLaren, I'm hungry!"

"Ok, ok, show me the way. Remember, you don't have to tell me that more than once!"

The women walked briskly the few blocks to the restaurant and since the dinner rush didn't usually pick up until a bit later, they were able to get a table immediately. Their waitress came over shortly after they were seated by the hostess and introduced herself, "Hello, welcome to The Carousel, I'm Cyrilla; I'll be your waitress tonight. Can I start you off with a drink?" she asked.

"Cyrilla, that's an interesting name," Fiona asked, looking at their young waitress and wondering the origin of her name.

"Thank you, actually my parents are from Greece and they knew a girl in their childhood village with this name and I'm named after her."

"I think that's really cool, I've been to Greece. Were you born in Greece or in America?" Harriet asked.

"I was born in the United States and yes, I've been to Greece many times, and we still have a lot of family there. We go over there every few years."

"That is really cool," Fiona said, "Can I order a glass of white wine?"

"Yes, certainly, do you want a Chardonnay?" Cyrilla asked.

"Yes, that would be great."

"I'll take a Leinenkugel's if you have it on tap," Harriet requested.

"Yes, we do. Tonight's specials are chicken marsala, sirloin steak and house fries, or veal parmigiana. I'll get your drinks and return to take your food order."

"Thank you," the women said in unison.

"Wow, I already feel better, just that little walking and a change of scenery and how about you?" Fiona asked Harriet.

"Yes, I'm feeling a bit better. I wanted to ask you what your answer was to that question about the 8 months pregnant patient with depression, and probable side effects from her prescription pain medication. What did you decide was the fluff in that question and what did you finally determine as the question?" Harriet asked.

"Well, I figured it was a two-part issue within the question. The first part was probably to throw us off in that the patient was pregnant. The second part was the side effects of her pain medication. I took it apart that way and answered keeping in mind that the patient was pregnant but was more focusing my concern on the side effects."

"Good, that makes two of us. That's what I thought too. That question was very similar to one of the scenarios we spoke about in class, remember?"

"Yes I do. After I finished reading the question, I looked up to the ceiling and smiled with my mind's eye back in our classroom and our professor explaining how there would be questions like this on our exam. I'm glad I was paying attention that day!"

As the two were nodding and smiling at each other, Cyrilla returned to their table. "Here you go, now, have you decided what you'd like to eat?" Cyrilla asked.

"Yes, I'll take the veal," Harriet said, "What are my other choices?"

"Well, you have a choice of a tossed green salad or home-made soup, then the choice of a potato, rice pilaf, or corn on the cob."

"Corn on the cob, it is only July. Hmm, I think I'll take a loaded baked potato and a salad, can you make it a Caesar salad?" Harriet asked decisively.

"I'll take the house green salad with Italian dressing, the chicken and rice pilaf," Fiona added.

"Wonderful, I'll be right back with your salads."

"Thank you," Harriet said, as Cyrilla walked away.

"Ok, which question was it you wanted to talk about?" Fiona asked.

"Do you remember the one about a nursing Mother with post-partum depression? I thought that question was more about what medications the Mother took, and which would cross into the breast feeding infant, more than about the Mother's post-partum status. What did you think?" Harriet asked.

"Yes, I remember that one too. I crossed out the depression and focused on the medications," Fiona replied.

Fiona looked up as Cyrilla approached with their salads. "Here we are, now you had the Caesar, right?" Cyrilla said, looking at Harriet for confirmation.

"Yes, I did, thank you."

"That means you have the house green salad with Italian dressing."

"Yes, that's right. Thank you," Fiona said reaching up her hands and accepting the plate and placing it in front of her on the table. "Harriet, could you pass the pepper, please?"

"Sure, here you go," she said, as she reached across to Fiona's side with the pepper, "Well, that's what I think that question was looking for."

"I hope that's how I answered it; I can't remember now. What do you think you'll review tonight?" Fiona asked.

"I think I'll just review general anatomy and psychiatric cases. What about you?"

"Besides the benefits of holistic care, I think I'll review narcotic medications, their side effects, and the risk of addictions."

"Did you see the poster in the auditorium bathrooms about the Lollapalooza tomorrow on River Island?" Harriet asked.

"Yes, I did. If we aren't too exhausted tomorrow, want to check it out?" Fiona suggested.

"That was exactly what I was thinking too. I'll meet you at the same spot or vice versa tomorrow and we'll go to the Lollapalooza together!" Harriet said, laughing so hard she almost snorted her soda.

"Here we are, chicken for you," Cyrilla said looking at Fiona, "and the veal for you, right ladies?"

"Right," they answered back.

"Enjoy your dinners."

"Thank you, I'm sure we will," Fiona admitted.

"Wow, I didn't realize how hungry I am. Taking tests is not only mentally exhausting, but drains all the blood sugar. I'm sure they won't put something like that on one of these tests!" Harriet said.

Before Fiona could respond, she looked at her meal and agreed with a big grin. "Harriet, I hope we do this again after the exam is over and before I go to Europe, but I think my schedule is too tight for that. How about after I get back; when are you moving to Florida?"

"I think I'll go down in January, spending the holidays with my family. One last time around the block, so they say," Harriet said.

"Well, then I'll be sure to call you when I get back and we can figure out when we can do this again. I mean dinner, not the exam!"

"Amen to that."

Their dinner long since consumed, they headed back on foot to the parking structure and the brief hunt for their cars. The garage was well lit and fairly clean. The only scent noticeable was the gas smell from someone's leaking gas tank. In short order both women found their cars and were headed home. Fiona headed north and Harriet headed south. They waved contentedly at each other after they returned to their respective cars. They waved again when they exited the parking ramp. Harriet followed Fiona's lead and they left the parking structure long after the rest of the garage's occupants from earlier in the day had taken their leave.

Fiona thought that most examinees had already headed home for a nap or dinner or both, before they themselves crammed in as much last minute studying as possible before retiring for the night. Since Fiona and Harriet had planned out their study preparation well in advance and both felt ready, they weren't too concerned about heading home immediately after the first day of the two day examination. Having dinner right after the exam was more important for these women than getting home in a timely manner.

Hopefully, Fiona thought, tomorrow will go just as smoothly as today, and, I'll be able to decide on every answer allowing enough time to review my choices and pace myself without feeling rushed. That had been her game plan today, her offensive strategy to take her time with each question. She would remember to check her watch for her pace and the signs at the front of the examination area for the remaining time left in each section. Overall, she felt positive about her performance.

Chapter 24 Nursing Board Exam–Day Two, 1985

After dinner that night, Fiona took to the porch for a last minute review of narcotic pain medications, side effects, addiction symptoms, and then a brief review of gross anatomy. At 10:30PM, she heard the faint rumblings of the living room stereo as her Father played one of his Herb Alpert & the Tijuana Brass albums. The high pitch strong tones, despite being on a low volume setting, permeated through the glass French doors and into the porch area, interrupting Fiona's last minute study session.

She opened the French doors and walked through the dining room and into the living room where she found her parents cutting a rug. They looked surprised to see Fiona and were slightly embarrassed at the same time. "Oh, Fiona, we thought you had already gone to bed! Did we disturb you dear?" her Father asked.

"No, I was almost finished anyway. If they have a question on codeine tomorrow, including expected side effects, before I answer, I'm going to hear that music! Good night now," Fiona said as she sashayed passed her dancing parents and headed to her room.

The next morning she woke up before her alarm clock. She got up, showered, ate what breakfast she could manage to get down her upset and nervous stomach, and then began the drive back downtown to the auditorium and the last day of the exam. Traffic was heavy despite the summer day, but there was still a bit of a rush hour for the work week.

Just outside the parking garage, Fiona was waiting for Harriet and they repeated the steps from the prior day and waited anxiously for the rancher to open their pen. "Sheep for the shearing," they would joke later. About the same time as the previous morning, the doors opened and the women made their way to their seats. While they waited in their seats, the gossip had begun about what had happened in other parts of the auditorium. "Had you heard it," Fiona could hear someone saying this not far from her table. And then she heard, "About the baby?"

"What about the baby?" Fiona heard the conversation continue.

"Someone from yesterday had a baby! They say she was in labor most of the morning session and didn't come back after lunch. She had a nice baby girl, named Kay. Least, that's what I heard," the whispered voice said.

Fiona sat quietly bemused at her thoughts on what she had just heard. Could someone really have been in labor and taking this exam? Urban legends likely started just this way, she thought, and then she said to herself, "Watch out for the evidence, listen to what people are saying and then make up your own mind about what could or did happen."

Fun fodder to keep our minds off the exam is what Harriet was thinking, when the rumor mill reached her side of the auditorium. She was interested in finding out more, just like Fiona. It would be interesting to poll those leaving today to see what other gossip, rumors, and stories, true or fictional, had been concocted or transpired, while they sat answering question after question and hoping that each correct answer was propelling them closer and closer to their chosen career.

As expected, the pesky proctor moved over a few rows and when Fiona raised her head noticing her, the proctor simply acknowledged Fiona's movements and began to walk further down the row. Fiona was determined not to let this proctor interfere with her ability to take this exam. "I'll show her," she said, under her breath.

One never knows the intention of these proctors. Perhaps their goals were to make the examinees more nervous, thus encouraging them to rise up against them. Showing their defiance and passing the exam being the goal and not interfering, perhaps that was the better way to think about it, Fiona thought quietly.

Before long, it was time for the lunch break period. The women met by the stairs and headed to the street vendor for sandwiches and sodas. They sat along the benches adjacent to the auditorium in a small city park. The sun was shining and a soft breeze was blowing. The dwarf trees planted here danced a slow dance to the sun. The tree branches reaching up to the sky and swaying in the enlightened breeze gave Fiona and Harriet a soothing performance.

Somewhere down the block they heard an alto saxophone. A street urchin was playing a woeful blues tune à la Miles Davis, John Coltrane, or Louis Armstrong. The combination of the dance of the dwarf trees, the jazz music, the company, and the friendship, gave these two women an overwhelming feeling: it was a perfect day, except for the exam, but they weren't allowing that one detail into their vernacular, not for this one precious hour. They hardly spoke at all, their energy reserved for the remainder of the exam and for consuming their respective sandwiches.

Finishing her sandwich first, Harriet was looking around at the other park occupants, the people passing by on the sidewalk, the cars driving by, and then she saw it. The embodiment of both of their nerves was a monarch butterfly twittering and flittering about just above a sidewalk heating vent from a large nearby building. While it wasn't uncommon to see butterflies in Minnesota, what was uncommon was the timing. Suddenly, she felt it too.

"Do you feel that?" Harriet asked Fiona.

"Feel what?"

"I don't know exactly what *it* is, but I know I'm feeling something." She paused briefly, listening to the saxophone running riffs, and then she continued, "I think that Monarch over there just took away my remaining nerves, do you see it just down the block, over there?" she said, pointing to the sidewalk just down a few yards from them.

"I see it too, yes, but I'm not sure it has taken away all my nerves. What I'm enjoying," Fiona said, standing up and walking from their bench to the grassy area just a few feet away, "is that music." At which point, she sprawled out face up on the grass, eyes closed and just listened to the music. While it wasn't her favorite musical genre, the blues jazz combination was very soothing none the less. "Don't let me fall asleep here, please!"

"I won't, we only have 15 more minutes anyway."

"Ok, give me a power nap of 5 minutes and then a 5 minute brisk walk and we'll be ready to go back and face the music!" Fiona said laughingly.

"Oh, you are SO bad," Harriet said, looking at her watch, checking the exact time.

Five minutes later, Harriet said, "OK! Time's up, ready for a walk?"

"Oh, man, I was just getting relaxed too. Ok. I'm ready." Fiona said woefully.

Getting up and beginning to make their way back to the auditorium, the music crescendo could be heard growing and echoing amongst the tall buildings that fenced in the park. The breeze was the accomplice, carrying the notes further along their escape from the instrument. The sun was still shining brightly and cast a warm glow on their faces as they made their way back to the exam site. It was as though the musician knew what his audience so desperately needed to hear. Could he have known what they were facing? Was he playing this music, his music, just for them? Did he know the impact his notes had on these young nurses-to-be?

Then Fiona interrupted their brief revelry of the music by saying, "You realize we only have a few more sessions of the exam and then it is over! Well, that is, only the exam would be over. Then we start the long and impatient waiting period for results. How long did they say we have to wait for results?" Fiona asked.

Harriet answered, "I remember them saying about 6-8 weeks."

"Yes, that's right," Fiona said as she opened the door to the auditorium. They had arrived expeditiously, faster in fact than they had planned and discovered the doors to the table area were still closed. Like sheep waiting for the shearing, they waited, huddled together, their eyes downcast, their hooves tapping expectantly about the tile floor. Click, clop, clunk, depending on the footwear each examinee wore.

Days, months, and years later, the women would recount this experience to any who would listen. The one odd experience they would repeat each time and one that the building planners and nursing board examiners likely heard frequently, was that there was always a line for the women's restroom facilities and hardly any for the men's. Why hadn't the organizers allocated a few of the men's rooms to women and globally speaking, why wasn't there a disproportionate number of women's facilities? The ratio of women to men examinees was likely 100 to 1.

Knowing that everyone standing in the line and waiting to use the facilities was a nurse-to-be, Fiona boldly stood in the men's line saying, "If we haven't seen it yet, no time like the present!" Everyone in line began to laugh, cutting the embarrassment and stress of the moment.

The last phase of the exam, unlike the rest of the exam, took a global look at a patient with multiple issues and the examinee was challenged to eliminate the fluff in the question in order to look deeper into what was really in question. Fiona found she was able to pace herself and finished a few minutes ahead of Harriet. She was waiting for Harriet on the steps and smiled broadly when she saw her friend exit the exam center.

"I'm glad that exam is behind us. Are you ready for the Lollapalooza?" Fiona asked.

"I've never been more ready for it!"

"Yeah, yeah, I'll bet you've never been more ready for it, me too!" Fiona said, laughing deeply.

"Let's take the Wabasha bridge across the river, we can hoof it over there don't you think?" Harriet surmised, pointing across the river at the Island.

"Yes, we can. Let's get out of here."

They walked at a slower pace but made good time. The walk across the bridge would have normally been witness to a genuinely awesome view, but these two nurse hopefuls had already taxed their brains enough not to notice the barge traffic gently rolling along on the river below. The current ebbed and flowed continuously. The energy of the waves would generate and regenerate all along this portion of the river. These waves here, in town, never lost their momentum even when they hit the concrete edged embankment reinforcing this part of the river from the city above. There had always been talk of refurbishing this area of lower town but so far, flooding, funds, and environmental protective frenzy had thwarted any attempts.

The closer they got to the island area, the more readily they could hear and eventually see the festivities. A small Ferris wheel had been set up, along with food vendor kiosks, tents with carnival games, and at the far end of the party grounds, there was a stage and amphitheater. Live music blasted from oversized stereos and the crowd assembled in the area was happily dancing in their seats, in the aisles, or on their way into the area.

"I need a beer," Harriet stated, speaking extra loud in order for Fiona to hear over the loud music.

"I see a bar over there," Fiona said, pointing off to her right. "I don't want a beer, but I sure could use something else, I hope they have rum and coke."

As the women approached the make shift bar vendor area, they were pleased to note that they had more than just beer. Harriet, who had worked part-time summer jobs as a bartender, saw bottles of liquor that would make margaritas, a tequila sunrise, piña coladas, and Fiona's requested usual: rum and coke.

"I see a fairly full bar here, including strawberry margarita mix. Fiona, do you still want a rum and coke?" Harriet asked.

"I see the margarita mix too; I'll take one of those!" Fiona said happily.

"Ok, first round is on me!" Harriet announced.

"Ok, I'll find us somewhere to sit."

"Ok, good idea!"

Fiona walked out into the tables and chairs area, which was located at the back of the amphitheater and stage area, where they could listen to the music and people watch to their heart's content. In a few minutes, she found an open and clean table. She quickly parked herself there and watched for Harriet when she had their drinks in hand.

"Over here!" Fiona yelled, and stood up to wave her hand over her head in order to catch Harriet's attention.

"Hey, this is a perfect spot!"

"Thanks, we were lucky to get here early enough that there were tables still available."

Over their first round of drinks, the band played songs they were familiar with from college. The lineup included: *Separate Lives, Mr. Roboto, Crazy For You, Don't You Forget About Me, Little Red Corvette, Raspberry Beret*, and many more Fiona could recognize but not name. She was always interested in the music but didn't concentrate on the words or the artist performing these songs. She just loved to listen to the music. Harriet, on the other hand, frequently knew almost all the names of the artists, the song titles, and the lyrics. That was what made their friendship interesting. Fiona appreciated Harriet's knowledge and Harriet appreciated Fiona's interest in listening to music.

The sunny day was also the perfect setting for one of her favorite pastimes. The pair would learn later that the afternoon high was 86F, with a clear summer sky and the severe July sun roasting everything in its path. The wind was also cooperating with a gentle 5 knot breeze. Harriet, while being attentive to the music, was also keenly watching the people as they walked by their table. She would love passing the time people-watching and wondering about their background story: what made them tick?

Her future position in Orlando would be working at a free standing psychiatric hospital and caring for patients with chronic mental illness. She was hired to work on a specialized unit catering to the type of patient population which would benefit most from her interest in wondering how people tick. Her observation skills and interest in people suited her area of nursing well: geriatric psychiatry. Her love of the sun would also be justified in the Florida sun.

Fiona, on the other hand, was still an open book. She hadn't set her sights on any type of hospital, clinic, unit, shift, or specialty area. She knew that her first nursing job would be dependent on her passing the boards. Since her literal eligibility to work was still several months away, Fiona wouldn't interview for any positions until after she returned from Europe. She thought she would apply for more general nursing jobs at only a few hospitals and would wait to do so until after she got back from her trip. Plus, she knew depending on the hospital and their associated experiences in the recent nursing strike, the hiring of new grads may not be a high priority. She would cross that bridge at a later time.

"This is great isn't it?" Fiona said, looking over at her friend.

"Yes, I could do this all day!" Harriet said with a chuckle.

"When are you moving out?"

"I'm moving to an apartment for a year or so and then down to Florida. I decided to put Orlando on hold for a while."

"Really, what brought this on?" Fiona asked. Then she learned that there was a man involved and Harriet changed her mind about leaving so soon and had decided to stay in town for another year following her presumptive positive results from the board exam. She could work at the board and care residence for the next year until she made the move south. Drew's House, as Harriet liked to call it, allowed graduate registered nurses (GRN's) to work as registered nurses, with supervision, until they got their board exam results. The only catch was a small monetary demotion which was reserved for these kinds of positions.

"When are you leaving for Europe?" Harriet asked.

"My flight is on August 26th, I fly from here to New York City and then to London. I have the directions for my cousin's flat and which tube to take to get there."

"What's a tube?"

"That's what they call the subway system in London. They have regular trains in London too, my cousin explained when she was here last summer, but in most cases, she told me I'll likely take the tube. She kept going on and on about tube stations, I figured out that was what she was talking about but wasn't 100% sure."

"When will you meet up with Ellen? Didn't you say she was already over there? Right?" Harriet asked.

"Right, yeah, I think she left already. She's camping in the south of France with Pierre and his sister, Francine. My Canadian cousin is getting married and I'm in the wedding party. My family will be driving to Manitoba to participate in the wedding and then return to Minnesota with a few days to spare prior to my flight. I am sure I'll have last minute shopping and packing to do. I think I have all the passes and tickets I need before I go. I showed you my international student identification card, right?"

"Yes, you did. That's what guarantees your ability to stay at youth hostels, right?"

"Yes, that's right. Did you use them when you were in Greece during your J-term class?" Fiona asked, knowing a J-term course at their college met for several hours every day in the month of January. She knew that Harriet participated in a J-term class abroad during their senior year. The art history class studied great works of art in Italy and Greece.

"No, the college arranged all of our accommodations and suggested a list of smaller hotels in Italy for us to use and then in Greece we stayed at a local college dorm."

At that moment, the band began to play the Otis Redding song *Shake*. In college, when anyone heard that song, they would immediately stop what they were doing and get out on the dance floor. Nothing had changed now either, for when they heard the song begin, they immediately made their way to the impromptu dance area in front of the stage and did their best interpretation of the *Worm*.

When the song was over, Fiona checked her watch and realized they hadn't eaten dinner. It was now 6:30PM. "Harriet, I'm getting hungry. I think we should eat something here, or maybe go somewhere else? What do you think?"

"Yeah, I'm getting hungry too. Let's see what kinds of food they have here."

"I see a few food vendors down that aisle," Fiona said pointing off to her left.

"I could really go for a slice of pizza with my beer, you?"

"Sounds good to me," Fiona replied.

As it turned out, there were several different food vendor options offering pizza, among other foods, and the pair settled for the pizza from Davanni's, a local pizza chain they both enjoyed. They got quite familiar with the Davanni's delivery staff when they were juniors and ordered pizzas for dinner in the nurses' dorm. Unlike their classmates back on campus, the nurses living in the metro area were expected to cook for themselves, attend classes, go to lab practicums, clinicals, and much more, all while cooking for themselves. Davanni's was their pizza of choice when faced with a time crunch or lack of groceries.

They decided to divide and conquer the food court. Harriet would get them some sodas to drink with the pizza. Fiona waited for their four slices of pizza and then returned to the area where they'd camped out. They ate quietly, listening to the band playing another familiar song from their college years, and watching the crowd around them who were also enjoying their food, sodas, and the music too.

After they finished eating, the strain of the day mixed with the recent food and earlier alcohol began to take a toll. Fiona was repeatedly yawning, and when she looked over at Harriet, her eyes were half closed. Fiona knew this day was one that would be remembered for a long time and yet one that was quickly drawing to a close. She felt it was time to indicate her thoughts to Harriet.

"Hey, don't fall asleep on me!"

"I'm here, I'm just enjoying myself."

"I hate to say it but I think I need to go home. I'm fading fast here, can you make it home?"

"Yeah, I'm fine. You are right, though, I think it is time to go too. We've had quite a day haven't we," she said looking at Fiona.

"Yes we have. I agree, time to go."

They finished their sodas and stood up looking for a trash receptacle. They walked much more slowly back to the auditorium and the adjacent parking garage. They were hampered in their walk as they were now walking against the grain, against the flow of foot traffic, against the volume of people finally off from work making their way to the Lollapalooza.

Finally they were up on the main road and heading west to the structure, and no longer fighting for their place on the cement. The city had built a pull-in area for cars to view the scenic overlook, which provided vehicle parking, a set of jogging/walking/bicycling trails, and a green area. Everyone was glad of the upgrade as witnessed by the increase in traffic on foot, or on wheels, along this stretch of only a few city blocks. The biggest growth spurt was the two-legged kind.

The cement sidewalk was relatively new as the city had finally resurfaced the adjoining street and replaced the sidewalks. There weren't any cracks, stubble, or pebbles along their path. The streetlights cast halos along the street and in the windows of the buildings next to their route. The relative humidity, frequently hitting tropical levels in Minnesota summers, must be high again this evening causing this optical illusion.

They eventually returned to the parking garage and they remembered its scent: old gasoline soaking into the concrete. Since they had arrived about the same time, they had parked on the same level. Most of the other earlier occupants of the garage had long since left, and while many people were attending the Lollapalooza, not that many people had parked down on the level where their cars had been parked.

"I'm parked just over there by the stairwell," Fiona announced.

"I'm just a few rows that way," Harriet said pointing to her left and seeing her brown Mercury Cougar waiting patiently for her return.

"Well, I guess this is it for right now. I'm heading to the cabin up north for the next two weeks and then up to Manitoba the second week in August for my cousin's wedding. When do you think is the next time we can get together before I go on my trip?" Fiona asked.

"I'm not moving up until after you leave. I'm going to work a few weekends here and there at the country club. We have a family reunion planned in August at the cabin, and I think my movers arrive at the end of the first week in September. By then, I'll be working full time at Drew's House. Why don't we shoot for dinner when you get back from Canada?"

"That sounds good to me. I'm glad we were able to share this event with each other. See you in a few weeks."

"I'm glad we did this too. I think it made it even more memorable for me, what about you?" Harriet added.

"Yes, for me too." Fiona said with a catch in her voice.

She was thinking of the future and whether or not their paths would cross, and if so, where, and why. Harriet saw the melancholy look on her good friend's face and closed in for a long and sincere hug. Neither nurse-to-be wanted this day to end, but they always knew that one way or another it would, just like all the others in the past.

"Well, drive safely and I'll see you next month."

"You too, see you sooner than we think."

They headed to their respective vehicles, Harriet to her own car and Fiona to her Mother's car, an apple red station wagon. They exited the parking garage and headed out into the city. Fiona's route was north and Harriet's to the south. As they came to a stop at the red light, they exchanged one more set of smiles and waves, with Fiona in the left turn lane and Harriet proceeding straight for another block and then right over the bridge. The summer night sky was blackening slowly as the reds, oranges, and yellows of the sunset were steadily growing eastwardly.

Chapter 25 Another Headache, Another Recollection, 1990

Relieving Jake, who needed to check-in with his office yet again, Ellen began to read a letter from Jane to Fiona. It was an old letter, from 1988 or 1989, one that Fiona had received months after Ellen and Fiona had returned from Europe, but when Jane had stayed on and visited with Kurt in Berlin.

From her bed, Fiona was curled in the fetal position, her stomach ache worsened now. Hearing Ellen's words as she read aloud the letter from Jane had created an alternate reality for Fiona with Kurt in Berlin. Fiona was out finishing the marketing for that evening's dinner party and had finally made her way to the train station and the last leg of the trip home to their modest student housing apartment.

The train station was busy and the oncoming train packed to capacity. Fiona knew that all the passengers needed to exchange positions from within the train with those waiting to board it from the platform. In the rush to get on the train and return from her marketing, Fiona's stomach was hit firmly with the umbrella of a disembarking male punker. His Mohawk hairstyle was reminiscent of those she and Ellen encountered back in 1985 in Düsseldorf. It was the sudden unrelenting pain and the force of his blow that felled her to the platform.

Gasping for air, it was all Fiona could do but lay and wait for someone to help her. Again, when she fell, not caring to protect her head, instead, her maternal instincts were to protect her now-protruding swollen belly.

Unable to protect both orbs was what sent her over the edge in pain and Fiona fainted, again.

"Herr Arzt Wilhelm," "Dr. Wilhelm," said the nurse, in a booming voice, "Der Patient scheint Aufwachen," "The patient appears to be waking."

"Ja sie ist wach," "Yes, she is awake," exclaimed Herr Dr. Wilhelm.

"Ow, oh my! OW, oh my goodness! My stomach hurt! What's happened, where am I, where's my husband Kurt?" Fiona managed to spurt out in rapid fire and clutching her belly.

"Now, now, lie still," said the nurse, this time in English. Her predictions now confirmed that Fiona was not a primary German speaker. Ever since the nurse was assigned to Fiona, Fiona never responded to soothing or calming words spoken in German. The nurse finally tried speaking in English and that was what Fiona had responded to, and, not only spoke back to the nurse in English. It just took some time, but only once she had come to more fully.

"You've been through quite an ordeal. Here have some water," she said, lowering a straw into Fiona's parched mouth.

Fiona mumbled something incomprehensible and grimaced again her face all screwed up. "There, there, now. Take this and rest, all in good time." The nurse managed to place a tablet on Fiona's tongue and helped her drink from the straw taking in the morphine pills. The pharmacy had run out of injectables-again.

After a few hours, Fiona woke again, still in pain, only this time it was her head and not her stomach. She opened her eyes into the darkness of her patient room and the buzzing of the cable car outside. She thought she saw the tall lanky shape of Kurt in the guest chair and in that soothing thought, fell back asleep. Kurt never roused from his dreams, missing her first glance at him since the accident.

A faint cool breeze touched lightly upon her face and the smell of fresh bread entered the room. The building next to the hospital in Berlin was a bakery and the benefits or deficits of the occasional aromas negated the permanent fusing of the windows on this side of the hospital. The patients would have to deal with the smells, good or bad, the medical facilities board had finally determined.

Kurt didn't mind the smell; he actually grew hungry as the scent of warm bread filled Fiona's room. Seeing his wife's unmoving slumbering body was cue enough that he had time to run out for a hot fresh breakfast and an espresso.

Having recently returned to Fiona's room, and in the middle of eating his second Pain Chocolat, Fiona stirred when she heard his familiar espresso slurp.

"It must be morning, did you bring me what smells so good too?" Fiona said softly.

"Good morning love, I'm sorry to wake you."

"Well it is morning and I should be up, right?" Fiona asked.

"Quite right my love, are you hungry?" Kurt inquired.

Rolling from her side onto her back was originally a good idea until she used her recently operated on abdominal muscles to move. Responding to her abdominal pain made her arch her back and in that bearing down movement, her blood pressure spiked and her head instantly screamed in alarm.

"Ow!" she said bursting aloud to echo the thoughts unsaid in her head.

"Oh, Fiona, does it hurt so much?"

"Yes."

"What hurts?" Kurt asked, not sure if he should hold his wife or get the nurse for some help. "Hold on, I'm getting the nurse," he said, decidedly.

Thinking to herself, what do I need a nurse for…then realizing that Kurt had already left the room and in opening her eyes she saw she was in the hospital in Berlin. Before she could determine her own state of health, the nurse walked in.

"Good morning, I'm Walda your nurse. Before I give you something for the pain, let me check you, ok?"

"Ok," Fiona said flatly.

"Your blood pressure is a bit high, but that is to be expected from the blow your head got when you fell. How is your abdomen?"

"Yes, my head hurts and my belly hurts." She said this again without much emotion or recognition of her state. But then, she looked at Kurt and as the tears began to flood from her eyes, she now understood why her stomach ached.

"Yes, well, let me see the incision, will you? That's a good girl," Walda said, urging Fiona to lay flat and easing up her gown as she lowered the blankets. "Nice and dry here. How about something for the pain? Ja?" she said.

"Incision?" Fiona looked up at Kurt.

"Oh, Fiona, what do you remember?" he said fondly.

"Well, let me see. I was doing the marketing for dinner. Emanuel and

Olivia were coming for a casual dinner before they went to the movies. I had my basket with me and was waiting for the train…" she stopped, well, she stopped speaking and crying ensued.

"Yes, the basket, they didn't bring it with you. They were in such a rush to get you to hospital; you were bleeding from both your head and…" Kurt stopped, reaching for his wife and holding her. "I'm so sorry, my love, they came to ask me what they should do. I had to make a choice to save… someone…" his voice trailed off.

"Save?" Fiona mumbled.

"Yes, you were knocked unconscious with the fall. You hit your head. They didn't understand why you were bleeding down your legs until they removed your coat."

Fiona was following carefully, hanging on his every word. "Bleeding down my legs?"

"Yes, my love."

"Save-somebody?"

"Yes, my love."

"Then?" she said. "The incision," she said, more loudly, "Oh Kurt, what did you let them do to me?"

"Now, now," Walda said, returning to the room at the sound of raised and frantic voices. "The doctor will be in to examine you on his rounds, shouldn't be too much longer." With that, she handed Fiona a small paper cup with two long white tablets. "Something for the pain," she added.

Swallowing them together with a mouthful of water, the distraction lasted only momentarily. "Kurt," Fiona exclaimed, "What about the incision?"

"Oh, Fiona, I'm sorry. I couldn't let them take you away from me. We can live our lives together, we can be happy…" he said, reaching for the tissue to wipe her reddening moist eyes.

"We can be happy together? Kurt, I can tell I can't feel the baby, but the incision, it is too big, too long. What did they do?"

"Ja, the doctor is here, he will explain," Walda said, trying to be helpful.

"Hello, miss, Fiona is it?" said the doctor.

"Yes, I'm Fiona. What did you do?" Fiona said in stifled shriek.

"There was too much bleeding and damage to the placenta. The police report indicated the blood loss as substantial. By the time I saw you, you were white as a ghost and had a blood pressure almost not distinguishable. We got you into the operating room most swiftly but the damage had already been done. The baby had no pulse, the wall of your uterus had a gaping hole in it, and the placenta was oozing wildly. We had to perform an emergency hysterectomy, I'm very sorry. You have given your husband and the hospital quite a scare. We've been waiting for you to wake up now for over a week."

Fiona was watching what the doctor was saying but whether or not Kurt thought she was actually hearing those words was something else altogether. It pained him to watch his young wife be informed that she will never be a Mother. It was only months past her 27th birthday, celebrating that night had produced their pregnancy. But not their family.

After the pills wore off and at least an hour of sleep, Fiona wiped her face and sat up in bed. "Forgive me?" she said to Kurt who was still sitting in the guest chair.

"There is nothing to forgive, it is I who ask your forgiveness. We've never discussed these types of life or death issues. I was lost without you there to help me, to guide me. I only did what I thought was best. The doctors all agreed that the only soul worth saving that day was yours. The baby didn't have a chance."

"I understand, but no children?" she said somberly.

"Not biologically, but there is always adoption," he said, hopeful.

"Well that's an idea, we'll have to talk more about it after I get out of here. I think you better find the nurse though, my headache is getting worse again."

He did as she asked and left the room in search of a nurse.

Fiona stirred when she heard the door to her room slam shut. She opened her eyes and realized the dream she'd had and reflexively reached for her abdomen. No stitches. No baby. No Kurt.

Chapter 26 Thoughts on the English Countryside, 1985

"Hello, bright eyes," Jake said, looking at his wife as she woke from a powerful dream. "Coffee and croissant today?"

Fiona sat up in her hospital bed and looked over at Jake. It was Jake sitting in the guest chair, not Kurt. It was Jake, it was Jake, it was Jake, she repeated. Then she said, "You're here early, anything special going on?"

"No, just the usual," Jake said, confused but playing along with Fiona's cover remarks.

"Coffee and croissant sounds good. But I'm wondering if they have any English Muffins? Toasted with butter and strawberry jam?" Fiona requested, hoping to have her order fulfilled.

"Well, if I can't order it now, I'll run down to the…" Jake stopped, corrected himself from saying the 'doctor's lounge' and began again, "Cafeteria and pick that up for you."

"Thank you," Fiona said, "By the time you get back, I'll have had a shower and will be more myself."

"I can't wait," Jake said, smiling as he left her room.

Fearing she wouldn't have much time in the shower, as soon as Jake left her room, Fiona quickly maneuvered herself into the bathroom and proceeded into the shower which included washing her shoulder length hair. It felt good to wash away the linger thoughts she had still remaining from her dream. Cobwebs replaced the fading dream. Why was Jake in her room so early? Hadn't he worked PM's last night, how is it he could be here so early, maybe he bunked with Sam in his apartment in mid-town.

Fiona wasn't able to be lost in her thoughts for long; she heard the heavier footsteps of a man walking towards her room, the nurses walked more quietly. She brushed her still damp hair into a style suitable for a hospital patient and then headed out into her room. Standing in the doorway was Jake, hands full with bags of pastries and two cups of coffee. Creamers and sugar were sticking out of his scrub top pocket.

"Here we go," he said. "Looks like I've got good timing?"

"Perfect," Fiona said, smiling hungrily.

"What story will you share with me during our walk today?" Jake asked, presumptively.

"Oh, I think since I've got the strawberry jam, I'd focus on the English countryside?" she said.

"I can't wait," he added.

They ate their breakfasts silently and once finished, headed outside to the gardens on the hospital grounds, as had become their routine. Once settled on the bench, Fiona began her story.

In the station, Fiona consulted the schedule of departing trains and discovered that her train to Salisbury from London was leaving from Platform 4. She followed the 'To Trains' signs and arrows pointing travelers to the various platforms, 1-2 were an immediate left, 3-4 were straight ahead, and 5-6 were off to the right. Waiting for the train to arrive, Fiona sat on a bench.

She thought back to the last few days. She had been through a lot and had realized more, finding connections with people, places, and the past. She was looking forward to returning to Salisbury, because she knew that after a day of rest and repacking, it also meant that she would be leaving for the remaining portion of her trip and finally joining up with Ellen.

Sitting on the bench, Fiona was lost in her thoughts. In a few moments, she would be replacing the feelings of wistful melancholy she experienced in Edinburgh and Oxford, to those of joy and the excitement of her European exploration about to commence. After visiting these emotionally charged locations, these places which for generations had been significant for her family, she would now begin to experience the exhilaration of exploring new places and meeting new friends.

For months, for years really, she had longed for the day when she could create a new history and make memories of her own. Perhaps someday, a family member or a friend would retrace her steps, look at her points along her path during this trip. Would they wonder what it was that she thought about in this city or country? Would they wonder what had she experienced along this journey that had touched her so? They would be following along from her trip diary, could they sense what it was like to be there at this time, did they sense what had she felt? Did they know how important this trip was to her and her own story?

Brought back from her reverie by the whistle of the incoming train, Fiona noticed the time on her watch. Like a finely tuned Swiss watch, the 9:15AM train arrived in the station ten minutes prior to departure, thus allowing for sufficient time to exchange the departing with the boarding passengers. Fiona was returning to Una and Gosnold's country home to retrieve her belongings she left behind during her side trip to Edinburgh and Oxford. On the platform, Fiona made a few decisions which would impact her packing.

She planned to ship the two urns, guidebooks, and the Dickens' books home. Una had originally made this suggestion knowing that over the next 3 or more weeks, Fiona was likely to make a few more purchases and shouldn't be overly concerned with these purchases when she could just as easily ship them home. Una would take her to the post office on their way home.

The train left on time and Fiona began to rely on the predictability of train schedules. Hopefully, the trains in Europe followed a similar pattern. Her train arrived about two hours later, and waiting outside the Salisbury Station were Una and Adele. They were waiting by the side of their car, more leaning against it than standing. They saw her walking out of the terminal and waved her over to them. The women looked forward to their lunch together and the time to debrief Fiona on her recent trip. Una explained that Gosnold was attending his cricket team practice, and would be home in time to prepare for the dinner party tomorrow night.

Once in the car, Fiona recounted a few of her experiences in Edinburgh and the sights she had seen. Along the drive from the terminal to the restaurant, the English women listened to their American cousin describe the northern land they knew quite well. Fiona sounded so consumed with her experiences, Adele was thinking, just wait until she returns and explores the Scottish Highlands.

Adele enjoyed hearing about the youth hostel while Una was eager to hear about Fiona's visits with the older women. What Una and Adele didn't say out loud, but shared with each other in their exchanged knowing looks, was that Fiona had changed. Something was different about her; she seemed somehow older, more mature, and calmer.

While Fiona wasn't exactly expressing fears about traveling alone, Una and Gosnold had discussed their concerns about Fiona's anxious looks or doubts when she was about to travel alone. Apparently, whatever Fiona experienced in those few short days, had been near monumental. This look was demonstrated on Fiona's face when she walked out of the terminal and was walking like a seasoned train traveler, and not like the young American girl who hadn't been on a train before her arrival just a week ago.

In the restaurant, Fiona finally sensed that these women were sharing information between each other, and in looking more closely, Fiona thought it was perhaps about her. "Ok, something is up between you two, what is it?"

"Let me ask you something first," Una began.

"Ok," Fiona replied.

"Are you ok?"

"Yes, I think so, why?"

"Well, now don't take this wrong, but you are different. I don't see the same American girl who was in my car just a week ago."

"I know. I can feel it too. I think visiting people and places from my ancestry made me think differently about who I was. Does that make any sense?"

"I think you connected with your roots, does that sound like what you are feeling?"

"Yes, that is it exactly. I think living so far away from my roots, as you say, I could talk about them, but I couldn't *feel* them. Now I do," she said.

"Yes, I believe that, now you do. Well done Fiona."

After the waiter came to take their order, Fiona explained to her cousins the experience she had in the taxi when she visited her Grandmother's childhood street. When she was finished with her story, and recalling her combing of the grass, Una looked directly at Fiona. With moist eyes of her own, Una thought she saw a tear in Fiona's eyes in the recounting of that poignant experience. As a Mother, Una was pleased to see the growth displayed in her cousin. Fiona's trip, if measured in miles, may have been a short trip, but the true distance experienced by her heart and soul was enormous.

Over the remainder of their luncheon, the conversation focused more on how Fiona would manage getting from London to Paris. They had finally settled on the train from London to Dover, then the Hovercraft to Boulogne, and then the train to Paris. "How long is that trip, do you think?"

"I think the last time I made that trip," Adele said, "I allowed at least 8-9 hours for all of it. Plus, it all depends on the weather on the English Channel and whether or not the Hovercraft is able to cross, or not, and the speed with which they can cross," she explained.

"Well, I have plenty of time; I just wanted to have an idea of how long it could take or could predictably take."

"Any other errands you'd like to complete before you leave? Like laundry?" Una asked.

"Besides going to the post office and shipping my bulky stuff, you mean?"

"Yes," she replied.

"Other than laundry, and a shampoo, nothing really comes to mind," Fiona replied.

"Well, besides needing to assist you with my washing machine, I wanted to make sure you didn't need me this evening. Gosnold and I have been invited for drinks by my young niece and her new husband. Charlotte and Charlie are in town briefly, before they take their honeymoon and then move to Japan for his job. We'll be back for a late light dinner," she explained.

"I'm sure I'll be just fine after you help me start my laundry. I need to pack as well. You don't need to worry about me."

"That's just it; I don't think I need to worry about you. I'm very pleased by this change, Fiona. I can't explain it exactly, but what I'm seeing makes me very proud of you. I'm going to try my best to express how this makes me feel in my letter to your Mother after you leave us."

"I know what you mean. I felt it last night; I'm still trying to figure out what it is. I think it is confidence with the unexpected. I'm no longer worried about what I don't know and finding it out is an exciting challenge. It is also the beauty of successful and meaningful encounters with other cultures. I now realize that I can manage just fine and I can go it alone. That was why I wanted to have this experience here with you and in going up north. I wanted to experience traveling by myself before beginning my trip with Ellen. I wanted to prove to myself that I could do it, and do it alone. I think I have done that and more, don't you think?"

"Yes, and more."

After lunch, the women returned to The Lodge and Fiona began her tutorial with Una's laundry machine. What Fiona hadn't expected was that the extent of Una's laundry machinery was only the washer. There wasn't a dryer. This fact now threw a kink into Fiona's plans for completing her laundry. She'd have to be careful with her choices in garments to wash, as she would have to wait for each item selected for laundering, to dry naturally.

Deciding to start with the bulkiest items first, Fiona set about placing those items into the washer. She managed her time well and soon had all the items declared 'laundry' washed and now placed on the line to dry. Next, she prepared the package for the post office and addressed the box to herself. Tomorrow, Una had said, they would go to the post office and mail the box.

Next, Fiona placed everything out on her bed and rethought her packing, similar to her packing procedure prior to leaving for New York. It was possible, she thought, that she had too many things and would have a second box to ship home. In the end, Fiona reconfigured where and how she placed her belongings into the suitcase and was able to get all items safely and securely inside. Satisfied with her successful packing, Fiona went into the study and relaxed in Gosnold's easy chair with a copy of *The Times* and a glass of port.

When Fiona had finished the first section of the paper, she heard voices coming from the kitchen's back door. She admitted to herself that she must have been so engrossed in the paper, that she hadn't heard the car approaching the house on the driveway. A few moments later, James and two other people walked into the study.

A bit taken aback at seeing Fiona in his Father's chair, James said, "Oh, Fiona, you've returned, and now you're sitting in my Father's chair!" he said with a chuckle.

"I know our secret ok?" Fiona asked sheepishly, yet jokingly.

"Done. Let me introduce you to my friends. This is Janet and Ruth, we went to university together. We came round to play a match of tennis, are you game, Fiona?"

"Nice to meet you," Fiona began. "I can play. I'm just waiting for my laundry to dry."

Janet smiled at Fiona and Ruth replied, "Nice to meet you too, Fiona. James explained your trip to us before, how nice is it that we actually timed our visit right so that we had the opportunity to meet you."

"Yes, very fortunate." Janet repeated.

"Just let me go change into shorts and a polo," Fiona said, getting up and walking to the doorway of the study.

"Wonderful, we'll meet you out on the court," James replied.

The tennis matches this time were less formal and mostly the fun of volleying the ball, with no score being kept. After a couple of hours, the group returned to the study and the cocktail hour resumed. Over drinks, they discussed their university experiences. Janet had studied English literature and was thinking of becoming a teacher in a few years. She wanted to explore her options after spending the next year volunteering at an orphanage in Guatemala. Ruth, conversely, was going back for a master's degree in architecture. Eventually, she was hoping to work for a non-profit organization that helped older buildings and historic places. Her conservancy, which she explained was like a lowly paid internship, would be starting in a few months.

While they were savoring the beginning of the cocktail hour, Gosnold returned from his cricket practice and was appropriately dressed all in white. "Well, Fiona, welcome home. Did you enjoy your trip?" Gosnold asked.

"Yes I did. I think it was the exact experience I was looking for," Fiona declared.

"Wonderful, I'm glad it was all you wanted. When are you going to Paris?"

"Tomorrow evening; Una said the two of you would take me back into London tomorrow night, and I can take the train to Paris the next day."

"Very good, I need to go to London soon for a meeting anyway. I'll just go up and freshen up before Una and I go out for drinks. We'll be back for dinner later."

"Speaking of dinner," Ruth said, "Janet, we should let James attend to his company and be off, we have dinner reservations ourselves at 'The Jackal,' and we don't want to be late."

"Right, well, thank you, James, for the tennis. It was very nice to meet you Fiona," Janet said, confirming Ruth's suggestion that it was time for them to leave. "James, we'll see you at the club before the end of the week, right, old man?"

"Quite right, I'll be down before week's end."

"Very good, well then, goodnight all," Ruth said, as she walked to the front door. It was obvious that these women had been here before and at least one of them, if not both, was a bit smitten on James. Fiona wondered though, if James was aware of this fact. He was always, at least to the American untrained eye, as cool as a cucumber.

"Goodnight then," James replied after them and seeing them out the door.

The smells had begun emanating from the kitchen before the women left, but no one wanted to make note of their dinner's progression. When Gosnold and Una returned, Fiona had set the table and made a green tossed salad to go with the baked ham and a legumes, rice, and spinach side dish. The ham was good, but the sauce Una prepared for it turned out to be too salty, and most people scraped it off to the side. Una didn't seem to be bothered by it and commented, "I'm trying a new recipe from the women's auxiliary, and I'm not too sure I like this salty sauce."

With this statement, everyone at the table was relieved. The laughter was emitted from all around the table. By explaining her recipe source and that this was the first time Una had prepared this dish, the diners' apprehensions and consternations regarding their entrées were relieved.

The dessert, however, was another matter. Una never planned a meal based on all first time preparation dishes. For dessert, she made her famously delicious cooked pears in chocolate sauce, with frozen mint sorbet pressed into the shape of leaves, which were displayed like actual leaves upon the top of each of the pears. Having skipped or removed a good portion of the main course, this decadent conclusion to their dining experience was superbly fulfilling.

After passing up the offer of coffee or tea, Fiona requested to be excused to her room. She prepared herself for bed in record time and was asleep before making an entry in her trip diary. If she dreamed that night, it was likely a game of tennis and her opponents were oddly pear shaped players with green hats and soft yellow uniforms.

The next morning, Fiona slept in later than she had planned. She walked into Una's kitchen just before nine o'clock and was busy wiping the sleep from her eyes. Another good night's rest, Fiona thought. She could smell the sausages Una was cooking, "Hmm, those smell good. Are they for breakfast?" Fiona asked hungrily.

"Most assuredly, would you eat them for any other meal?" Una asked, a bit astonished.

"Oh yes, some people eat breakfast food at all times of the day, but I usually try to just have breakfast at breakfast. May I have some cereal too?" Fiona suggested.

"Sure, the boxes are on the counter. Do you want some coffee or juice?"

"Yes, both please," Fiona replied.

"Gosnold is already off to cricket practice. It seems they are bound and determined to win this season. I'm sorry to say they usually do better than they have been; their timing just seems a bit off," Una explained.

"Just tell him you can't win them all, and if I'm not around tell him, I said for you to tell him that. I bet he'll laugh."

"American sporting humor?"

"Yes, something like that."

"There is an art exhibition near here today; do you fancy going to that this morning?"

"Sure, what time did you want to go?"

"Whenever you are ready; I was just waiting for you in case you'd like to go to it with me."

"I'm sure after I finish eating I can be ready in fifteen minutes."

A little while later, Una and Fiona were driving along the same road with the towering grasses, and Fiona was again concerned that they were like rats in a maze suffering from tunnel vision. The art work at the exhibition was explained to them as amateur, but in Fiona's estimation, it was way more than amateur. There were a few artists in several different genres, including impressionist and post-modern. Overall, there were only 40-50 pieces, and it didn't take the women long to complete the tour of the gallery that was displaying the exhibition.

On their way home, Una stopped at the greengrocer and the butcher in preparation for their uncharacteristically early dinner party tonight. James and Adele were in charge of clean up after the party as Una and Gosnold were going to drive Fiona into London in preparation for her trip to Paris.

While waiting in the parking lot outside the butcher's shop, Fiona wondered who was coming to dinner. When Una returned with multiple packages, Fiona asked, "Who's coming to dinner?"

"Well, it is an interesting mixture of people. Actually, you've seen some of them already."

"I have?"

"Yes, we've invited Gosnold's cricket team over, they heard you were leaving and wanted to meet our American cousin. So we thought, might as well have them over for an early dinner and then duck out to drive back to the city."

"That sounds lovely," Fiona said, using her new British slang.

"Quite right," Una replied with a wink.

"Can I help you cook?"

"I was hoping you'd offer, as there are quite a few things to prepare, and knowing how much you like to cook, I thought you'd never ask," she said.

"I'm only too glad to help. You and the family have been so kind to me. It is the least I can do to repay your kindnesses."

"I asked the other women to bring a few parts of the meal; Lance's wife Helen offered to bring a salad, Peter's wife Amelia said she'd bring a side dish of vegetables. That's all I know so far. In fact, not everyone said they were able to come. It will be a bit of a surprise when each guest arrives. I'll be thinking who is at the door each time the bell rings, and then after each one comes in, I'll wonder are they the last ones to come?"

"That makes it hard to plan what and how much food to prepare," Fiona commented.

"Yes it does, that's why I sent Gosnold out to practice and make confirmations from those we hadn't heard from. When he returns, he's supposed to share with me who will be coming and if there were more than we had talked about, he'd also go back to the butcher and get a few more steaks or chops."

"Flexibility and ingenuity hard at work here this morning," Fiona declared

"Quite right," Una replied. "We've had meals like this before, and they are usually rather amusing. We've not been the host, though, in several years."

In the end, Fiona helped Una not only prepare a large table in the dining room, but also put out flatware for those unexpected extra guests. They'd be placed in the green garden, in the study, or in the kitchen. The food would be presented on the sideboard and everyone would help themselves single file through a make-shift buffet line.

Before the guests were due to arrive, Gosnold returned from the club and explained that no one else was able to come to dinner. Knowing how many were coming to dinner made preparing for the evening easier for all. Una enjoyed hearing this news and in short order was ready for her guests. Knowing the exact number of guests attending her parties always put her at ease.

Their guests arrived at about 4:30PM and were all in good moods for the earliness of the dinner hour. They had been told that Una and

Gosnold were taking Fiona back to their London flat later this evening so that Fiona could take the train to Paris in the morning. When asked why they didn't just go out in the morning, Gosnold replied, "We don't want to be rushed."

Una said, "Let me show you to the study. Gosnold will fix you a drink. We'll eat shortly."

As they walked out of the foyer, four men from the cricket team and their wives joined Fiona and Gosnold in the study. Additionally, Una's niece, Charlotte, and her new husband, Charlie, arrived shortly after the cricket members. Last night at dinner, Una explained that after they'd gotten together for drinks with Charlotte and Charlie, they wanted to spend more time together before the younger couple left for Japan.

Fiona helped pour out drinks or bring them to their guests after Gosnold made them. "Fiona," asked the first guest, "I'd like to introduce my wife," Lance began, "This is Helen. Helen, this is Fiona, Gosnold's cousin."

Lance was a middle-aged man with dark blonde hair, clean shaven, with blue eyes and a twinkling smile. He had a stocky build and was likely more of a football player type than a cricket player. Helen was about 5'5", with blonde hair and blue eyes. She wore her hair straight with a few bangs. Fiona thought perhaps she was a bit of a hippy but never asked.

Helen said, "Nice to meet you, Fiona, and welcome to England."

"Thank you, it is nice to meet you too, Helen."

Eventually, Fiona met the following couples: Roger and Donna, Peter and Nadine, and Woodrow and Jeannie. The men ranged in age from early 40's to late 70's, as best as Fiona could determine. Their wives, however, didn't necessarily mirror their husband's ages. Nadine, Fiona was told, was Peter's second wife; his first wife had died about 5 years ago from breast cancer. Nadine was more than 10 years younger than Peter. What struck Fiona more than their ages or differences in age was how well they all knew each other.

Roger explained that when he was close to Fiona's age, he was working as a school counselor at a local high school when he met his wife Donna. She was working in the school's library as a technical assistant. She was the liaison from the library to the faculty, and worked with all the various audio-visual equipment and prepared said equipment according to teachers' requests.

"That was many, many years ago; I'm retired now and looking forward to spending time with my grandchildren and figuring out my next career. I've returned to university three times already," he said.

Roger was about 6'2" with a square frame and grey hair with green eyes. Donna was also grey haired and her hairstyle was cut short, which suited her small frame and height.

"He's never settled down for one career," said Donna, "That fact helped keep our marriage interesting. Next month, we'll have been married 55 years."

Peter and Nadine were the quiet ones of the bunch and were soon lost in the crowd of couples and other guests. What Fiona did learn about them was that Peter was likely in his mid- 60's and Nadine was likely 45-50. She had chestnut colored hair and brown eyes. She was a small, diminutive woman likely no taller than Fiona. Peter was a taller man, with dark brown, almost black, hair, flecked with grey, and a full beard. His slight build was evidence of a healthy lifestyle, and a fondness for jogging.

Woodrow and Jeannie were practically Una and Gosnold's clones. They were both in their late 60's to early 70's, and had greying hair. Their sagging frames showed that the cloning ended at the shoulders. Woody was a medium build, but was now out of shape, and carried a noticeable paunch. Jeannie had ample curves that were accentuated by her high cheekbones. Her crisp white hair was worn severely short; it was an extremely appropriate look for a pixie.

Returning to their conversations, "How long have you been a team?" Fiona asked.

"I haven't had any other team than this one." Peter said, "When I was looking for a team and I happened upon this one, I stopped looking any further. They seemed to have a great time together, whether or not they won."

"I agree. It seemed to me that this team had more spirit and history than any other I had been a part. I've been on the team the longest, and am our token elder statesman" Woodrow replied.

Laughing at his remarks, "Woody, when you get old and decrepit, would you please inform the rest of us!" said Peter.

"Fiona, you must know, Woody here, is one of the best bowlers we have. Peter, there, he's our best fielder," Roger explained.

"You know, I did see a match of yours a few days ago. Unfortunately, you lost," Fiona said.

"We don't lose them all. We just really enjoy the game, we don't all care about the outcome. For some of us, we are just glad we can still play at all!" Woody confessed.

Charlie was a tall young man with a slight build, like a marathon runner, Fiona presumed. He had medium brown hair that he wore fairly short. He kept his gaze on Charlotte most of the time. Charlotte was a shorter woman, again like Fiona and Una. She had strawberry blonde hair that just brushed her shoulders. She wore little to no makeup and her hair seemed to curl in natural waves about her face.

Fiona observed Charlie and Charlotte talking with Gosnold at the bar and was glad they had been invited for a bit more face time with her cousin's wife. What Fiona didn't see was Una. Fiona figured Una was in the kitchen, and at her first opportunity to leave serving drinks at the bar, Fiona made tracks to the kitchen, where she found Una. "How can I help?"

"Hello dear, I'm just plating the brisket. Could you take the vegetables from their cooking pots and place them in their serving dishes? Then when you've done that, see if James can carry them out to the sideboard for you."

"Will James know you need him or do I need to go find him?"

"I'm not exactly sure, but if I know my son, he'll just magically appear." As she said this last statement, James did walk magically into the kitchen.

"Hello Fiona, I see you are ready for the heavy lifting."

"Good timing James, please carry those out to the sideboard," Una replied.

After the food was positioned in the dining room, Una asked James to begin gathering their guests and to alert Gosnold that he could open the wine. Moments later, Gosnold appeared from the wine cellar with several bottles of merlot. He dusted off the bottles and placed them strategically about the table so that those wishing to drink wine could serve themselves. Thus was his style with groups of this size, for he figured it would take too long at this juncture to pour out individually ordered wine requests.

Once the bottles were placed and after receiving the nod from Una, Gosnold announced that dinner was prepared, and would everyone find a seat at the formal dining table. Customarily, he'd ask couples to sit together, but knowing how this group liked to mingle, he just asked them to be seated without further ado.

Chapter 27 The Night Train: Paris To Amsterdam, 1985

Fiona and Ellen exchanged smiles as they waited to board the train to Amsterdam. They had in their free hands their tickets, Eurail passes, and passports. Ellen used a large backpack like those used by serious backpacking climbers in the mountains of the United States. It was a well thought out piece of luggage except for one thing: Ellen wasn't strong enough to put the full pack up on her back. Fiona had to hoist it up for her and steady her until she got her bearings. Fiona hoped this exercise wouldn't occur too often.

While waiting on the platform, Fiona and Ellen made notice of how few passengers were waiting for the train. Perhaps others would arrive just a few minutes before departure, they surmised. But, once the whistle blew announcing open boarding, the women began the search for their compartment. Fiona's bag was just a little too wide to easily manage the walkway or hallways on this train, so she was forced to nudge it ahead of her lengthwise. She hoped that that wouldn't happen often either. If both of these luggage issues worsened, they would go shopping for alternatives, but only as a last resort.

After walking or shuffling through 3 long train cars, they finally came to their compartment. It was a triple decker couchette, with three bunk berths on each side of the compartment. The berths were positioned perpendicular to the flow of the train. The women unpacked their items needed for the overnight trip to Amsterdam, and then stowed the remainder of their bags in the overhead storage area. Ellen climbed up first to the third bunk on the right and waited for Fiona to hand her the luggage. Once both bags had been hoisted into the storage area, Fiona turned to the compartment door and confirmed that the door was locked and the privacy curtain was in place. Then she climbed up to the top berth on the left.

The storage area was connected to their compartment, and was literally situated over the center companionway of the train. It was just like the way airplanes were designed to use the unused headspace from seated passengers; these trains were designed to use the unused headspace in the hallways. Fiona made a note of this ingenuity in her trip diary, since she had never thought about how a train was configured.

Fiona had kept out her daypack, bottle of Evian, and her trip diary. The rest had been packed away in her suitcase. Ellen had done similarly. After the women were situated, they chatted and waited to fall asleep until the conductor had checked their tickets. Then they would finish preparing for bed, go to the restroom at the end of the car and finish their 'toilette.' A short time following departure from Gare du Nord, they heard a knock on their compartment door.

Fiona climbed down and raised the privacy curtain. As Ellen had supposed, it was the conductor. Fiona unlocked the door and opened it wide enough to produce their tickets and Eurail passes to the conductor. He looked at the women with a bit of confusion and said, "Passeports, s'il vous plait."

The conductor wore the uniform of the SNCF; the badge on his breast was the company emblem, and his cap was indicative of his rank as a conductor. He had dark brown hair and was clean shaven. His brown eyes were difficult to see in the dim light of the compartment, but when he looked up at Ellen, they glowed like a wild animal in headlights. He was of average height, a medium build, and smiled a lot. It appeared as though he enjoyed his job, especially when it came to dealing with young, but not so naïve, American women.

"Oui, d'accord," Ellen asked. "Yes, certainly."

The conductor noted the deep navy hue of the American passport and smiled, saying, "Where are you two going tonight?" in perfect English.

"Thank you, we are going to Amsterdam. Tonight is the beginning of our big European trip," Fiona explained, quite excitedly.

"Oh, I see," he said. "Well, my name is Jean; everything seems to be in order. If you need anything, my post is 4 cars up, the car after the dining car. Come find me there, all right, ladies?"

"Thank you sir," Ellen replied. "We'll keep that in mind if we need you."

"Oui, merci beaucoup," Fiona said, still trying to practice her rusty French whenever the opportunity presented itself.

The conductor offered a formal parting thought. "Je vous souhait une bonne nuit de sommeil," Jean said, "I wish you a good night's sleep."

"Oui, bonne nuit, merci," said Ellen and Fiona. "Yes, good night, thank you."

He left after punching a hole in their tickets, and handing their papers, tickets, and passports back to Fiona. They could hear his shuffling gait as he walked to the next compartment and rapped on the next door. "He seemed nice enough," Fiona commented.

"Yes, we were lucky. Pierre warned me that sometimes they assume American women aren't familiar with train travel, and they attempt to impose additional fines after the train has left the station. That's why it is always good to be as polite and positive as possible. Plus, what they don't know about what we know, could work in our favor."

"Do you want to take turns using the restroom? You can go first if you like," Fiona suggested.

"Great, I'm ready to try to sleep on here, but I'm not sure how much sleep I'm going to get tonight. I'm so excited and upset at the same time, you know?" Ellen reported.

"I'm just excited; I am so ready to go. Thank you for going with me on this adventure," Fiona said.

"Thank you for going with *me*. Now watch your step, I'll knock 5 times and then you check the curtain before opening the door, deal?"

"Deal," Fiona replied.

After about twenty minutes, there was a knock on the door, which was followed shortly by four more. Fiona grabbed her daypack, now filled with toiletries, and climbed down from her top berth perch and opened the privacy curtain. As she predicted, it was Ellen returning from the restroom. Fiona opened the door and after Ellen entered, she made her way to the restroom.

"There is a line, just so you know," Ellen informed.

"Ok, I was beginning to think that. I didn't think it really took you twenty minutes to get ready for bed. I'll knock the same way when I get back."

"Ok, see you in twenty or so," Ellen projected.

Ellen it turned out had the better timing that night. When Fiona found the line for the women's restroom, it was now 9-10 people long. After about 15 minutes and still 4-5 people ahead of her, Fiona thought about looking for an open restroom in a different car. She made a mental note of the car their compartment was in, and then began the search, walking towards the rear of the train.

About four cars later, Fiona found an empty women's restroom and completed her toilette. She had her bottle of Evian with her to use as the water source for brushing her teeth. Similar to traveling in Mexico, several family and friends had suggested not using restroom water on trains for brushing teeth.

The companionway, the train's inner corridor or hallway, was lit at only about 50% of normal, making her movements through the train a visual strain. Forty-five minutes after she left, Fiona knocked on their compartment door 5 times just like Ellen had done. Except unlike Fiona's snappy response and descent from the top bunk, no one came to the door. Fiona knocked five more times a little more loudly this time. There was still no response from Ellen. Fiona tried the door, but it was locked. Figuring that Ellen had fallen into a deep sleep in the short time that Fiona was away, she thought that the next best thing, instead of yelling in an abandoned companionway, and waking other passengers, was to find Jean, and see if he had a key to open the door.

This task turned into a bit of a marathon as Jean's car was located in the busiest part of the train. Walking 4 cars up felt more like at least 10 cars further than from where she started. But Fiona was resolved to find help, and she knew that Jean likely had a key. It wasn't like Sophie's apartment where a mailbox was positioned conveniently next to the apartment door. No, she'd have to hoof it if she was going to get help.

She already knew which car they were in from her trip to the bathroom, but this time she counted the cars so she'd have an idea on the return trip where she'd started. "A little like Hansel and Gretel, how appropriate," Fiona said, smiling to herself. She had counted to the number three before the smells of a dining car met her nostrils. Jean had said that his post was the car after the dining car, "I must be close, thank goodness," Fiona mumbled.

The throng of travelers that were heading downstream to Fiona's upstream now made sense. They'd all been in the dining car for one reason or another. The return trip of going back to her compartment wouldn't take as long as the one getting here, she surmised. Inside the dining car, at this hour of the night, was still a bustling scene. Perhaps for some Europeans or other travelers, night trains were an excuse to party. One example was not a scientific certainty and therefore, Fiona thought, not something one could conclude.

Eventually, she made her way through to the end of the dining car and opened the door to the next car. The train must be going through a curve, Fiona thought, as the movement of the train shifted so dramatically to the right; that she was softly slammed to the side of the companionway. Just as suddenly, the shift went to the left and appeared to have overcorrected, just like a sleepy driver weaving through oncoming traffic. "But this was a train, how and why does it move like this?" Fiona said to no one, and made note to ask Ellen about it.

Fiona knocked on the door marked "Conductor," and waited for a response. Unlike the door to her own compartment, there wasn't a security or privacy curtain. This door didn't even have any windows, it was solid metal. And, unlike her compartment door, it opened after being knocked upon.

"Hello, young lady," Jean said, "Can I help you?" He spoke in English remembering their prior conversations and knowing that if she was seeking him out at this hour, she likely needed his help and a good start was to speak in her native English. He was respectful and attentive to his customers; something not lost on a not-so-novice a traveler as Fiona.

"Hello Jean, I went to the restroom and when I came back, I used our coded knock, but no one opened the compartment door. I'm afraid Ellen fell asleep, and I didn't want to wake up the other passengers, so I came here to see if you could let me into my compartment?"

"Surely, just show me the way," he said, grabbing a large key ring and connecting it to his utility belt in one swift movement like a modern day Batman.

"Oh, great, then follow me," Fiona said. "I'm four cars back, compartment number 526B, see, I wrote it down in my trip diary." Fiona said, showing her diary to Jean.

"Such a clever girl," Jean said smiling.

"Well, you see, I really, really, don't like getting lost. You should have seen what happened the other day!" Fiona exclaimed, and then shared the ordeal at Sophie's apartment, the post office, and then the hotel search.

By the time she talked about their dinner party with Jessica and Milton, she was at her compartment door. Having heard Fiona talking, Ellen had climbed down from her perch and opened the door before Fiona knocked.

"Hey, what's going on? Why do you need the conductor? Fiona, are you all right?" Ellen asked, a bit alarmed.

"Am I all right? Where were you? I knocked on the door almost an hour ago and you didn't open it. Were you sleeping?" Fiona demanded politely. "I went to get help, since you didn't open the door. Jean here, agreed to open it for me."

"I've been here all the time. I've just finished writing a letter to Pierre and then I was reading my book. I thought the line got too long and you were stuck in it. Where did you knock?"

"Our compartment is 526B, I knocked right..." Fiona stopped in mid-sentence. As she was about to finish saying the number of the compartment that she'd written in her trip diary, she pointed outside the compartment to the number posted. It was 526E where Ellen was standing not 526B. If she'd been knocking at a compartment, it was obviously now the wrong one.

"B and E, in this light, looks a lot alike. Anyone could have made that mistake. Come on in, no harm, no foul, right Jean?" Ellen assured.

"Oui, c'est vrai. Bonne nuit, mademoiselles," he said, realizing that he was no longer needed and left for his post, where he could finally get to eat his dinner and go to sleep, all other emergencies aside.

"Well, now I feel about two inches high," confessed Fiona.

"Don't sweat it; you're both tired and excited. I could have made the same mistake. In fact, I almost walked right by our compartment. Come on, let's turn out the light and call it a night."

"Ok, I think you are right. I am more tired than I realize."

They locked the door, turned out the light, climbed up to their sides of the compartment and tried to sleep. It was now well after two o'clock in the morning and both young women were staring at the ceiling, with sleep a long way off. It was odd trying to get comfortable in a train bunk bed that rolled against the grain. Instead of rolling or lolling them to sleep, they discovered that the train's movements were more head to toe up and down lengthwise, and not side to side like a cradle or hammock. Later, they concurred that this peculiarity of train travel might preclude truly sleeping on a night train, and it might force them to make some adjustments to their mode of travel down the line.

About five o'clock in the morning, Fiona rolled over and looked out the compartment window. The train was still moving along, but the sun was faintly rising. The light danced along the sides and top surface of their compartment, in time with the click, clack, of the mechanical sounds of the train. Fiona rolled back to her other side, confident in the notion that they were closer to their destination than to their departure point. That knowledge relaxed her enough and she fell back to sleep.

Later, Fiona sensed the train slowing, much like that of a jet airliner cleared for landing, and the beginning of its gradual descent back to earth. In this case, the gradual slowing was indeed the train, most noticeably due to the clanging sounds coming from the coupling of the cars, and when the brakes were applied. Fiona looked across to the other top berth and saw the sleeping form of Ellen curled up in the fetal position. The sudden clang of metal on metal, as more cars slowed, jarred Ellen from her restful slumber.

Ellen looked across at Fiona now and said, "Wow, what was that?"

"I think they just applied the brakes, we seem to be pulling into a station. Do we have time to freshen up, or do we have to go right away?" Fiona asked.

"I never asked Pierre about that, good question. I'd say let's get presentable and be ready to freshen up in the station. If we run into Jean or another railway worker, I'm sure they could tell us when we ask them."

"Ok," Fiona said looking out the window, "Did you sleep very well?"

"Not a lot but enough. How about you?"

"I woke up just before sunrise; I remember watching some of it. The transition from starry skies to a pink sky had luminous streaks of light flittering about in our compartment. The light was bouncing off something just outside the window. It was mesmerizing."

"I woke up a lot, but slept through that part, sounds beautiful. Are you sure you weren't dreaming?"

"No, I'm pretty sure I was awake. What do you think the temperature will be; it looks like it is raining right now."

"I would think it could be fairly mild, we'll have to get a newspaper to know for sure. I guess I'm going to dress in the layers I have and be flexible. I'm sure we'll need our slickers," Ellen said, looking at the raindrop streaks forming on their compartment's window. "I hope it doesn't rain all day," she said.

"Makes it kind of hard to sight-see in the rain. I'm going to wear my jeans and polo, just like yesterday. I can always keep a sweater out for later in my daypack. The slicker will likely keep me warm enough."

"Hey, I forgot to show you this last night. Look what Pierre got for us; it is a hostel directory. Here, while I get dressed, you look up Amsterdam and see what time we can check-in," Ellen said, handing the small guide to Fiona who was already dressed.

"Ok, let me see. Looks like this one allows us to check-in whenever. We'll have to find out from the front desk if they allow us to stay during the day. Didn't Francine say, or was it Sophie, that some hostels kick you out all day?"

"I'm not sure who it was, but I remember someone saying it, you are right about that. Let's take our chances, if it stays raining we can always hang out at a restaurant or go shopping."

"Shopping sounds good to me!" Fiona said; she was always up for shopping, whether or not she purchased anything was the true tale of the tape, the cash register tape.

As they were discussing their wardrobe options, the youth hostel's rules, and how to spend a rainy day, Jean walked down the companionway, announcing in French and English, "Terminus, Terminus, Station Centrale. Il faut sortir en trente minutes," "End of the line, Central Station, you have 30 minutes to exit."

"That answers that; how much more time do you need," Fiona said to Ellen.

"I'll be ready in a few minutes. If you want to see about the line for the restroom, go ahead. I know my bladder can't wait for the terminal."

"Ok, I'll go see; be back in a few minutes."

As it turned out, there were very few passengers lingering on the train. Most had already disembarked and were in or already out of the train station. The stragglers, Fiona called their pair, didn't have anywhere important to go, so they took their time. She didn't find a line at the restroom and completed her toilette in record time. In returning to their compartment, she thought about where they could get breakfast. Night trains likely closed the dining cars well before their arrival at the terminus; they'd have to plan ahead better than this if they wanted to eat when they got up.

Back at their compartment, Ellen had finished dressing, changing her attire three times before finally deciding on her jeans and a karate tee shirt of Pierre's. "No need to be gussied up if it is all covered over in a slicker," Ellen stated, as Fiona walked through the compartment door.

"Not at all, not for me either! But I do appreciate the effort and the thought. No line for the restroom, your turn now," Fiona instructed.

"Good, I need to go. Be back in a few minutes, I'm all packed up. Here, wait a second," she said, still speaking from her top bunk, and now handing Fiona her large backpack. "Keep that with you on the floor and I'll be right back. Then I can help you with your bag," Ellen said.

"Good idea. I'll study this hostel guide, what a fantastic little book. I'm so glad Pierre thought to give it to us."

Ellen finished her toilette, and she too returned to the compartment in record time. By now, Fiona was fairly familiar with the contents and format of the little hostel book. Like maps from when she was a child, lots of photographic symbols were used to depict various services or attractions. From the guide, she read that the small letter 'i' meant information. But so far, there was no information in the guide listing the hostel's policy for daytime hours. They'd just have to wait and find out when they got there.

Fiona climbed back up to her berth and handed her bag and the carrier to Ellen. She reloaded everything so that when the aisle was unobstructed, it would roll smoothly behind or in front of her. She placed her daypack on her back and assisted Ellen with her backpack. They were beginning to orchestrate their morning rituals this morning, but as of yet, weren't aware of this repeated collaboration.

Ellen thought it would have been a nice touch to thank Jean for all his help the night before, if they ran into him when they exited the train. Unfortunately, he was nowhere to be found. Before they found the train station café, they found an information desk, unattended at this moment, but with free maps of Amsterdam. They helped themselves to a map, and exchanged about $20.00 each into Guilders for cab fare or other transportation, since the hostel guidebook said the hostel was too far away from the train station to walk to.

Then they stopped at the café for breakfast. More thirsty than hungry this morning due to lack of quality sleep, Fiona settled for cereal and coffee. Ellen appeared able to eat a bigger breakfast and ordered French toast, juice, and coffee.

The service and prices were good and within about half an hour, they were on their way to Vondelpark Youth Hostel. From the train station, the directions were quite clear and said to take the electric tram. They got off the tram several stops away, and within ten minutes after they left the train station, they had arrived at the hostel. The local time was now 8:00AM.

The clerk at the front desk allowed them to check-in and stow their luggage in a locker, but they had to leave for the majority of the day. They were told, "The rooms are closed from 10:15AM to 3:30PM. You can retrieve your bags then and at that time we'll give you a room key. You are reserved now for room 11-12. We are still serving breakfast, if you are hungry," she said.

"We didn't know if you'd still be serving food when we got here, so we ate at the train station. But thank you for offering."

"We serve dinner here at 6:00PM; tonight is taco salad night," she added.

"Can we exchange money with you?" Ellen asked.

"Why of course, our rate today is," she paused, "1.96 per dollar, almost 2 to 1."

"I'd like to exchange $50," Fiona replied.

"Me too," replied Ellen.

"Very well," she said, handing them their guilders using the conversion chart she kept behind the desk. "Here you go."

"Thank you. We'll be back in time for dinner if not sooner. I know I didn't get enough sleep last night. Can you suggest some local shopping or other sights?" Fiona asked.

The clerk was about their age and wore glasses with a thick plastic frame that were at least 5-10 years out of style. She wore no makeup and her mousy blonde hair was pulled back in a braided ponytail. She was dressed in a youth hostel uniform of jeans and a black with gold lettering sweatshirt. In view of the clerk's odd sense of fashion, Ellen wondered why Fiona was asking her where to shop. It didn't appear that she'd been shopping in several years, at least for glasses anyway.

"There are a lot of shops a few blocks away in the city centre, I'm sure you'll find something you'd like there. That's where my Mother shops," she said. "Thank you for filling out these registration forms, I won't be here when you return, so just tell the duty clerk that you are all checked in and what your room number is; then they'll give you your key."

"Thank you for the shopping tips," Fiona replied.

"Let's get these bags stored and then go explore. Shopping, here we come," Ellen declared.

Chapter 28 Amsterdam, 1985

After storing their luggage in a locker, Ellen kept the key for the locker in her pocket. Fiona kept with her the daypack, in which she had a bottle of Evian, her trip diary, and both of their passports. Again, she wore the money belt safely tucked inside her jeans. They discussed what to do for the day and decided to go to the shopping area suggested by the hostel clerk. But, before they left, they heard a loud clash and then a boom. They were the unmistakable sounds of a thunderstorm. Donning their slickers and bracing for the inclement weather, they headed towards the shopping mall where they knew they could pass the time in a dry and enticing environment.

The temperature, they estimated, was in the low 70'sF, but coupled with the fine misty rain and slight breeze, to the unsheltered body, it felt more like 50'sF. Just like the clerk said, the shops were only a few blocks away, and further down the street, the women discovered a small enclosed shopping mall. As the rain changed from misty to a mild downpour, they headed inside to wait out the weather.

What they thought was a mall was instead a department store, similar to the ones at home or Edinburgh's Jenner's which Fiona had patronized just a few days ago. Something Fiona had resolved to shop for was a multifold or double-sided change purse. She'd watched as the waiters or waitresses in Paris made change out of a black wallet with multiple dividers for all levels of currency. They also had another one for coins. They knew about using up coins as they left each country, knowing that when they returned to America, they would morph from usable currency into mementos of the trip once they left the country that disbursed the coins.

On their way into the store, they passed an obvious tourist booth which was selling interesting items about Amsterdam, as well as postcards. Fiona purchase 3 postcards and stamps. Ellen purchased 5 and stamps too.

So their next stop, they agreed, was the purse section. On display were various sized handbags and pocketbooks. The wallets and change purses were behind the counter, too tempting to walk away by "mistakenly" being placed in someone's oversized pocket or bag.

"Look at those black ones over there; don't they look like what the waiters carried?" Fiona asked Ellen.

"Yes, they do. They are rather big for what you want, though, aren't they?"

"By looking at them up close, now I can see that. Maybe these," Fiona said, as she turned to the counter and looked through the glass display at the change purses on the shelving unit inside. At this point, a young man walked up, asking, "May I show you something?" He spoke in English having already heard the women speaking to each other. Unlike anywhere at home that Fiona was familiar with, no one would listen to your conversation and then ask to help you in your language. At home, guests were expected to speak English.

"Yes, could I see that blue leather change purse, no, not that one, yes, that one." Fiona said, correcting the clerk as he grabbed alternatively the wrong and then the correct purse.

"That looks good, how much is it?" Ellen asked.

The clerk informed them, "The prices are inside the purse, I believe that one is about 5*f*, five guilders."

Fiona pulled out from her daypack her conversion chart and read that the Dutch Guilder was about 2 to 1, or $2.50 depending on the current exchange. She explained the information she had to Ellen, who said, "That's a great deal! Do you like the purse Fiona?"

"Yes, I'll take it. Do you see anything you like, Ellen?" Fiona asked.

"Yes, I really like this handbag," Ellen said, looking inside at the price and then with a gasp, put the purse back. "Fiona, I think you have a nose for the deals, can you pick one out for me? That one was priced at over 300*f*!"

"Well, Ellen, we always knew you had good taste. What kind of purse are you thinking about getting?"

"Something small, more like yours, but bigger, and in black. Do you see anything like that?"

"If you want a regular handbag, I suggest you go to a handbag shop, they will have better deals for you," the clerk offered, sincerely. "Our bags are more for locals replacing worn out coin purses, not really handbags and such. We don't get all that many tourists shopping in here; it probably has something to do with our prices on purses," he explained.

"Ok then, let's go look at clothes," Ellen replied, losing the impulse to make a purchase here.

"Women's clothing is upstairs, you can access the stairs from around that corner," the clerk said, pointing behind his display and over a bit.

"Thank you," they said in unison.

Fiona tucked her new coin purse into the daypack and was smiling as they hit the stairs. She knew they'd be shopping a lot on this trip, and she had consulted another area of the youth hostel guidebook that made suggestions of local fineries and shopping must-sees. Amsterdam was known for leather goods, silks, china, and of course, wooden shoes.

Reminded of these famous shoes, Fiona made mention that they should at least try them on, see how heavy or bulky they were, and see if they really wanted them. The novelty, she thought, might wear off soon after returning home. Those kinds of purchases, they would try to avoid. They knew those kinds of things were impulse driven and primarily for tourists. They had made an agreement that although they were tourists, they would try to live like locals and embrace the cultures of each country instead of pillage it for profitable property.

Upstairs the women each let out a "woo" sound as they entered the women's clothing section. They were like children in a candy store, trying on many items each. What caught them off guard was the single changing room for ALL women, used at the same time. Multiple mirrors were dotting the exterior walls of this massive changing room, and were accentuated with pegs jutting out of the walls to hold the clothes each shopper had shed.

Fiona brought with her into the large changing room 8 items and only purchased one, a rich purple silk blouse. Ellen on the other hand, brought in 12-15 items and purchased 4-5. They included other silk blouses like Fiona's, a pair of Capri pants, some woolen socks, and a pullover red sweater. Fiona was still buzzing about her change purse, and the steal she felt she had with that purchase clouded her ability to shop upstairs. She knew there would be many more opportunities to shop and wasn't concerned. Plus, the change purse was light and didn't add much to the weight of her daypack.

Back downstairs, new blouse in a bag for Fiona, and multiple items for Ellen, they came upon a section selling key chains and other touristy trinkets. Keeping to the mode of the day, Fiona looked at but didn't purchase, a small key chain with guilders imbedded in it. She did keep it in mind, since this was their first stop along their journey, and she knew that they would encounter many tempting items to purchase. She knew she would need to pace herself.

"I'm getting tired. Do you want to head back to the youth hostel?" Ellen suggested.

Before they left the mall, Fiona spotted a newsstand with chocolate bars, gum, candy and *USA Today*. She walked over and purchased a large chocolate bar called *Verkade* and a newspaper. After she paid, she turned to Ellen and said, "When we get back to the hostel, we can look for the weather forecast in the paper. Let's hope the forecast is a prediction for good weather."

"I agree, I've had enough of the rain," Ellen replied.

They found the exit from which they had entered the department store and retraced their steps back to the youth hostel. They remembered that it was called 'City-Hostel of Vondelpark,' and they now saw the signs for it again. The last time they were walking up this sidewalk, the rain had stopped, but it was back now with a vengeance. They attempted to walk briskly, trying to avoid the puddles. Their slickers kept their upper bodies dry, and the plastic bags their purchases, but the puddles and angle of the rain were too much for their pants. They were fairly soaked upon their return.

They retrieved the key from Ellen's pocket and gathered their luggage. At the front desk, they explained to the new clerk standing there that they had checked in earlier and now just needed the key to room 11-12. "Thank you," Ellen said.

"Top of the second flight of stairs to the left," said the clerk as he watched them dripping all over his formerly dry lobby. "For those who purchased tickets, we start serving dinner in about twenty minutes."

"Can you tell us if we bought tickets for dinner when we checked in?" Fiona asked.

"I know you didn't because we only sell them at dinner time. Go get yourselves situated and when you are ready, I'll sell you the dinner tickets. Do you have enough change for the lockers?"

"Yes, I think so, but if not can we make change with you?" Ellen asked.

"Sure, we keep a lot of it here just for that reason. See you in a while," he said.

"Thanks!" Fiona said, over her shoulder. Before they proceeded upstairs, each woman removed her slicker and gave it a final flick out the front door in an attempt to remove excess water. Then they found the stairs and headed up to their floor. They found their room was the first one just a few feet from the landing. Using the key, they opened the door and walked into a large room with over 12 bunks. Along one wall was another row of luggage lockers.

"Wow, this is a huge room. I hope it doesn't fill up," Ellen said, hoping to be more private once they'd left familiar grounds of Paris.

"What do you want to do, keep one bunk between us?" Fiona asked.

"Sure, sounds fair, in case it does fill up. I'll climb up to the top bunk, I'm taller than you and I don't mind it," said Ellen.

"That's good because I might try to sleepwalk right out of it!" recalled Fiona, and explained how as a child she frequently walked and talked in her sleep.

They took the next few minutes to unpack those items they needed and then placed the luggage in a locker in their room. This time, Fiona kept the key, placing it in her money belt.

Next, Fiona took out her new postcards and this time she wrote one to Una, one to Sophie, and lastly, one to Stephanie. In the notes on the cards, she explained where they were now and what plans, if any, they had for the rest of Europe.

Ellen sat on her bunk and wrote out a card to her fiancé Pierre:

"Ma chéri,

> *Je suis en Amsterdam mais il pleut toujours. (I am in Amsterdam but it has been raining all day.) Je pense que nous n'allons pas rester ici longtemps. (I don't think we will stay here much longer.) Je ne sais pas notre destination d'ici. (I don't know where we will be going afterwards.) Et autre chose, Fiona est très agréable. (And another thing, Fiona is very agreeable.)*

Je t'aime beaucoup, Ellen. I love you, Ellen."

After writing their postcards and stamping them, they spent a few minutes freshening up before heading back downstairs.

While they were approaching the front desk, they found a small mailbox just before the lobby, by a business office, and inserted their postcards. They then proceeded into the lobby, where they went back to the front desk where they asked to purchase dinner tickets from the clerk. This time he was wearing his name tag, Alec, it read. Fiona picked up on this fact and said, "Hi Alec, my name is Fiona. Thanks for your help earlier, can we buy our tickets now?"

"Certainly, it is nice to meet you Fiona. That will be 7.50*f* each." He said looking at them both.

"I'll be buying the dinner tickets for both of us. Can you take the charges out of this large bill?" Ellen said, suggesting she purchase dinner and then Fiona could get them something else later. This way they both didn't need to get out their money.

"I like how you think," Alec said, "Here's your change. Follow the signs to the dining hall and attached kitchen. Trays are set up cafeteria style and beverages are at the end. Enjoy."

"Good idea, Ellen. We can keep track, maybe I'll pay for a taxi or something. Thank you, Alec," Fiona said.

"Thank you, Alec," Ellen repeated.

Watching the others in line proceeding ahead of them, Fiona and Ellen figured out what was offered for dinner. It was taco salad just like the morning clerk had said, but also other items, like hot dogs, chips, and cold sandwiches. Their tickets indicated admit one, so they assumed that meant one entrée. Ellen grabbed a cold ham and cheese while Fiona was adventurous and helped herself to the taco salad. At the end of the line was a soda fountain with cups, lids, and straws.

They placed their trays down on an open table and then one by one returned to the soda fountain, as they had watched the person just ahead of Ellen. She was still trying to balance a full tray of food in one hand and slightly stumbling to fill a glass with her preferred flavor. Ellen and Fiona exchanged knowing glances as they shared the unspoken common idea that they thought perhaps the filling of a glass was a two handed job.

Without a tray, it was a simple process, press the ice button and then press and hold down for the soda while holding the waxy plastic cup. Ellen opted for orange crush and Fiona served herself a 7UP. Neither wanted any more caffeine. Over dinner, Fiona recalled a memory of a time when someone at college stumbled and dropped their meal tray. To Ellen, she said, "Remember at school what would happen if someone dropped their tray in the caf?"

"I most certainly do, it happened often enough, even once to you, right Fiona?"

"It was one of my most embarrassing college moments. The resulting applause from the gathered diners was most deafening, especially when your face is two shades of red!"

"I think you were eating with Stephanie and me that night, I remember it all too well. You know, you really aren't a klutz. Did you know that while I didn't fall or dump my tray, I slipped on the same patch of spilled food, you just didn't see it?" confessed a slightly embarrassed Ellen.

"You never told me that, wow that clears up a lot!" exclaimed Fiona. "After dinner, we should do our best to fall asleep before any bunkmates arrive; I imagine I'll sleep better if I get to sleep before any roommates arrive. I'm tired from the night train, how about you?"

"I'm tired too. I bet we sleep pretty soundly tonight," Ellen replied.

"How's the sandwich?" Fiona asked.

"Really good; the bread is really fresh and doughy. How's the salad?"

"It's good too, just spiced differently than my taco salad. Maybe I should have gotten a sandwich."

"Live and learn. You could always eat your chocolate bar if you get hungry later," Ellen suggested.

Their conversation, unbeknownst to them, was being overheard by a woman sitting at the back of the dining area. She was intent on the two women, ever since she heard them speaking in English. She figured they were Americans too. As they were finishing up their dinner, she decided to head over and introduce herself.

"Hi, my name is Jane. Are you guys from the States?" she asked.

"Yes we are, you too?" Ellen said.

"Yes, I'm from North Carolina, where are you from?" Jane said. She was about 5'4, small in frame and light in pounds. The length of her dark brown hair was just over her shoulders and appeared to be naturally curly, with a soft wave curling under at the ends. She had suffered through a lengthy divorce and her grown children were now out of college themselves, getting established in their careers. From what the women could tell from the first few minutes with Jane, she was a very upbeat, down to earth, youthful, middle-aged woman.

"I'm from Minnesota, nice to meet you Jane. My name is Fiona."

"I'm originally from Minnesota but my family is now living in Georgia, I'm Ellen. It is a pleasure to meet you Jane."

"What room are you in tonight Jane? We are in 11-12," Fiona shared.

Jane answered, "I'm also in 11-12. How coincidental is that?"

"Very," Ellen replied.

"Did you arrive today? I didn't see you last night," Jane asked.

"We just got here this morning on the night train from Paris; this is our first night here," Ellen explained.

"It might be our last, too, if it keeps raining," Fiona said, grabbing for her newspaper and the weather forecasts.

"I heard it was supposed to rain for a few days, they said a few days ago in the paper," Jane said. "So I've given up and am ready to leave Amsterdam. Where are you headed next?"

"We hadn't really decided yet. But if it keeps raining, we'll be leaving too," Fiona shared, without consulting Ellen.

Nodding her assent, Ellen said, "I agree, no need to stay somewhere while it is raining; that isn't any fun. We are close to Germany, what if we go there?"

"That works for me, besides, I asked Sophie for some suggestions of places to go to and she said 'If you are going to Germany, you have to go to Bavaria and see King Ludwig's castles; they were dedicated to Wagner, you know, the composer?' Let me go back to the room and get the *Cook's* book, then we can check the timetables for train departure times and destinations? Ok?" Fiona asked.

"Works for me," Ellen said.

"Ok, I'll be right back," Fiona stated, rising from the table and going back to their room.

Fiona ran up to the room and quickly found the book they now knew was quite valuable to those traveling Europe by train. Their room was still mostly unoccupied. Returning to the table, with the book in hand, she said, "Here we go, Ellen, can you find us a destination?"

"Sure, let me look," Ellen offered happily.

"Mind if I tag along and travel with you two? I am very easy to get along with, and frankly, I'm tired of traveling alone. My forty-five year old body needs some younger traveling companions. You two just let me know when you're tired of me and I'll go off on my own, ok?"

"Deal. We are the three musketeers in the making," Fiona said, laughing out loud at her own joke.

"I want to be Aramis," Ellen declared. "He always reminded me of

Pierre." Ellen went on to explain to Jane that she was engaged to Pierre and that he was waiting for her back in Paris.

Jane explained that she was on an open ticket, taking the year off to travel Europe and regroup. She said the word regroup with a slight catch in her voice, so the women knew she was working through some problem and when she was ready, she would explain it to them. They may never know and that was fine too.

Finished with their dinner, Ellen and Jane followed Fiona back to their room and the *Cook's Timetables* to determine their next stop on their European adventure. 'The book,' as they called it from then on, was invaluable to them, for it would probably help determine all their future destinations. They would jokingly call it their holy grail of train time tables. It delineated routes to many German cities, including Hamburg, Hannover, Bonn, and Düsseldorf.

While the book also had information about many other cities, the women discussed traveling the first leg, in distances of train time, of about 2-3 hours. If they liked the city, they could stay there overnight, if not, they could move on. This way, they could take smaller steps but eventually make positive progress to places they knew they'd go to, like Munich and other cities in southern Germany.

Ellen spoke first, "You know, I know a little something about Düsseldorf; the orchestra tour, from college, went there last year, so I know my way around a bit. That is, if I can remember anything. It is a nice city, what about going there first? The book says there are trains leaving Amsterdam every few hours and by train it takes about two and a half hours."

"Düsseldorf sounds like a plan, what do you think, Jane," Fiona asked.

"Düsseldorf, here we come," she said, with a big bright smile.

Fiona said, "Now I'm full and exhausted. Mind if I excuse myself? I really need to get to sleep. Maybe we can go look at the timetables and decide which train to take to Düsseldorf in the morning? You know, we aren't in any rush; we can take our time tomorrow and see when we are ready to go. Are you up for that Jane? Ellen?"

"Sounds like a great idea, Fiona. I'm fading too. Sorry to bail on you the first night, Jane, but last night on the night train we didn't sleep too well. At least, I know I didn't. Each time I looked over to see if Fiona was sleeping, she was looking at me to see if I was sleeping," Ellen said, erupting in laughter.

"Sure, you go to bed, my old bones could handle an early night." Jane replied, rubbing her hips like an elderly woman.

"Jane, the first hint of an old woman I get from you, I'll let you know!" Fiona said with a smirk.

"I like you guys a lot already, look out Düsseldorf, here we come!" Jane said, smiling.

That night while Fiona slept, she dreamt about a large castle with operatic music playing in the background, and the white nights of an Alaskan sky keeping her awake during the day. Or was it the dark Alaskan nights and a large white castle? Fiona roused from her dream and discovered the multi-bunked room was now filled with women speaking in foreign languages. Some spoke in what sounded like Russian while others sounded German. They certainly didn't sound like the Austrian women Fiona met in Edinburgh. And they certainly had a complete disregard for anyone trying to sleep.

The lights of the room had been turned on from the off position that the trio had left them in when they went to sleep. They were on full now as the rest of the room's occupants were preparing for bed. Jane saw that Fiona had been disturbed from her sleep and they shared a quick glance of sympathy for each other. Jane simply shrugged her shoulders from where she stood and made a shushing sound, placing a finger over her mouth.

This action only slightly silenced the verbal barrage and instead was replaced by boisterous laughter. Fiona decided that if their response to being shushed was laughter, they were either as tired as she was or drunk, but quite likely both. There was no peep from the upper bunk as Ellen apparently slept through the thoughtless and boisterous chatter of the latecomers. Fiona did her best possum imitation and attempted to return to sleep. She accomplished this task long after the rowdy crew had fallen asleep before her.

Thankfully, Fiona didn't experience any strange new dreams on account of their new roommates. She had her normal accoutrement of oddities, including a dream where she was walking on a train platform, waiting for a small train that just never seemed on time. When she woke the next morning, she'd been enjoying one of her favorite dreams, watching a fantastic vista on a grassy hill in the mountains with a slight breeze and the chirping of a loud bird.

"Fiona!" Ellen said from her top bunk, "Turn off the alarm. Fiona!" she called again.

"Uh, what's going on?" Fiona said dazedly.

"Hit the alarm!" Ellen shouted.

"Oh, I'm sorry. I was dreaming that loud birds were chirping. There, it's off now," Fiona said, unnecessarily, as the room full of women was now looking at her, obviously aware of the now silenced alarm. They were glaring at her from their respective bunks. Feeling the many sets of eyes glued on her, Fiona first looked around the room, then to her new friend Jane, and then to her old friend Ellen. Then she muttered softly, "karma."

Since they were now all awake, Fiona suggested they get dressed and discuss their plans for the day over breakfast.

"Good idea," replied Ellen.

Downstairs over their breakfast of hard rolls and hot chocolate, Jane announced that while she was waiting for Ellen and Fiona, she had gone out to the street to buy a newspaper. She now spread her copy of the *USA Today* paper and said, "The weather in Germany, Düsseldorf in particular, is looking pretty good about now." Jane said, pausing slowly to point out the nearby window, which was again proof of ongoing rain.

"I'm all for a change of weather, what about you Fiona?" Ellen replied.

"Düsseldorf, das ist gut, ja?" "Dusseldorf, that is good, yes?" Fiona confirmed.

To this, Ellen and Jane replied in unison, "Yes!"

Chapter 29 Amsterdam to Düsseldorf, 1985

The forecast for Düsseldorf, Ellen had read in Jane's newspaper yesterday, called for low humidity with overcast skies and temperatures in the 60'sF. While traveling, the women discovered you don't dress for the forecast; you dress in layers for comfort. Today, Ellen decided to wear a dark gray sweater over a red tank top, with jeans with black leather shoes. Jane was wearing a long sleeved white shirt over a light blue tank top, and blue jeans with tennis shoes. Fiona opted for a fuchsia polo shirt and jeans with tennis shoes, and around her waist, she tied a rain slicker. At the outset, both Ellen and Jane carried their jackets, still unsure of their necessity yet.

After breakfast, on their way back to their hostel bunk bed room, Fiona said she wanted to ask the front desk clerk a question. Stopping at the reception area, Fiona approached the oddly dressed, yet helpful clerk from the previous morning.

"Good morning," Fiona began. "I was thinking we'd take the tram back to the main train station just like we did in getting here yesterday. Do you know the tram schedule?"

This morning the fashion faux pas female was wearing her name tag, which read: Maelle. She replied, "Yes, following a short walk, the tram stop is just a few blocks down, you remember from yesterday. The schedule on weekdays is about every ten minutes until noon, then it changes to every 30 minutes for about 3 hours, and then it changes back to every ten minutes. They try to have the trams more frequent during high occupancy times," she said, with a seriously knowing tone, and a bright smile.

Maelle was better dressed today, Fiona noted, with a short sleeved red cardigan sweater set, with matching knit tank top, and khaki pants. Perhaps, Fiona thought, when they first encountered Maelle yesterday, maybe she was going to a costume party with a retro or off-beat theme. Thinking better of it, Fiona asked, "I really like your sweater, did you buy that locally?"

To this Maelle smiled, "Yes, these sweaters are sold at my Mother's boutique; it is a few blocks from Centraal Station. I can give you the address if you like. Yesterday, I was in a before and after fashion show and," she added with a girlish chuckle, "My Mother dressed me as a 'before' so that women would know how not to dress!"

Ellen spoke up hearing this admission, "Well, I like this look a lot better. It makes sense to use your daughter like that. I used to make clothes at school and try to show the difference in good construction and poorly made clothes. Your outfit from yesterday would have worked in my presentation too!"

Jane merely said, "Looks good to me. Let's get packed, I want to see the punk rockers in Düsseldorf! Did I tell you about that?"

"Punk rockers?" Fiona repeated, questioningly.

"Yes, before I met you two yesterday, I had been asking people I'd meet in youth hostels or on various trains, where had they been and if they had any suggestions for me. I never planned out where I was going before I came to Europe, and I knew the local people, the twenty-somethings, or the old farts like me that I'd meet along my journey would tell me interesting tales or of must-see locations. One recently told me of the punk rockers that hung out in the old town part of Düsseldorf."

"Ellen," Fiona began, "Do you remember freshman year when a friend of mine from high school came down for our Halloween Party?"

"Yes, I do, she came as G.I. Joni, right?" Ellen asked. "Pronounced like Joni Mitchell, if I remember right?"

"Yes, that is right. For my classmate's outfit, but do you remember what I wore?" Fiona inquired.

To this, Ellen was lost in a far off glance, it was as if she was trying to pull up a photographic image of that night and everyone's costumes. "Didn't you go punk?"

Fiona replied, "Well, preppy punk!" Jane immediately asked, "What is preppy punk?"

By this time, the women had walked back to the bunk room and had begun the packing process and preparing themselves to leave the hostel.

As they packed, Fiona began her tale. "Well," Fiona said, "It is when you don't really have punk clothes in your wardrobe, or are you able to say your hairstyle suits either. Since I dressed, well, still dress, fairly preppy, we simply added that word in front of punk. It was a bit of a joke on my part but everyone got it and enjoyed what I wore. I had on soft petal pink thin wale corduroy pants, an aqua with black and white striped polo shirt that I rolled up the sleeves. We then used that green hair gel," she paused for help with the name and then continued, "Yes, that's it. Well we plastered back the sides of my hair and tried to give me a mini Mohawk. I looked odd, which was my plan."

"Maybe if you see some real punk rockers in Düsseldorf, you'll know firsthand how they dress and no one will ever ask you 'And what are you dressed as?'" Ellen exclaimed, laughing heartily.

"Good idea," Fiona replied.

After a quick laugh, Jane chimed in, "I can't wait to see them. I hope I can snap a few photos without their knowing!"

"Are you all packed and ready to leave?" Ellen said.

"I'm ready," Fiona said.

Jane said, "Me too! Let's go find some punk rockers." Jane had finished her packing before the other two and had been consulting their *Cook's Timetables* book. She quickly learned that this book had been given a definitive nickname. She learned that the book was 'the book' and in it she read that there was a train leaving for Düsseldorf at 9:39AM, and they planned to be on it.

The trio left the bunk room, laden with their respective luggage, and as they passed the reception desk for the last time, they waved and smiled at Maelle. She was helping other guests check out from the hostel, but happened to look up as they were leaving, and waved back at them with a broad smile.

She mouthed to them, something Fiona thought was, "Have fun in Düsseldorf!"

The weather outside was overcast and humid just as the newspaper's forecaster had predicted. The threat of rain still felt imminent and they were glad to be leaving the depressing nature of it. Even with the humidity, the temperature felt slightly brisk, enough for a light jacket. The street was busy with cars, trams, bicyclists, and other pedestrians just like them.

The youth hostel was situated in a more residential part of Amsterdam, but nowhere near suburbia like in the United States. There were few distinctly 'green' areas, mainly pavement, sidewalks, and driveways. As they made their way along the sidewalk, they frequently encountered partially empty bicycle racks. Amsterdam was a city known for the bike riding of its inhabitants. Had the weather been better, Fiona thought they might have stayed and toured the city by bicycle instead of on foot as they were now.

Their route to the tram stop was the sidewalk which was positioned next to a fairly busy street. There were 2-3 lanes of roadway for cars, although, the roadway wasn't painted as such. This reminded Fiona of the lack of road markings in Paris too. She knew after watching Francine's driving, that if she was ever going to drive a car, in Paris or any other city for that matter, she'd need a serious lesson in understanding the markings on the road, especially when there aren't any. To Fiona, this lack of paint felt more like a free-for-all along the road at speeds of up to 40-50 mph.

Not only would a driver along this unmarked road need to know the 'rules of the road,' they would be sharing the space with the trams. This made Fiona wonder, as on any body of water, more powerful larger boats would yield or give way to smaller, less powerful ones. So in this case, on this street, who yields first? Fiona spoke softly out loud, "Maybe it is me."

Ellen overheard her friend's muttering and said, "Maybe it's you what?"

"Oh, I was just looking at the driving going on in the street there," she said pointing to the street and the cars in it, just next to them. "I wondered, who gives way?"

The path along the sidewalk was strewn with puddles or their remains, and they walked cautiously so as to keep their feet dry. "Well, with all the puddles along here, I was thinking more about how to keep my feet dry, that's hard enough for me. As for the other pedestrians, I don't want to imagine more than avoiding all these puddles just now!" Ellen exclaimed, doing a little dance down the sidewalk as she skirted another puddle.

While walking along the sidewalk and dodging the puddles, the women discussed the need for purchasing train tickets, and what kind of accommodation they'd get. The book had indicated that this 9:39AM train was a direct express to Düsseldorf and would take about 2-3 hours. They agreed on 3rd class seating, like rows in a bus or plane, since this time they wouldn't need to eat and didn't want to waste the required fare increase for better seating for such a short trip. If they had been traveling longer, over a meal, or like a few nights prior, they'd have had a longer discussion about their seats. This decision was swift and easy.

Just like Fiona and Ellen, Jane had also pre-purchased a Eurail Pass. So far Jane hadn't upgraded very often and usually stayed at a hostel, small hotel, or bed and breakfast. As their discussion continued about what else they might encounter, and as they were looking forward to making more decisions about their future train accommodations, it was a good time, they determined, to discuss each other's opinions.

Jane explained, "Since I'm traveling alone, I wasn't feeling secure enough to purchase or upgrade to a sleeping car." Then she added, "Perhaps when I'm not traveling solo, I'd rethink that possibility."

"Good point," replied Ellen. "We hadn't really discussed that, had we Fiona?"

"No, we didn't. You both have good points. Maybe when we have more time we can make some plans or at least discuss this more."

While they were talking, Ellen turned around to look at oncoming traffic and noted a tram was heading their way. On the header sign, she read, "Centraal Station."

"A tram is coming up behind us, how far to the tram stop?" she asked.

"I think it is at the end of the next block," Jane answered.

"Want to make a run for it?" Fiona asked them. "I can pull my carrier well enough at a slight jog, but what about you Ellen, can you handle it with that heavy pack?"

"If you can, I can. If you beat me, just ask the tram driver to wait for me!" Ellen exclaimed.

"I'll get him to wait," Jane said, as she instantly pulled ahead of them, as if it was now a race. She was showing off her skill of running with luggage, and, for the moment, was far superior and she beat the other two with ease.

Ellen and Fiona walked up to the tram stop just as the tram was slowing to its stop. Unbeknownst to them, the tram they were racing to catch had been delayed due to a red light at the last intersection. This extra time allowed them to catch up to Jane and practically walk right into the tram, no waiting.

The tram ride lasted about twenty minutes this time, allowing them to arrive at Centraal Station at about nine o'clock. Upon entry into the station, they found a restroom to utilize first, and then, remembering that Jane also had a Eurail Pass, they bypassed the ticket window, and instead they just followed the signs to their waiting train and hopped on.

They knew this ride wasn't too long and agreed that their choice of seat assignments was satisfactory. At 9:39AM precisely, they all felt the sudden movement of the train as it lunged and lurched out of the station. The bumpy momentum would continue for many kilometers until the train was cleared to proceed at the assigned speed.

About an hour into their journey, the skies cleared and the sun shone so brightly, that despite being inside the train, they were tempted to wear sunglasses. The temperature was also rising and they shed their jackets and slickers. Fiona hung her slicker on a hook conveniently placed not too far from her seat. She wanted it to dry out fully before scrunching it up and repacking it in her bag.

They sipped on juices or water that they purchased in the train station after they used the facilities. It was a good stop, they discussed, not knowing if an express direct train for a 2 hour journey would have a dining car or beverages for sale. They never bothered to look since they were sufficiently supplied.

They also sensed their imminent arrival as the train began to slow as the women could see more and more buildings along their route. These buildings converted from the occasional house to apartment buildings to a business district the closer they got to their arrival time. As the train limped along the final legs of their route, they consulted the book for a list of additional destinations and routes to get to them.

"Without sounding like a broken record, do you mind if we go to the punk rock area first? I think I remember it is in old town. Does the book list it?" Jane asked.

"Let me see," Ellen replied, since it was her turn to schlep or carry the book. "I see it on the map; they list it in the section on Düsseldorf, it looks like old town is within walking distance. I'm sure we can lock up our bags in the train station and just carry our daypacks. Sound like a plan?" she asked.

"A plan to me," Fiona giggled.

"Me too, thank you for going to my suggestion first. After we've had enough of old town, we can check the book for other places to see. Maybe a park and a picnic," Jane suggested.

"A picnic!" Fiona shouted. "Great idea, we even have dishes!" Fiona went on to explain that while they were shopping in Amsterdam, they happened to see a section in one department store displaying camping gear or picnic wares. They realized then that neither of them had thought ahead to pack a cup, plate, or utensils. They took turns carrying the book and the picnic set. Fiona purchased a cup and saucer, and a knife-fork-and-spoon red plastic set.

The train finally came to a stop and they were allowed to disembark. They headed into the main terminal and found the lockers. Stowing their bags was not a problem since there were plenty of lockers available. They would make a mental note of lockers at every stop, just in case they'd want to use them again.

The next step was to find the exit that would lead them to the street the book claimed would lead them to old town. They all looked in various directions before Ellen spotted an exit and said, "I see an exit over there," pointing off to her left.

"I see a different exit over there," Jane said, pointing to the right.

"I don't see one so I'll just follow one of you!" Fiona said, since she was still figuring in her head if she had all she wanted inside her daypack and hadn't joined in the search for the exit. "Maybe we need to just take one and see where it leads to outside. Does the book say which direction to take once we are on the street, for that matter, does it even say the name of a street?" Ellen suggested, thoughtfully.

"Good point, let's just go outside and see what we can see. It may be quite obvious when we are no longer in the station." Jane said, turning to head towards Ellen's exit.

"I agree, good idea," Fiona said, as she too turned to follow Jane.

"Ok, then. My exit, here we come."

Their discussion and storing of bags took about fifteen minutes, and once they were out on the street, it was actually exceedingly obvious how to get to old town. Once they cleared the terminal building, there was a huge street sign and an arrow pointing to the right and indicating Altstadt or Old Town. Next to it, there was a sign that pointed to the left directing travelers to the Hauptbahnhauf, the main train station.

"Oh, man, all of that and look what we find. I can only think that if we ever get lost, the best thing to do will be to go outside and see if we can see any signs directing us back the way we came!" Fiona exclaimed, feeling a bit insignificant about their prior discussion to get to the punk rockers, which all started with how to exit the train station. It turned out to be a lot easier than any of them had ever thought.

They made their way up Kasernenstraße, a wide one-way street that took them to the intersection of Grabenstraße, and it was here they turned left. From there they found a small alleyway of cobble stones, for pedestrians only, with quaint shops and taverns. It was in one of these taverns that they decided to stop and grab some lunch. The smell of sausages, French fries, and sauerkraut filled the air. Smells Ellen adored.

"I like this place, just take in all those glorious smells!" Ellen rejoiced.

Fiona thought her friend must be really hungry to find sauerkraut a tasty smell. She had never quite established a place for that side dish in her food repertoire. But, she did take in the aroma of French fries, or in Germany, she learned, were pommes frites, the same as in French. According to their pictorial menu, pommes frites were listed under a picture of French fries.

The hostess sat them quickly at a table for four, near the window overlooking the cobble stone alleyway. Within a few moments a waitress appeared and asked, "Was mochten Sie zu trinken?" "What do you wish to drink?"

All three women, in rapid-fire said, "Coke!"

"Sehr gut," "Very good," she said, and then the waitress was gone.

A few moments later, distracted by their conversations about finding the punk rockers, their drinks arrived. They looked at their three glasses of coke, in tall clear glasses, without ice. They had a mutual common thought, either they were going to get used to drinking coke warm, or they needed to learn the German words to ask for it on ice. In the future, if they wanted to continue to drink cold cokes, they'd need to learn the necessary phrases in each of the countries' native languages that they visited.

At this point in the day and along their journey, they were quite happy drinking warm coke. Perhaps that would change, but now, they just wanted to have a nice lunch. Not long after the waitress disappeared after delivering their drink order, she returned to take their food order.

"Was mochten Sie zu essen?" What do you wish to eat?" she said, smiling at the notion that this table and these women were obviously tourists. She was glad to know it.

Jane ordered fish and chips, Ellen ordered Wiener Schnitzel and Fiona ordered chicken salad with pommes frites. Their food arrived in good time, they ate in relative silence, realizing that they were hungry and had ordered really tasty food.

"I have been waiting for real Wiener Schnitzel ever since Fiona and I planned this trip. That has got to be one of my most favorite dishes. That was really yummy! How were your meals?" Ellen asked.

"One of my favorites is chicken salad, but you know me, anytime I can get my hands on small cut fries, I'll order them every time. Just like popcorn, or jello, there is always room!" Fiona declared. She turned and looked at Jane who was still finishing her lunch.

"Hmmm," was all Jane could muster since her mouth was full and her taste buds were very happy.

"Is it that good?" Fiona asked Jane.

Again, without talking with her mouth full, Jane merely smiled and nodded vigorously.

There was another pause in their conversation, as all of them continued to savor their respective dishes. Fiona, often wont to daydreaming, was looking out the plate glass window next to her and watching the people walking by along the cobble stone path. Where were these people going, how many of them were tourists like her, and how many of them were locals. Did the locals even come through this area, was it all for tourists? Would she meet anyone else as interesting as Jane, Farahilde and Annaliese?

Jane was traveling with them now, how long would that last? She seemed like a wonderful lady, going by what they knew about her so far. For her age, which was likely close to double their own, she was more than capable to keep up and quickly added benefits to the original pair making the trio that much stronger. Her sense of humor, her southern perceptions, and her inability to speak badly about anyone or complain about anything, were all things that made her a wonderfully perfect traveling companion.

Fiona knew that Farahilde and Annaliese weren't heading home for well over a month now; she remembered spending some interesting times with those Austrian women. They added some culture and spice to Fiona's familial quest while in Edinburgh. Wouldn't going to Austria, in November, be a great idea? "I wonder how long my money will hold out," Fiona thought.

What about Steven and Amy, the Colorado couple she met while touring the Salisbury Cathedral? Had they already returned to the States? They were an impressive couple taking in the sites and history of the majestic cathedrals in England. Fiona thought if she could manage it, once she'd begun her career, she'd like to return to England someday and take tours like Amy and Steven's.

"If I only had the time," Fiona said, not realizing that this thought was actually spoken until Ellen responded.

"Have time for what, Fiona?" Ellen asked.

"Oh, did I say that out loud? I'm sorry, you caught me daydreaming."

"Daydreaming already, Fiona, haven't you got enough to think about here with us?" Ellen teased.

"Well, I was just thinking about coming back to Europe, visiting my Austrian friends from Edinburgh, and going back to England and Scotland. I really want to do that and I was trying to figure out how that could happen."

"Don't fret about it, Fiona. I daydream all the time. In fact, I should tell you, if I don't respond when you are telling me something, it isn't that I didn't hear you if I don't respond, it's that I really didn't hear anything at all. When I'm daydreaming, I'm in my own little world; all I hear are my own thoughts. I could imagine that if I had the experiences like the two of you are having at your age, I'd want to come back too. A lot sooner than at age 45, believe you me." Jane confessed, knowing that the more she got to know these two women, the harder it was going to be to break company, whenever that happened. Jane met Ellen and Fiona less than 48 hours ago, and yet, it felt as though they had known each other a lifetime.

Ellen chimed in at this point, saying, "Well, I can remember many a time when Fiona didn't respond and not for a lack of hearing. Sometimes at school, we'd just let her be until she came back to the present. We all figured she was hopefully having more fun daydreaming than with whatever we were doing, right Fiona?"

"Right, more fun!" Fiona replied.

Within moments of Fiona's statement, their waitress returned to their table asking if they needed anything else. Blushing slightly, Fiona wondered if the waitress had heard Fiona's shout about more fun and rushed back to their table.

By this point, the waitress had also overhead them speaking in English and when she spoke, this time, it was in English, "Can I get you some dessert? More coke?"

"No, thank you," Ellen answered, "We just need our check and we'll be on our way."

Thoughtfully, Fiona said to the waitress, "Are we far from Altstadt, old town?"

"You are going to Altstadt?" she asked.

"Yes, we want to see the punk rockers," Jane offered.

"Ja, the punks," said the waitress. "I know dem."

To this, Jane, Fiona, and Ellen erupted in veracious laughter: the punks. Fearing she had made a mistake in English, the waitress blushed, and appeared as though she would walk away. Jane reached out for her arm, not letting her get away.

"No, don't leave. You made a joke!" Jane said.

"A joke, ja ist gut," she said, her German and English now a bit blended.

"Can you give us directions to Altstadt?" Fiona asked.

"You are right on the edge, the alleyway just der," she said, pointing out the window to the cobble stone walkway that brought them to the tavern. "If you leave here and go to da corner, there will be a large square with a fountain. You know dis, you throw coins into dis fountain and make wish?" she asked.

"Yes," Ellen said nodding.

"After da fountain, take a right on Mittelstraβe and about 3-4 blocks down is the center. Der you will find da punks." She said it again and received the same laughter. She still didn't quite know why these Americans were laughing but they seemed nice enough about it. Someday, someone would explain to her that punks are thugs and punk rockers are a fashion style, similar to other style trends like surfer, preppy, grunge, or classic.

The women didn't take the time to tell her either, but paid their bill and left saying as they were walking out the door, "Let's go find us some punks!"

Chapter 30 Two on Land, Two at Sea, 1991

That morning, Clifton was out finishing the last items of his list: servicing the car, the last of their packing list purchased, picking up repairs for their generator, spare parts for the engine, and another few miniature tanks of kerosene. Bette completed their sorting of washable items and dry good supplies for their journey northward.

On Monday, they went over their standard trip list and reviewed each item on the list very carefully, such as, replacing batteries in flashlights and confirming the supply of new batteries, checking the motor service log, taking a good look at the sails, jibs, and rigging. The list, they knew, was essential to surviving on a sailboat when at sea for weeks at a time.

They were still planning to leave Fort Myers by dawn on Wednesday and in their discussions last night, they knew they were on pace to be ready to cast off with the outgoing tide. They had fervently watched the weather reports and they were lucky that they storms had passed to the north and seas would be prime.

Bette went out to the mailbox to retrieve their shipped copy of the paper and picked up the other mail that had straggled in. They had already put their mail on hold, but their service was less than perfect so a check and recheck pre and post departure of their condo mailbox was routine. One of Bette's typical morning routines, outside of trip preparations, was a stiff cup of coffee, or two, and a crisp tart apple, with the New York Times Crossword Puzzle.

Bette smiled as she read Fiona's brief note and saw the fireworks she'd drawn in the margins. The men had come up with the idea after Clifton had explained to Jake their next voyage of the Ceilidh: to New England in the fall. Bette remembered Jake's reaction to their new home away from home, a floating retirement home; other's had RV's, Jake's parents had a sailboat. She remembered watching his face when Clifton removed the paper stencil he had so painstakingly made with the name. He painted the name himself while sitting in the dinghy. Jake was a bit stunned having been told to present himself for the unveiling or 'else.'

"Nice, very nice, again, how do you say it?" Jake asked.

"Like this," his Father said, "Kay-lee."

"Do you like it?" Bette asked.

"Yes, it looks great to me. But how are you going to manage all the questions about the name?" he said.

"By making new friends-hospitality goes a long way on the open seas," Clifton said simply.

"Sure enough," said Jake.

They no longer really spoke about the name; it stood alone both in position and in their hearts.

When Jake heard about his parents' plans, he knew *the* port of call had to be New York City. What a better way to show off the town than by land and by sea. Bette and Clifton had previously plotted out their itinerary with side trips to the mainland all along the eastern seaboard. They'd wondered about seeing the kids in New York, but liked the idea of staying there a few days even better when it was Jake and Fiona's idea.

Fiona was a very thoughtful girl, Bette knew, and the idea of seeing a bon voyage note in their mail just hours before departure was incredibly kind and special. She waited to read it with Clifton and placed it aside with the other mail that had infiltrated their restrictions request.

Next, she moved on to the puzzle before her coffee was cold. By the time she had downed her third cup, she finished her half of the puzzle and left the rest for Clifton. They liked to share, she'd complete 'across' and he'd complete 'down.' She headed to their bedroom to shower and change before Clifton returned looking for lunch-which she hadn't prepared. Such a busy life they lead, she thought, retirement was supposed to be less busy than your working life.

Tuesday night they went down to their slip and checked their packing and supplies one more time. Invariably, they would find something either forgotten or needing attention, but also not life-threatening had they missed it. This trip though was different.

No, they always triple and quadruple checked supplies that would sustain them should the unthinkable occur. Besides, this trip, they thought, was really not out in so called 'open water' as much as it was the distance they were planning to travel. They could easily pull into marina after marina every few days, but being more accustomed and seasoned sailors, they preferred to manage on their own.

Bette tossed and turned a bit that night as Clifton noticed since he was not sleeping most of the night. He was still running lists and supplies well into the wee hours, even if that meant just in his head lying in bed next to his bride. This trip was one they'd planned for some time and the added bonus was near the middle of it, a rendez-vous with Fiona and Jake in New York City for the 4th of July celebration in the Hudson.

He recalled writing in his boat log just before turning in:

"After 13 months on the land, we had to go, just had to go. Bette started in February getting Ceilidh spiffed up for the trip. We'd taken all the cloth goods home to be washed and stored them there away from Marina moisture and mildew. I had all the tools out, and we'd borrowed a number of items from the galley rather than duplicate them in the condo. April came and lots of boats at the Marina had moved out, so there was a slip for Ceilidh there, near to home for the last fixin and loading. We found enough fixin to keep me busy....foot pump, fresh water pressure pump, head hoses and three-way valve, varnish teak .....and the list goes on. A boat doesn't fare well sitting in place, not being used."

Still smiling about the upcoming trip with his best friend and wife Bette, Clifton noted a small tear well up in his eye as he thought about their journey through life together, he and Bette, and what Jake and Fiona had ahead of them. He hoped like his marriage to Bette that there was smooth sailing, charming winds, and calm seas. Should the forecast turn stormy, he hoped Jake would adopt the motto which Clifton had spun off from that popular song to which he danced with Bette, "Let the waters rise to meet you, and never let them run you aground." His interpretation of that meant, be the bigger man and apologize to your first mate and never go to bed angry or mad.

By the time Clifton and Bette left their marina in Florida that first Wednesday in May they planned to be arriving in New York City by the end of June. They would spend time in the city before heading north for a few weeks and then returning to Florida by the beginning of September. The sailors would be arriving in Florida about the same time that Fiona and Jake would start their honeymoon.

Jake and Fiona planned two months off and had tried to coordinate that much time off with the schedulers from their respective units. Fiona knew how easily they could either trade shifts or work all their shifts in a row, but she put in for the vacation request just to be safe. In the end, the hospital staff, they discovered, had faked the schedules on both of their units, all along planning to accept both of their vacation requests, but making them sweat a little in the process, which didn't hurt either. They had the blessings of their peers.

Clifton and Bette's voyage on the Ceilidh would be just at the beginning for the honeymooners. Europe in the fall had fewer tourists, somewhat cooler temperatures, better prices, and more options for accommodations. They couldn't think of a better way to celebrate the Davies' trip of the decade than a party on the Ceilidh and the New York City harbor fireworks.

In Clifton's nautical navigational plan, they allowed themselves two to three months at sea in order to reach New York City harbor by the end of June. They'd make it by the 4th of July celebration if it meant getting in a car and driving! Fiona and Jake had expressed to their fondness of watching the fireworks and had made the suggestion for them to arrive in time for that event. Jake had called the local yacht club and as a thank you honeymoon gift, had arranged a temporary slip space inside the marina in lieu of a mooring outside it.

The nautical plan was filed, the yacht prepared, the sailors rested, while the New Yorkers only had to wait for their arrival. The celebration would be fantastic under a dark starry sky and with more than bottle rockets bursting in air; it would be quite a sight that night.

The morning of their departure, Clifton posted a letter to Jake with their itinerary, including the hops to the mainland and local marinas. It was in that letter that Jake got the idea of booking them a slip in the upper harbor off Liberty Park, just west of the Statue of Liberty. They could also take a mooring in Atlantic Highlands, and in Great Kill.

Everything was set, now they just needed to relax, sit back, work, and enjoy the ride. Prayers were said by all who knew of the Davies' journey, no doubts were on hand for their abilities, but the weather has made afoul even experts at sea.

They were ready.

Chapter 31 Eilean Donan Castle & Isle of Sky, 1991

Their bodies and souls refreshed from their dance and slumber, they left the B & B in Pitlochry and headed west towards the Isle of Skye. The ever growing heather-covered mountainous terrain was dotted with sheep and goats. Jake drove more carefully whenever encountering a blind turn, for one time along this stretch of lonely country they'd encountered a small flock of sheep walking casually in the middle of the road, no shepherd in sight.

"Wait here Jake, don't get too close," Fiona cautioned, she was concerned that the beasts might actually take a liking to their vehicle and ram them.

"I'm fairly certain these are docile creatures and more afraid of us," Jake offered, still heeding his wife's suggestion.

Fiona rolled down her window and listened to the baying and bleats. Turning to Jake, she flushed a bit before turning back to the opening and shouting "Baah, baaahhh, baaahhh."

The sudden noise turned multiple heads of sheep nearest the car, and a few "baahs" in return. "I think I'm going to keep the fact that you might be a sheep-whisperer a secret," Jake said with a toss of his head.

"Only between us," Fiona replied, "Only between us." She leaned over then for a long, drawn out and moist kiss. It was one of their longest, especially since their road was blocked anyway.

They waited a few more minutes before gently easing the car through the sluggish sheep. Once on their way again, they began to watch for a particularly picturesque vista upon which to have their picnic lunch. They'd found a butcher and baker in Pitlochry on their way of out of town and had managed to obtain enough non-perishable food stuffs to sustain even Jake's appetite until they arrived in Kyle of Lochalsh. They knew their reservation at Grants' would hold as they had pre-paid with their credit card, in full. They hoped that wasn't a foolish notion but thought the best approach when finding accommodations on an island was to be secure in having a room waiting than wanting a room.

The air grew a bit brisk the higher they drove and a bit of fog had settled in as well. Driving was still smooth and easy, just the sights were less visible the further one looked. Fiona wondered what they might be missing that had been enveloped in fog. Perhaps picturesque mountains with freezing creeks and crackling brooks, at that thought her head bobbed suddenly, she thought she had been feigning sleep, but instead shocked herself when she awoke with a start. "Dreaming again," she muttered.

Jake hadn't heard what she'd said; he was focused on the road ahead of them and the fog.

The roadway, A9, direction Inverness, skirted the Cairn Gorm Ski Area and National Park. Jake knew this from studying their map. He figured the fog had rolled down from the still snow-covered mountains where the air was cooler and the moisture and growing balminess of mid-sixties created the fog and was blocking that view. Fiona appeared to be napping again and he let her rest.

When he saw a petrol station in Invergarry, he pulled in to refuel. The lullaby from the car's constant motion stopped gently and Fiona roused. She took in her surroundings and looked for Jake, spotting him at the back of the car with the gas hose. She hopped out of the car, approached him, and gave him a quick peck on the cheek and a squeeze of his firm buttocks.

"I'm in search of a loo," she said.

"I'll be here darling."

Fiona walked towards the main building and cashier area of the petrol station and disappeared through a double door. Jake continued with the maintaining of their rental car in checking the tire pressure, adding windshield wiper fluid, and cleaning the windows and mirrors. He was just about to go inside to pay when a man approached him.

"Excuse me," the man said.

"Yes sir?" Jake replied.

"My wife just came out of the washroom and said there is a woman in there needing some help. She said her name was Fiona…" the man's voice trailed off as Jake's face grew concerned and he began to hyperventilate. "You must be Jake. Your wife is ok, but she needs you, follow me, my wife showed me where she is waiting for you."

Hastily following the man, Jake's mind began to wander and run through a whole host of problems. As he approached the restroom area, he could see a few people hanging about and could hear the high pitched muted wale of Fiona from within.

"I'm here Fiona, what seems to be the trouble?" Jake announced.

"Jake, is that you?" she said.

"Yes darling, what's wrong?"

"When I came in to use the toilet I peed red. I can't tell where I'm bleeding from," she said.

Jake said quickly, "Are you lightheaded?"

"No, pulse is a bit rapid though."

"Can you open the stall door?" he asked, having shooed out the remaining observers save the woman who found her and sent her husband to get him.

"Yes, but there really isn't room for both you and me in here," Fiona remarked, unlatching the stall door. The tiled room grew dark as the timer light went out and the shadow of light from the open restroom door was the only available light. The assisting stranger, a local to the area, knew about the timer and hit the switch again. She pointed to her husband who was just outside on the door landing to keep an eye on the timer and hit it again and again if needed. He nodded agreement with a shrug of his shoulders.

"Will ye be needing a doctor then, deary?" the woman asked.

Jake began, "My wife and I are both nurses, I think we can handle this, but if you know of a clinic we could go to, we may need it." Turning to Fiona, he began a series rapid fire questions like on their hospital admission forms, practically conducting a complete history and physical in front of the woman and within earshot of her husband. The remaining crowd of onlookers grew bored with the commotion and had already dispersed.

After completing his questioning and confirming a few of Fiona's ideas, the couple deemed this an urgent medical issue but not emergency. They should see a doctor in a day or so. They both knew what to watch for and so far, Fiona's symptoms did not include fever, racing pulse, headache, lightheadedness, dizziness, or heavy bleeding. Her bleeding, while red in color, was not in large quantities. They both remembered how little blood it took to discolor any liquid.

Now a bit embarrassed, Fiona agreed to exit the stall and return to the car. While they were reviewing her systems, the helping woman mentioned the location of a clinic in Ratagan. When Fiona mentioned the location of their room reservation, the woman said it was only a few kilometers away. She said the reception desk at Grants would have the name and number of the clinic and doctor for her to use while she was in town, should she worsen and need to see the doctor for a more thorough examination.

Out at the cars, Jake and Fiona thanked the couple for helping them and for the information. "It was so kind of you to assist me, in that state," Fiona added, blushing.

"Yes, thank you," Jake said, holding out his hand, and shaking the man's proffered hand firmly.

"Well, our daughter loved her time in your country; it is all we can do for any traveling Yank in our own."

"Goodbye, safe journey," the woman said.

"Goodbye," replied Jake and Fiona, now holding hands for support.

Back on the road towards the Isle of Skye, Jake and Fiona returned to discussing her symptoms. With a quirky smile, Jake believed he'd concluded her diagnosis but hoped he was wrong.

"You are sure of the source of the blood, from the urine and not…" he said.

"Yes, I'm sure as best as I can be. I say let's just keep an eye on it, and if I feel any pain or other symptoms, we know where a doctor is up the road, we can go in if needed. Ok?"

"Ok."

"No cramping?"

"No cramping."

Chapter 32 Altstadt, 1985

They found Mittelstraβe just as they were instructed, and the fountain. Not overly superstitious, but also not wanting to pass up the opportunity to change their fates, they each reached into their pockets, tossed a coin into the fountain, and made a wish. Ever the romantic, Fiona wished that fate would interfere with a young man equal to the task of loving someone like her. Ellen wished for an enjoyable trip, but that it would soon take them back to Paris and her awaiting fiancé Pierre. Jane, the oldest of the trio, wished not for something for herself, not this time. No, she wished that the women she just met had their wishes granted.

As they turned to walk away from the fountain, a slight wind picked up and blew debris into Ellen's eye, caused Fiona to blush at the idea that fate had just heard her request, and created a catch in Jane's throat, thinking that all wishes were indeed going to be fulfilled. All she needed to do now was hang on and enjoy the ride. For the other tourists and locals alike who were also taking part in the fountain's ritual, the wind signified something else: stormy weather.

The fountain was in a public square and adjoining the square, were a couple of sidewalk cafés and a few smaller shops. Ellen popped into one of the small shops when she saw postcards in the window. Fiona quickly followed. Not all postcards, Fiona thought, were for mailing. Some, she predicted, she would use in her memorabilia album that she planned to make after she returned home.

In the shop, they found large chocolate bars, a small jar of strawberry jam, and a few other knick knacks. They both bought chocolate and postcards, Fiona also purchased the strawberry jam. She wanted to see if it could at all compare to her Mother's home made jam.

Back outside, Jane was waiting for them. She didn't think about postcards today as she was mesmerized by the view back down the alleyway they'd just walked. When Fiona and Ellen rejoined her on the cobble stone path, they understood why. There was a small troop of younger men dressed in lederhosen and positioning themselves by the fountain. In their hands, or by their feet were the assorted musical instruments that they each played.

Altstadt, they later learned, was a Mecca for tourists, and the locals did their best to oblige. This small brass band was all the proof Fiona needed to feel entertained. She took out her Canon T70 and began to frame her shots before she actually took them. Using the natural beauty of the alleyway and the fountain as her backdrop, Fiona took a few shots hoping that at least one of them captured the essence that was old town. She focused on the band, the costumes, the cobble stones, and the audience; she even captured Jane and Ellen in a few frames in an entirely candid fashion. They were completely unaware and perfectly innocent in their positioning in the photographs. If the process of taking these pictures turned out as expected, Fiona would most certainly need to share them with both of the women and perhaps the Düsseldorf Chamber of Commerce for their marketing campaign.

"I should be so lucky," Fiona said softly.

"Lucky about what?" Ellen asked.

"Oh, I just took what I think is a really good photograph, and I was just thinking if they turned out as good as I expect, then I'd be so lucky."

"Get a good shot?" asked Jane.

"Yes, I hope so."

When Mittelstraβe intersected with Flingerstraβe, they took another right hand turn. Here, after about thirty feet, the alleyway opened up onto a smaller street, with a sidewalk for them to walk along. This street had enough room for one car in each direction. Again, there were no lane painted markings to guide them.

"I'm glad I'm not driving around here, I'd be so slow and lost without all the painted markings. I'd likely go the wrong way down a one-way street!" Jane exclaimed.

"Me too," Ellen agreed.

"I think I'd have to take some serious lessons if I change my travel plans from biped to automobile," said Jane, who still looked a bit perplexed about the roadway adjacent to their sidewalk. "I'm so glad you two let me join you on your trip. This is going to be so much fun!"

"I agree, this is fun, right Fiona?" prompted Ellen.

"Agreed!"

They didn't walk very far along Flingerstraβe before they were back on Kasernenstraβe, the street they knew would take them back to the train station. Instead of turning right, in the direction of the station, however, they turned left when they saw the view up the street to the left.

"Look up there!" Ellen shouted.

"Oh, how beautiful, let's go in there!" Fiona suggested.

In turning left and walking about half a block, they reached that which had caught their eye. It was another small square which was positioned in front of an old church. This area of town was completely built up and the only 'green' areas were those that were planted, a few trees that lined the larger streets or in this square, the hanging baskets full of petunias in assorted colors of deep purple and a most vivid fuchsia. Amongst the petunias were assorted spiky or feathering greens and a few light colored tiny blossomed wildflowers.

Fiona recognized the petunias but not the rest of the plantings. It didn't matter, everyone marveled at the effect. These baskets were hung in pairs opposite each other, hanging from ornate metal arms on lampposts that presumably at night, lit the street. Again, Fiona took out her camera and framed a few shots, but this time, she asked for posed shots with Ellen and Jane in the foreground, the hanging baskets lined up, pointing to the old church in the background. Fiona hoped that these precious shots also turned out.

They took turns taking and posing for each other's photographs, changing the pose slightly with each other, allowing for some bit of differences instead of having them all be essentially the same. As they were finishing up, the clock tower from the old church chimed three o'clock. "Three bells, three women, that's just right," Fiona said, thoughtfully.

Jane added, "Exactly, it is *just* right. If I forget to tell you when we part ways, I had a great time with you two."

"If I may, Fiona," Ellen said looking at Fiona for permission, "We did too."

They toured the small old church for the next hour, where they took shelter from the growing temperatures and climbing sunshine outside. They were delighted by the refreshing climate inside the limestone structure and in their good fortune of no further rain. They had traveled far enough east of Amsterdam to outrun the downpours of their time there.

Looking at her watch, Ellen noted the time was closing in on four o'clock and they hadn't decided their final destination for the day. She said, "Well ladies, have you seen enough of Düsseldorf? Do you want to stay here or shall we move on to somewhere else?"

A concerned Fiona said, "We've only just gotten here, I guess I thought we were staying here. But, we only stayed in Amsterdam a little over a day; I suppose if we are going to see the most of Europe on this trip, perhaps we do need to move on. What do you think Jane?"

"I'll be happy with whatever you two decide. If I can help in that decision-making does the youth hostel guidebook indicate hostels in Düsseldorf?"

"Good question; let me look." Ellen replied, and then she opened her daypack in which she carried the youth hostel guidebook. It was Fiona's turn with 'the book.' "There is a hostel listed, I have a suggestion. Why don't we call the hostel and see if there is room for three tonight? That will certainly help us with our decision," Ellen said.

"Good idea, both of you," replied Fiona. "We need to find a pay telephone, or a post office. I don't see one in the church, but then again, it is highly unlikely that I would!"

Back on Kasernenstraβe, they quickly saw a bank of public telephones and they immediately made their way over to them. "What's the number?" Fiona asked. "Oh, wait a minute, you better call," she said to Ellen, "You speak a little German and you have more experience with European phones and phone numbers than I do!"

"Good point. I've got the number," she said, as she dialed the number while consulting the guidebook. "Ringing," she concluded.

Fiona and Jane could only stand back and wait while Ellen completed the call. Fiona based her understanding of the one-sided conversation from the body language and the intonation of Ellen's voice. Interpreting what she gathered to Jane, she said, "I don't think they have room at the *inn*."

"What makes you say that?" Jane asked.

"I can tell by the way Ellen's speaking. I think we should think of somewhere else to go, let me get out the book."

"Ok," Jane replied.

Now Jane stood back and listened to Ellen and watched as Fiona flipped through pages in the book. "We could catch a train to Würzburg at 5:36PM," Fiona announced to Jane.

"Works for me, does the book indicate hostels there?" Jane asked.

"Yes, I see the icon for them. Get Ellen's attention and let's see what's up."

Jane tapped Ellen on the shoulder and she halted her call politely, "Yes?" Ellen said.

"No room, right?" Jane assumed.

Ellen replied, "Right. So I've been asking the receptionist if they had any suggestions or knew where else we could stay. I was on hold for a minute or so and she just came back to the line. If you two figured that out, did you look for a destination for us?"

"Yes, what about Würzburg?" Fiona asked.

"How far away is that?" Ellen questioned.

"Well, the 5:36PM train is scheduled to arrive at 9:45PM; if we take that I think we better have a reservation or some kind of guaranteed lodging. Don't you think?" Fiona surmised.

"Yes, I do. Let me ask her," Ellen said, then returning to the phone and continued with the inquiry.

After what felt like a long time, as Jane and Fiona watched, Ellen's face grew into a smile. They could hear it in her voice too. "Sounds like we have a reservation," Jane said.

"Yes, it does. I wonder for where though." Fiona added, thinking that it was growing late and they still needed to get on the 5:36PM train.

Just as Fiona was checking her watch for the fourth time, Ellen concluded her call. "We are all set, we have reservations for 3 women at the Würzburg Youth Hostel. The receptionist said the hostel staff will wait for us knowing that we are coming in on a late train. They said it happens all the time, and, the receptionist taught me something rather important."

"What is that?" Jane asked.

"Well, she said since this is still high tourist season, we may want to take a little time to plot out where we are going, a few days at a time, so that we don't end up arriving somewhere too late and without a place to stay."

"Good idea. I never thought of that!" Fiona admitted. "I just assumed, wrongly, that we'd always be able to find a place to stay. Perhaps we should also have an alternate plan, just in case our primary plan has a problem."

"What about dinner," Jane asked.

"Good thinking, are either of you hungry?" asked Ellen.

"I'm not, it's only a little after four o'clock. Let me check the book to see if it says that 5:36PM train has a dining car." Fiona said, then turning her attention back to the book. After a bit of reading, she looked up and informed them that, "No mention of a dining car, actually, I couldn't determine if the book does tell you that. Maybe when we run into a really nice conductor, they would know more about this book and how to read the legend better."

"Even if we don't get the information, we can just be prepared with having enough of our own food, which we bring with us. You know, food that either we decide to eat if perishable or food that could keep. Take Fiona's strawberry jam for example, it would be tasty with some brie and a baguette. If we can find a butcher shop or even a small grocery store, perhaps we should watch for one on our way back to the train station, we could buy ourselves dinner and snacks."

"Ellen, you read my mind, well, at least about the strawberry jam. I'm all for finding a grocery store, even if we have to ask for directions or go a little out of our way to find one." Fiona said, beginning to walk in the direction of the train station. "Keep your eyes peeled and your step light," Fiona said, smiling.

Jane replied, "I'm so glad I hooked up with you two. I'm taking notes about how you plan and travel. I would have just raced to the train station, maybe grabbed something there, or tried my luck on the train. Either way, now, I know I won't miss dinner. Not with the way you two make plans!"

"Fiona and I have always been good planners, haven't we?" Ellen said. "Remember back in college when you helped me by entertaining Pierre while I took a mid-term exam?"

Smiling, Fiona said, "Absolument!" "Absolutely!"

The walk back to the train station, along Kasernenstraβe, took them right by a small grocery store with a tiny pastry department. They immediately exchanged knowing glances at each other, Fiona winked, Jane gave two thumbs up, and Ellen said, "What luck!"

Inside the grocery store they separated to hunt for that which they would each eat for dinner. "Can I suggest, before we buy anything, that we meet up by the cashier and compare purchases before we spend our money? I was thinking that way we wouldn't duplicate what we are buying and may actually plan to buy things that go well together. What do you think about that?" asked Fiona.

"Good idea," said Jane.

"I agree; good idea." Ellen said, as she opened the door to the store.

They didn't take long to meet back by the cashier. Jane found a stash of beef jerky, string cheese, and some hard rolls. Ellen found some brie, a baguette, and another cheese that she said was 'smelly.' Fiona arrived with a large bottle of Evian, chocolate bars, a baguette, sliced ham, potato chips, and a smaller log of what she assumed was like summer sausage at home. Fiona also found a small jar of mustard.

They agreed that they had shopped wisely and that no one truly needed to return anything, their luck was still going strong. They paid for their items with Fiona's credit card since they realized they never stopped to change money, even after paying for lunch with Ellen's card. They never saw the 'exchange' sign or actually went out of their way to find an exchange. That little bit of carelessness would need to stop if they expected to have cash to pay for things, since not all merchants, vendors, or attractions would accept a VISA® card. They only had the change from the youth hostel in Amsterdam and they threw that in the fountain a few hours ago.

"How about some wine," Ellen suggested.

The attentive cashier spoke up saying, "Are you Americans?"

"Yes, we are," Fiona answered. "Why?"

"Oh, I really liked Chicago and New York City."

Fiona was curious how this cashier had such a good command of English. "When were you there?"

Wilma blushed and replied, "I lived in Chicago for a little over a year."

Fiona swallowed softly and said, "We live in Minnesota, did you ever get up there?"

"No, I didn't."

"How was it that you came to Chicago?"

"I saw a baseball game in Chicago on my last trip over. Friends of mine from university convinced me to go with them on a foreign exchange program. I enrolled in their university just for that class. I was studying at the Robert Schumann University, here in Düsseldorf, and they were studying at the University of Bonn, in Bonn. Do you know Bonn?"

"I've heard of it," Jane said, still amazed at the connection with this young woman.

"What were you studying," asked Ellen, her musical curiosity now piqued.

"Violin performance," she said.

"What a small world." Fiona replied, then thinking back to their purchases and time constraints, she said, "Do you sell wine here or will we need to go to a liquor store?"

"We sell a few varieties of wine and beer. I can show you, it will only take a moment, we don't have much left in stock our next delivery is tomorrow." Wilma said most assuredly, yet knowing that these women were either planning a picnic or maybe were leaving town. She assumed it was a bit of both. As she led them to the store's small cache of alcoholic beverages, she said, "Are you planning a picnic?"

"No we, well, not exactly," began Jane. "We are taking the train tonight, going to Würzburg, and we needed to buy food and drinks for dinner. So I guess if you call buying food and eating while riding a train a picnic, then yes, we are going on a picnic," Jane said.

"I've been on that train, it is a nice ride. You'll like Würzburg, here we are, some wine over there," she said, pointing to the shelves to her left, "And bottles of beer are over there in the cooler."

They looked at the various bottles of wine and selected an Australian Rosé, and a German Riesling, the latter seemed most apropos. Ellen picked up a few bottles of Heineken, to which Fiona snubbed her nose. She wasn't planning on drinking beer anytime soon. Ever since graduation, she would always say when asked if she wanted a beer, 'No, thank you, I drank all the beer for my entire life in college.'

They returned to the cash register with their bottles in hand. No other customers had entered in the ensuing time and while a few looked in from the street, they all but one walked away without entering. That tourist smiled as he walked past Fiona and the other women. In this instance, Ellen caught Fiona noticing a man noticing her; it made her smile for her still single friend.

Back at the cash register, Jane realized as Fiona carried the bottles of wine, to ask if they had a cork screw or a bottle opener. Jane didn't have one and this was something they had yet to discuss. "Do you have a bottle opener," Jane asked Fiona, and then turned to Ellen when she saw the vacant expression on Fiona's face. "Well that answers that!" Jane announced pointedly.

Ellen and Fiona hadn't brought a bottle opener with them and they were both busy looking around the register to see if they sold them.

When Ellen didn't see one, she said, "What do you think Fiona, shall we add to our picnic set?" Fiona asked, "Do you sell corkscrews?"

That pretty well answered Ellen's question and she looked in her daypack for her credit card so that they could proceed with their purchases and head back to the train station.

Wilma replied, "Yes, I keep them hidden here under the front counter, they too often walk out on their own if I don't do that. Here you go." She smiled as she handed one to Fiona.

"Thank you very much. So, when was it that you were in Chicago, and what about New York City?" Fiona asked.

As Wilma punched in the items for purchase, she quickly told the trio about her initial one year in Chicago in 1980 and then adding another year of touring about the United States, ending with a few months in New York City. She took a job as a cashier, no less.

Keeping track of the time, Jane began to move towards the door indicating that it was time for them to leave if they didn't want to have to run or take a taxi to the train station. Ellen and Fiona knew she was right and after Fiona took down Wilma's mailing address, they were back on the street and making good time for their train.

As they walked into the train station, they continued with their habit of seeking out the restroom facilities knowing that while still less than optimal, a train station's toilet would be nicer to use than one on a train itself. Finished with their 'toilette,' they proceeded further into the terminal and consulted the big board of arrivals and departures. They were getting better at deciphering all the posted information and noted that they were seated in a compartment that had bench seating to the right and left of the entry door and a small convertible table by the window. After boarding, they were finalizing their picnic when the train left the station causing each of them to hold onto their various food and beverage stuffs so that they didn't end up on the compartment floor.

Once the train was steadily underway, they opened the Rosé and a bottle of Evian. They each took a chunk of their respective baguettes and made sandwiches. Ellen's creation included smelly cheese and sausage. Jane used a sharp knife to cut her log sausage like pastrami or pepperoni and added some cheese similarly to Ellen's. Fiona's sandwich, on the other hand, was concocted of thinly sliced ham and brie on a baguette with a little bit of dijon mustard.

Everyone sat back to enjoy their sandwiches, shuffling from their seats to the newly accustomed rhythm that was train travel. Each train, they would discover, had its own rhythm and seasoned travelers would adjust faster than any novice. Before finishing their sandwiches, they wanted to share a toast with the Rosé wine, and this time, Fiona made the toast:

"Here's to finding friends, fiancés, and family!"

"Here, here!" announced Jane and Ellen in unison.

Each of them spent the 4 hour journey differently. Fiona slept, Ellen wrote out another postcard to Pierre, and Jane sat back and took it all in. By nightfall, their stomachs, minds, and hearts had been well fed.

Chapter 33 Islands & Bridges, 1991

They agreed that Jake would continue driving and let Fiona rest. They didn't want this small blip to further affect their honeymoon. They found a small quiet meadow amidst the fog and pulled over to have their lunch. They went down a winding wooded hillside, keeping clear of the brush, gorse, and heather. They were off-road and loving it. They made sure to keep out of visual range of the road before they stopped. Exiting the car, Fiona walked carefully to the make shift wayside rest, and Jake carried their luncheon and a blanket from the boot.

They ate in relative silence taking in the mountain vistas, listening to the earth, the animals, and their hearts. They each consumed a turkey on rye and a roast beef on whole wheat, shared some pickles, olives, crisps, and a large bottle of orange crush. The shops in Pitlochry were overdue for their orders for diet cola products, so they selected the orange. It reminded Fiona of childhood and the luxurious beverages at a particular fast food chain with excellent fries.

After their stomachs were filled with all that Fiona had purchased, they lingered on the blanket for a while, glad to be holding each other and continuing to take in the picturesque mountain views. The snow was still upon the highest peaks, but the temperatures in the meadow weren't unseasonable, but typical for fall weather. Though it could be unpredictable this time of year, they had enjoyed crisp nights and sunny days, dressing in layers and shedding as the temperatures rose and fell.

Instead of dessert, they lay in each other's arms. With the events of the morning still fresh on their minds, they discussed the risk of making love on their picnic blanket. Feeling isolated and refreshed from their lunch, they, being typical newlyweds, opted in.

Jake took extra care with Fiona's body; he mentally took his time and making note to himself that this time, for sure her crescendos were prior to his own. He unbuttoned her blouse first and nuzzled upon her bosom. The gooseflesh responses were all too common when Fiona's breasts were exposed to dropping temperatures, or to Jake's touch.

Fiona rested her head upon a rolled up jacket and arched her back in response to Jake's suckling mouth. Her hips were also rising and falling, calling for the coupling of their bodies. A small sweat grew upon her brow.

"You are sure you feel ok, darling?" Jake asked questioningly.

"Baby, I always feel ok when I'm with you."

"You know what I mean."

"Yes, I know. I want you, is there any doubt?"

"No, I can see that," Jake said, and in saying so, undid the remaining fastenings of her pants and slid his hand upon her mound, warm and moist. He smiled as removed her remaining clothes.

She let her hands roam about his torso, sculpting his chest and shoulders, pulling him to her. Then she sought out the zipper to his jeans and relieved his growing manhood. Not wanting to wait much longer, she allowed her body to rise to his hand and come upon it. Her back both ached and arched under his touch. She found his mouth and kissed him deeply. Then let out a scream he knew was only for him.

For some reason, however, that scream sounded a bit more like a bleat and he laughed as his wife baahed for him again and again and again. He held off joining their bodies until she had advanced in their dance more times than he could count. Viewing her face told him she was more than pleased and ready for more.

He removed his strangling jeans and allowed her to mount him. He wanted to watch the peaks of his wife bounce to the scenery of white capped mountains. Her moans and satisfaction were echoing above and below them. He almost thought he heard a sheep bleat in response from a neighboring mountain top.

Their blanket oasis was like an island in the greenery and purple heather and muted gorse that was the highlands. The red and black tartan pattern of the blanket, while likely a clan they would recognize, was, in the moment, one that neither of them could identify. The woolen fibers were rough on their naked bodies, that rash of love they had called it.

After their lovemaking ended, they relaxed into each other's arms and slept. Her body was more overwhelmed with joy and inattentive to the small but growing catch in her right lower quadrant. Their love juices flowed from their bodies, mixing, and spilling upon the plaid. They lay there, still joined.

They woke just before tea time and hustled back to the car and retraced themselves back to the A87. Within the following fifteen to twenty minutes, a mileage sign appeared indicating 38K to Ratagan; Grants would be along the main street, according to their directions. The heater on the car took the edge off the falling temperatures and the fog dissipated upon their return to the highway.

They looked at each other, kissed quickly, and as best one could, held hands with a manual transmission, rode the remainder of the journey lost in their own thoughts. Jake was looking forward to dinner and a nice bottle of wine. Fiona was thinking about dinner and the strange feeling ebbing in her abdomen.

Once off the main highway, signs were posted directing them to Grants. The moderate sized croft stood solo amongst the heather and gorse, whitewashed against the greenery. They were met soon after pulling into the drive by a tall man sporting a large woolen sweater. Fiona thought perhaps the weather was turning cool by the looks of his outfit and by her wanting a sweater too. She also noticed that she was still slightly sweaty.

The driveway was unpaved, but lined with small granite chips which made it noisy. Not likely that many cars arrive unannounced in a place like this, Jake pondered. He pulled into an available parking spot and turned off the engine. The tall man began to approach the vehicle at a leisurely pace, not being intrusive but as a welcoming host to new guests-who he always treated like family.

As Jake exited the car, he heard the man speak, "Aye, ye've arrived then laddie. Did you have a good journey? I'm Mr. Grant, we are so glad to have ye with us."

"Yes, we have and yes we did. Thank you." Jake replied.

Fiona hadn't gotten out of the car just yet, so Jake walked around to her door to open it for her. He eyed the trunk to see where their overnight bags were and saw they were on the seat behind her. He first opened her door and then turned back to the passenger door to claim their bags.

"Jake, I feel strange." Fiona whimpered.

"What's that, Fiona?"

"I've got a tugging in my stomach, just here." She said, pointing to her right lower quadrant. "I think I've developed a fever too, even though I know I'm warm, I'd want a blanket or a jacket just now. Perhaps we can ask Mr. Grant for directions to the clinic?"

"Do you want to go inside first, see if a change like lying down will help?" Jake inquired.

Fiona said, "Yes, let's try that. I don't feel that bad, could just be something I ate. You feel ok though?"

"Yes, good as rain."

Looking back at the building, Jake could make out the front door and how wide it was, a single door, more like the homes in Connecticut or Long Island than what he expected here. He'd thought a draw bridge about the door more appropriate and was a bit let down that the building was as it was.

He didn't get much more time to reflect on the building once they were inside. It was warm and welcoming. He got Fiona settled in a chair in the parlor and then returned to the car to get their bags and her purse. When he opened her car door, he saw it. Blood. She hadn't mentioned feeling any bleeding but still, he ran back into the house.

"Fiona," he exclaimed, "You're bleeding!"

"I am?" Fiona said softly.

"Yes, look," he said, holding up a towel he'd taken to the seat in attempts to clean it. "Mr. Grant, can you call ahead to the clinic and explain we are on our way over?"

"Aye, laddie, but there's no way you need to go to the clinic just now. It's closed, the doctor is out," he said.

"How do you know that?" Fiona asked.

"Because he's out back playing cards with the rest of me cronies, today is poker day! Wait and let me fetch him for ye!"

As Mr. Grant removed himself from the parlor, his voice was loud and alarming. He yelled for the doctor from just in the hall, not fully outside. Jake waited with Fiona and could hear, "Fitz, come quick now, there's a lassie that is a needin' ye presently in the parlor!"

"Come down here Tony, it's ye turn!" said a card player.

"Aye, it may be that, but I need Fitz," said Tony.

"Aye, what's the clambering about then?" Dr. Fitz asked, beginning to rise out of his chair, hearing the alarm in his friend's voice.

Tony replied catching his breath, "Aye, a young couple just arrived, ye ken the couple we've been waiting for, and well the lassie is bleeding and not feeling well. Please come!"

Dr. Fitz got up, "Alright Tony, I'm on my way, where is she then? At the clinic?"

"No, in the parlor!" Tony yelled and returned to the house.

Inside, Jake and Fiona weren't as frantic as Mr. Grant, but their level of restraint was also apparent.

"Hang on lassie, the doctor will be here presently," Tony announced. "Yes, most presently."

The heavy boot steps coming from the hallway to the parlor echoed in pairs. In the end, the entire poker game participants came bounding into the house, but only the doctor entered the parlor. The not too quiet whisperings from that area of the house were a bit unsettling, and Mr. Grant shooed them outside.

"There now, lassie, the doctor is here."

Twenty minutes passed as an anxious Mr. Grant, his poker party, and now Mrs. Grant were waiting in the kitchen for word on how their new guest was fairing. It was Jake who emerged first and was shortly followed by the doctor. Fiona was still in the parlor. Jake looked drawn and fatigued, the doctor, in concentration.

They had agreed to wait this out at the Grants and see how Fiona felt a few hours hence. The bleeding was vaginal, not urinary, as they had once thought. She was resting quietly on the towel-reinforced sofa of the parlor, the cramping, sweats, and clamminess abating. As far as she could ascertain, she wasn't due for her cycle either. She was comforted knowing that the pain she had silently in the car was now shared and in the hands of Jake and Dr. Fitz.

Jake checked them into their room and unpacked their overnight bags, returning with a sweater for Fiona. Mrs. Grant served them soup and scones with strawberry jam and hot tea. They were in a holding pattern, an island awaiting the dropping of the draw bridge, and the continuation of their honeymoon.

Chapter 34 Würzburg, 1985

Back on the train, Fiona was dreaming and she felt an odd sensation poking her in the shoulder. In her mind, she saw a lush green valley nestled in snowcapped mountains and a small brook bubbling near her boot-covered feet. She was slowly becoming aware that there were voices in her dream, female voices, but a far way off and somewhat muted. She was gazing into the sunshine that was gradually melting the snow, filling the brook, which fed the green grasses in the valley. She heard the crickets chirp and the birds singing.

"Wait a minute," she said, in her mind. "Birds don't usually sing at the same time as crickets."

Then she felt the cool water of the spring splashing her face, washing away the cares of her day. But wait, it wasn't her hands that were washing her face. It was a splash of cool water all right, but her hands remained clasped under her head as she lay looking around her at the greenery that was the valley. Fiona remained confused, recumbent in the splendor of the valley, in the warmth of the sun's glow.

She heard the drums of the woodland folk as their parade recessed further into her mind's eye. And then the timpani rang out, boom, boom, boom, in concert with the shrill flutes and violins. The symphony, Fiona knew, was one of nature, one that could be somewhat off key. To her, this was her music; it was always her first opus, the sounds of spring.

Ellen looked at Jane and said, "I don't know what else we can do; she's probably dreaming and incorporating all we are doing to wake her up into her dream. I can see a small smirk growing on her face. She's asleep all right."

"How much wine did you have?" Jane asked, looking at the empty bottle.

"Fiona must have had some of the wine, right? That can make her so sleepy…" Ellen's voice trailed off as Jane started to speak.

"Has she done this before, slept this soundly?" asked Jane.

"I heard of one incident when she was living off-campus and was late for clinicals. She'd forgotten to set her alarm clock and was only woken up when Harriet, another classmate of ours, went into her room and shook her," said Ellen, as she demonstrated on Jane, grabbing her shoulders and gently rocking her back and forth.

"Well, maybe that's what we need to do next. Banging on our bottles with the spoon, clanging the guidebooks like they were cymbals or us jumping up and down haven't worked. You might as well grab her shoulders, I'll get her feet," suggested Jane.

"Ok, that's a good idea." Ellen realized that they had only a few more precious minutes to disembark the train before it continued the route to Stuttgart.

"Ok, ready?" Jane asked.

"Ready," Ellen replied.

"Ok, on the count of three, one, two, three!" They said the countdown in unison.

On three, as they had agreed, Ellen grabbed Fiona's shoulders and Jane her feet. In their combined efforts, they were able to right Fiona and get her sitting up. She had long ago slumped over taking up most of the seats on the one side of their compartment. The two women would learn, with Fiona's short stature, she could curl up or stand up in the smallest and most convenient spaces. Especially if it meant to sleep, in that, they learned, she was a master contortionist.

A newly righted Fiona opened her eyes and said, "Hey, watch out for the little brook…" She stopped there as she realized she was no longer dreaming, but being intently watched by her two very concerned friends. "Hi," was all Fiona could muster amid her increasingly flushed face.

"Welcome back, have a nice trip?" Ellen joked.

"Actually, I was," Fiona began, and then realized she was being teased. "Why did you wake me up?" she asked.

"We were getting worried. The train is going to leave Würzburg very soon; we've packed up everything and are ready to go. Come on now, wake up, this is our stop!" Jane said, more forcefully than intended, but still sounding like a mother hen too-which had been her first intention.

"Oh, yeah, er," Fiona stuttered, "I'm awake now, thanks. Würzburg, here we come!"

Thinking that it was fortunate that the other two kept track of their belongings and took the time to pack up their picnic and what not, Fiona was the modicum of poise in the train station and on the walk to the youth hostel.

"Glad to have you back with us," Jane said.

Over the faint rumblings of the departing train, she said softly to her old and new friend, "Thanks."

"You are welcome," Ellen said, "Just don't make a habit out of it. You scared me to death!"

As they exited the train station, they were refreshed by the crisp autumn night air. While Fiona was sleeping, Ellen and Jane had researched the location of the youth hostel in Würzburg and after looking at a map in the book, they determined that they would need to take a taxi to the hostel for it was too far to walk. Time, at this moment, was not on their side. The hostel, they knew, would close and lock their front doors at eleven o'clock and it was now after ten.

"Fiona," Ellen began.

"Yes?"

"Jane and I did a little investigating while you were dreaming of 'little brooks.'"

"I'm sorry you had difficulty waking me up. I'm rather embarrassed." Fiona said, as put up a hand to cover her face. She had finally flushed.

"No, it's ok. We got off the train in time; it's just that the hostel is too far away, we'll need to take a taxi to get there." Ellen said, looking from side to side, as they left the train station building.

"Ok," Fiona said, following where this was going. She, too, helped look for the taxi stand, but Ellen spied it first.

"There is the taxi stand over there," Ellen said, pointing to the queue of travelers waiting for taxis.

"Wow, it is really dark tonight, just look at all the stars!" exclaimed Jane.

The town of Würzburg, the guidebook indicated, had a population of about one hundred thousand people and it physically straddled the *Main River*. The ridgeline of the buildings here was that of residential, up to 5 stories maximum, mostly two to three stories, like many older European cities.

While they waited in the taxi line, they each took a turn at the currency exchange window, figuring that they would be in Germany for a few more days. They wanted to have sufficient cash on hand, so they each exchanged about $100. The train terminal gave a satisfactory exchange rate, they learned after the fact. They waited about ten minutes before they were at the front of the taxi line. Ellen was selected to explain to their driver that they wanted to go to the Jugendherberge Youth Hostel. The cabbie answered in German and then in English, "Ja, Ja. Zehn minuten!" "Yes, yes. Ten minutes!"

They were a bit surprised that he spoke English. Perhaps the advice they'd received at school was a bit outdated; they encountered more and more people who were either fluent or conversant in English. Ellen's German was good, but sometimes limited. Jane and Fiona spoke almost no German, albeit counting, travel terms, and food, those kinds of things didn't really count, not according to Ellen.

After they confirmed that the driver knew of their destination, they climbed in. Their route took them down many quaint streets and drove across a bridge that connected the city over a wide river. It was difficult to see the city too well at this hour and they vowed to take a better look in the morning.

While they were driving to the hostel, the cabbie had told them that at this hour of the night, the main gate to the hostel would be closed. They would have to ring the buzzer to get in. He had described to them to the doors and the courtyard through which they could enter and locate the hostel's front door.

When they stopped midway up the stairs, the cabbie said, "Now just go up those few remaining steps. At the top, turn right and look for the gate where there is a large set of double doors, they guard the courtyard. Just through there," he said, as he pointed to the staircase about 15 paces away. "Will you need help with your bags?" he asked.

"No, I think we can manage, but thank you," Jane said, as she paid him. She had exchanged some dollars at the train station while Fiona was helping Ellen maneuver with her heavy backpack.

"Good evening to you then," he said, and as he drove off, they were left in the shadows of the great beam of light.

Fiona looked up at the night sky, then up and down the street, and then back again to the staircase that the driver said was the entrance to the hostel. "Wow," was about all she could muster.

"Ditto," replied Ellen. "The guidebook didn't say this place was massive!" Indeed, the hostel in question was easily 5 stories tall, and longer than an American football field, or at least it looked that long while they were standing curbside in the dark. Unfamiliar shapes are difficult to estimate in the dark.

"Look at all the light," Jane noted, and then they noticed what Jane had seen. It was a sharp beam of light, the column of which was heading skyward not far from where the taxi dropped them off.

"Where is that coming from? Don't go into the light!" Fiona joked.

"Oh, Fiona, don't be so macabre, we are NOT Carol Anne! The hostel knew we were coming in on a late train and they just wanted to make sure we didn't get lost from the curb to the door!" Ellen declared, snubbing out her friends attempt at haunting humor.

At this hour, the street was relatively dark, only a few lamplights were lit, and they were interspersed up and down the street. The dark autumn sky was so clear and the air crisp, had they been out in the country, the illusion of plucking a star from the sky would have been hard to miss. But here at the dooryard to the hostel's gate, the lights shone like a beacon to the heavens. These lights were so bright; the stars were camouflaged in the sky.

Softly, Fiona said, "I wish we could see the stars from here."

"Me too," said Ellen.

"I was watching them from the train, but now they've vanished for the night, and so must we," Jane said, philosophically.

They climbed the steps and the closer they got to the courtyard door, the clearer it became that the beam of light was coming from the youth hostel courtyard. They all thought how kind that the 'innkeepers' had thought to leave a light on for them.

At the top of the stairs, they found the double doors and the buzzer. Ellen, the first at the top of the stairs, turned to the other women and said, "Shall I take the honor?"

"Go right ahead," Fiona chimed.

"Yes, you are ready, go for it. Buzz away." Jane retorted.

What caught them off guard now was the sound that was emitted following the depressing of the buzzer. It was like a deep gong or carillon sound. Not a buzz as they had expected. "Wow," again, was all Fiona could say.

"Ditto," Ellen said, turning and making a face of utter surprise at the same time.

"Is this place a castle or a hostel?" Jane asked.

"We'll see if we can get in!" Fiona quipped.

Just as Fiona uttered this remark, the latch on the door popped and the wide double doors spread open. Their eyes took some time to adjust to the brightness of the courtyard and to realize that a short older woman was now looking back at them. Her smile beamed just like the light from the courtyard.

"Guten Abend," she said swiftly.

The trio chimed in together saying, "Guten Abend."

From their American accent in the spoken German, the woman greeting them said, "Good evening, I am Frauke Feierabend, head mistress of the hostel. Please come in!"

"Thank you. You are so kind to meet us at the door. We apologize for coming in so late. We completely forgot to plan out where we would be staying tonight. Thank you for having space!" Fiona said, somewhat stammering. Under her breath she said, "That won't happen again!" She was growing tired and the dream state she had been in was keeping her from fully waking up.

"Don't give it any more thought. My Greek Mother used to tell me to keep a light on for wayward sailors; you never know if one might take a fancy to you! Besides, the remote latch is broken and I'm waiting for my husband, Wilhelm, to fix it. So in a way, I'm not doing anything extraordinary. Please come in," she said kindly.

They followed the little older woman as she turned and headed across the courtyard. She must have been a model in another life, for her beauty was not lost on them, but her height, it was almost the same as Fiona; short. Surely, a woman as charming as this would work in front of the camera, just not a runway model; she was too short for that. This much Fiona knew all too well. She was wearing a woolen brown skirt, off-white blouse, and a brown shawl. Her sensible shoes indicated a history of wearing high-heeled shoes and the related sequelae of sore feet later in life.

Frauke walked through the cobblestone courtyard and disappeared behind an open over-sized door. When the women caught up to her, she was standing behind a counter with a registration book opened for them to sign in. They quickly completed the necessary paperwork and followed her upstairs to their room. Unlike the hostel in Amsterdam, with its grand room and rows of bunk beds, this hostel had smaller rooms that had 4 beds in each room.

As Frauke opened the door to their room, switched on the light, and handed a room key to each of them, she said, "Here you go, you three have room number 27. Breakfast begins at 6:00AM sharp, but I don't expect to see you until at least 8! It is after eleven o'clock now; I do hope you sleep well. We can talk more tomorrow. Now good night!" she said, leaving the room.

The sleep well comment caused a snicker from Ellen and Jane, as they knew Fiona had a head start in that department. They completed their preparations for bed and had successful lights out at 11:50PM. Shortly after their room lights went out, the broad beam of light in the courtyard dimmed, leaving a much smaller beam, like an outdoor night light. Fiona fell asleep with a smile on her face.

In the morning, after completing a refreshing shower and shampoo, they got dressed in relative silence. Ellen wore a soft pink tunic with grey pants and flats. Jane wore another of her favorite crisp white shirts with blue jeans and tennis shoes. Fiona wore a hot pink polo shirt, also with jeans and tennis shoes. These clothes would, they thought, be suitable for the day, but later, they would discover otherwise.

The trio found their way to the great room of this hostel and the ever present line for food. Breakfast, Frauke had explained last night, was included in their overnight fees, and they eagerly awaited their turn to see what this hostel offered their young travelers.

Armed with another large pot of hot water, Frauke recognized the women as they were waiting in line. "So happy to see you this morning, I trust you slept well?" she asked.

"Very well," offered Fiona.

"Yes, very well," confirmed both Jane and Ellen.

The women were a bit worn out from their walking about town in Düsseldorf and catching the late train. Sleep, especially as they saw for Fiona, was a commodity that they would have to monitor regularly. If they were unfortunate to run low on quality sleep, as was the case near finals in college, Ellen knew someone was likely to get sick. For reasons such as this, Ellen didn't really put up much of a fuss when it came to waking Fiona. She could only hope for the chance to catch up to Fiona's nap time or become a good traveling sleeper. Exhaustion or a good day of sight-seeing would likely be a sufficient drain, and that sleep, when it was afforded, would be more than welcome.

Jane noticed the hard rolls and jam, helping herself when it finally became her turn. Fiona decided on oatmeal with hot chocolate; Ellen corn flakes and tea. They found a table with three open seats and made their way over to it. There were round tables at this hostel, not the long tables that reminded Fiona of her elementary school lunchroom. Here, 6-8 diners could share food and conversation; always open to the thought that both would be good enough.

The rest of the occupants finished their meals before the women, and since no one was waiting for more hot drink or food, Frauke saw fit to come over and speak to her newest temporary tenants.

"So, please, tell me, where you are from? I love to gather visitors from faraway places, in my guest book I keep a log of where people have come from," Frauke said, looking at each of the women in turn.

"Well, I just joined up with these two," Jane said, pointing from Ellen to Fiona, "a few days ago in Amsterdam. I've been traveling about Europe with no real directional plan. When I met these two, I knew I needed to ask them if I could tag along. So far it has been terrific and I'm so glad I got up the courage to ask them. Hello, my name is Jane; I'm a school teacher from North Carolina."

"Nice to meet you Jane," Frauke said, smiling like a mother hen. "I've been to North Carolina; your countryside and the mountains are very similar to Bavaria, but nothing like my native Greece."

"Yes, that's what I've been noticing," Jane confirmed.

"I'm Ellen, and this is Fiona. We just graduated from college a few months ago and are traveling Europe. We didn't really discuss a plan either and when Jane asked to join us, we couldn't see any reason why not. I'm engaged to Pierre; he's waiting for me back in Paris."

"Ah, gay Paris," Frauke said. "I like to go there for Valentine's Day with my lover, Wilhelm." At this comment, she started laughing when the looks on the women's faces were of confusion. They were correct in remembering that Frauke had said she was married, and now they had each heard her divulge a lover. "Wilhelm, he is my husband too! But when we travel, we like to refer to each other as lovers. It is more romantic that way," she said with a knowing wink. "When he retired, we moved here and bought this hostel. It was our dream retirement position to run an inn, and, what better way to do that than with a youth hostel in this ancient city!"

"You are retired?" Fiona asked.

"Yes, a few years now. We moved here from Greece. And who are you?" she said.

"Oh, I'm sorry. My name is Fiona. Like Ellen, I just graduated from college and before I left for England and my visit with family, I learned I passed my nursing boards. So when I go home, whenever that may be, I'll be finding my first nursing job. Probably in a hospital, I should think," Fiona said, distractedly. As she was speaking about passing her boards, a young man entered the great hall. She thought silently, Europe has some of the best looking men.

Her gaze at the young man was not lost on Frauke and she encouraged the young man to join them. It turned out to be one of her four sons. "Come here Bröckel, come meet my new friends," his Mother said, waving him to the table.

"Ja, ja," he said, in German, thinking that these women were German speakers.

"Son, I'd like to introduce you to our latest batch of Americans. This is Jane, Ellen, and Fiona."

"Oh, Americans, how nice to meet you," he said, instantly changing into English. "Americans usually call me Brock, it is easier for them to say," he added.

"Nice to meet you too, Brock," the women said.

"Are you going to the castle and the museum?" he asked.

"I think that's what the guidebook suggested," Jane confirmed. "Would you recommend it?"

"Oh, yes. Both places are very good, you will have a great time walking about town. Lots of good restaurants and places to take in the wonderful vistas we enjoy here in Würzburg."

"I love castles and Ellen loves museums. Sounds like a great day to me. Can we walk to all of these or do we need to take a taxi, or something else?" asked Fiona.

Frauke answered, "Oh, very easy to walk. That way you get to see more and experience our people, right son?"

"Right!"

When they had packed their daypacks, filled their Evian bottles, and sorted out cameras, money, and incidental supplies, they were ready to meet the day. Outside, they stopped in the courtyard just past the front door of the hostel. No one had checked with Frauke, or Brock, or any of the other travelers regarding the temperature outside. It was unseasonably cool and before braving the day inappropriately clad, they retreated back to their rooms, their respective tails between their legs.

"I know we'll learn as we go along, but that was a basic thing to forget!"

Ellen said, looking at her friends. "We really need to be prepared for the weather and for our accommodations. Can we agree to try to remember all of this as a group? I don't think we need to break it down into the minutia for respective duties, do we?"

"I like the idea of divide and conquer; we are in Europe after all. We can all take a primary role and have the other two as backup. I'll take on the weather," added Jane, sounding very resolute.

"I'll manage the accommodations!" stated Fiona.

"All right then, I'll work on food. It is my specialty! Then it is all settled, help each other, but have a primary duty." Ellen declared, holding out her hand for them to collectively shake on it.

Fiona said to Jane, "Ok kiddo, you are up. What's the forecast?"

"Today, looks unseasonably cool with a 40% chance of showers later in the day," Jane said, reading from her pretend newspaper. "We'll have to buy a real paper in town. But by looking out the window, I'd say it is a layers day."

Each of them changed part if not all of their wardrobe for the day. Ellen was now sporting a grey turtleneck sweater with red Capri jeans, Fiona in a light pink polo, navy sweater and jeans. Jane, the minimalist, simply pulled on a hooded sweatshirt over her other clothes.

"Ready?" said Jane, as she looked at the other two as it appeared they were finishing up.

"Ready," said Ellen first, and then Fiona.

This time when they left through the hostel front door, they agreed they were now properly dressed and asked another guest to take their picture. They posed as if they were fashion models in a pinup for Calvin Klein jeans. Their pose, in the cobblestone courtyard, was a significant juxtaposition from old world to new.

When they had arrived the night before, the hostel building was both cloaked in darkness and also brightly strewn with floodlights. The stark outline of the beams of light had limited their view of the entire building, the light so powerful to blind anyone from seeing the full structure. Besides a bicycle resting next to the front door, there were a few cars parked inside the courtyard, presumably for workers, not travelers like themselves. The ornate lanterns, which the previous night had lit the courtyard, were now dormant.

They could now take in the edifice that eluded them only a few hours before. Standing in a cobblestone courtyard, the front door from which they came, was now to their backs, the front gate, which they passed through the night before, ahead. To their left was a large marble-like fountain, which was set off to one side, water spewing from the fifteen foot obelisk and collecting in the pool below. Fiona thought to make a wish but decided against needing any further help on having a great day.

As they proceeded further into the courtyard, they could take in the building more readily. The mammoth structure suddenly captured their attention as they took in the details of its design and construction. The aged stucco siding was broken up by the limestone framed windows, with dark mahogany panels. The glass was paned in an old looking way, it gave Fiona pause. She had already spent time in some ancient cathedrals and hundred year old homes in Edinburgh, was the rest of her trip going to be a discovery into the past?

"Look up there," said Fiona, as she glimpsed the structures above the hostel higher up on the mountain bluffs. "Just look at that!" She was pointing to the rooftop of an altogether different structure that was perched higher on the hillside, above the hostel. "Now I know that this building wasn't always a hostel, obviously not. I wonder if in town we'll learn the history behind this building."

"And then some," added Ellen.

"I'm ready to go learn and explore," said Jane.

"Right, let's go find out!" Fiona concluded, guidebook in hand following the map into town.

It was settled; they spent the day following the guidebook directions to the ancient castle and the museum. They walked along the ancient bridge that united the two sides of the city like the septum of a heart. While each side was independently self-sufficient, together, connected by the bridge, they lived as a whole and were more abundantly thriving.

They learned that the structure above the hostel was the Fortress Marienberg. As they were walking the grounds, they discovered that there were cut out sections in the stone wall. These window-like alcoves, they knew, were likely used as a security stronghold and from which rifles would be shot to protect the Fortress.

They took turns posing and poking through these holes in the wall. Only, this time, it wasn't to point a gun and shoot, it was to wave and shoot a photograph. Ellen stayed below and took photographs of Fiona and Jane as they poked their respective heads and hands out their windows as they posed for a picture. Then Ellen exchanged places with Fiona and they repeated the picture taking. Ellen sent a postcard to Pierre with this wall as the cover photo.

They returned to the hostel and found Frauke in the front hall looking over her register of reservations. She was speaking on the telephone and making reservations. She saw them enter and waved them over, holding up a stubby finger indicating she was almost finished.

They patiently waited for her to finish, drinking the remaining water in their Evian bottle and looking at the book for the times of trains to Bavaria. They still hadn't decided if they would stay the night here, where they knew Frauke would be sure to give them a room, or if they wanted to move on. It was early afternoon and trains, according to the book, were leaving at regular intervals, they would eventually learn that they always did.

"Well now girls, have you decided if you will stay the night here?" Frauke said to them.

"Not yet, do you have room for us?" Fiona asked, true to her role as captain of accommodations.

"Oh yes, we have room for you. I saved spaces for you just in case!" Frauke admitted.

"How kind of you," Ellen replied. "If you could give us a few minutes to discuss it, we'll go to the great room and figure it out."

"Very good," she said, as she watched them walk down the hall from reception to the great room.

"I like it here," Jane said first.

"I do too, but there is more to Europe than just one city. What do you want to do Ellen?" Fiona asked.

"Well, since we can stay here and don't have to race to a train and another late night check-in, what if we stayed here again tonight and left on a mid-morning train. That way we aren't rushing," Ellen said logically.

"Train to where," asked Fiona. "Where should we go next?"

"What's on your must-see list from Sophie? Isn't there something about King Ludwig?" Ellen asked.

"Yes, there is. She said to make sure we took in all three of his castles. Are they nearby?" Fiona questioned.

"How far away are we from those castles?" Jane asked, more interested now having heard places of interest to her too.

"Well, it is probably as far away as the train last night. Do you want to see the countryside by daylight or take a night train south to Bavaria?" Ellen asked.

They realized she asked a very good question. Even if they grew tired and slept during the day, they certainly knew they wouldn't see any of the German countryside if they took a train at night. Further, they knew that, as Fiona and Ellen initially discovered, they didn't sleep all that well on a night train.

"Good point," said Fiona.

"Yes, very good point." Jane agreed.

"How long is the train ride and what is the destination city for one of the castles?" Fiona asked.

"Let me look," said Ellen. After several long moments, Ellen looked up and smiled. "I think I figured it out. The guidebook indicated that one of King Ludwig's castles was near the city of Füssen. So once I figured that out, I had to find a train that went all the way there. It is a rather small town. I found it, though. See, look," she said, as she took the next few minutes to explain what she had learned.

"So if we take the train around ten o'clock tomorrow morning, we arrive in Füssen, after changing trains in Munich, about three o'clock? Is that what you are telling us?" summed up Fiona.

"Right, München is German for Munich. If we took that train, we'd arrive in time to get dinner at a decent hour and to bed early for the long day of sight-seeing around the castle. We can ask Frauke to make us a reservation at the hostel in Füssen, yes, Fiona," Ellen said, "I looked at accommodations. I know that's your job, but I helped just this once."

"I like your plan, don't worry about me!" Fiona said.

"That sounds like a good plan to me, too." Jane was always agreeable and explained things she knew or had experienced since she'd been traveling on her trip longer than Ellen and Fiona had been on theirs so far.

"Which castle is in Füssen?" asked Fiona.

"The guidebook indicated that all three are not too far from Füssen, but the closest one, it looks like, is Neuschwanstein." Ellen said slowly, pronouncing the German word carefully so that Fiona and Jane would comprehend the name of the castle.

"Neuschwanstein, you say?" Jane asked.

"Yes," Ellen replied.

"Isn't that the castle from *Sleeping Beauty*?" asked Jane.

"Yes, that is also in the guidebook." Ellen confirmed, pointing to the information in the helpful book.

"That sounds so romantic! So dreamy!" exclaimed Fiona.

"Then is it settled?" Ellen asked.

"I think so," replied Jane.

"Very well, let's ask Frauke for a reservation in Füssen for three tomorrow night." Fiona replied, standing up and beginning to walk back to reception.

When they returned, Frauke had just finished helping a worker from the kitchen with the menu for dinner and she looked up hearing the women approach. "So, staying?" she said with a broad smile.

"Yes, staying tonight and then we will seek out our futures in Füssen come tomorrow afternoon." Fiona said, predicting the romantic nature of their next destination was not lost on her.

"Wonderful, so glad you can stay with us again. Füssen is such a very charming place. You know, it is a good place to figure out the rest of your journey. Perhaps you will try to stay there several days? There is so much to see and do there, even in a town so much smaller than my Würzburg. Would you like me to book your reservation?" she said.

Looking at each other, the women realized that they had again left out one crucial detail in their deliberations: how long to stay in Füssen. Smiling coyly at each other, heeding Frauke's suggestion of staying in Füssen for more than a day, each of them took turns suggesting the length of their visit.

"3 days?" Ellen began.

"4 days?" said Jane.

"What if we start with 4 and see if we can add on as we need?" compromised Fiona. "Or, go for 5 days and see if there is a penalty for leaving prematurely?"

"Good point," Jane noted.

"4 days it is, with the option of leaving early, or staying on. Agreed?" Ellen asked.

"Agreed!" their unison was becoming a mutually shared joke and their smiles could not belie their satisfaction with their plans.

"Very well, let me ring up the hostel-keeper, I'll be but a moment." Frauke said, dialing the telephone almost instantly. Moments later, she replaced the telephone receiver and smiled, "Ja, ja. You have a reservation. They told me to tell you that they are looking forward to the three of you and your stay in Füssen. They were glad of the length of your reservation! It seems you are unlike other travelers who only stay one night and leave before they find out why they came to Füssen in the first place!"

Her comments made them blush and giggle like schoolgirls, as was the intent of the message. They hurried themselves upstairs to freshen up for dinner and a quiet evening discussing Füssen and the next few stages of their time in Germany. Würzburg, would be a pivotal moment in their journey, one that held the foundation in a wall that kept in those you desired and kept out those one did not. It also led to several days in the romantic setting that would be Füssen. Fiona wondered what kinds of water fountains they had in there and whether or not she'd actually decide to make a wish. This trip was becoming a wish fulfilled, and it had only just begun.

Chapter 35 A Würzburg Family Dinner, 1985

Frauke was glad they had decided to stay. Tonight, her family was planning their next trip to Greece, one which they hoped all their children would join in on. As the women went back upstairs to change for dinner, Frauke was waiting for Bröck to return to the front desk so she could leave the reception area to check on her own kitchen and the family dinner. She wanted to invite the women to eat with them, in their private quarters.

Frauke had taken a real liking to all of them, especially Ellen. It was like watching her own child on a trip when she looked at Fiona. She knew the younger women were very close to the same age as her son and she was playing matchmaker. Ellen hadn't explained thoroughly enough about Pierre, as it was her Frauke was thinking of for her older son, Christopher. As Frauke was lost in thought, Bröck returned from his afternoon chores and checked in with his Mother.

Frauke, now relieved of front desk duty, retreated to their private home within the vast expanse of the youth hostel; it was located on the opposite side of the main hostel kitchen. In that way, she could share the amenities of the larger kitchen, especially when all her sons and husband were home for dinner. The hostel's kitchen staff was preparing an assortment of traditional German dishes, including: cabbage rolls, bratwurst, sauerbraten, as well as standby tourist fare of hamburgers, pork chops, and baked chicken.

In Frauke's side of the kitchen, she was preparing Wiener Schnitzel with sauerkraut, asparagus and a warm German potato salad. She had some Riesling wine chilling, as well as a full bodied Cabernet for Wilhelm, his favorite. She filled their carafes with the red wine and set them to breathe. Next, she turned her attention to the table setting and placed a cotton table cloth on the table. Wilhelm will like this, as it was from his Mother's house.

Finishing the final touches of setting the table, Frauke added three more place settings in the hopes that the women would accept her invitation to dinner. On a monthly basis, she enjoyed pretending that they lived in a single family home and that this spacious expanse of rooms was within the confines of her home and not the back rooms of a large European youth hostel. Additionally, she dressed all in her finest Greek clothes, serving German food, to her guests from faraway places. In this case, it was for three American women, and hopefully, new friends of the family.

The paradox of their nationalities, combined with the menu, suited her personality and she hoped their guests would pick up on this little tidbit. Wearing her "Greek Eye" jewelry would certainly get the conversation heading in that direction should anyone inquire as to the nature of her adornments. Not to be undressed, she also put on her *Gucci* wrist watch; it was the one she bought from a street vendor the last time they went to New York City. She couldn't resist it, even if *Gucci* was spelled 'Guci." The sharp silver lines always brought a smile.

Satisfied with her preparations for dinner, and having discussed the remaining cooked portions of the meal with the head chef, Frauke walked right passed Bröck, who appeared interested in being relieved from his current post. The disappointment on his face was replaced with a smirk as he knew where his Mother was heading and her plan once he saw where she was going.

Frauke kept on walking and made her way to the women's side of the hostel and to the young Americans' room. When she reached door 247, she knocked firmly. It was opened slowly by Jane, who was rubbing her eyes with her hands.

"Yes?" she said sleepily.

"I'm sorry to disturb you, perhaps you were sleeping?" Frauke said apologetically.

"The other two are still sleeping, but I'm awake, is something wrong?" Jane asked.

"No, no, nothing is wrong. I wanted to invite you three to have dinner tonight with my family, in our residence."

"Oh, how nice. We hadn't thought of dinner yet; I think we were playing that one by ear. What time were you thinking?"

"7:30PM?"

"Very good. I will tell them when they wake up. They haven't had a chance to catch up on their sleep since the night train a few days ago. If they don't wake up on their own just after seven o'clock, I'll wake them up myself. That will give them enough time to get ready for dinner. Thank you, that is so kind," Jane said.

"Gut, gut," Frauke said in German with a Greek accent. "Wonderful, see you then!"

Jane closed their room door as quietly as she could and went back to fulfilling her one luxury, reading a book. Before she was able to get too engrossed in the pages of her borrowed paperback, there had been a small book nook off to the side from the reception area. When they returned from town earlier today, she moseyed through the volumes kept there and helped herself to this particular little tome. It was Ellen who woke up first.

In a whispered tone, Jane said to Ellen, "We've been invited to dinner with the family, in about forty-five minutes."

"Well, that is very nice."

"Do you think we should wake Fiona now or let her sleep a bit more?" Jane asked.

"I'll bet she'd appreciate a little more time," Ellen replied.

"Don't bother, she's awake," Fiona said echoing their whispered tones. "Remember, she's a light sleeper!" Smiling, Fiona sat up from her bunk, scratched her scalp and said, "What's this I hear about dinner?"

"Boy, we can't put anything past you can we?" Jane said jokingly.

"Nope."

"I wonder if they get dressed up for dinner, what do I have that is clean?" Ellen said, muttering to herself as she opened her backpack. "What about this?" She said holding up a khaki skirt and white blouse.

"Looks good to me, I'm switching my sweatshirt for a sweater. What about you Fiona?" Jane asked.

"I've got a clean shirt to change into and I can put my sweater over my shoulders. I can always put it on later if it gets cool enough."

They spent the next quarter hour freshening up their hair and makeup and setting aside appropriate clothes for train travel for the morning. That way, if they had a late night, they'd be more prepared for morning repacking than if they just left things alone. Fiona also grabbed one of her packages of wild rice for a gift.

Back downstairs, Frauke went back into the kitchen to speak with the chef on the stages of dinner preparation. The chef explained that dinner for the family would be ready to serve any time after 7:30PM, just give him the signal. All was prepared, now Frauke concentrated on coordinating their schedules for their family trip to Greece. She was so engrossed in her studying of timetables and maps that she didn't hear Bröck explain that the women had arrived.

Here she was at the breakfast table with her books on Greece, her European version of the Cook's Timetables, the monthly subscription variety, plus all her photo albums from their last trip 5 years ago. It was a trip for their anniversary but Frauke and Wilhelm make it a family affair. Someday soon, their sons will have families of their own and will no longer be able to make this trip.

Caught with her materials still on display, Frauke blushed deeply saying, "Oh goodness, look at this mess. I'm so sorry you had to see this. I'll just put it away."

Fiona was first in the room and saw the display of maps and books on places she knew were in Greece. She'd heard enough from Harriet's tour to Greece and that she'd also been to Corfu. In addition, Fiona spied maps of Italy and a variety of cruise line pamphlets. In particular, which Fiona now picked up, was the brochure that depicted Venice.

"Wow, sounds like a great trip," was all Fiona could muster at the moment.

"Yes, it is. But, you don't want to hear about it," she said, somewhat baited.

"Sure we do, we love to travel or we wouldn't be here!" announced Jane.

"Are you certain?" Frauke said looking from each woman to the next. It was agreed. Looking at her watch, she saw that they had a few minutes until dinner would be ready. "Here, then, please sit." To her husband, who she knew would by now be in their sitting room, she called out, "Wilhelm, please attend to the drinks. Our guests have arrived."

From the recesses of their quarters, the women heard a faint, "Ja!" and then a chuckle. Momentarily, a shorter stocky male, with hints of grey hair, erupted from the family area. He smiled similarly to his wife, pleased that they were again entertaining guests.

"Was mochten Sie zu trinken?" "What do you wish to drink?" he said, his smile broader still.

In English, the women ordered wine and moments later Wilhelm produced several glasses and a carafe of chilled Riesling. He seemed very proud to serve.

"Have a look at my plan for our trip this time," began Frauke. "I think we will go to Venice by train and pick up our cruise line there. The cruise is a 4 day cruise, long enough to experience ocean travel but not too long," she said winking. "Then we will stay in Corfu for 5 days, with all the family there. By the end of 5 days we can either cruise or fly home, depending on the weather and Wilhelm's temperament!"

"Yes, I'm sure. If you encountered nasty weather, you'd want to leave as conveniently and quickly as possible. When Pierre and I were camping with his sister last month, on the French Riviera, we planned our trip the same way. If we couldn't stay dry in our small trailer, we'd coop up in a small hotel for the duration or simply drive home."

"Pierre," Frauke said confusedly as she looked at Ellen. "Who is that?"

"My fiancé," Ellen beamed.

"Your fiancé?" Frauke repeated, "You mean to say you are not single? But you just graduated from college. I'm so confused."

"Ellen is engaged to be married; they met in high school! Jane and I are single though," Fiona spoke before thinking.

"I'm still confused, what bothers you that I'm engaged?" asked Ellen.

"Oh, I took a liking to you for one of my older sons. He isn't very sociable, too shy I'm afraid.

Blushing, Ellen said softly, "Thank you for the compliment, I'm only sorry to have misled you. I'm very engaged. Someday, your son will find someone, just like Jane and Fiona will. I can feel it, you know, Cupid's arrow is aiming at our trio, just missed on the first try."

"That is very kind of you to say; I can see Pierre is a lucky man."

"Thank you, now that we've sorted out the confusion, please do tell us about your trip!"

Still a bit flustered that her prowess and matchmaking skills were a bit rusty, Frauke said, "Oh yes, our trip. Please come in and see the plans for my family's trip."

As if on cue, Wilhelm stood to fetch a refill of the wine carafe as he took stock of his guests' wine glasses as they moved to sit about the table and began to listen to Frauke's tale. As he left the breakfast area, over his right shoulder he encouraged them to take a seat, they might be there a while.

"Oh darling, we would miss dinner if they did that. No, tonight I'll limit my tale, trust me!" She said, pushing up one finger and a fist into the air in triumphant glory.

He knew his wife better, though, for after twenty minutes and exhausting their supply of chilled Riesling, Wilhelm took his final trip back and forth to the kitchen to refill the carafe and returned with the Cabernet. His wife was still so engrossed in her trip planning and storytelling that she missed his exchange of glasses and change in beverages. Finally, the chef caught her attention when he declared he could no longer hold dinner and still claim to be a trained culinary chef; spoilage was imminent.

"Frau Feierabend, Wir müssen jetzt Abendessen zu servieren," said the frustrated chef. "We must serve dinner now, Mrs. Feierabend."

"Ja, danke!" Frauke shrieked, realizing that she had forgotten about the dinner portion and was completely distracted with the entertaining of her guests. Who, as she looked at them, appeared to have enjoyed her wine selections this evening? Their rosy faces could not be fooled. "Please follow me to our dining table, the chef insists on serving our dinner before it spoils. I've completely forgotten about it, I was having such a good time explaining our trip plans."

"We did too," Jane said as she looked from Ellen to Fiona and back again.

"The wine is delicious!" Fiona added.

"Well, hopefully, so too will be the dinner I asked the chef to cook for us."

To this, Wilhelm said to his flustered wife, "Oh darling, we can only hope."

Frauke and Wilhelm were joined by three of their four sons at dinner that night. Over the next several hours, the trio of women was witness to the rituals of a Greek family eating a prepared German meal, in their dream retirement job of being youth hostel keepers. The eight of them were attending to her every word.

Their dinner was served and special graces were said, first in Greek, then in German, and then in English. The entrees were served with recipes from Frauke's and the chef's compilations and most certainly the enjoyment had commenced. The women heard the stories of trips to their Greek homeland, by air, by sea, and by rail. They also heard stories of courtship, marriage, and family life; love among them was a constant. What no one that was a guest at this table had seen was the Greek Eye at the center of the table, taking everything in, not missing a moment.

Frauke had placed her favorite blue and white porcelain Greek Eye as a centerpiece to be shared between guest and family. She purposefully used it tonight to ward off any ill-will, misconceived jealousy, or unrequited love. What this matchmaker had wished was for the potential of love to bloom at her table, while maybe not between those seated at it, but in their respective futures. She wanted these women to enjoy a marriage like hers with Wilhelm and the lifelong happiness they had derived from it.

She was ever the Mother, ever the wife, ever the bride. Near the end of the evening, Fiona thought she caught the exchange of a wink between them, either way, she didn't let on if she had. This was indeed a time to share in and join with this family and not one to report and expose the happenings of the evening.

Later in her bunk, still slightly dizzy from all the wine, while Fiona drifted off to sleep, she listened to the faint snores and ever so slight sounds of breathing from her sleeping traveling companions and friends. She reflected on the time they had shared tonight with this family and how open they had been to these three strangers.

As she drifted further into sleep, it occurred to Fiona, that in the span of only a few days, she had seen or experienced several signs people associate with superstitions: wishing wells, throwing coins, debris in the eye, and lastly, an odd centerpiece in a rich blue that was almost purple in color, and at its center a pearly white mixture, the depth of which was lost in its luster.

In her dreams that night, the birds were singing, and the geese were honking in their traditional V-shaped formation, as they headed south for the winter. Fiona wondered if the geese in Germany were also called Canadian. She would have to ask someone, she said in her dream voice. That is, if she remembered to ask, since she was so distracted by the thoughts of wishing wells, coins, and eyes.

If she had looked more closely, she would have seen that the geese had purple eyes, the bird's song was in operatic tones, and the wishing wells no longer spewed water. Instead, a rich full bodied Cabernet came forth from the main fountain and drained down along the pattern and out the eight spouts and into the goblets adorning the fountain, in an octagonal pattern. The excess, never left the collecting pool, but, somehow, was redistributed in a never-ending cycle. Love, she thought, was the same way, never-ending and best when shared often amongst friends.

Chapter 36 Calm Seas and Good Intentions, 1991

Eager to arrive in New York to see the newlywed's before they left for their honeymoon, Clifton was busy cleaning the deck after entering updates in the ship's log. Bette took a few casual moments on deck to review the log and add to it as she saw fit, but only in the capacity of first mate. She read with interest how her husband loved to put pen to ink.

The log read:

"We made our way in the channel toward Naples about a 1/4 of a mile until we turned to the north into one of our favorite all time anchorages. The scenery.....multimillion dollar houses in a lush tropical setting.....is matched only by the peaceful tranquility of the place and it's security as an anchorage. We've been in here many times before, but it's been awhile. A wee dolphin welcomed us by flipping his tail high in the air....they usually just roll up when they breathe, breaking water with their head, breathing hole and dorsal fin, but this tyke flipped his tail in the air and gave a "smack" with the flat end. We dropped anchor.....brought out the cushions and proceeded to enjoy being "on the water again."

Bette looked up, smiling and remembering, it was a great feeling. She looked across her legs and watched Clifton struggle with a particularly dirty spot on the deck. Smiling again, she returned to reading the log:

"The evening's entertainment was three-fold. Two other boats came in and anchored. Then a party broke out at the newest mansion just off our stern. We watched it being built several years ago....it looks just as strange in its finished condition as it did during construction. It is about 25' deep, but stretches across 250 to 300 feet. The party was outside with lots of chatter. It quieted only when they were seated and dinner was served. The servers were in white jackets and bow ties, quite posh. The third entertainment was the cruise boats who take visitors through...to watch dolphins, or big homes. They pass unnecessarily close to our anchored boat, so we converse with the passengers. It's a hoot.

"The sun set in fiery golden splendor through the silhouette of royal palm trees to the West, while in the East, a full moon rose to light the night. It was a very special welcome to our first night back on the water.

"May 2nd -- Today we'll make 73 miles to an anchorage in the Little Shark River. The Little Shark is only 20 miles north of Cape Sable, the southernmost tip of mainland Florida. It's a remote, untouched, natural river draining the Everglades into the Gulf. Theonlyevidence of "Man" or the 21st Century are the few day marks to mark the entrance. The rest is just as it was 200 or 500 years ago. We pass Marco Inlet, Cape Romano and continue on course until we've passed the Cape Romano shoals, another 15 miles down the coast. Then it's 40 miles to the Little Shark.

"The Gulf water is clear, aqua against a blue sky dotted with low lying cumulus clouds, typical of tropical areas. We're accompanied by half a dozen other sails, all heading south in order to begin their journey north, all forced here by the shallow waters of Lake Okeechobee. At one point, a 3 mile circle included 11 sailboats with a number heading up the West Coast. The wind was 10 knots and just enough north of east that we could sail. What a delight! This area is dotted with crab traps, so it takes good attention to avoid the floats. Being the designated driver for Ceilidh, I'm strongly motivated not to snag one ourprop. On another trip to the Keys....we'd sailed all night in strong winds and in the channel into Marathon we'd hooked a trap. I was the designated diver at that point. I suggested we try reversing the gears to see if it would wind off. I was elated to see the float pop out of the water on our stern and our speed return to normal.

Bette rubbed at her eyes as Clifton approached. He saw that she'd been reading the lob, smiled, and began to gently massage her should. Bette smiled at his touch and said, "I can't wait to share this log with Jake and Fiona in New York City."

"Me too, honey, me too," Clifton said, smiling at his bride.

"It is our new narrative you are writing here darling," Bette said.

"Indeed it is, indeed it is."

He turned the Ceilidh into the wind, let out the sails, and secured the rudder. While he listened to the sails flutter ineffectively, he took Bette's hand and they headed below. Still smiling, Clifton closed the cabin hatch and began to remove his shirt. Bette was way ahead of him smiling mischievously from their berth. She was naked in just moments, having read the log and her husband's own signals.

Prior to setting sail, when they were filing their route plan with the harbormaster, they had allotted extra time along their route for impromptu excursions. They were both glad of it now for it allowed them to navigate, without restraint, the eastern seaboard and into New York harbor. When they took breaks, such as this, it was in these delays that they relished the most important part of this journey; their shared time together as a married couple.

They too were on course.

Chapter 37 Positive Progress, 2015

Meanwhile, back in the hospital, the next morning while Fiona took her shower and then consumed her bland hospital food breakfast, Jake headed over to the bio-medical library in search of cases similar to hers, with positive progress, and perhaps, an outcome strategy they could implement.

Fiona was curious why Jake felt the need to stay overnight in her guest chair. He must be working an awful lot of odd shifts to sleep here. She would ask him about that when he came back, if he came back.

Her thoughts were interrupted by a phone ringing. "Hello?" Fiona answered.

The crackling on the line made her suspicious of the proximity of the call's origins. "Fiona," said the caller.

"Yes, this is Fiona."

"Fiona, this is Bette Davies, Jake's Mother?"

"Hello Mrs. Davies, how are you? Are you looking for Jake?" Fiona asked.

"Bette, please, and no, I wanted to speak to you. Besides, Jake is at the clinic seeing patients this morning."

The comment was not lost on Fiona. Over the last few days, as she seemed to be coming back to them and back to Jake, the parents, Jake, and Gabriella concocted a plan. They were no longer willing to wait for Fiona. They would push her, if they had to, into remembering; into remembering her life with all of them; especially with Jake.

Fiona thought slowly about what she just heard and Bette didn't push her, waiting on the other end of the silence for Fiona to put things together. They knew she had the pieces of the puzzle but unless you have a frame of reference in which to guide you, having all the pieces doesn't matter much if you don't know what you are making. For Fiona, that was more of a remaking of her history, tagging onto the narrative that was her story, her life, and her marriage to Jake. Not in so much as a do-over, but as a do-again remembrance.

"Yes," Fiona finally said. "Seeing patients, when is he planning to come visit me?"

"If you are up for it, he told Clifton and me sometime later today. He's got a full load in neurology clinic." Bette added her husband's name and the type of clinic patients hoping to snag a memory in Fiona.

Instead, Fiona kept the conversation neutral, "How is Clifton? Are you calling from Florida?"

Glad to hear that she had some recollections about her in-laws, Bette said, "Yes, I am. He's fine. He's out checking on Ceilidh just now. We are planning a cruise through the Panama Canal and up to Cabo. We are going to be gone for several months, weeks at sea at a time and before we go, we wanted to fly up to see you. Would that be alright with you?"

Fiona heard all the words but her brain was slowly processing them. She knew all the places too and had memories come flooding in about crewing sailboats to Cabo but the pieces didn't paint the picture of sense. But she knew something was beginning to connect when her headache returned. Maybe thinking and remembering are the source of my headaches, she thought.

"Fiona?" Bette repeated after several minutes of silence on the line.

"When would you be arriving; I'd need to get the house cleaned," Fiona said abstractly.

"By the weekend, Clifton made the booking already. We arrive a bit after noon on Saturday," Bette said, quite aware that Fiona had said house and not apartment. She hoped that meant the house in Elizabeth and not their studio apartment in Manhattan.

Their house was in Elizabeth, New Jersey; it was a modest Tudor style home. They had learned that the previous owner was a landscape architect and had used the own home as a model for his master's thesis. The architect took a significant amount of time and paid attention to every last detail as was evident in their artfully adorned property.

Fiona immediately took a liking to the exterior gardens which included a large variety of native shrubbery, perennials, annuals, and ornamental grasses. With over an acre of turf and tall mature trees, the house was strategically placed within the property. Jake knew they would need to hire a gardener to keep all the natural accoutrements to their new home or palace.

"Sure, that will be fine. It will be nice to see you before you leave," Fiona added, with no further comment on her living arrangements or the fact that she was still in the hospital.

"Wonderful, perhaps your parents are still in town and we can all go out for dinner," Bette said, still pushing. On her end, Clifton was standing next to her and his mouth continued to drop in awe of what his wife was doing. He almost said something but in watching Bette's face as she talked, and only hearing half of the conversation, he just waited, although impatiently at best.

Bette was watching him frustrated in his chair, and cradling the phone on her shoulder, she gave two thumbs up and a wink.

"Yes, they are. That would be very nice." Fiona replied again, absently.

"Ok then, I won't keep you. Keep up the good work dear, and we'll see you in a few days."

"Thank you, I will?" Fiona said, a bit confused and then added more confidently, "I will."

"Goodbye dear, see you soon!" Bette said energetically and smiling at Clifton.

"Did she get it," he said impatiently.

A Cheshire cat wouldn't smile any more broadly, "I believe I chinked the armor."

"Good, let's call Jake with the news. That plan he concocted with Gabriella worked. Keep hitting her with logic and pieces to her life's puzzle and our beloved Fiona will come back to us.

As she hung up the phone, scenes from the distant archives in her brain began appearing, nautical themes, bright rooms with sunny windows, with the smell of coffee and the music of Wagner. Fiona began to hum her favorite Wagner opera: Füssen-Opus 1.

At the neurology clinic, Jake couldn't help daydreaming out the window. He was recalling when Fiona first came home from the hospital and how he'd 'nursed' her. It was in the fall, over their anniversary, the one and only anniversary she'd missed. Now it was Monday morning and he was recalling the past weekend.

Chapter 38 An Autumn Breeze, 2016

A year had passed since Fiona was roused out of her coma and in that time the roles this couple shared in their marriage had evolved and changed. Jake became the nurturer in the family as it was he who would care for Fiona and help her traumatic brain to heal. Throughout that slow and emotionally painful recovery process, Jake had reprised his nursing role as Fiona did not remember him as either her husband or as a neurologist.

On this beautiful autumn afternoon, Jake had suggested Fiona return to their bed and rest, now that it was an hour after lunch. It was a lazy Sunday afternoon in late autumn and he hoped her headache would subside while being relaxed and recumbent. He was the doting husband.

He looked up from the paper and saw the dance begin. Outside, the sun was still shining. The trees were in their full exchange of the season. It was as if the crimsons, deep oranges, and gold colors mixed with the fading greens of the leaves, were like the silent symphony of color performed by the deciduous trees during their final bow before the transition into winter.

He read from the paper the times for the tides, sunrise, and sunset. He looked up again and could see the beginning notes of the clear blue sky as they transitioned to sunset. The music had begun at sunrise, gave way in late afternoon from the stanza of blue, and finally concluding with the sharing of the sunset between the sky and the land. It was where the trees and the sky mixed their colors and appeared as one.

He checked his watch and confirmed that sunset was less than an hour away. He could see the sunset's bloom, where the colors stretched across the sky, and the sharp tendrils of color beginning to skim across the tops of the tress. He could see the dance repeated on the glass of the windows here from his perch and watched as they danced and flitted across the family room wall. Sunset was expected just after six-thirty. Checking his watch, he realized it had been several hours since Fiona had retired to work on her headache. He had begun to read the paper when he no longer heard his wife's movements upstairs.

It was time to check on her and see about plans for dinner.

When they made modest remodeling changes to the master suite, the hallway leading to their sanctuary had been opened up with one wall of windows. Walking along the bank of windows now, he watched the sun's dance upon their stucco walls, enhanced by a small crystal wind chime.

In the hall, in the sun, he had felt the warmth of the sun's fading rays, but once inside the room, he felt chilled. He smiled, knowing how his wife loved to sleep under heavy covers in a cool environment.

Upon entering their master suite, he first noticed the sleeping form of his wife who had cocooned herself in their comforter. She was practically camouflaged within their bed among the quilts and decorative pillows. He listened to her mumbled murmurs and knew she was dreaming. He knew his wife was happily dreaming when he listened to her dream speak.

He also knew that if he closed the open window his wife would wake from the change in room temperature. He liked this plan, he liked it a lot.

In Fiona's dream, she felt herself walking up a hiking trail and into patches of snow. Having lived in a region known for snowy winters, Fiona enjoyed the thought of hiking through the snow, of breaking a sweat. She could hear the sounds of a babbling brook, and she imagined icy cool water flowing along the mountain stream where it was forced to create a new direction of flow with each change in condition, frozen or thawed.

The weather was growing warmer, the ice would surely melt soon, she thought. That was when she heard it, "C-R-A-C-K!" It was the ice beneath her feet. She was now standing on a collecting pool that had once been frozen over. "But, no," she thought, "I can't be standing here."

"C-R-A-C-K, C-R-A-C-K, C-R-A-C-K!" There it was again. She looked to see where her feet were and became aware of the warmth about them.

"F-I-O-N-A!" Someone was calling her name, what were they doing here with her by the stream, would they come and find her before she fell through into the icy depths?" she continued, dreaming.

Again, she heard her name, but it wasn't a woman speaking, it was a man, "F-I-O-N-A!! Wake up," said the male voice.

"I'm over here," she thought she spoke in her dream, but her voice wasn't the loud shout she had planned, it was merely a whisper. It was nothing anyone would be able to hear outside, not here in the snow, on the noisy collecting pool of melting ice. "Come and find me over here. I'm on the cracking collecting pool, quick, hurry, I'm going to fall through."

Then, she heard the cracking noises again. "What was that, if it was the ice, surely, it wouldn't play with me this long and allow my torment to continue, would it?"

It was then she realized she was dreaming of dreaming but still didn't wake. She was too interested in hiking the cool snowy trail up to Füssen and the castles in Bavaria. In the background of her mind, she heard the operatic sounds of Richard Wagner, the composer heralded by King Ludwig II, who was a local to those parts of Bavaria.

By now Jake had also heard the crackling noise and his head turned to view their stereo turntable. The collection of records she'd been absently listening to in her sleep had finally finished. He wondered if she was listening to the crackle noises too.

"The music," she thought, "It was the sound of the needle hitting the vinyl record. C-R-A-C-K, then, C-R-A-C-K-L-E, and then there it was: music. Yes, that was it. It was music. This was the music she learned in her Music Appreciation class in college, yes, that was it." She thought.

In her college classroom, she would daydream while the professor played the wonderful melodic symphonies of Wagner. She would often visualize herself climbing a snow-capped mountain whenever the professor laid down the turntable's needle and began Wagner's masterpiece, which she called, "Füssen: Opus 1."

It was her favorite, and realizing this made her smile. "Were the mountains snow-capped in September?" she thought in her dream.

Jake saw her smile and he smiled reflexively.

"F-I-O-N-A!" finally she recognized the fact that someone was indeed calling her name; perhaps, she wasn't standing above a precipitous cracking pool, maybe she was dreaming. In her head, she allowed herself a few more bars of Wagner's symphony and then turned her head.

She opened her eyes to her see her husband Jake lying next to her and smiling back. He said, "Were you dreaming of Füssen again, darling?"

As she smiled, he enveloped her in his arms and they joined the trees and the sun's dance with a dance of their own.

Coming back to his present situation, and his awaiting clinic patients, Jake prayed things would continue to show improvement, just like the seasons. While predictable in that they always came, when and what type of weather was a unique annual event. He loved to be a spectator of the weather, especially in the fall when the seasons took turns in their own dance.

That's not what was bothering him on this sunny fall day. While they were somewhat secluded by the flora, and as private as they had hoped, today, of all days, the noise from the neighbor's lawnmower was polluting the tranquility of their bedroom.

The move to Elizabeth was planned down to the last detail. It was the next natural progression in their marriage: home ownership. While they knew the commute for Jake was longer, they agreed that the price for this home was too good to pass up and it allowed them to keep Fiona's small apartment in the city.

Her apartment was just a few subway stations away from the hospital: it held many memories of their dating and falling in love and it was just simply too convenient to give up. Jake had the option of staying close to the hospital for a cat nap while on call or he could make the train in time for a late dinner at home when he'd finished his appointments for the day. They were hoping over time that his rising seniority within the neurology practice would reduce the number of overnight on call shifts. In the end, they were both pleased with the decision.

Keeping the apartment in the city worked for Fiona too. Since her preferred shift began at three o'clock in the afternoon, instead of heading out to Elizabeth, she'd stay in the city each night after work. Well, they both did. They worked vigilantly to coordinate his on call shifts with her minimally part-time hours. Once they were married, she didn't want to accept the position of being just the doctor's wife. She had her own nursing career and was still working hard in it.

The apartment, located on East 78th Street, wasn't fancy and was a small one bedroom apartment. It had originally been Gabriella's apartment, Fiona's classmate from college who had been the driving force behind Fiona's move to New York in the first place. They both lived and worked together. It was not a coincidence that they worked opposite shifts at NYU Medical Center; they rarely saw each other or slept in the apartment at the same time.

After Gabriella and Nate's wedding, the newlyweds moved out, leaving Fiona with a serious decision. She finally decided that if she managed her money well enough she could afford the apartment on her own. About the same time, she and Jake were spending more and more time together on and off the golf course and in the end, she didn't live alone for long.

When designing their new home, Fiona asked the interior decorator to recreate one of her favorite nautical themes. In stunning detail, the designer captured Fiona's vision as the room was decorated in a motif of navy, white, and red. The colors were used throughout the room, and included boating pennants and the communication flags used by sailors and boat captains. Miniature anchors were positioned as accent pieces.

The interior designer hired a seamstress to fashion an impressive king-sized comforter for their master bed. A local muralist painted about the dresser mirror as if the painted ropes were literally holding the up mirror in an optical illusion. It became the focal point of the room.

When they were dating, Fiona learned that Jake's family had experience with yachting and sailing just like hers. They would find solace in their bedroom retreat. In addition, for Fiona, she often took comfort in this room to help heal her recurrent migraines or ringing of the ears.

Prior to climbing into bed, she'd opened their bedroom window to let in the cooler outdoor air, dropping the ambient temperature to her desired temperature for sleeping. Despite the sunny day, the temperature outside was in the high 50's, much cooler than their windowed hallway which frequently baked in the natural light.

He further noted that before she crawled into their bed to sleep, she placed her favorite stack of vinyl records on their turntable. It was from this stack of records that he now heard cracking and scratching. He could see that the stack of records had been played out and the turntable was now spinning without sound as the final recording had concluded and the needle was quickly tracking to the label. First a C-R-A-C-K and then S-C-R-A-T-C-H, it repeated in an oddly rhythmic tone.

He slowly grabbed the needle's arm and replaced it in the receptacle. He then walked to their bedroom window and in shutting it he felt the cool breeze coming in as it struck his face. Turning to the sleeping form in the bed, he watched her sleep and noticed the smile upon her face. This he hoped meant relief from her headache and pleasant dreams.

Meanwhile for Fiona, the sounds of ice crackling had slowly begun to cease, thus bringing her back to a more wakeful state, and back to him. If that didn't rouse her, his second option to wake her was to increase the room temperature. He wanted her coming back to him in their sanctuary. If those didn't work, he knew how he would wake her. A smirk came across his face at the thought of it.

In one movement he cut off the audible pollution from outside and arrested the remaining incoming cool air. An insomniac, she used the pleasant whirring of a fan or the outside obtrusive noise as a lullaby effect. The sudden cessation of the cacophony to which she had been sleeping, roused her and he knew the silence of their bedroom would wake her.

Before she appeared undisturbed from dreamland, he'd gone back to the turntable. The final selection was by Richard Wagner; he knew that was her favorite piece of music. Füssen: Opus 1 was what had been cracking and scratching when he entered the room.

Lastly, he removed her record selection with replacements of his own. He set the records upon the turntable, switched on the revolving disk, reached for the needle and gently dropped it at the beginning of Marvin Gaye's, *Heard It Through the Grape Vine* from the sound track of the movie *The Big Chill.*

He thought that she was feeling reminiscent if she chose to listen to these songs and ending with the piece inspired by Füssen. What better way to ease away a migraine than by reliving a great moment from her life and remembering those people and events from it. He knew that it always set her mind into a relaxing frame, helping her recall her trip to Europe, with Ellen and Jane, and the extraordinary time they had there, especially in Germany, in Bavaria, in Füssen.

Besides her life with him and the children, their home in the suburbs, and her work at the hospital, he knew that it was returning to Bavaria that was her favorite place to remember and her favorite destination of her dreams. He looked over at her now and saw that her face had changed from the concentration of sleeping and dreaming to the possibility of waking. He cleared his throat slightly as he looked at her for any glimmer, any hint that she was waking up. Then he knew.

She knew too that she was waking up and returning to him. As she realized this, it made her smile. Still, she was thinking of the words she was speaking in her dream, and unknowingly said out loud, "Were the mountains snow-capped in November?" and that was the last thought she had in her dream before waking.

"Fiona," he murmured softly in her ear. She finally recognized the fact that someone was indeed calling her name, perhaps she wasn't standing above a precipitous cracking ice-covered pool or in the wintery arms of the

Bavarian Alps. Maybe she was dreaming. In her mind, she allowed herself a few more bars of Wagner's symphony, even though the matching music coming from her turntable had long since stopped. But it hadn't in her mind. When she finally let the music play out, she turned her head and opened her eyes.

She discovered her husband Jake sitting on the corner of their bed and smiling back at her. He said, "Welcome back, were you dreaming of Füssen again, darling?"

"Guilty," she said, with a slight smirk. Looking up from her pillow on their bed and out the window which was now sporting the beginnings of a beautiful sunset, she said "I guess I was more tired than I thought. How long have I been sleeping?"

"Well, it is after eight o'clock in the evening now, you've slept almost all day. How is the headache?" he inquired.

"Headache?" she said, slightly confused. Her thoughts had returned to the last moments of her dream and her standing on the cracking ice.

"Yes, that was why I suggested you take a nap; I couldn't help you make the headache go away so I thought you needed more rest."

"Oh, yes, now I remember. I'm only a bit foggy now. You know the dullness after the migraine."

Pulling his cardigan sweater firmly about his waist, he said, "I don't know how you sleep when it is so cold and noisy in here." He was dressed in light brown corduroy trousers with a soft pink oxford shirt and navy cardigan. His burgundy tasseled penny loafers had been kicked off and were now resting near the end of the bed to his right. His brown socks had a hole in the heel, which he now stood on to camouflage. He looked back at her and smiled.

"I just sleep better when the room is cold. As to the noise, even with this migraine, it is music to my ears and my only distraction from attempting to listen to anything else. I wouldn't be a good patient then, would I doctor? Besides, the outside noise and the cool breeze are actually soothing to me, even with a headache."

Unwinding herself from her position in the cocoon of comforter and blankets, she asked him to join her. "Would you climb in with me, my headache is gone, but I think I'll need your special touch," she said.

For over 25 years now, they had learned how to sooth each other with their healing gifts. He readily admitted that her skills came naturally and his were learned in years of study from books. He had decided to go back to school after 5 years of nursing and was now a physician; his specialty was neurology. He had a keen interest in neurology since his wife had been in and out of a coma since her head injury she suffered during the second year of their marriage. Her only remaining deficits following her head trauma were the recurring migraines and the occasional dizzy spell. She thought for a moment and had to check her diary to recall the last time she'd fainted.

She keenly recalled the first time she fainted, for other reasons than head trauma. It was during her trip to Europe and a particularly warm telephone booth in Salzburg. She was calling home to complete her weekly check in with her parents and helping put their minds at ease with her traveling so far away. The overwhelming heat of the booth coupled with her excitement had been all she could contain and she simply fainted.

Before climbing into their bed, he returned to the turntable and began her favorite piece of music, and he looked over at her in their bed, and said to her, "Do you remember what happened in September, 1990?"

A slight blush came to her cheeks. She said, "Yes, I do. But will you tell me the story again, please?"

"Ok, if you insist." He climbed further into the bed having disrobed and greeted her body with his. By now the turntable had advanced to the second selection and their dance that night was accompanied by the allegro of Wagner's piece: Füssen- Opus 1.

Chapter 39 A Bavarian Train Ride, 1985

After leaving the family residence in the wee hours of the morning, the trio of women didn't have the complete luxury of sleeping in. Remembering their agreement to divvy up duties, Fiona realized that her duty assignment was accommodations. To her, this included the method of arriving at their destination, as well as where they stayed. Predominantly, their choice of overnight accommodations would be youth hostels.

Prior to going bed, after the other women had fallen asleep, Fiona took on the challenge of determining if they had an additional option of trains and arrival times, especially since they had stayed up so late. She scoured over the book and the hostel guidebook and found her answers. In their best interest, Fiona felt it better to sleep until at least nine o'clock and left a note for the other women. In that note she included the following key information:

"Good morning ladies, don't worry, I'm sleeping in! I've changed us to the twelve-thirty train. It gets to Füssen at five o'clock, and we can have lunch on the train. See you in the morning-again! Fiona."

In the morning, it was Ellen who found the note and after reading it, agreed with the plan and went back to bed. Jane was stirring as Ellen went back to bed and gradually woke up looking around her realizing it was indeed morning. She, too, found the note, and looking at her watch, went happily back to bed with the forethought of resetting her alarm for ten o'clock.

In what felt like a few short moments, each woman instantly awoke when the alarm bleated. B-E-E-P! B-E-E-P! B-E-E and Jane turned it off before the end of the third beeping sound. "Good morning," she said in a startled but whispered voice.

"Good morning," said Ellen.

"Yes, good morning. You found my note! Thank you for letting us sleep in." Fiona said, grabbing her brush and pulling out the remainder of her pink foam curlers. "I found out that there were several other express trains tomorrow that still get us into Füssen in good time. You agree with me about the train at half past twelve?" "Yes, we do, ah, did."

"Well, it still takes us to Munich where we must make a change, like the others, and yet it still arrives in Füssen a little before five o'clock."

"That's good. What else did you find out, I see you are really taking to your duties?" Jane said, smiling.

"Yes, I am, better a little late than not at all! So, here's what else I found. The hostel guidebook indicated that the hostel is within easy walking distance of the train station and open for reservations at nine o'clock in the morning until eleven o'clock at night. I suggest we take this train just after noon, gather food for lunch and possibly dinner. After we get dressed, we need to call this number for the hostel in Füssen and make our reservation. Then we can grab breakfast and get on our way."

"Last night, I asked Frauke if she could pack us a lunch from leftovers. She refused, stating, 'No leftovers for my new friends. I'll make you something proper for the journey.' Isn't that great?" said Ellen.

"Sounds like the only thing we need to know is the weather! I neglected to check last night," Jane began and then reached under her bunk for the newspaper she kept there, "But in the paper, yesterday's forecast for today was in the 70'sF. So, if you look at it, we all took care of our respective jobs, for the first time, we are prepared! Awesome!"

"Wow, we finally got everything lined up, that is great. Now all we need is the train to be on time and the hostel to have a room for us. I'll go make the call before breakfast," said Fiona. "I'll meet you in the great room."

"Ok, sounds good, see you in a few minutes."

Fiona was dressed rather quickly since she knew the forecast was for warmer weather; she dressed in her jeans and fuchsia polo shirt with her tennis shoes. They would be walking and sitting a lot today and she needed her traction. As she left the room, she looked at the other two who were almost dressed. Jane was in her staple white oxford shirt and khakis with tennis shoes and Ellen in a black shirt with jeans and her red espadrilles.

Fiona was dressed and out of their room heading downstairs before the other two, even though she got up after them. She quickly found Frauke at the front desk and gained her permission to use the phone. With some assistance in dialing, Fiona reached the youth hostel in Füssen and made reservations for three women without a hitch.

Her task mostly complete, she left the front desk and Frauke, heading down to the great room and breakfast. As she entered the great room, Fiona saw that Jane and Ellen were just ahead of her standing aside the line for breakfast; they were waiting for her.

"Good morning again," began Fiona, "We have our reservations. Next?"

Jane and Ellen said in unison, "Breakfast!"

"Ellen, what's on the menu this morning?" asked Fiona.

"Looks like everything you like, pancakes, bacon, apple juice, oatmeal, waffles, coffee, hot chocolate, tea. Need I say more?"

"What, no cold cereal or hard rolls?" Fiona joked.

"Well, I thought perhaps you'd be tired of those, so I didn't bother to tell you about them. They are there, but I thought you'd enjoy more of what I just mentioned being better, right?" Ellen asked.

"I think you are right on that one!"

"I'm right behind you," said a hungry Jane.

In the end, Ellen had predicted Fiona's breakfast fairly well. She chose pancakes, bacon, apple juice, and hot chocolate. Jane found the corn flakes, sausages, toast, and coffee. Ellen, true to form, found the waffles, sausages, and tea. They found seats at a nearby table and began to discuss the remains of their preparations and packing. Like Fiona, the other two had taken a few moments the night before to place most of their possessions back into their luggage.

Being nearly packed before leaving for the breakfast line also helped the next process of keeping them on time to make the twelve-thirty train. They knew saying their thanks to the Feierabend family would take some time, especially, with their new Mother-like friend, Frauke.

Individually, each woman knew that by traveling like this together, to these wonderfully historic and scenic places, they would certainly meet some incredibly interesting people and make new lifelong friends. They quickly made their way back to their room, finished their packing, freshened up, and each, one at a time, checked and rechecked the room for any stray belongings. Convinced they were ready to leave; Ellen closed the door and kept the key in her spare hand to return to Frauke at the front desk.

Farewells can be a difficult ceremony; they can bring joy, or they can bring clarity. For Jane, it was difficult knowing that her own Mother was so far away, of this Frauke had reminded her so many times over the last few hours. For Ellen, it was joyous as she'd made another connection in Europe, one that she would return to and share with Pierre. For Fiona, it brought clarity. She knew that she was on the right path, selecting good choices of locations to see and meeting friendly, interesting people. And while she was taking in all the history that is found in any corner of Europe, she knew home would also be the right choice too.

Outside the hostel, Wilhelm was waiting for them in their family car, a Volkswagen station wagon. He clicked his heels together and made a sweeping gesture, as if he was the chauffeur to Cinderella and they were off to the ball. The women were a bit stunned, having already discussed and planned on taking a taxi to the station. They stood looking back and forth, first at each other and then individually to Wilhelm, whose grin only grew larger as his intentions were realized.

"Ja, ja, here is Wilhelm, he is to take you to the station!" announced Frauke.

"Are you certain of this, you must have work to do?" said Ellen. She realized, finally, that this grand gesture of the transportation was the Feierabend family's final attempt at treating these three women like the new family members they had become.

"Ja, this is correct," Frauke confirmed. "He will drive you to the station. We don't want you to be late! You will never know how much fun or how thankful we are that you came to our hostel. Please tell your friends about us, but remember, you were like family, extra special!" And with that, she could no longer contain herself and ran blubbering into the hostel no longer wanting to create a scene out front.

"There she goes," said Wilhelm. "Please climb in and we'll be at the station in a few minutes. You do want to make the next train, ja?" he assumed.

"Yes, we do," said a still stunned Jane.

"Yes, we do. Thank you for all your kindnesses. I will send you a postcard and hope we can continue to write." Fiona, the pen-pal collector, beamed as she climbed into the car having placed her bag securely in the way back.

Not to be left behind, Jane quickly mimicked her friend and climbed in. Ellen followed but sat up from taking the front passenger seat. Since Ellen was easily the tallest, the other two naturally headed for the backseat. It was something that none of them spoke about, was concerned about in the least, it was just logical.

They arrived in short order at the station and found the overhead schedule board. Their train was departing from track #10. As was their ongoing ritual, they used the restroom facilities in the station and then headed towards the train. They planned on sitting in 2nd class, with the rest of the locals. Their first leg to Munich would take a little over 2 hours. They found a 2nd class car and began determining where to sit. Their discussion was short lived as they agreed on the section of the car at the front. They sorted out their luggage and once it was secure, began to pass out their items for lunch. The leftovers were just as delicious as the night before, the memories of that dinner still fresh in their minds.

Ellen set out her new bottle of Evian, which had been purchased in the train station while, Jane unpacked the lunch Frauke had her chef make for them. Fiona wondered what they were going to eat, being not familiar with cold German food other than a German potato salad.

"Here we go," Jane said. "Fiona, do you want one?"

Looking over at Jane, Fiona was relieved to see what looked like sandwiches and chips. "What kind of sandwich is it?" Fiona said, still a fussy eater.

Smelling and tasting the sandwich, Jane said, "I think chicken salad. Tastes great. Here, only way to know if you like it is to try one," she added.

"Ok, all right." Fiona reached over the waxed paper wrapping that contained a sandwich. She took a tentative bite and then looked at each of them and made a seriously cautious face. Coughing and spurting, she said, "Oh, my goodness!"

"What is it, are you ok?" asked Jane.

"She's ok," Ellen announced, "That's just her way of teasing us. I know you like it, so you can stop pretending that you are choking. Remember the international symbol for choking isn't a cough," Ellen finished.

"You are right, I do like it. Chicken salad is one of my favorites."

"That's what I told Frauke last night when we were in the kitchen. She took me aside, one cook to another, and asked what it was we all liked. I knew you really liked chicken salad and that since meeting Jane, she did too. So I just offered that as a suggestion. Turns out, the hostel chef had made chicken breasts for the other hostel guests last night. This morning, he cooked the remaining chicken just for our sandwiches this morning. I told him to concoct something we would remember. Do you taste the spices?" Ellen asked, breathing in through her mouth, similarly to wine tasting.

With a mouthful of sandwich Fiona replied, "I don't care about what spices are in here, it tastes great to me!"

"Here you go, there are two for each of us, some carrots, chips, and fruit. Do you want an apple or a banana?" Ellen asked each of them as she was handing out the other sides.

Jane spoke first, "I'll take an apple, I like green apples, if you spill them on your shirt, no one can really tell."

"I'll take a banana," said Fiona.

"Great, I'll take the orange. Bon appétit!" Ellen declared as she took a large bite of chicken salad. As she tasted the chef's spicing ability, she was pleased in having had the discussion with Frauke about it. It was a delicious sandwich.

"Is there any mustard?" Fiona asked, "I think I'd have a little more mustard."

They took turns sitting facing the rear of the train; it was an odd position watching where you had been instead of where you were going. For some people, the trio had noticed, it was a bit overwhelming. Sometimes they'd seen entire families sitting all in the same direction. They thought it was likely that some of the members got motion sickness facing the rear.

Within the hour, it felt as though the train had both reached maximum speed, and before long, begun to slow down. What was actually happening, they would eventually learn, that trains often had to change tracks if the initial tracks weren't a direct line to their destination. Sometimes, it was to slow down for a tunnel, others for no apparent reason. It was something they would discuss but never fully understand. These direct trains never stopped between destinations. So comprehending their speeds, without direct knowledge of the railway systems, was out of their reach.

Having consumed her sandwiches, carrots, and her orange, Ellen looked into the picnic bag to see if Frauke had left them anything for dessert. She found something that made her smile. "Anyone interested in dessert?" she asked.

Still finishing her banana, Fiona looked over at Ellen with a surprised look. "We have dessert too?"

"Yes, want to guess what it is?" Ellen teased, stringing them along.

"Well, unless she packed an ice box in there, I'll wager $100 that it isn't ice cream," said Jane.

"I'd agree with that wager, but far more interesting things have surprised me on this trip, I wouldn't put it past Frauke to figure out a way to do it if she could," Fiona surmised.

"No, it isn't ice cream, next guess?"

"Apple pie?" Jane said, "She'd manage that if she wanted to help us feel American."

"No apple pie, but good guess."

"We already, well, I already had an apple, but pie is a good guess or apples?" Fiona said.

"Yes, it is."

"Blueberry?" said Jane.

"No, not a fruity pie," Ellen hinted.

"Not a fruity pie?"

"No."

"What kind of pie can you have without fruit?" Fiona said, a bit befuddled. But just as she made that statement, she thought of something. "Pecan pie?"

"Yes! Good guess, how did you figure that out?" Ellen asked Fiona.

"Yeah, how did you?" Jane added.

"Well, Ellen's fiancé is from Paris, perhaps she made us some mini pies, tarts, or tortes?" Fiona began. "So knowing that Frauke had asked for tips on the luncheon, she instructed her chef to make for us, I figured the sandwiches were for me, the fruit and vegetable sticks for you Jane, and a tart or sweet portable dessert for Ellen. What better than large slices of pecan pie?"

"Well, they aren't exactly large slices," Ellen corrected.

"They aren't? They didn't put a whole pie in that bag did they?" said Fiona as she strained to see what was at the bottom of the bag Ellen had carried with her from the hostel.

"No, there are several little pies, you know, tarts."

Handing one to Jane who bit into it immediately following finishing a mouthful of green apple, said, "Now, that is a tart, tart!"

Both Ellen and Fiona knew the joke and were careful to cover their mouths so that their laughs didn't display the delicious pecan tarts they were now devouring. They were having so much fun with their lunch that they hadn't noticed the train slowing down. They had begun the gradual process of converting from an express direct train to one working in combination with local trains as they came closer and closer to Munich's central station.

"What does the guidebook say about Munich? Should we make a trip back here after we tour the castles?" asked Fiona as she was looking out the window at the gradual transition from farmhouses, greenery, and cows, to cement sidewalks, streets, and tall buildings.

"Yes, it is a growing metropolis. I think the concentration camps are also near here, look here, Dachau isn't far away," Ellen said, leaning towards them and speaking both quietly and reverently. Pointing at the small map in the guidebook, her fingernail pointing out the location of this 'place,' "Do you want to go there?"

"I think it is something from history we should experience while we are here," Fiona agreed, as she too leaned in and spoke in hushed tones.

Jane, following her new friends' lead, leaned in and whispered, "I'd like to go there too, I may be older than both of you but still too young enough to know firsthand what people went through during that time. Perhaps we can see it in a few days?"

"I agree with you both, I think going there is something we should do while we are in this part of the country. We can certainly learn something, right? I mean, it can't all be fun, games, shopping, eating, and drinking, can it?" Fiona said, looking first to Jane, then to Ellen. "Can we add that to Sophie's list?" As she uttered these words, the train's brakes grabbed hold, it was a message. The women were literally moved in their seats as the train lurched suddenly, swaying them into the aisle near their luggage. Fiona, already within sight of her bag, reached for the side compartment of her suitcase, retrieved Sophie's list, and with a handy pen, she added simply the word, "Camp." They would all know what it meant going forward.

Within the hour, they were greeted with the serious look of a conductor who was making his rounds of the train; this stop was the terminus. He had a playful smile despite his serious look and his graying red hair was neatly cut and styled. Having walked past when the train lurched, he was checking his charges for injuries, and had overheard the women discussing the limited time to change trains to catch the train that went out to Füssen.

He also had heard their more recent discussion about going to a concentration camp; his family would have appreciated their demeanor and candor in their decision to see this piece of German history. He enjoyed listening to conversations in all sorts of languages and his private lessons, therein. He wanted to practice his English and as he walked by, he overheard that they were on their way to Füssen.

He decided to offer them his more playful side and winked at the women who seemed to be slow in disembarking. To them he said in his best English, "Better hurry now, you don't want to miss your connection!"

Fiona was closest to him and overheard his comments the best. The last one out of their seats, she turned and said back to him, "I don't want to miss it either! Thank you!"

Running to catch up to Ellen and Jane, Fiona said, "We have to hurry!"

Even though this train was on time, they still had to walk all the way into the main terminal in order to see the schedule of departing trains and their assigned tracks. Ellen, donning her backpack, was slower than the other two who could pull or lift their smaller bags more readily. She caught up to them just as Jane saw the train to Füssen. It was leaving from track #14.

Ellen said to them, "You two run ahead, I'm slow with this big pack, make sure not to leave without me."

Fiona and Jane agreed to walk on ahead but neither would board the train and risk being separated. Instead, they sat on a bench opposite the train car where they had decided to board. It was again, 2nd class, since it was another shorter trip, only about two hours. "Let's wait here," Jane said.

"Good idea."

"Does the guidebook say we need to be in a specific car?" Jane asked.

"What do you mean?"

"Well, let's check with Ellen and then the conductor, he'll get us to the right car or we might end up in Brazil!"

"Very funny," Fiona mused.

"I'm not kidding; I realize Brazil is out of the question but some place we don't expect if we don't pay attention. We want to get to Füssen tonight."

"Yes, I made our reservations for three women, all set."

"Good, I forgot to ask you, I was so busy and groggy this morning. Here she comes, I can see Ellen now," Jane said.

"WOO-WOO-WOO," the metallic train whistle indicated the whistle code for departure.

The women stood and gradually crossed the platform as Ellen finished her approach. They boarded together and after finding their seats, they were still searching for the conductor when the train left the station.

"Just in time," Fiona said, smiling, as they left the station.

Chapter 40 Füssen, 1985

She briefly made note of the other travelers in their compartment, as seating was limited. Next to the trio were a smiling Asian-looking man and another man with a large backpack. The Asian man told the women his name was Masato. He smiled the entire trip, and was really a man of a few words. The other man introduced himself as Kurt, a student on his last few days of holiday before beginning graduate school at the University of Berlin. He'd won an award for the Master's program in Linguistics; it included room, board, and classes. A small stipend to live on was forwarded to him and he chose to spend it seeing Bavaria.

Kurt told them about growing up in Canada and how he learned to speak German. Fiona hung on his every word. After an hour or so she grew tired with the motion of the train, the wine they'd been sharing, and hearing of each others' travel stories. Everyone seemed to be in a good mood and looking forward to the climb skyward into the wintery snowcapped mountains of the Bavarian Alps.

Fiona was excited to be going to such a magical place and to the land of castles. Sitting next to an open compartment window, she quickly nodded off in her seat as soon as the locomotive pushed the train along its uphill journey. She faintly heard the conductor speaking, but now she was off in dreamland dreaming of the train's route into the Alps, to the castles, and to King Ludwig's favorite musician, Wagner and his music.

In her dreams, she felt herself walking up a hiking trail and into patches of snow. Having lived in a region known for snowy winters, Fiona enjoyed the thought of hiking through the snow. She could hear the sounds of a babbling brook, and she imagined icy cool water flowing along the mountain stream where it was forced to create a new direction of flow with each change in condition, frozen or thawed.

The frozen areas of the brook dammed up the flow, much like the beaver from her native Minnesota. But here, she could hear the constant sound of the waters flow; it was almost in time with her resting heart beat. She could feel the thrum, thrum, thrum, of the water as it cascaded along the rocky path.

In her dream, the weather was growing cold, the brook would likely freeze over soon, she thought. That was when she heard it, "C-R-A-C-K!" It was the ice beneath her feet. She was now standing on a collecting pool that had frozen over. "But, no," she thought, "I can't be standing here."

"C-R-A-C-K, C-R-A-C-K, C-R-A-C-K!" There it was again. She looked to see where her feet were and became aware of the coldness about them.

"F-I-O-N-A!" Someone was calling her name, what were they doing here with her by the stream, would they come find her before she fell through into the icy depths?" she continued dreaming.

Again, she heard her name, but it wasn't a woman speaking, it was a man, "F-I-O-N-A!! Wake up," said the male voice.

"I'm over here," she thought she spoke in her dream, but her voice wasn't the loud shout she had planned, it was merely a whisper. It was nothing anyone would be able to hear outside, not here in the snow, on the noisy collecting pool of ice. "Come find me over here. I'm on the cold collecting pool, quick, hurry."

Then, she heard the cracking noises again. "What was that, if it was the ice, surely, it wouldn't play with me this long and allow my torment to continue, would it?"

It was then she realized she was dreaming of dreaming but still didn't wake. She was too interested in hiking the cool snowy trail up to Füssen and the castles in Bavaria. In the background of her mind, she heard the operatic sounds of Richard Wagner, the composer heralded by King Ludwig, who was a local to these parts of Bavaria.

"The music," she thought, "It was the sound of the needle hitting the vinyl record. C-R-A-C-K, then, C-R-A-C-K-L-E, and then there it was: music. Yes, that was it. It was music. This was the music she learned in her Music Appreciation class in college, yes, that was it." She thought.

In her college classroom, she would daydream as the professor played the wonderful melodic symphonies of music by Wagner. She would often visualize herself climbing a snow-capped mountain whenever the professor laid down the turntable's needle and began Wagner's masterpiece, which she called, "Füssen: Opus 1."

It was her favorite, and realizing this made her smile. "Kurt," she mumbled, "Were the mountains snow-capped in September?"

She thought in her dream of her life with Kurt, fought to stay asleep and remain with him, but she was losing.

CHAPTER 41 A HONEYMOON INTERRUPTED, 1991

As was her custom, Fiona wrote out several postcards. They'd mailed one of them to her parents and another to Gabriella. Postcards. Thinking back, Jake remembered the ones she'd sent last week, it was a sunset photo of the "Old Course" at St. Andrews. Before he placed it in the post box, Jake took a minute to read the first postcard:

"Dear Mom and Dad, spent a great day yesterday drove by St. Andrews, high tea in Perth, found great B & B in Pitlochry. Thursday heading west to Isle of Skye. Seeing lots of sheep and more fog. Weather holding parts of each day. Thank you for all you've done for us and in making this trip not only possible but so memorable. We love being here together and miss you both. Love from both of us. F & J."

Then he looked over the card to Gabriella, who was looking after their apartment while they were away. Jake figured it was just a customary thank you card but was curious enough to read her card too. It was written after they'd left Pitlochry, but before their mountain meadow picnic, which Jake could tell by the events written on Gabriella's card. Her words in this card touched Jake's heart. This card read:

> *"Gabriella, I now understand what you've meant when you speak of Nate. I hadn't ever put the amount of love you could feel for someone in perspective, like you've been telling me, until I've been here with Jake. You can't believe how I feel. It is just really special. When did you know the first time? Love Fiona."*

Jake wondered what Fiona meant by the 'first time' and made a mental note to ask her. Right now, he was more concerned with calling her parents and sharing their recent news than in interpreting a postcard. It could certainly wait. He would wait too. He was always waiting for her.

Hearing the phone in ringing in the middle of the night wasn't something unexpected, but it can be a bit shocking. Jake knew that the MacLaren's would want to know as soon as he did what was going on. It was the source of the call that shocked the MacLaren's more than the time of the call. Maureen answered, as the phone was on her side of the bed.

"Hello?" she muttered, still a bit groggy.

"Mom?" Jake said. Long before their final wedding vows, both sets of parents had encouraged their new son or daughter-in-law to call them 'Mom' or 'Dad.'

It was Jake calling in a panic. She urgently motioned to Ian to get on the other phone in the kitchen.

"Yes, son, is something wrong? Why are you calling now?" Maureen said, uncertain.

"Well, that's why I'm calling. Fiona's in the hospital here. We had a touch and go day and evening at the hotel and she got admitted to the hospital a few hours ago. This was the first time I could get away to call. She's sleeping now. It is just a precaution but, oh Mom, I'm so worried..." his voice cracked in his effort to speak.

It was all Jake could manage at the moment.

"Jake, take a breath," Ian said, "Now tell us what has happened."

Over the next few minutes Jake outlined their trip thus far including the bathroom scare at the petrol station and through yesterday afternoon until when they discovered Fiona's bleeding.

"Ok, so what does the doctor think, what is the plan?" Ian said.

"Right now it is just to keep her under observation. I'm scared Mom, she's never been sick before, nothing like this. She won't eat or drink, she slept all day. She is a bit weak too, but her vitals were normal."

"Did they run any tests?"

"Just a few minor ones, you know, an abdominal ultrasound. They don't have an MRI or CT scanner here. I don't want to evacuate her either, so we are staying put and going by how she feels."

"How does she say she feels?" Maureen managed.

"Well, her abdominal pain comes in waves, she feels like it is gastrointestinal, and then she feels weak, she just keeps repeating that."

"Ok, Jake," Maureen began, knowing a bit about her daughter's interpretations of symptoms, being trained as a nurse. Maureen was a

Mother and had an itchy feeling about what Fiona wasn't saying. "Please have her call us when she wakes up. I have some questions for her. Don't worry terribly, if she wasn't well, she'd say so. She'd want to be moved to a bigger facility."

"That's why I called, I, we, I mean, haven't discussed what to do if we are sick or what our intentions or wishes, oh, I don't know what to do."

Ian chimed in at this point, "Jake, hang on son. The doctors would have asked you 'those' questions already if they were needed."

"I'm sure you are right, if you say so," Jake said, absently.

"Well, son, it sounds to me like this one is out of your hands. Be patient and wait. We'll send our prayers your way and hope when you call us again, you will have better news. Let us know if you need anything. Are your parents back in Florida? Did you call them yet?"

"Yes, they are, but I called you first. She's your daughter after all. I knew she'd want you to know. I'm calling them next."

"Listen son, if you need someone, if you need any money or help, I have friends in Edinburgh and Maureen has cousins in London. We can always call them too.

"Yes sir, you are right. I'll be patient and let you know what and when I know it. As for the friends and the money, I don't need it now; we really don't know much of anything right yet. I just wanted to call and let you know. I need your strength and your prayers," Jake said formally.

"I completely understand Jake. It isn't fun going through that over there all alone," Maureen replied. "It would be no trouble to alert my cousins about Fiona's condition, they are her cousins too. Perhaps one of their children can drive up to be with you?" Maureen said, absently, already thinking of calling her cousin and making the request.

"Good idea, dear," Ian said to Maureen through the phone. Then to Jake he said, "Listen Jake, I can put out a call to lease a private jet at any time. So we could be there tomorrow if you need us there. But so far, I don't think you do, just know that is an option, ok Jake?" Ian added.

Nodding at her line in the bedroom, Maureen said, "Yes, Jake, we leave as soon as you say the word, right Ian?"

"That's right, Jake."

"No, I just wanted to let you know what's going on and how Fiona's doing. I'll keep in touch."

Jake hung up, knowing that Fiona's parents were up to speed with her condition, next he'd try his parents.

The phone rang three times before a cheerful voice picked up, "Hello?"

It was his Mother. "Hi Mom, this is Jake calling," he said, glumly.

"Quiet down, everyone, please, go ahead Jake!" Bette said, loudly.

The room of guests quieted down almost immediately, the yacht club was having a progressive dinner and as was the typical result, a few stragglers would hang out at the Davies for a few rounds of 12-year old Scotch that Clifton kept hidden in the not so deep recesses of their condo.

"Hi," Jake began and stopped.

Bette sensed his alarm, "What's the matter Jake?"

"Mom," Jake tried again, his muted sobs traversed the ocean between them.

Bette excitedly, and without caution, hailed Clifton from the lanai and rapidly instructed him to get on the other extension in his office. "It's Jake, hurry, something's wrong."

"I'm heading to the other phone Jake," Clifton shouted, from the lanai.

Clifton picked up the extension in his office saying, "Ok, I'm here son, what's going on? Were you in an accident, are you ok?"

Bette listened from her line in the kitchen, her guests watching her nod breathlessly, as each moment unfolded. They knew Jake would only call if it was an emergency. The group split up, most of the couples remained with Bette, while the rest infiltrated Clifton's office trying to learn what was going on. The stragglers at the party were good long-term friends of the Davies and Clifton would have never even considered shooing them back to the lanai or home for that matter.

Jake, thousands of miles away, painstakingly explained what he knew so far. It wasn't much but it was something.

"Oh, Jake," Bette began when he'd finished. "You tried to call earlier I'm sure, I'm sorry we were out. What can we do?"

"Yes, Jake what do you need?" Clifton added.

"I just need you to be strong for me," Jake said, "I'm holding myself together ok but it is hard this far away from home. Healthcare and their system here are so foreign to me."

"How long has she been sleeping?"

"Only a few hours, we were up most of the twilight hours here, I just got her transferred and admitted to the hospital."

"What hospital is it?"

"Broadford, it's about a 30 minute drive towards the coast from Ratagan."

"You're on the Isle of Skye then?" Clifton asked.

"Actually, that's a good question. We were on our way, we were stopping for the night in Ratagan, and going to drive this way tomorrow. We wanted to go down to the coast and drive about there for a week or more. We didn't really have much of a schedule," he said.

"Ok, let me get the atlas. Bette talk to him, I'll be right back." Clifton set down the receiver with a bit of a clunk and could be heard rummaging through the bookshelves of his office library. Any good sailor had a slew of charts, maps, and a good world atlas. He happened to have one by the folks at Oxford, circa 1957.

Picking up the receiver, "Ok Jake, tell me that again, where had you just gotten to?"

"Do you see Inverness and A82?"

"Yes," he said.

"Ok, follow A82 down past the loch, which was fantastic, I'll tell you about that another time. We took the A887 to the A87 west, do you see that?"

"Yes," he said, again. This time he looked more quickly along the lines of the curvy road, and out onto the Isle of Skye. "Yes, I've found Ratagan. Ok, I see Broadford too. What size of town is it?" his Father asked.

"Well, I suppose big enough to support a local hospital. I already spoke with Ian and Maureen, if I need them, they said they'd hop a flight in the morning."

"Perhaps he could swing down here and pick us up," Bette said, having listened to the map discussion and wondering where that was going. She wanted to know how Fiona was doing, not the size and location of where she was presently. "Right?"

"Ah, I'd suppose so," Jake said.

"Bette, I don't think that's a good idea, we'll make our own bookings, do you want us to come, Jake?"

"Not now, I just wanted you all to know and knowing that you know and that you could all come is helping me no end," he said, sighing.

"We love you and Fiona, son. Remember that," Clifton said.

"That's right, remember that, dear," Bette put her hand over the mouthpiece not wanting Jake to hear her soft sobs. Her eyes moist, the unshed tears running down into her nose, she knew that if she sniffed, even if quietly, both of her men would hear. She didn't really care if they heard though, she was emotional and that was the important part of her deception.

"Listen, I've kept you guys up too late, I'll call back in the morning, my afternoon."

"Hang in there son, you'll have some information soon enough. Bette, are you still there?" Clifton asked.

Squelching a sniffle, "I'm here, yes, I'm here."

"Thanks, Mom, thanks, Dad," Jake began and then paused, "Listen, the doctor is walking this way, I have to go." Jake said.

Clifton and Bette got in a quick, "Ok," and "Love you," before they heard Jake hanging up the phone; the line was still open when they heard Jake say, "You found out what?" Then the line was dead.

Clifton and Bette hung up their respective handsets and reunited in the living room. "What do you make of that?" Bette said.

"I think we should be packing a 3-4 day bag," Clifton said. "I'm calling Ian, I don't care what time it is."

"Please, call them. We need to talk to them, now!" Bette agreed, heading back to her line in the kitchen and waiting for the shout from Clifton's den when he'd completed dialing the MacLaren's phone number.

"It's ringing," Clifton shouted.

"Hello, Jake? Son, what's the latest?" It was Ian's fast-paced pitch.

"No, Ian, this is Clifton and Bette, we've just had a call from Jake and gather you have too. We wanted to compare notes, get on the same page, make plans, you know..." Clifton said, his voice interrupted by Ian.

"What did he say, anything new?"

"Who is it dear," Maureen chimed in, wearily.

"It's Clifton and Bette, Jake just called them too."

From her side of the bed, Maureen sat up and turned on the bedside lamp. From her bedside table drawer, she removed a small pad of paper and a pen; both had the markings from the 'Waldorf Astoria' on them. She'd helped herself during the wedding...a memento.

The men were talking for about ten minutes before they hung up. The plan was in place, if Jake called with unfortunate news, Ian and Maureen would charter a plane and go immediately to the UK. Clifton and Bette would fly commercial standby in hopes that they would get two passengers to give up their seats if all flights were booked. They knew pleading their case at the gate would get a rise out of some willing and booked passengers.

But Jake didn't call back and not soon enough for Maureen. She had her bags packed and ready to go, pleading with Ian to book their flight anyway. It was Ian who showed restraint knowing his new son-in-law and his only daughter were medical professionals and would call if they were in trouble.

"No call, no trouble. Any trouble, I make a call. Ok?" Ian said.

"Not in my book, but ok." Maureen scoffed.

"Well dear, it will have to do. Our little girl has grown up and married the man she loves. We need to be patient and wait for our daughter to let us know where and when we are needed. It is her affair now; we are just happy observers to her new life with Jake."

"I'll never get a wink of sleep tonight now," recalling the two sleep-interrupting calls so far, "It's the not knowing that is going to really bother me," Maureen confessed.

"I'll stay up with you dear," Ian said, comforting his wife of so many years by reaching for and holding her hand as they lay awake in bed.

That night, in the United States, two couples tossed and turned waiting for more information and results. One had night interrupted and another cut short.

While across the pond, the newlywed couple was waiting for results with information. Jake was doing his best to be patient with the patient-who, like her parents miles away, was also finally sleeping--holding her hands atop her belly.

Before turning out the light in their bedroom, Ian and Maureen looked intently at each other and said another quick prayer. Despite their anxiety in waiting for another call, they did finally fall asleep too, spooning in their bed.

While Fiona continued to sleep, with what looked like a tolerable amount of pain, Jake was out in the hall speaking with the doctor. What Jake didn't know was that Fiona wasn't asleep; she was meditating to tolerate the ache from her belly and the strangeness going on down below.

In the hall, Jake was speaking with Fiona's doctor and a redheaded nurse named Jennie. He wasn't smiling, hadn't fainted, but he wasn't sure if he should be happy either. From a patient's room across the hall, he heard the television and the station announcement that the BBC was hosting a Wagner concert in the coming weeks, for tickets call the station. Jake didn't hear anything further than Wagner and recalled Fiona's favorite piece from college music appreciation class: Füssen-Opus 1.

Chapter 42 A Honeymoon Rescue, 1991

As the music from the television concluded and the Elvis song, "Suspicious Minds," brought him clarity, he refocused his attentions to what the doctor was telling him. Prior to their honeymoon, Jake had picked up as many open shifts as possible. He hadn't yet told all his co-workers about his engagement, he just hadn't had the right opportunity. Instead, his co-workers would play certain songs on the radio at the main desk, wondering if and when he'd pick up on the fact that the music and lyrics were the unit's way of easing him into confessing.

He'd tried for many months to suppress his feelings and plans with Fiona from the unit, that when this song had come on just as he walked up to the main desk he knew the jig was up. Now, suppressing a smile from that musical memory upon hearing the song again, Jake did his best to listen as intently as possible. He feared he would end up listening as a nurse and not as both a husband and a nurse.

"Mr. Davies, perhaps this would be best discussed in the family lounge. You are alone here in the UK, that is, you two are alone?" said the doctor, turning to have Jake follow him to an alcove just down the hallway from Fiona's room.

"Yes we are, lead the way."

"We've conducted a few tests as you know, the abdominal ultrasound ruled out any involvement in the gallbladder, liver, stomach, and intestines, as sources for her bleeding. While you were on the phone, I had a gynecologist examine Fiona."

"A gynecologist would be appropriate," Jake concurred.

"I assisted the doctor," Jennie offered.

"Yes, that's good," Jake said, aware that the medical team seemed to be hesitating. "What's wrong with my Fiona?"

The doctor and Jennie looked back and forth at each other and to Jake. Taking a deep breath, the doctor began to explain their findings.

"Jake, I now know the source of Fiona's bleeding, fatigue, and mood."

"You do, please tell me what it is! Is she going to be alright?" Jake demanded.

Jennie couldn't wait any longer as a broad smile came across her face, but looking down again before she looked Jake squarely in the eyes, "What the doctor and I have been waiting to tell you is that…"

"Allow me." Dr. MacGinnis interrupted, "Jake, you may continue on your honeymoon, but Fiona will need some bed rest first. You're going to be a Father young man, a Father." The doctor paused briefly, allowing Jake a moment to let the good news sink in.

"A Father? Bed rest? Fiona's pregnant?"

"Yes, son, she is."

"But there is something wrong, is that it?" asked Jake.

"I believe the gynecologist will explain it better than I but essentially, Fiona has a problem with the placement and condition of the placenta. The twins will need more time to mature and will do better if she is on bed rest a bit longer. She has a mild form of abruptio placentae, when the placenta prematurely separates from the uterus. It can be stopped with plenty of rest. We have a wonderful B & B that I recommend you stay at, for the next week or so. I believe Dr. Morgan, the gynecologist, would concur and his clinic isn't far. Fiona could come to see him at the office at the end of a week to get a status update. If she is cleared, then I'd suggest you continue with your honeymoon and just keep to the sights and low key activities. Nothing too stressful just yet," said Dr. MacGinnis.

Jennie was watching Jake as Dr. MacGinnis was explaining Fiona's condition. She hoped he would handle the news well and keep it together. She was pulling for him.

"Yes, twins Jake. Do you want some water?" Jennie said, looking at Jake who seemed a bit parched. She left the family waiting area in search of a glass of water. She didn't like that she always offered to fetch things because she knew the juicy details of the rest of the patients' story would or could be told while she was out of the area.

"Twins. Wow, are they ok?"

"Yes, they do not seem to have been in any distress. Fiona is suffering from classic Level I symptoms, some mild vaginal bleeding, tender lower abdomen which is actually her uterus contracting, normal vital signs, and fatigue."

"When will she be discharged?" asked Jake.

"Probably tomorrow, I'll confer with Dr. Morgan once more. I'm her primary physician but if Dr. Morgan wishes, I can sign off the case and sign it over to him, now that we have her diagnosis. By the way, you'll likely want to make some calls stateside; let's go see if Fiona is awake and I'll ask Jennie to bring you a room phone."

"That would be fantastic Dr. MacGinnis, thank you for all your help."

"My pleasure son, anytime I get to bring someone good news along with the bad, I enjoy my work. It can be very rewarding to figure out the puzzle of your patients," he added, rising to leave and proffering a hand.

Jake shook his hand firmly. "I know. I've been thinking about going to medical school myself, after the honeymoon, I was going to look into what was needed to get into local programs and start getting myself prepared to be in school again. If we are expecting twins, well, I may have to put that off. I'll talk to my wife about it. Oh, that sounds so good! To talk to my wife," Jake muttered, hands on his face, walking back into her room, holding his breath.

"Good luck son," the doctor said softly from down the hall, "Good luck." Smiling, the doctor exited the floor through the door at the end of the hall.

Jake pushed open the door to Fiona's hospital room. He found her sitting up looking out the window; a bit of flush to her cheeks made her look more alive than she had the night before when she'd scared him so being so pale. "Hello, sweetheart."

Fiona turned to see who was speaking, turning her head towards the voice and at the same time knowing it was Jake. "Hello, darling." She said, suppressing a grin.

"You sure know how to pull the carpet out from under a guy! But I love you all the more for it!" With that, his voice cracked and he lunged forward and enveloped her sitting form into his long arms and crouched in front of her. "Your timing could have been better," he ended.

"I don't think there really is such a thing as a good time to tell you that!"

"Well, how long have you known?"

"I suspected it when we were on the picnic blanket, our lovemaking felt different," she said.

"You are a good forensic detective, I'll grant you that! What did Dr. Morgan tell you? I never saw him," he asked.

"His office has made a reservation for us at the Broadford Hotel, his patients are upgraded into one their suites. Dr. Morgan said the staff at the hotel will be expecting you sometime this evening to give them our information and arrange for my transfer tomorrow, that is if I feel up to leaving in the morning. They said you could stay with me here or in our room there, whichever you want."

"I'm still reeling about twins, Fiona, T-W-I-N-S!"

"Come here, sweetheart," Fiona said; her voice had a new Motherly tone to it.

"Oh, I love you so much." Jake bent his head onto her chest and let her caress him. Everything would be fine, he knew it now. Medical school, like he had explained to Dr. MacGinnis, could wait until the twins were perhaps in kindergarten, then they'd all be in school together! "Fiona, I was thinking while I was waiting." He began, "I think I'd like to go back to school."

"Oh, school, what kind of school? Get a master's degree in nursing?" Fiona asked.

"Not exactly," Jake said, "I was thinking more like medical school."

"I think I like your thinking!" Fiona agreed, "Maybe you could help me first with the twins as they are smaller and then go in a few years?"

"Fiona, those were my exact thoughts. I'm so glad you agree."

"Jake, we've been partners in many things since we've met, why not that? And, hey, who knows, maybe someday when I'm not so young, my hair is gray, the kids are gone, I'll want to go back to school too!"

"Deal, darling, it's a deal. By the way, while I was waiting, I put through calls and spoke to both of our parents," he said.

"Yes, I figured you were. I looked for you a few times and when you weren't here I thought you'd be on the phone," Fiona stopped short as her room door opened.

It was Jennie; she had an old cradle topped phone to plug into the jack near Fiona's bed. "Now this is a better way to make calls."

"Yes, it is. Thank you Jennie," Fiona and Jake said.

As Jennie left the room, they both looked at the phone. They kissed passionately, wanting to share in this moment privately a little longer. Jake stood and pulled Fiona to her feet. He then sat down in the oversized chair and pulled her to his lap. In this makeshift coupled posture, they could be on the phone, paired together and be able to hear together as they shared the news.

They decided to call Maureen and Ian first, knowing that Maureen would be struggling not knowing her daughter's condition. Condition it was indeed. Looking at Jake, Fiona nodded as he fingered but didn't dial her parent's area code. Silently, he too acknowledged who they'd call first. After all, he'd called them first before too, asked their permission first, there were a lot of firsts. Twins, however, weren't a first.

"Should we wait, what time is it in Minnesota?" Jake said.

"Approaching dawn I suppose, they'll be glad if we woke them, it won't even faze them if the news doesn't wow them, the time of the call will." Chuckling, Fiona dialed the number but handed the receiver to Jake. "I'll come on after you get them. Ok?"

"Ok."

The phone took a bit to connect and then they both heard the distant tones of a call ringing. It was answered almost immediately.

"Hello?!?" said Maureen, "Jake, is that you?"

"Yes Mom, it's me."

"Oh my son, you have had us in such a dither. What, er, how is Fiona? Do they know what's wrong with her?" Maureen motioned to Ian, who was still trying to put on slippers, tie his robe, and run to the kitchen extension without missing anything. "Ian stay here, come listen with me," Maureen instructed. "Ok, Jake, we're ready."

"It isn't Jake," Fiona began, softly, "It's me." While the emotional toll of what she was about to do was about to overtake her, Fiona did her best to not let on her feelings. She failed.

"Yes, Fiona, so good to hear your voice. Please, dear, tell us," Maureen said. Then to Ian she said, "She's crying, oh Ian!"

Ian began, "Ok, Fiona, it's all right, what do you have to tell us, what has the doctor diagnosed?"

"Well, I was examined by two doctors," Fiona explained, still trying to keep from full on crying but struggling. "The internal medicine doctor cleared me…"

"Oh that's marvelous," Ian and Maureen said, interrupting.

"But that's not all," said Jake. "Hold on," he said.

"What, there is more?"

"Yes, there is." Fiona said, obviously taking a deep breath before beginning and not covering the receiver in the process. She was milking this moment. She pulled her head away from the phone and looked at Jake. She mouthed the words for them to say it together. He nodded.

"What is it?" Maureen said, "Oh, dear god, Fiona, what is it?"

"Twins," Jake and Fiona shared together. "It's T-W-I-N-S!"

"What? What did you say dear?"

"Twins! Mother, I'm pregnant with TWINS!"

"Oh mercy, my baby is pregnant. Ian, did you hear that!" Maureen shouted. Ian was less than 6 inches away, now pulling back. He announced he was going to the kitchen extension. Kissing Maureen, he left the room.

"Ok, I'm here," Ian said, a bit breathless. "I heard TWINS, is that right?"

"Yes, Daddy, twins. But," Fiona said.

"But," Maureen and Ian said together.

"But I have a problem with the placement and strength of the placenta. It is called abruptio placentae, it means that I could be fine if I rested a lot, didn't exert myself and had a calm 4-5 more months, then the babies and I should be fine. They estimate I'm at 10-11 weeks now." Fiona announced, Jake didn't even know.

Blushing, Fiona paused on the phone to kiss her startled husband.

"Wow," was all Ian was able to stammer.

"How are you feeling, my dear. Oh, how you gave us such a scare. I have packed my bags and your Father was just about to book a private plane to come to the UK. Fiona, oh how this is good news."

"How will you spend the remaining honeymoon?" Ian, the pragmatist asked.

"Well, so far they've booked me in a local hotel, it's their version of a B & B, and I'll stay there for a week. They said if I'm feeling ok afterwards, we can resume our trip. We could continue with the Isle of Skye and then head back to Edinburgh. I think," she said looking at Jake, "We'll keep to the bigger citied areas and head back early. We can spend a week at home or so before returning to work."

"Work? Will you work pregnant?" Ian asked, astonished.

"Sure, why not?"

"Really?" Jake said, "If the doctor approves her, I'd suspect with a change of duty level Fiona could work several more weeks. Or, we'll be home in one week and she'll be on bed rest for the rest of the pregnancy. We'll just pray for the best and fate will work out all the details."

"Right, my thoughts exactly," Fiona agreed.

"Listen folks, we need to call my parents too. We'll be in better contact with you, likely checking in each afternoon our time, morning your time, sound like a plan?" asked Jake.

"Good plan, oh thank god you are fine dear. We love you, thank you for giving us this exciting news! I can't wait to tell my friends." Maureen expressed, animatedly.

"Mom, I think you should wait a bit, at least until we get home, ok?" Fiona suggested.

"Oh, good idea, I'll keep it under wraps."

"God bless you dear Fiona, my baby is giving me my first grandchildren!" Ian couldn't smile more broadly.

"Ok then, goodbye for now," Jake said.

"Goodbye, we love you."

"We now, love you too."

A similar phone conversation was had with Jake's parents who were relieved at their news as well. Jake also asked them not to tell their friends until Fiona's pregnancy was further along. They reluctantly agreed on the non-announcement for now. Jake and Fiona spent the rest of the afternoon spooning in her hospital bed. Jake was smiling like a Cheshire cat while Fiona was fast asleep. While he was lying there, he was doing the mathematics behind their news. If Fiona was 10-12 weeks along, he concluded, that means we conceived on or around the 4th of July. It was their most special holiday- next to their wedding day, now for even more reasons, make that two reasons at that.

Comforted by his conclusions, Jake whispered a faint, "Hmmm…"

Chapter 43 Reframed Recollections, 2015

When Jake was driving from Elizabeth to NYU Medical Center that day to see his wife, he was thinking and hoping that after all these days of recounting to him her European trip with Ellen, and most certainly without Kurt, that Fiona would begin to remember, and begin to return to him. He'd been waiting patiently through many, many stories, and several times had caught himself wanting to add to them, knowing the details from when he'd first heard about her trip when they'd been dating. No, now was the time for intense restraint. He so wanted to kiss and make love to his wife, she seemed so lost in her thoughts of the most recent years, those beautiful years they'd spent together. Instead, she harbored in the past, one actual and one fictional.

She seemed so fragile too. "Maybe," he prayed, "Maybe that fragility is actually her breaking point to return to me," Jake said aloud in the car. "What if I push her through those memories, push her so hard that while initially it feels like I'm pushing her away, when in actuality I'm pushing her back to me. Oh, my god. I've got to check this out!"

Jake pushed down on the car's accelerator and unlike Fiona, the car appropriately responded. Hopefully, today, so would Fiona. He pushed a button on his steering column and his car made a faint beep. "Call ready," the car said.

He smiled, that voice which Fiona had programmed into the voice activation system, he'd never liked it, and she'd opted not to record her own voice. He was wishing now that she had.

"Car, call Gabriella," Jake said.

"Calling, Gabriella," the car said, somewhat robotically.

Jake held the steering wheel listening for the tones indicating the call was going through. Gabriella answered on the second ring.

"Hello?" she said.

"Hi it's Jake. I just had an epiphany!"

"What, about Fiona?"

"Yes, I think I figured it out."

"Tell, tell, do tell me!"

"I think if I use logic today as she is recounting the phase of the trip when she's leaving Fussen to go to Salzburg, if I ask her about the hospitals there, you know, press her about events that never happened. Didn't she write to you that after the three of them went on the sound of music tour that Jane left to go to Germany and she and Ellen went to Italy? Why isn't she telling me about that part of their trip? What do you think?"

"Oh goodness, Jake what an epiphany, I think it is a perfect idea. I know I've read her trip diary and my postcards to her. They went to Salzburg briefly after their 2-3 days in Füssen and then on to Milan. That's where she got pneumonia and they left for primary French speaking folks, like Ellen's friend in Lausanne, Switzerland. After a few days at high altitude and cough syrup with codeine, Fiona told me she was good as new. That's when Ellen got home sick for Pierre and they headed back to Paris. She stayed with Sophie's parents in the country and met up with Ellen and Pierre everyday by train."

"Ok, I'm going to do it, I'm going to push her to the logical side of things. We haven't taken this approach. We've just been waiting and I think I'm ready to move from the waiting room to the living room. Allegro!" he shouted.

"Allegro!" Gabriella shouted back. "Call me later; I want to be one of the first to know what happens!"

"Ok, I'll call you later, bye!" Jake said, then to the car, "End CALL." The car disconnected the call and an ever more energized husband was now in charge, the doctor was out.

Jake parked the car in the doctors' parking area and with a kick in his step climbed the 10 flights of stair equivalents to Station 51 and swooped into Fiona's room. It was empty.

Like a hot air balloon losing ballast, Jake left her room in search of her nurse. He checked the duty roster and discovered Fiona was assigned to Laura, a tall blonde woman Jake knew from his time working on the station. He knew Laura was fond of Fiona and would have a good answer as to Fiona's current whereabouts.

Looking up and down the hall without peering into patient rooms, Jake finally spied Laura in the med room. She was putting together some I.V. drips and their partner fat emulsions. She smiled as he approached.

"Hi Dr. Davies," she said.

"Hi Laura, where's Fiona?"

"Oh, she's not in her room?"

"No, I just came from there. Did she go down for tests?"

"No I don't think that any were ordered. Let's check at the desk," Laura said, putting down the I.V.'s and walking up to the front desk with Jake.

From behind the desk and on the phone, their latest neuropsyche intern/ward clerk Todd looked up at them. He silently motioned for them to approach more closely, holding up a finger indicating he was almost finished with the call.

"Hi, how can I help you," Todd said, having hung up the phone and then addressing Laura and Dr. Davies.

"Hi, Todd, you know Fiona's husband, Dr. Davies?" Laura said.

Todd replied, "Yes, I do." He spoke quietly looking from side to side, "Not so loud, I thought we weren't supposed to mention his relationship."

"Well, you've got me there. But, Fiona's not in her room, do you know where she is?"

"Hi Doc, well, I think I saw her with shoes on, I think she may have gone for one of your legendary walks. Have you looked out the window to see the common garden areas?" Todd asked.

"Good information, let's look there," Laura said, turning away from the desk and heading to the incidental waiting area with windows she knew faced west and towards the memory gardens. They were so named by the Davies and MacLaren's, in a quiet ceremony a few months after Fiona was hospitalized. They were hoping that their donation would jog Fiona's memory. Both sets of parents and Jake had discussed the donating and planting of a Bonsai tree. It was like the one in her parent's garden in Minnesota.

"There she is!"Jake said, peering out the window. "She's sitting on the grass next to the Bonsai."

Joining him at the window, Laura said, "Yes, she is and I think she's crying. Look."

"Yes, I think you're right. I'm heading out there now; if anyone calls, tell them to come to the hospital, it could be tonight! It could be tonight that Fiona *finally* returns to us," he said. Out of earshot, he said, "And back to me!"

Down the stairs in a flash of lab coat, tie, stethoscope, and jeans, Jake repeated more loudly, "Coming back to me! Coming back to me!"

Back on Station 51, Laura wondered who would call. "He must have told someone his plan before I got here, we'd best be ready for guests," Laura said to Todd, "People are definitely heading our way."

Outside, Jake took in the scene first, relishing in the sight of his wife sitting on the grass, legs strewn to one side, and her hands combing the grass. As he grew closer, he could see that her eyes were closed, so his encroachment was not revealed. He also saw that her face was quite moist with tears. He could only hope that they were tears of joy at the realization of the return of her true memory and that finally, she had come back to him.

He stood there waiting, edging ever closer as he sensed she was talking aloud. He walked to the side and around to the back of her position. She was indeed talking. There was no audience save him, whether he was intended or not; he stood in awe of what she was saying.

To the grass, her hands combing and peeling each blade practically individually, "Do you remember me?"

He believed she was back, she had returned from the past memory that was askew of her real life. Back to him, this was real. Back to him, it was very real. His mind spoke what his heart had been feeling, he repeated, and repeated. And he smiled. It was a knowing smile, one that had ached for over a year for his wife of over 24 years. She was coming back! She remembered what was real. She remembered me! As if he could not smile any further, he did.

He continued to stand there, quietly behind her. He noted that patrons of the hospital, and the workers who would be coming and going as shifts changed; all took a wide berth of passage around them, watching Fiona's oration or monologue without interruption. Despite having a psyche unit, a locked one at that on this hospital's campus, it was strange to see a patient in a patient gown sitting alone on the grass and talking.

It must have seemed strange to some, but for those who knew her, seeing her here, on the grass and talking, they knew too. He smiled at those who silently acknowledged him and were giving them the space they so dearly earned, for which they had yearned and for which they had worked so hard. He nodded at others, showing his assent. She was coming back, he knew it. They did too.

Her eyes opened then and took in the curves and crooks of the Bonsai tree. "Did my Father take care of you too?" she asked. "I remember you, do you remember me?" she said to the tree.

Her hands were still wringing the grass, careful to not pluck any blades but simply to massage the tendrils of the weeds, and hold onto them with a mighty grip.

Jake's eyes were moist as he listened to his wife, he could only imagine the journey and distances she was traveling in her mind. She had unknowingly created this alternate life and family with a man she only met for a few days. Ellen and Jane had confirmed that when he spoke with them that first week she was hospitalized.

They'd come up from the Carolinas and from Minnesota to be with their friend, reading her trip diary back to her. They had been there with her and had not only seen her writing in the diary, but sometimes they took turns making entries, gathering bits of data or details, or helping her recount a particularly eventful day. It was like the day they spent in Füssen, walking up to Neuschwanstein and taking the English tour, listening to Wagner from the multiple speakers set up throughout the castle.

They'd confirmed her illness, which began in Salzburg and concluded in Lucerne with a good bottle of cough syrup. By then, Fiona and Ellen had parted ways with Jane as she'd gone off to Germany to go through Check Point Charlie and East Germany, East Berlin. In Jane's letters to Fiona, received after returning to Minnesota, Jane had mentioned how she'd spent time in Berlin, going to bistros, bakeries, and a brunch with Kurt, the man they'd all met in Füssen. By then, Kurt was studying at the University of Berlin, earning his Master's degree in Linguistics. Prior to his departure from Füssen, he had shared his contact information with Jane. When she got to Berlin, her letter had said, they'd met for brunch. Jane wrote how the two of them had had such a pleasant afternoon and how much Kurt had enjoyed meeting the three women, especially Fiona. He had asked Jane to give her his remembrances the next time the two women spoke or wrote with each other. Fiona had indeed left an impression on him but not as she had remembered it when she woke up from her coma.

Before long, Jake noticed someone whispering his name and he turned to find Gabriella standing a few feet away from him. Fiona's musing and monologue continued uninterrupted. "How?" he said, for it was all Jake could muster.

"Laura saw where you were headed and called me over on cardiology. I've transferred all of my assigned patients to the charge nurse. They let me come down here to help you, that is, if you need it, that is," she stammered, "If this is what I think it is!" She too smiled.

"Yes it is, yes you are, please stay with me. This is too incredible for words. Just watch her," Jake confirmed, pleased that their friend was there with him, with them.

Fiona was still unaware that she was 'on stage,' that her one woman show was gathering the attention of a slightly growing crowd. Jake continued to acknowledge people as they arrived and stood near the grassy area on which Fiona was still speaking.

With yet another handful of grass she said, "I think I remember you, I think I used to play here. Like my Grandmother Winnie," she said to the grass, "Do you remember me? I know I've been here before and 'played' with you," she said again to the grass. The tears were still rolling down her cheeks.

The bench opposite where Fiona sat on the grassy patch suddenly became the source of Jake's attention. He eased himself ever so slowly, Gabriella beside him, taking seats on the bench. It was a memorial bench honoring those whom the hospital had served, a gift from a grateful patient's family, one of Fiona's patients actually.

When word came to the hospital by the family that Fiona's favorite heart transplant patient had passed away, everyone was saddened. The family, wanting to show their great appreciation, reached out showing their gratitude. Ian sat on the hospital's charity board and when the idea of a donation of this kind crossed his desk in Minnesota, he had an immediate thought: a special tree to sit near while sitting on the bench.

In the end, the bench donation was coordinated with her Father's donation of the Bonsai Tree. Her Father knew how much the deceased patient, Lloyd had meant to his only daughter, so donating a tree, something that would live on in his honor, seemed only fitting. Lloyd's wife, Sophie, had heard so many stories about Fiona's Father's business pursuits, from Fiona directly, when she cared for her husband that it all seemed so perfectly right. The decision and means to contact him weren't at all difficult to find.

The ceremony was held several years ago when Fiona, Jake, Sophie, and the MacLaren's could all be present. The hospital held a small dinner to commemorate the garden, which had been named: Lloyd's Memorial Garden. The cardiology department had all been there, and also the off duty nurses from Fiona's unit, other philanthropic patrons, and dignitaries from around town.

Looking up at the bench and the tree, still lost in her thoughts, Fiona once again said to both objects d'art, "I remember you, I remember you. Do you remember me?"

Jake took Gabriella's hand and they slowly and silently approached Fiona from the side. What had been obstructed from their previous view of her back was now clear. Fiona had found her trip diaries. The small collection of cloth covered books was placed haphazardly in front of her, one hand leafing through the pages, the other leafing through the grass.

"Do you see what I see," Jake said to Gabriella.

"Yes, if you mean her trip diaries," she replied.

"Where did those come from?"

"I'm not sure, I thought they were stashed away at your house in New Jersey?"

"So did I," with that, Jake scanned the collection of onlookers and discovered standing amongst them was Ellen. The tears were streaming down her face too. "Did you know Ellen was here," Jake said at last.

"No, where is she?"

"Just there," he said.

They both pointed at Ellen who nodded back and began to ease her way towards them. Behind her was Jane, someone neither Gabriella nor Jake had seen in many, many years. Jake began to wonder if there wasn't some master plan unfolding and that he was just a pawn upon it.

"Hello Ellen," Jake said as he kissed her cheeks in the French custom.

"Jake, I'm so glad this day has come. You remember Jane, don't you?"

"Yes, hello Jane, it has been quite some time. You look well. Ellen, do you care to tell me what's going on?"

In whispers, Ellen confessed at bringing out Fiona's travel diaries and showing them to her. She also showed Fiona her own diary, one that Fiona never knew she'd kept. They had spent the morning comparing the entries and then the shock of the past was clear. Fiona had flown out of her patient room, ran down the stairs, and stopped here at the memorial garden.

"I'm sorry Jake, I just couldn't sit by and wait for my friend to come back from the past into her true life. The narrative she'd claimed to have written wasn't the truth, and I could see how much pain you were in, how much pain she was going to be in if her mistaken beliefs weren't exposed for what they were, mistaken beliefs, nothing more."

Jake stood and listened to the description of how the morning's events had unfolded. He'd been on rounds and at his clinic to see patients all morning and had missed coming in to see Fiona until this afternoon. Gathering himself together he said, "I thought Dr. Logan had expressed grave concern about such an overt approach. I'm sorry I listened to him, surely this has had a deep impact, just look at her."

"Yes, it has. I'm glad to see it. You know, when I arrived this morning, she was mumbling in her sleep. I could only make out a few words but those words really concerned me." Ellen had explained overhearing a dreaming Fiona utter the words, Kurt, incision, and baby.

"You think she's remembered about the twins?" Jake asked.

"I haven't asked her yet; she only said she had to go, to go, to go. She'd repeated that and then ran out."

Gabriella added to the conversation now as she had been listening and thinking about how this must have been for her old college friend. "Did she say anything about Jake?"

"Yes, did she?" Jake asked.

"No, just that she had to go. That's when I saw you down the hall. You were talking to Laura and seemed all flustered. I didn't want to yell to you and you high-tailed it off the unit before I could close the gap and speak with you. I've been watching from the window with Laura," Ellen said, looking over Jake's shoulder as Laura approached them.

"Hi everyone, how's Fiona?" Laura asked.

"I've been afraid to approach her," Jake admitted.

"I've put in an emergency call to Dr. Logan; he said he'd be over in a few minutes. I thought I'd wait for him with you all down here," Laura recounted.

"Did he say what to do in the mean time?" Jake wondered.

"No, just to wait for him."

"Ok, so we wait."

Again.

Chapter 44 Honeymoon Finalé, 1991

Fiona was discharged from the hospital to the Broadford Hotel suite and everyday about tea time, Dr. Morgan came to evaluate her. She slowly tired of the mundane and wished to continue with their vacation. They now had the time and Jake the energy to exact a plan of action. There would be no more flitting about the Scottish Highlands, they now had a fairly rigid itinerary, one that kept them close to main cities with hospitals.

Even Dr. Morgan had contributed to their route. He gave them information about doctors he knew in the areas where they had planned to visit. By the end of the first week, Fiona was still weak, but busting to be released. They met on a Friday night to confer with the doctor once more and work out the details of her physical activity for the remaining three weeks of their romantic holiday.

"I insist that at least once a week, barring any further bleeding or cramping, that you keep your appointments that I've set with my colleagues along your route. We don't want you to lose these precious moments. Can we all agree on that?" Dr. Morgan began their meeting.

Looking back and forth at the men in her life at the moment, Fiona said, "Yes, I can if you can sweetheart."

"Yes, I can."

"Good, now as of yesterday, you mentioned that the bleeding had stopped, is that still the case?" the doctor asked.

"Yes it is."

"Very good, and the cramping?"

"Only if I am up and about walking too much," Fiona confessed.

"Yes, I'd agree with that doctor. Fiona has been growing edgy and wanting to go outside in the garden, sitting on the grass, listening to the wind in the trees…" Jake added.

"If you leave here, say as soon as tomorrow, will you agree to limit and slowly ramp up the walking about as you see the sights? Can you be honest in that level of activity? Or will I need to instruct your husband to wheel you about in a wheelchair?"

"No wheelchairs!"

"She can agree," Jake said, looking at his young bride and the shock of a wheelchair ride. "I'll keep her to short walks, drive her to the door and I'll carry her if I must."

"Fiona, will you agree to such a plan?"

"Yes, doctor, yes my darling Jake, I will be a good patient."

"Very well," the doctor began, "I will discharge you now allowing you to leave in the morning. I have approved of your travel plans, the itinerary seems straightforward and you will be having 3 more doctor visits before the flight home. I suggest having a few days in Edinburgh, just the two of you taking in all that has happened here."

"Before you go, doctor, Jake has a question for you," Fiona chimed in, as the doctor had started collecting his instruments and placing them in his black bag.

"Yes?"

"Well doctor, you realize we are on our honeymoon, what about having sex, when can we resume having it?"

Smiling, the doctor replied, "If the last doctor visit allows for Fiona to have full activity privileges, I'd say in Edinburgh, you'll get quite accustomed to the view inside the room than outside it."

"That soon?" Fiona said, with a smile.

"Yes, that soon. You are a young healthy woman, with the proper amount of rest, you should be able to rejoin your sex life by the time you return to Edinburgh."

"Great!" Jake said, triumphantly.

"Thank you for all you've done caring for me, doctor. I am glad to have known you," Fiona shared.

Jake agreed, saying, "Yes, thank you. You have been more than kind. I hope to be as good a doctor as you some day."

Fiona turned her head sharply at her young husband's comments. "Really?"

"Really."

"Cool, married to a hunk of a man, who knows how to care for me and others. Can't beat that now can I?"

"I'd like to see you try."

"Me too."

The doctor left, smiling all the way to his car. Americans have quite a different sense of humor than we Scots. "I'll have to remember that," he muttered as he opened his car, climbed in, and drove off. He had no worries about Fiona's ability to carry the twins to term, as long as she got plenty of rest.

The next morning, buoyed on renewed hopes of good health, fair weather, and low traffic, Jake lead Fiona by the hand and gently placed her in the car. He had already packed their overnight bags and arranged for the mistress of the Broadford Hotel to pack them both snacks and a lunch. Since they didn't have a cooler, only a picnic basket, they had been purchasing cool or hot drinks along their route whenever their thirsts needed quenching. Ironically, in the last few days prior to the onset of Fiona's bleeding, that quenching usually came from each other. They'd have to artificially fortify their thirsts for each other with a diet soda or other potable.

From Broadford they headed northwest to the village of Portree. The A87 motorway took them inland for most of the morning and they arrived at Portree by lunch. They found a nice park in which they took their luncheon and Jake let Fiona nap while he perused the maps. He wanted to walk throughout the wee village but didn't want to leave Fiona's side. They'd have to return some day and rediscover each aspect of their trip from Broadford on. He looked forward to that indeed.

After a two hour nap, Fiona woke to see Jake smiling. "I'm ready if you are?"

"I'm ready too. I know just how we'll go back to the mainland, this time by sea. Look at the map," he said, holding it down and pointing to the road that skirted the edge of the tiny island. "The A855 goes all the way around the island coast. That should be breath-taking."

"Sounds absolutely beautiful, how long until we reach Sligachan Hotel?"

"I haven't calculated it exactly but it's a small island, can't take us too long. That way we've seen a lot of it and tomorrow can head back to Kyle, Kyle of Lochalsh. That's where we are staying tomorrow night."

"We aren't venturing too far from Broadford in the process, kind of going in circles. I suppose that's a good way to handle my symptoms, not to venture too far from that hospital. From Kyle, then where?" she asked.

"While you were napping, a few locals had approached me wondering if I needed assistance since I seemed to be so intently studying the map," he confessed.

"Ok," Fiona agreed.

"From Kyle we head south to Fort William. If the weather holds, we can see more craggy mountains, if not, we'll see 10 feet in front of the car! I read that in Fort William, they get 300 days of rain a year!" Jake announced, shocked.

"Really?"

"That's what folks who dropped by today told me."

"Well then, let's pray for a rain-free and fog-free day!"

They packed up the lunch and got Fiona situated in the car. They took the route discussed and arrived in time for a late dinner, the sun just beginning to set behind the hotel. Jake hopped out with his camera to capture the golden, red, orange, and lavender hues the scene was creating.

They slept in that next day and were on track for the remaining days. They visited Kyle, Kyle of Lochalsh, and took a quick tour of the Eilean Donan Castle. In Fort William, they spent a few days, one with socked in fog. They made it to Oban for just an overnight. From there, they took the coastal route to Carrick, and took in Kilmory Castle along the way.

That day in Kilmory, Jake allowed Fiona to tour the castle on foot. Back at Eilean Donan, he view had been from the car. She'd fallen asleep most of the morning and he had awakened her when they drove up the drive to the castle. He knew that breath-taking sight was worth waking her. She thanked him with a very passionate kiss. They lingered in their embrace for what seemed hours in the car park, with no other tourists in sight. They wouldn't have noticed them anyway, even if there had been any tourists on hand.

They drove through a village named "Furnace" and made the obvious jokes. They loved learning about the less populated side of Scotland; it had really welcomed them and took them in. A few hours later, the A83 motorway lead them to a town called "Rest and Be Thankful." Pulling over, they took in the views of the greenery covered mountains. They saw a few signs leading them to a parking area and took refuge there. Taking a short walk, they encountered a sign that told them the story of the place so named.

The sign read:

"O're the roads you have come
Many a gentleman have done
Rounded up the rocks to carry
So future travelers could rest not weary."

Beneath the sign was dated the completion of the road, circa 1750. Fiona pointed out the date to Jake and they wondered of their relatives who were in the area at that time, if any of them had passed through this high mountain pass and taken refuge in the crossing. They sat on the grass near a picnic area, with benches lining the edge. Fiona absently combed the green blades, bringing them home.

"This is some place," she said.

"Indeed." he said.

They took a quiet moment to reflect on the history of their families, their ancestors and the lay of the land. It struck a chord in both of them, bringing them together for a long embrace. Tears flowed from Fiona's eyes, while Jake's were merely moistened; they were lost in their own private reflections.

"Look at the time; if we want to reach Balloch and Balloch Castle by dinner, we'd best leave now." Jake said, keeping them to the itinerary.

"Where are we staying there?" Fiona asked, having forgotten that portion of their plan.

"They made us a reservation at 'The Maid of The Loch,'" Jake stated having checked their papers prior to speaking. "We are supposed to spend two days in Loch Lomond, they said the timing of our arrival was on a weekend, you see the doctor at the clinic on Monday."

"Well then, let's not keep this lady waiting for the Lady," Fiona mused.

They arrived at sunset, ate a quiet dinner and were in bed early. Lights were out by 9:30PM with a leisurely morning planned at the Inn and then the afternoon at Balloch Castle. Then on Sunday, they looked in the telephone book for a list of local parks. They first purchased postcards and stamps, and then set out for an afternoon in the park, writing notes home about their trip thus far. They didn't describe any of the pregnancy details, only where they'd been and the sights they'd seen. The state of Fiona's body was best left for in person dialogues.

Tuesday morning, they drove to Glasgow and spent three days there. It was the last few days out in Scotland before returning to their home base of Edinburgh. They quite easily took in the differences in the two anchor cities of Scotland. It was in Glasgow, that they discovered the work horse of industry and in Edinburgh, the holder of pomp and circumstance, history and pageantry.

They saw the clinic doctor in Glasgow on Wednesday. They were 5-10 minutes early to Fiona's 10:00AM appointment. They knew this was the appointment where they would learn if their love-making could resume. They weren't the least bit anxious at all, hence their earliness to the appointment.

The nurse called Fiona's name and they stood to follow her back into the clinic. They noted the similar styles of décor which were lacking yet consistent in all the clinics. It truly reminded them that they were far from home. No two clinics were all that alike, but there certainly weren't a cookie cutter process like some in Manhattan clinic chains.

The doctor came in after a brief wait and in short order began her evaluation with a history of the symptoms and concluded with a physical examination of Fiona. She'd introduced herself as Dr. Samantha Frances.

"Please call me Sam. I understand that both of you are registered nurses back in America, what areas do you work in, aye?" she asked.

"Nice to meet you Sam," they said.

Fiona explained her work area first, saying, "I work on a telemetry step-down unit."

"I work on a neurology medical-surgical unit, upstairs," he said.

"So ye work at the same hospital, is that how ye met?" the doctor asked.

Jake gave a brief description of their meeting to play golf after he'd posted the need for a 4th on a golf outing. "The rest is history," he said.

"We've got quite the honeymoon story too," Fiona quipped.

"Indeed ye do," agreed Sam. "Well, I have some good news and some bad news, which do ye want first?"

"Bad news," Fiona burst out, "I need that first."

"Aye, well, I believe your honeymoon is coming to an end in a few days, is that correct?"

"Yes, it is."

"Aye, well, I think when ye get home; ye'll need to see ye own OB/GYN to see whether or not ye'll be cleared to work. At the moment, ye are doing quite well. I don't see any signs of maternal hypertension, no bleeding, and no tenderness."

"Yes, that's correct."

"What about her work troubles you?" Jake asked.

"Aye, well, any sort of physical exertion such as what I suspect she endures at work may or may not be off limits. For the immediate future, I'd say she'd be just fine working, but in a few weeks, that might change. Many women with abruptio placentae are on bed rest at the end of their pregnancy. I wouldna want to hasten that by her over exerting at work, aye?"

"I see," Jake said. "What if she worked in the monitor room or in a management position?"

"Yes, I could work in the MR or be charge nurse. I haven't been promoted to management but perhaps they could find something for me to do in lieu of patient care?"

"Aye, lassie, I'd pursue that," Sam said.

"What about the last few days here, can I walk more and be a tourist?" Fiona asked.

Jake smiled, saying, "Or more?"

"Yes, ye can, I don't see anything impeding yer progress. Just don't begin too much, be gentle and careful, aye? I wouldna want to hear ye overdid it as a couple only to hear that ye were admitted in Edinburgh, or back home for that matter. Mark my words, slow and steady, should win the race. Aye?"

"Thank you doctor, I'll go slowly. I'm making arms and legs I need to take my time!" Fiona said, with a smirk.

"Indeed!" Jake flushed.

"Very well, do you have any other questions?"

"Do you have any recommendations for a quiet, steak dinner in a Glasgow restaurant? You know, where you'd go to celebrate news like this?" He paused, "Where do you go with your husband?" Jake asked.

"Aye, we love the Ceilidh at 'Sloans;' many people get engaged there," Sam said.

Shocked at the words the doctor had just used, Jake stammered, "The what?"

"The Ceilidh at 'Sloans,' it is the best, aye," she said.

Smiling and looking back and forth at each other and the doctor, Fiona and Jake said together, "That's the name of his parents' sailboat. We will definitely go there! We know Ceilidh!"

"Aye, small world, isn't it?" said Sam.

"Yes it is. Thank you doctor."

"Please, call me Sam."

"Thank you Sam," they said.

In the car they shared another laugh and a knowing glance. They couldn't get themselves to the hotel fast enough. The bulge in Jake's trousers was growing as the miles remaining on their itinerary shrank. It only took them a few attempts to find the hotel, as they encountered too many one way streets. Eventually, they found it. Jake sent Fiona on ahead with her purse; he'd park the car and follow with their bags.

"I'd like to check-in," Fiona had said to the desk clerk.

"Absolutely lassie, name on the reservation?"

"Davies," Fiona said proudly. She hadn't used her married name much this trip, Jake had done all their check-ins.

"Aye, I see you have the Honeymoon Suite and there is a letter for ye. Please wait right there and let me fetch it straight away." The desk clerk disappeared into a back office.

He returned a few minutes later with an envelope addressed to "Fiona MacLaren Davies, eyes only" she was when he handed it to her. "We've been wondering when ye may show, with the title like that and all," he said.

"Well, I best open it then!"

Inside was a letter signed by Clifton and Bette. They had spoken with her parents and arranged this room as a new Mommy-to-be present and hoped that they would be using it before heading home and that she'd be on the mend by the time they'd arrived in Glasgow.

"It's a note from my new in-laws, they wanted to let me know that this room is a gift from them to me and my husband. Nice, huh?"

"Verra nice lassie, here's the key," the clerk said handing over an oversized skeleton key with Gaelic writing and a large purple thistle blossom upon the handle. "Ye room is Suite #311, just take the small flight of stairs out of the lobby to the lift and press 3, it will be the last room on the right. We do hope ye enjoy your stay with us, if you need any further hospitality just let me know, you know, 'Ceilidh,'" he said.

"Thank you," Fiona said, and smiled as she turned to the stairs and began the brief journey to their room via the elevator. "Verra nice, indeed," she said, out of range of the clerk, attempting to speak with the clerk's particular brogue.

Just as the clerk had indicated their room where he'd said, with the key in the lock, Fiona turned it and opened the door into the room. Stepping inside, she saw it. A catch of breath caught in her throat. Jake was strewn naked across the king sized bed, a tempestuous smile across his face. Rose buds were tossed about the floor along with rose petals, peonies, and purple thistles. His anticipation and arousal of her arrival was quite well noted.

"Hello my love," he said, in his most seductive tone.

"How did you get up here so fast?"

"Well, when you were freshening up this morning, I called my folks to update them on our status. Father and I concocted this ruse, do you like it?"

"So, the letter I read down stairs, who wrote that, who is paying for this lovely room?"

"Well enough, my parents are paying. Clifton wouldn't have had it any other way. He called ahead and dictated the note. It was all a stall tactic for me to have time to prepare the room. There isn't a car park here, but a wonderful valet. Dad called the florist down the street and they instantly knew what to do. All I had to do was beat you up here and, uh, be, uh, ready for you," he said, smiling wantonly.

"Well, I won't make you wait any longer. Come hither Mr. Davies, take me, I'm all yours, all three of us."

"I will take all three of you, again, and again, and again. Slowly, gently, and repeat, I'm just following doctor's orders. Aye?"

"Aye, laddie."

They missed dinner in town that night and instead raided the mini bar, their bodies once again joined and full of sustenance from and of each other. The honeymoon finale was accompanied by the pipers of the highlands, for somewhere in the distance they heard the familiar wail. It came through their slightly ajar room window, the piping of bagpipes.

The next morning at breakfast they saw the flyer advertising what they'd experienced the night before. It was a festival of pipe bands, notable participating bands were from the clans MacLeod, McKay, and Stewart. They had heard the first night of the festival last night while celebrating themselves. They heard the wail of the piping band. The flyer listed the performances last night as the McKay Pipe and Drum Band and it listed that their last song of the evening, the one unending song that had kept Fiona and Jake accompanied in their own orchestrations, had been the band's favorite anthem, the 'Skye Boat Song.'

Looking at each other, together they read the flyer. Jake knew it would be a top 10 list of their songs as a couple for it would now replace Fiona's prior favorite of Wagner, Füssen: Opus 1, with their song of love. This one song echoed his sentiments exactly, for they were, Fiona, Fatherhood, and family. He loved their choice for their duet set in allegro.

Chapter 45 Many Returns of the Day, 2015

Fiona continued to speak of remembrances, still unaware of the growing crowd about her. Jake and Gabriella sat quietly on the bench and looked for the time when they would finally interject. He seized the moment, he had waited long enough.

"Fiona," he said, "Fiona, look at me."

Fiona was startled by his voice and opened her eyes, following his wishes. "What are you doing here?"

"I was about to ask you the same thing?" he said, as Gabriella looked on. "Hi Gabriella, you are here too?"

"Yes, Fiona, I'm here."

Jake began tenderly, speaking from his seated position on the memory bench. "What do you have there?" he indicated in her hands by pointing to the trip diaries, both Fiona's and Ellen's.

There was also the lavender folio containing their love notes as husband and wife. Gabriella caught Jake reading them knowing that the notes documented their married life together. He'd replaced it in his briefcase when Fiona returned to her room. Gabriella simply removed it from the bulging case and tucked it into the magazine she'd been carrying. Later, Gabriella placed it where an unattended Fiona could find it.

"Well, I'd love to say it was just a little light reading, but it is more than that."

"Yes, it is."

Gabriella took this as her cue, "What do you remember about those books?"

"Yes, Fiona," Jake asked, "What do you remember?"

"Well, a lot actually. I've just been sitting here remembering the time in Edinburgh, with the taxi driver and speaking to the grass. I wanted to know if the grass remembered me, if the bench, the bonsai, if they remembered me?"

"What have you discovered?"

Turning to Gabriella, Fiona said, "Did you put these out for me?"

"No, I did." Ellen approached from out of view; she'd remained standing behind Fiona. Stepping forward now, she said, "I couldn't wait for you to come back to us. Fiona, please tell me you remember me?" In her hand was a get well card from Jane, as yet, unread by Fiona.

"Ellen, of course I remember you. And Gabriella, I've known you two since college, I wouldn't forget you." Fiona said, fresh tears moistening her eyes as she peered up, and looked at first at Ellen and then at Gabriella.

The classmates acknowledged their complicity; it was the unspoken expression on their faces that gave them away.

Jake was waiting to say the words for which they'd all been waiting.

For months now, it was what they'd all been sworn to secrecy about. They'd been on pins and needles around their friend, for to them, she wasn't only Fiona, she was the colleague, the wife, and the woman they knew and loved.

Was it time they wondered?

Was it time that she would remember?

Was it true and real for her, as much as it was for them, just watching, like a movie on the screen. They watched rapt in each movement, and awaiting the utterance of each new word. Was it finally her time?

"Fiona, do you remember me?" There, he said it, the longing in his face evident, how he had missed his wife all these months. It broke his heart each time she retold the known stories her European trip, with Ellen and Jane; and her conjured up memories about Kurt and their so-called lives together in Berlin.

Finally, finally, he wanted to know if he waited long enough. Had she finally remembered him?

Fiona regarded Jake directly. She looked at him for a long time, so long people in the crowd began to murmur and mumble their concerns. Jake returned her gaze, never faltering, never giving in; he was waiting for her to return to him.

In many situations, there is an exact instant when the realization of memory occurs. In that moment, in that millisecond of time, the countenance upon one's face changes forever. It was her 'aha' moment, when her memory light bulb went off. It is captured frequently in films and in still photography. In this case, it was captured by everyone. The exact moment, at 5:16PM, that Sunday evening in Manhattan when Fiona's face changed and she finally was looking at the face of her husband and not the face of a colleague, of a co-worker: it was Jake.

The realization proved overwhelming and again, Fiona fainted. Her imminent fainting and landing this time were couched by her husband of over twenty years. He caught her in his long outstretched arms, he was there, he knew, for he had been waiting. As always, waiting, but this time he smiled, she had remembered him. She had remembered him. She had remembered me.

He laid her down upon the grass she so wanted to remember. Did she leave an impression this time? Would the grass remember her? It didn't matter any longer, he knew she had returned to him and from now on, he would remember enough for them both.

The kiss they shared was more poignant than all the other kisses they had previously shared. For it was this kiss that was shared with the flooding and flurry of memories returning. The overwhelming joy of being in the arms of the man she loved, being kissed by him so deeply that it brought her back from not only her fainting spell, but from her amnesia following her brain injury and coma.

It brought her back to him and to her children. They were waiting too.

Chapter 46 Expectations, 2016

F-I-O-N-A!" Finally she recognized the fact that someone was indeed calling her name, perhaps she wasn't standing above a precipitous cracking pool, maybe she was dreaming. She had been listening to the music of Wagner in her dream. She allowed herself a few more bars of Wagner's symphony, her Opus 1 of Füssen, and then turned her head.

She opened her eyes to see her husband Jake was smiling back at her laying next to her on their bed. He said, "Were you dreaming of Füssen again, darling?"

"Guilty," she said, before rolling over and kissing him more passionately than he had expected and giving into her, his body joining hers, eager for the moments they shared together, alone. For he was no longer waiting.